Presidential
Migraines

★ ★ ★ ★ ★
A Dr. Jack Stevens Novel

Presidential Migraines

FRITZ STROBL

FIRST
EDITION

Presidential Migraines

Additional copies of this book are available at www.PresidentialMigraines.com

First Edition

ISBN 978-0-9844940-0-2

Produced with the assistance of literary developer Lance Wubbels and designed by Koechel Peterson & Associates, Inc., Minneapolis, MN.

Manufactured in the United States of America

for

★ ★ ★ ★ ★

Debi,
the best addition ever to my life,
without whose love, encouragement, and ideas
most of my joys and accomplishments
would not exist

★ ★ ★ ★ ★

The Author

FREDERICK (FRITZ) STROBL, M.D. is a Board Certified Neurologist who graduated from college in electrical engineering, computer science, and control systems. At Rensselaer Polytechnic Institute he was the recipient of the four-year Lockheed Leadership Scholarship, its highest academic award, given to one entering freshman yearly at each of the top ten engineering schools in the United States. He later transferred to the University of Minnesota, and as a student, he worked part time for the Systems and Guidance section at Honeywell. This section was responsible for the development of various control systems, including the Apollo moon program, X-15 rocket plane, various military and commercial aircraft, including the 747 aircraft guidance.

At the University of Minnesota Medical School, Dr. Strobl was in an accelerated program such that he graduated in three years instead of the usual four. He was the recipient of numerous awards in engineering, medical school, and during his neurology residency, including the Shapiro Award, given by the University of Minnesota Neurology Department to the highest ranking Neurology Resident based on competitive national practice board examination. He still holds the record for the highest score in the history of the university.

Dr. Strobl did part of his residency training at the National Hospital for Nervous Disease, Institute of Neurology, Queen Square, London, and Fellowship training at Mayo Clinic, Rochester, Minnesota. He has been a practicing neurologist for thirty years and Director for many years with the Minneapolis Clinic of Neurology, the largest independent neurology clinic in the United States. He was formerly the Chairman and President of CNS, Inc., a company he cofounded, best known for Breathe Right Nasal Strips®.

His wife, Debi, helped start CNS and was one of the first four Directors on the Board. He has co-invented several patents and more are in preparation.

Acknowledgments   ★ ★ ★ ★ ★

AS USUAL WITH MY ADVENTURES, my wife, Debi, put up with a lot while I wrote this book. I have also been blessed with two wonderful daughters, a terrific son-in-law, and my first grandson, all of whom also gave up personal time with me. My two Havanese, Machiavelli and Remy, gave physical support and literal lap warmth in the preparation of this book. They also were the first to see my writings at various stages. Although they rarely said anything, their silent love and approval was always a plus, regardless of the book's success.

Ed Flaherty met with me numerous times and helped me through the new author learning curve. He put writing into the best business framework I have seen so far and taught me much. Al Horner was probably my first author contact, and Al helped to start the pragmatic phase of writing. Vince Flynn, at whose table I was seated during a YPO/WPO meeting, provided inspiration, although he probably doesn't know it since I never told him I was writing a novel.

John and Deb Esmay, great friends for the last twenty years, were always there encouraging whatever I was doing, including offering good feedback for this book.

Gerry Timm, Ph.D., was instrumental in my decision to attend medical school instead of law school and fulfill my dream of starting an engineering company.

W. Albert Sullivan, M.D., the Associate Dean of the University of Minnesota and one of its finest surgeons, was always an inspiration—more than he knew for many medical students. He died tragically of a brain tumor. I will always cherish the fact that when he said his final good-byes, I was one of those whom he called and told me I was special to him. I never knew he thought that much of me. I wish I had known him better.

Terry Balfanz, retired from the Minnetonka police force, was helpful in some of the investigative parts.

Bonnie and Marv Eimiller kept me fed and encouraged during this process. Marv Eimiller coached me through some of my golf endeavors and put up with my attempts to relax from neurology and writing by playing golf.

My mother and father were always there when I needed them and supportive. I don't think they ever understood all my "inventions," although I never mentioned some of them since there was some damage from time to time to the basement.

Lance Wubbels, who worked as my literary developer, helped a lot in putting a more readable style to this first novel as well as deleting parts that were too wordy. He is a super person with whom to work.

Jack Vogelgesang has always insisted he be the first person to buy the first edition of my first book. This is certainly appreciated, and I wish I could clone a million Jacks.

I have had many wonderful teachers, professors, and mentors over the years at every level of education and later in life. Thank you all.

There are others who are shy about having their names here or want to remain anonymous. They know who they are. Thank you.

Then there are the nameless men and women of the army, navy, marines, air force, CIA, NSA, FBI, and numerous other government agencies who protect our dear United States daily, in ways usually never known to the general public. Without them no form of government, political party, or our vast, precious freedoms and opportunities could exist.

Last, but never least, the women and men who are doctors, nurses, technicians, therapists, and all the support staff that keep American medicine the best in the world. It has been my privilege to work with these people. Accept no substitute. Medicine in every other country is so much worse.

Debi and I have traveled throughout much of the world. We have a great country—not perfect, but the best there is. As Churchill said with respect to democracy, all the other countries are so much worse.

1

Nothing endures but change.

Heraclitus, Greek philosopher (540 B.C.–480 B.C.)

CHAPTER 1

"PLAY YOUR CARDS RIGHT," her mother had said years ago, "and you might just end up becoming a doctor's wife. Physicians might not be as rich as they once were, but they're never hungry; they're kind to their families, and they always have work."

Margaret Baxter smiled at the memory as she walked down the long hallway toward the Department of Neurology Conference Room, carrying a freshly brewed carafe of French roast coffee and a plain white cake box. With her long white-blond hair and the body of a ballerina, the twenty-seven-year-old assistant had turned a lot of heads for several years and been hit on constantly, but to date she hadn't had any serious relationships. Now that she had finished night school, she was ready to settle down and start a family, and she had her eye on a cute neurology resident who had "husband" potential written all over him.

She walked a little slower than usual this morning, feeling a bit of sadness about the 9:00 A.M. meeting. The research group had been meeting for several years, and this was their final scheduled meeting. Depending on what the group was discussing on any given meeting, they might meet at the University of Minnesota's Neurology Department or in the Department of Electrical and Computer Engineering. Occasionally, they met at Minntronic, a large biomedical manufacturing company. Three M.D.s, three professors of Electrical Engineering, and three Ph.D. electrical engineers from Minntronic formed a lot of talent. They represented some of Minnesota's and the United States' brightest and finest minds.

The research had gone well, far better and faster than expected. They had developed a small biomedical device that had vast potential. Held up to the scalp just above the ear over one of the temporal lobes, it had the potential to speed learning for students, perhaps help visually or hearing impaired patients see and hear as well as possibly be able to help people who suffered with schizophrenia, stroke, or cerebral palsy. Simulators for new airplanes might be learned more quickly by pilots. There seemed to be no limit to the device's potential. It was still in a primitive level of development, but the groundbreaking work was done. The finished product and design specifications had been delivered to the sponsor months ago, so this meeting was more of a celebration of a job well done.

Margaret loved working with the group. The members had all quickly come to enjoy one another, which seldom happened within research groups, and she knew there was a lot of personal sadness among the group now that it was ending. She hoped their friendships would continue and there might be more projects on which they could collaborate. Regarding this project, though, the members were strictly forbidden to make or use any related devices. Still, they had learned much, and they thought that knowledge would serve them well in developing different, noncompetitive projects in the future in good faith.

Initially, the group had been quite skeptical that the project was even feasible, but they repeatedly reminded themselves that Einstein said the best ideas seemed crazy at first. It was a brilliant idea that came seemingly out of nowhere by a sponsor of Iranian descent with deep financial pockets. The group members were required to sign confidentiality agreements, as they had with many other projects. Although there were a number of other people supporting the lower level research and development efforts, the project was set up so that only this group of nine understood the whole scope of it, which helped protect the intellectual property and patents that would belong to the sponsor. They were also required to turn over to the sponsor all related notes, disks, paperwork, and any other information in any form relating to the project. They had done all that and electronically shredded the related parts of their hard drives so as to permanently erase the materials, as contractually agreed.

Margaret stepped into the conference room and walked past photographs of former Chiefs or Heads of Neurology, among them some national legends whose books were references for neurologists around the world. Individual photographs of the Chief Neurology Residents of the university hung on the walls along with the photographs of each group of graduating residents. This was a select group personally deemed to be the best and picked by the Head for this honor; less than half of the residents in any year were so selected. *If there was such a thing as mental osmosis,* she thought, *this is the room in which to spend some time.*

"Fresh coffee," Margaret announced as she set the cake box in the center of the large walnut conference table and passed the stainless steel thermal carafe to one of the three M.D.s who had worked on the project.

The current group in the room sat in comfortable burgundy leather chairs on casters around the long rectangular table and was engaged in several lively conversations. Crimson and gold University of Minnesota coffee cups that sat on similar logoed coasters were placed around the table, and the members were drinking coffee that Margaret had brewed for them earlier. They were happy for the freshly brewed refill.

The conference room was a corner room in the University of Minnesota Hospital, with two sides of windows through which could be seen part of the university campus as well the Mississippi River. Margaret stepped to the window and gazed out. She never tired of seeing the huge green lawns bordered by red geraniums with the blue Mississippi in the background. It was a beautiful sunny morning in the first week of August in Minneapolis, dry and pleasant after a couple of weeks of thick humidity and scorching heat.

This is why I love it here, she thought. *It's a perfect day to walk around Lake Calhoun and work off some pounds. I'm going to sneak out of here early. I should call Dr. Burns and see if he'd like to come along. Someone said he has a sailboat down there.*

The Minneapolis campus of the university was quiet below her, only an occasional pedestrian walking on the sidewalks, and it would not be busy for another five weeks when the herd of students starting the fall term would stampede in. However, a smaller and older herd of media personnel had already started to form, whose stampede sounds would crescendo in three weeks for the first presidential debate that would be held in Northrup Auditorium, then that herd would rapidly disperse.

Funny how the summer pace is slower, she continued to daydream. *Even the mighty Mississippi flows more leisurely in the dry times. Goodness, I love the summer.*

With some reluctance, Margaret turned back to the table, coughed loud enough to get everyone's attention, and pointed out the white cake box tied with a beautiful blue ribbon, a present sent from their very pleasant Iranian sponsor, Mr. Adel Jalili.

"Mr. Jalili called and some emergency has come up, so he will be unable to attend," Margaret said. "He sends his deepest apologies because he really wanted to be here. He wanted you to know how pleased he was with what everyone did and that he will miss seeing you. He sent over a cake from D'Amico and Sons. . .your favorite. . .and hopes we all enjoy it. He asked me to wait for everyone to come, then to open the envelope and read the card to you all."

The group all liked Jalili, a single man who attended all their meetings and was generous with both his praise and money. He would at times take them to dinner at Manny's, arguably the best steakhouse in the country. So it was sad that he couldn't make it for this final meeting.

Margaret lifted the plaque with their names engraved on it that they'd gotten Jalili as a gift and said, "We can send him this, but it's a shame we can't give it to him in person. Maybe we should wait, just in case he asks us to do one more dinner at Manny's."

With that, Margaret passed out the paper plates, plastic forks, and napkins. She reached for the envelope holding a card that was attached to the white cake box. *Wow, that's tight,* Margaret thought as she struggled with the envelope. Finally, she pulled harder. . . .

* * * * *

To the university hospital personnel walking toward the tall building who survived the explosion, there was a blinding flash they could see whether their eyes were turned toward the building or away, whether closed or open. One second the hospital was normal, and the next second, part of the building was missing. The survivors on the street were the ones who were the farthest from the blast.

Expanding at 26,400 feet per second, or about 18,000 miles per hour, the blast instantly killed everyone in the Department of Neurology conference room as well as some in adjacent offices and hallways, people who would later be termed "collateral damage." Windows in nearby buildings were blown out, and some of the men mowing the lawn below the conference room were killed. Unlike the movies, there was no outrunning the blast, even if you had known it was coming.

Most of the survivors on the front lawn were dizzy and somewhat deaf from the barotraumas. Those closer to the building experienced severe breathing trouble. Individuals in the closest group were deaf, breathing poorly, and blinded. Then there were those who died from the flying debris, both human and inorganic.

There was no hope of survival from the shockwave for those inside the conference room. Most of the elite group of researchers' bodies stayed in the room, more or less, but Margaret Baxter was one of the few who was propelled through what had been the window and onto the lawn by the Mississippi River that she had been admiring moments before, leaving all her hopes of marriage and dreams of summer walks in the smoke and rubble.

2

Obviously crime pays,
or there'd be no crime.

G. Gordon Liddy

CHAPTER 2

PULLING HIS BLACK H3 Alpha Hummer to a stop next to his wife's matching black Mercedes Benz CLK350 convertible, Dr. Geoffrey Jellen smiled as he shut off the engine and glanced at his completely remodeled office building in Edina, a wealthy community just a few minutes southwest of Minneapolis. Located just down the block from a street lined with colorful Victorian homes and magnificent gardens, the single-story free-standing building represented the latest piece in the fulfillment of his dreams.

Stepping out of his Hummer and slipping on his Loro Piana cashmere jacket, Dr. Jellen surveyed the empty parking lot twice before closing the door and locking it. He walked quickly to the front door of the building and went inside. Stepping into the spacious waiting room with its ceramic and glass tiles, marble countertops, and leather chairs, he stopped to admire the 48" x 84" three-panel impressionistic oil painting of an Italian bridge that dominated one entire wall. His clear brown eyes sparkled with pleasure.

"Don't you just love the old world flavor?" he commented, then turned toward the receptionist desk.

Camelia Jellen, who served as the office manager and receptionist in his solo practice, glanced up from her computer screen. "You're late," she spoke sharply. Her flashing green eyes fixed on him with an expression of contempt. "I told you that we have to talk about the numbers."

"Oops, I forgot. . .again," he answered with a careless shrug and a half smile as he stepped toward his office. "I told you to not worry about it. I've got two more guys who are ready to start up."

"You said that a week ago," she replied stiffly, pushing back some of her long, tangled red hair.

"I'll make the calls. I just needed time to get them ready. I'm aware of the bills, including your last trip to Saks. What was that about?"

"Just a little something for all the charity banquets you drag me along to," Carmelia replied. "It's paying for your two past wives and all those little brats you sired that you need to be concerned about."

"I'll call today," Dr. Jellen answered, raising his hands in mock surrender.

"Did you hear the news?"

"No, what?"

"You won't believe it," she said, motioning to his office. "I turned your TV on."

He walked into his office and glanced at the flat screen TV that hung on the wall. Before he got to his large mahogany desk with the gold detail around its leather inlay, he froze in his tracks at a sight he immediately recognized—the blown-out and burning corner of one of the medical buildings at the University of Minnesota.

A young female reporter from one of the local stations was live at the scene, her voice tense with emotion as she said, ". . .a violent explosion rocked the main hospital at the Minneapolis campus of the University of Minnesota less than an hour ago. You can see behind me the power of the explosion."

The cameraman panned the smoking building and the sizable crater that had been blown out. A myriad of flashing colored lights and the wails of ambulance and police sirens all seemed to blend together. Uniformed policemen from the University of Minnesota and the city of Minneapolis as well as firemen and members of the bomb squad were moving in and out of the building.

"The Emergency Medical Response Team from the University of Minnesota hospitals is inside the building at this time, doing triage on the victims, with a smaller triage group outside helping those who survived being hit by barotrauma, flying glass, and debris," the reporter's voice continued as the camera swept the general area.

The cameraman kept out of the field of view the scattered human parts that had blown out of the conference room and were being numbered, logged, and photographed by local CSIs. It was standard procedure at the television network that *If it bleeds, it leads; but too much guts is nuts, at least the close-ups.*

The reporter's eyes looked dazed as she turned and looked at the scene, and her chin quivered in a vain attempt at self-control. "The bomb squad has inspected and cleared the area. The CSI teams have cordoned off the area and are combing it for evidence." As she spoke an FBI team appeared on camera walking behind her, which the cameraman followed. "We don't know much at this time. The best information is that this apparently occurred in a conference room of the Department of Neurology. As you can see, the windows are blown out around the blast site and debris is scattered over a large area of the lawn in back of me."

The cameraman panned the once green, neatly cut lawn that was now covered mostly with glass and bricks and littered with gray and black pieces that once fit together to make usable objects, again avoiding close-ups of anything that might be human remains.

"The FBI will be assessing the possibility of terrorism. Stay tuned for further developments that we will bring you live as we learn more."

As the screen changed back to a morning game show, Dr. Jellen shook his head and whispered, "Oh my God, not here." It was as though he was hoping it might drive back the ominous foreboding that had suddenly possessed him. Exhaling a deep breath, he slowly sat down in his chair, then noticed that Camelia had followed him into the room.

Twenty-one years younger than him, Camelia was tall and slender with alluring curves he had paid for and features that were almost too perfect. She was by all accounts the trophy wife he had always wanted, with *ethics du jour*.

"Wow. . .I've been in that conference room!" he said in something of a smothered exclamation. "I cannot imagine an explosion there."

"What could be explosive there?" Camelia asked.

"I don't know," he replied, picking up the TV remote and clicking off the game show. "The hospital is extremely careful about any type of explosive compound."

"Do they use ether? That stuff is explosive."

"No, no," Dr. Jellen answered, breaking into an unconscious grin, "not in that setting. Years ago one of the older surgeons at the U insisted on still using ether, which had a distinct smell. The anesthesiologists had switched to newer, safer anesthetics, so in order to satisfy the old guy, they spilled a few drops on the floor for smell whenever he operated. He never figured it out, and everyone was happy."

Camelia broke into laughter, and her expression softened. "Sounds like a trick you'd pull. What about acetone, though. Don't we use that to remove EEG electrode glue from scalps of neurology patients?"

Dr. Jellen nodded and said, "It is, but it's not going to be in a conference room. I wonder if I knew anyone who was in that conference room?"

"Gosh, I hope not," Camelia said, but her tone switched back to its typical cool, even colorless tone. Then she turned to step out of the room.

"Is the first patient here?"

"Not yet," Camelia replied. "But Mr. Harvin is one of your big users, so keep pushing him. I'll bet he's got rich friends who are looking for the same supply."

"Let me know when he's here," Dr. Jellen said. "It's not that simple, and you know it."

A mask of indifference slipped back over Camelia's face as she walked out the door.

Alone in his office, Dr. Jellen pushed some of the papers around on his desk, but his mind refused to settle down. His emotions were in a ragged state from the news report, but he wasn't sure what he was feeling. *Sadness, at the loss of life?* No, it was on a different level, but he couldn't place exactly what it was. *Something from the past. . .*just beyond his mind's reach.

Geoffrey Jellen, M.D., was a chronic pain doctor, and as was true of most of his colleagues, he was benefiting from the fact that the average life span had increased from 47 years in 1900 to 80-something at the present. Much to the credit of American medicine and research, there were many blessings about living longer, but living longer was accompanied by some curses as well for many people, such as chronic pain. However, unlike most of his fellow chronic pain doctors who wanted to do something meaningful by relieving pain for those patients for whom nothing seemed to help, he just wanted to make money easily in a specialty field that desperately needed more doctors. And he was, and then some.

Dr. Jellen had trained at two excellent institutions, the University of Minnesota and Mayo Clinic. Although not highly intelligent, he had a near-photographic memory, making most schooling easy for him. He often didn't really *understand* what he memorized; but if the test questions were similar to what had been in the books, course syllabi, or lectures, he could regurgitate it for the test. Never one who was willing to work hard, he found ways to slide through and thought nothing of cheating whenever possible. Coming from a poor family, he was able to get a free education and a ticket to what he thought was the American Dream.

After finishing the university medical school and residency at the Mayo Clinic, getting his first job had been easy, especially in a newer specialty. As was true during his residency, there were more positions in chronic pain to fill than specialists to fill them. Nevertheless, he had not been able to keep a job for more than a few years at any clinic for which he worked. As was true of other sociopaths, he was adept at lying and weaseling his way out of jams, but working daily among a group of astute M.D.s, he ultimately slipped up and was exposed for who he really was. One former wife said it was because of his gambling habit, and the next said it was his affairs and abuse of alcohol. He said it was the idiots who ran the clinics.

Having been fired from yet another clinic soon after he moved in with Camelia, Dr. Jellen took the big step and went into solo practice. *This time* he intended to make it on his own and reap all the benefits. There was no way he was going to work more than forty hours a week, but his dreams of wealth drove him to rise far above the comfortable lifestyles of many of his doctor friends. To add to his stress, Camelia was most kindly referred to as "high maintenance" by her friends, although it was debatable if any of them were actually her friends.

Even before he went into solo practice, Dr. Jellen had realized that for a chronic pain doctor who wasn't hung up on the medical ethics that had been jammed down his throat in medical school, it would be easy to make money selling narcotics. Any medical doctor with a BNDD number could prescribe narcotics. Although the federal watchdogs kept an eye on prescriptions for narcotics, certain specialties were expected to write more—chronic pain being one.

For Dr. Jellen, it started with writing one prescription to a real patient, then he had Camelia get the narcotics prescription filled at a pharmacy not used by that particular patient, which he then sold at an enormous profit. It was so easy to do that before long he was writing dozens of prescriptions. There were plenty of pharmacies to which Camelia could go and always pay in cash. He laughed when Camelia had suggested that they change the name of the clinic to "Jellens' Drug Store." He had to admit that they had given the word *drug store* a whole new meaning.

At times the bigger laugh was that *if* a pharmacist questioned a prescription, he or she would call Jellen to confirm it was legitimate. Jellen told Camelia that if she was too bossy, he'd tell the pharmacist her "script" was a forgery, and she'd be arrested.

Distribution turned out not to be a challenge. Some of Dr. Jellen's patients went through the monthly maximum of narcotics quickly and requested more before it was time to refill; sometimes the story was they had "lost" their bottle. For the ability to refill early, he discovered they were willing to pay a premium. Whenever he found one of his patients selling extra medication on the side, in return for not turning them in, he made them split the money with him. He had recruited enough patients to form an illegal narcotics pyramid, where they made money too. Camelia dubbed it the "Frequent Refillers Reward Program." If he expanded his "prescription business" to his winter home on the west side of Florida by Naples, where many Minnesotans went, he was assured of an unending stream of tax-free cash.

After seeing all his scheduled patients that morning, Dr. Jellen looked up from his desk as Camelia walked into his office and asked, "Would you like me to get some lunch?"

"That would be great," he replied. "Are you going to do takeout from Byerly's?" Byerly's was a famous Minnesota grocery story a few blocks away on France Avenue that is known for its upscale class, food quality, and décor.

"Yes. Do you want the usual?"

"Wild rice soup," Dr. Jellen said with a shrug as Camelia turned to leave.

"Looks like that last patient is a no-show," Camelia added. "The next patient isn't due until 12:30. I suggest you make your calls. Time to cash in on the time you've given these guys."

"Whatever you say, *Dear. . ."* he spoke sarcastically, not covering up the anger he felt when she kept pushing him to come up with instant money. Only he knew how to pull the strings at the right time. He knew there was a lot of easy money out there, if he was careful, and he believed his version of the American Dream was finally going to reward him with everything he wanted. . .and deserved.

Picking up the TV remote, Dr. Jellen clicked on the local news for an update from the scene at the university. The network had hardly interrupted its live feed during the entire morning. As the image of the same female reporter came on the screen, she said, "We have been told that there were ten people meeting in the conference room at the time of the blast. However, there were many others in adjoining rooms and in the courtyard in front of the building who were either injured or killed as well. We still do not know how many deaths have occurred here."

The same feeling of oppression he'd felt earlier in the morning washed over him again. Something heavy and menacing. Something was wrong, but he just couldn't place it. Nevertheless, he felt it to his core.

3

Life is pleasant. Death is peaceful.
It's the transition that's troublesome.

Isaac Asimov

CHAPTER 3

"I GOT BOTH CLIENTS ONBOARD, just as I said, and one of their wives," Dr. Jellen said with a smile as Camelia brought in their takeout lunch and carefully set the sack from Byerly's on the credenza in back of his desk.

"Get me the prescriptions, and I'll get them started," she replied matter-of-factly, lifting his Styrofoam container of soup out of the bag. "We need to keep building this if we're going to pay for all your toys."

Dr. Jellen shook his head and turned back to the TV. *And you're my most expensive toy!*

"The powerful explosion at the university Neurology Department may have been caused by military-grade explosives, according to informed sources," the reporter Cheryl Nelson said. "Given the size of the explosion and the number of people killed, it is being considered a terrorist attack by Homeland Security until proven otherwise. The FBI agents from the Minneapolis office were some of the first to arrive on the scene, and there's additional support from Washington on its way."

"So much for *Minnesota nice*," Camelia commented, glancing up at the screen. "What is the world coming to? Terrorists killing neurologists? Ridiculous."

"I can't believe it," Dr. Jellen replied, his eyes fixed on the reporter. "What motive—"

"No one has been identified by authorities," Nelson continued, "pending identification of the bodies and notification of next of kin."

"I'll bet I knew every one of those doctors," Dr. Jellen broke in.

"You know just about every M.D. in Minneapolis," Camelia said, then she chuckled to herself. "As if you give a rip if somebody thinned the herd a bit for you. It might actually mean more business. Don't go getting all teary eyed about it."

"Why don't you just shut up for a while," Dr. Jellen snapped, his anger flashing. "What do you know about what I care about?"

"Oh, boy, I know what you care about," Camelia whispered to herself as his attention went back to the TV.

Cheryl Nelson was joined by a gray-haired man with a strong chiseled jaw and a dark suntan. She said, "I have with me Dr. Jason Volatta, a retired FBI explosives expert. I understand, Dr. Volatta, that we may be dealing with a C-4 type of military-grade explosive. Is that true?"

Volatta nodded and answered, "It's very early in the investigation, but the appearance of the scene would suggest C-4, at least as a consideration."

"Can you explain for the viewers, please, what C-4 is?"

"C-4, or Composition 4, is a plastic bonded explosive, also called PBX, or simply a plastic explosive. It consists primarily of an explosive compound, a binder, and a plasticizer. The plasticizer makes it highly malleable, with the consistency of modeling clay. In this form, it is extremely stable. You can roll it into a ball and play catch with it safely or even throw it in a fire and it will burn slowly. For C-4 to explode requires a detonator to be shocked. In the United States, C-4 is tightly guarded and all but impossible to steal from the military. It comes typically as M112, 1.25 pounds each."

Nelson glanced at some of the CSIs who were walking in back of them and continued, "So how does the FBI determine who did this? Isn't a plastic explosive such as C-4 totally destroyed or vaporized when it blows up?"

"The analysis varies with the type of explosive and detonator. If, for example, there was a small plastic electronic timer, there might be pieces left, depending on whether it was electronic or mechanical. If the bomb was more sophisticated, using an attached cell phone as the detonator, the metal parts might survive the blast."

"It's hard to believe you can find anything traceable."

"You'd be surprised what we find. If any part of the timer survives, we look for the make, and if we get very lucky, we might get a fingerprint off, say, the battery."

"So far," Nelson continued, "the cleaning crew did not see anything suspicious in the room last night, at which time the room was reported to have been locked by security. There is a report that a cake box was delivered to the meeting this morning. If that package contained a bomb, what might the FBI find?"

"If it was a bomb, and we don't know that yet, a simple 'trip-wire' type of device, that is, a detonator cord, could have been attached to the cover. Or an electronic sensor for when the box was opened would do it. Those methods of setting off the explosive are harder to find."

"In that case, what would you do?"

"If a plastic explosive was determined," Dr. Volatta answered, "we would look for the taggant."

"A taggant," Nelson repeated, looking somewhat puzzled. "What is that?"

"A taggant is a chemical substance, such as 2, 3-dimethyl-2, 3-dinitrobutane, called DMDNB for short, which functions as a chemical marker and is added to any C-4 that is legitimately manufactured for the military. Different manufacturers in different countries would add, as the name suggests, a tag—that is, a chemical that survives the explosion and is unique to where it was manufactured."

"So it would be simple to trace?"

"Yes, but only if the C-4 was made in a non-terrorist country and stolen, for instance. The terrorists, if sponsored by a government, might have had it made in their home country where no tag was added."

"Then what?"

"Then from the chemical analysis we could determine a plastic type of explosive, but not the country of origin. This isn't as bad as it sounds, however, because we would have eliminated many countries and could surmise a terrorist origin. The untagged PBX would have been made in only a few places in the world."

As Dr. Volatta talked, Nelson had been holding her hand over her ear, clearly listening to something from her producer. "I have a breaking report from the station that the financial sponsor of the research project that was the topic of this morning's discussion in the Department of Neurology conference room was missing from that meeting. He is also said to have sent the cake box to the meeting. Attempts to reach him by phone have been made, but his number has been disconnected. He is an Iranian, whom we are pursuing leads on. . . . What do you make of that, Dr. Volatta?"

"Well," the bomb expert said, shaking his head, "I'm not going to jump to conclusions before the facts are established. There are many fine Iranians who live in and love this country and are as loyal as the most patriotic citizen."

"But you can't dismiss the source."

"Of course not. Iran is the classic case of state-sponsored terrorism with a violently radical, amoral leadership that has been at war with us for decades. For an Iranian man to miss a meeting like this is highly suspicious, especially if he sent the box. You can bet the FBI is checking every lead."

"Dr. Volatta, the first presidential debate is scheduled here at the university in about three weeks. Do you think there is a relationship?"

"It certainly is intriguingly coincidental. The lead teams for both candidates will arrive in town over the next few days as will the Secret Service. I can guarantee there will be much discussion between those groups and the explosives investigative team. What doesn't figure is why terrorists would blow up part of the Neurology Department."

"Do you think this could be an attempt to disrupt the election process by the Iranians? Or to intimidate the candidates?"

Volatta responded, "Anything is possible. President Kozdronski has had a 'zero-tolerance' policy toward Iran, which has worked to restrain their level of terrorism. And part of the president's policy was retaliation, so when Iran tried to attack one of our navy aircraft carriers operating in the Persian Gulf, his immediate response was to sink two of their navy's ships. While I am not an expert on political terrorism, there's no question that the president is despised in Tehran."

"Thank you for your insight, Dr. Volatta," Nelson concluded, then turned back to look directly into the camera. "We will continue our live coverage and report to you as more information breaks regarding this horrible tragedy here on the Minneapolis campus of the University of Minnesota."

Camelia had her cup of soup and drink in hand, standing at Dr. Jellen's doorway. "Iranian terrorists bombing your old neurology buddies," she said sarcastically. "You might be next. 'Anything is possible,' right? The Iranians hate drug dealers, you know."

Dr. Jellen didn't bother to look up. There was something about this that had his stomach turning in knots, and it had nothing to do with who had died in the blast. He walked to the window in his office that overlooked the parking lot and street and wondered what it was.

Communism is like prohibition,
it's a good idea but it won't work.

Will Rogers

CHAPTER 4

"YOU'RE GETTING SLOPPY AGAIN," Camelia warned, stepping into Dr. Jellen's office with a handful of paperwork after one of his midafternoon patients had left. "You can't just keep dealing Vicodin to everyone who comes in here. The more you vary the prescriptions, the less chance we have of being noticed."

"Paul. . .whatever his name is. . .was on it before he came to me," Dr. Jellen replied, "and he's really got an appetite for it. I'm doing him a favor by schooling him on keeping sober and not mixing. Just get him what I say, and he might develop into more than just a user."

"I don't know about that. . . . I don't trust him yet," said Camelia. "He's a weird guy, and he hits on me every time he's in the waiting room."

"They all hit on you. That's why you're out there. Like bees to honey. They're not blind. And it's good for business."

"Well, Paul is weird, and Vicodin isn't his only addiction, I can assure you of that," ventured Camelia. "Speaking of addictions, you have about forty-five minutes before Mrs. Lindahl gets here. Remember, I can listen in on what's going on after you shut the door. She's got the hots—"

"Like I'd be interested in that cow, for crying out loud," Dr. Jellen snapped. "Don't you have something to do. . .like bill someone?"

Camelia broke into a twisted smile and laughed to herself as she turned and went back down the hallway to her desk.

Dr. Jellen glanced at his watch and pressed the cable remote to "9." He found his clients were easily impressed by his observations on world events, so he had become something of an astute news junkie over the years.

The cable political reporter Signe Larson was seated at her desk with a guest next to her and saying, "We are counting down to the U.S. presidential election that is now three months away. With both parties' national conventions being held early this year, the candidates agreed to move up the date of their first presidential debate, which is to occur in three weeks at the University of Minnesota, only a few blocks from the site of this morning's deadly explosion. There has been no word on whether this first debate will take place as scheduled. Reliable sources close to the investigation of the blast indicate a connection to Iran, but this may simply be coincidental. We will keep you updated on the explosion as more information becomes available."

As everyone had expected, President Felix Kozdronski, the incumbent for the last four years, had coasted to an easy win through his party's primaries and the national convention. He was popular, personable, and looked impossible to beat, since during his tenure the economy had boomed until recent months, and no one credible dared to blame him for the downturn. Even through the downturn, unemployment had remained relatively low, and through a series of discerning spending cuts, Kozdronski had actually been able to *reduce* taxes for all income groups, for which the leading economists and the stock market applauded loudly. He had been able to get economic and ethnic groups across the spectrum "to work together for America."

Meanwhile, other than a few regional hot spots, the world was relatively at peace. U.S. troops were only serving overseas in peacekeeping roles in a few places, and none were involved in combat situations. Early in Kozdronski's presidency, after he stated in his

Inaugural Address that he would have a "zero-tolerance" policy for terrorist nations, specifically calling out Iran by name, Iran had condemned his administration and issued a warning. A month later the Iranians sent a small surface boat that launched a torpedo against the USS *Abraham Lincoln* (CVN 72), a Nimitz-class of nuclear powered aircraft carriers, which was on patrol around the Persian Gulf. The attack was unsuccessful, and in retaliation to the threat on the 5,000 men and women on the supercarrier, Kozdronski ordered the carrier to attack two Iranian destroyers, both of which were sunk. Following that incident, the Iranians had made a lot of noise, but caused no real trouble, until possibly now with the bombing on the University of Minnesota.

The Kozdronski administration had also been very effective in improving national energy supplies. Despite waves of opposition, he pressed through legislation for speeding up the licensing process for nuclear plants for electricity, made breakthroughs in extraction of shale oil, and helped make it financially feasible for the home use of solar and fuel cells. He had also been able to get all the states to agree to a uniform and year-around Daylight Savings Time, which alone had saved a stunning 3 percent in national electrical costs.

While President Kozdronski's approval ratings were relatively high for a sitting president, after four mostly stable years and few high-water achievements, he suffered from the usual wear-and-tear of partisan politics and general boredom that often goes with the office. Meanwhile, the non-incumbent party's primary and national convention had been hard fought and had captivated the news.

Signe Larson, an attractive blond thirty-year-old journalist, turned to her guest and said, "In the studio today is Dr. Deborah Steinberg, a Wharton School of Business economist and a Nobel Prize Laureate in international economics. Thank you for joining us."

"You're welcome," Dr. Steinberg said and smiled pleasantly. In her late fifties, she had a quiet dignity to her expression. "Thank you for having me."

"Dr. Steinberg," Larson started in, "given today's shocking events, it appears Iran could resurface as an international relations problem, but China's economic concerns are already coming into play in this year's presidential election. Although the United States' manufacturing, which depends on cheap labor to compete globally, is still moving overseas to China, the Chinese contend that our manufacturing is moving increasingly to cheaper labor sources in other countries of the Far East and, in the last few years, Africa, thus hurting China's economy, particularly with the mild slowdown in the American economy. What do you think about the Chinese concerns?"

Steinberg took a deep breath and replied, "Let me back up and say that the Kozdronski administration has made a strong case for the economic fact that as long as the business sector is strong, the morphing of displaced U.S. manufacturing workers from unskilled to more skilled ultimately means cleaner, better paying jobs, which has happened continuously since the beginning of the Industrial Revolution. As far as Communist China, however, the movement of manufacturing to other countries is a huge concern, because their economy is state-run and not able to easily change its labor force into different jobs, as one can in a free-market society that responds naturally to change. I won't comment on the politics of communism versus democracy other than as pertains to economics."

"Kozdronski has stood firm with Taiwan, even though the Communist Chinese government has continued to cause problems with the Taiwan issue because of economic concerns. Give us your perspective on the issue."

Steinberg replied, "Actually, Taiwan and Beijing represent almost a perfectly paired scientific experiment of two radically different economic systems, because both systems have an identical ethnic base. In the experiment analogy, mainland China would be the 'control group' and Taiwan the 'test group.' Taiwan relies heavily on exports and has far fewer natural and human resources than the Beijing government, yet Taiwan has always outperformed them. With their free-market economy, Taiwan responds with the integration of millions of mini-experts on the front lines of business making instantaneous decisions based on the present economic reality. Meanwhile, a few bureaucrats with centralized and politicized plans in Beijing try to do the same."

"Can you simplify that down?" Larson asked.

Steinberg nodded and chuckled. "Certainly. Think of it like this. The economy of any large system—in this case a whole country— works best if very small 'microeconomic' units that are trying to make a profit every day, such as individual business owners and family businesses, are allowed to do just that without excessive government interference. Putting all those small microeconomic units together, or integrating them, makes a large 'macroeconomic' unit—a country in the largest case—and forms a powerfully successful economy with jobs for all who want to work."

"Sounds like you're making a political statement there."

"No, not at all. I was raised in a liberal family, and I still vote left-of-center for many candidates. But as I have been doing my research over the last twenty-five years, the facts have changed my view from a centrally run economy to a decentralized economy."

"Many of your colleagues don't agree."

"That's an understatement," Steinberg agreed. "But remember, most politicians, economists, and reporters have never run a business. So even with the best intentions, they don't know what it really takes to make business work on a daily basis. Most of us academicians base our theories on ideals, not facts, unfortunately. I did for a long time."

Larson continued, "Some economists say it isn't so much the island of Taiwan being independent; rather, it is that the mainland Chinese don't like the comparison to Taiwan, which, like Hong Kong before it when it was free, is booming economically with a huge capitalist middle class of whom the *least wealthy live much better* than almost all of the mainlanders. True or false?"

Steinberg answered, "When it comes to economic systems, no one likes to hear that their neighbor who has fewer resources is doing much better than they are, whether it's the Joneses up the street or the smaller country with an identical ethnic base. Mainland China had done well economically, and the communist dictatorship or dictatorial oligarchy in communist clothes is richer than ever. Make no mistake, they love the influx of capitalist money, and some of that has filtered down to the tiny but growing middle class. Now that the mainland middle class can afford computers and see the prosperity of Taiwan, it's creating real problems."

"So the Internet is making that much of a difference?"

"For decades, a communist or any other dictatorship could control the media and tell their citizens that they had it better than anyone else. How would the people know there were much better and fairer economies out there? They could block radio and TV, outside newspapers, burn books, and so on to prevent the truth from reaching their people. They cannot prevent satellite transmissions, but by making ground receivers punishable by death, they in effect shut that down. The Internet is harder, though, because there are enough honest low-level government workers who see the truth and share it with trusted friends and relatives. Now that some of the mainland Chinese population has enough money to afford computers, there is a secret underground circulation of CDs, DVDs, and USB memory sticks that shows the truth about economic systems. That is bad news for Beijing!"

"Dr. Steinberg, with so many differences between the United States and China, what brings them together?"

The Nobel economist responded, "It is an interesting, *symbiotic* relationship...and fairly simple as well. China has a huge labor force that makes decent goods cheaply, and the U.S. has the money and the markets for those goods that many Americans couldn't ordinarily afford if produced domestically. The Chinese are now the world's largest exporting nation, finally surpassing Germany. Despite China's population being about four times that of the U.S., its GDP or Gross Domestic Product is only 25 percent that of America's. On a per capita basis, China produces only one-sixteenth of the United States. Sales to the U.S., its largest trading partner besides the European Union, make up 10 percent of the Chinese GDP and 20 percent of its exports. China needs America to buy their goods as well as to have the economic strength to outsource their manufacturing there for the other half of the symbiosis. If China's productivity improved, it would depend less on the United States, but this poor productivity is typical of a communist system."

"Thank you, Dr. Steinberg, for your perspective on how relations with China are affecting this year's presidential election," Larson concluded, then turned toward the large screen next to her right and continued, "We have another guest joining us from our studio in San Francisco, the former Ambassador to China, Dean Richards. Ambassador Richards, do you have any comments regarding Dr. Steinberg's assessment of the Chinese situation?"

Richards, a tall and stooped older gentleman in a black suit, noted, "I agree with Dr. Steinberg's analysis, although I will say that the mainland Chinese communists are adapting much faster today than in the past. The party ideologues came out with their new interpretation of Mao's doctrines, stating that *limited* capitalism that helps pay for all the needs of the *true* communists is right and proper. As such, they *aren't really* capitalists; rather, they are *using* capitalism to further communism. This, they say, is *not* a shift in Maoist policy."

"But you disagree?"

"Absolutely," Richards said, shaking his head. "Capitalism is capitalism. By way of contrast, although their puppet government in North Korea should have been a good source of manufacturing and income for Beijing to further exploit, as well as to become a competitor for any business going to Africa, North Korea is a black hole that refuses to adapt politically to the new world economics. China has sent over hundreds of advisors and massive financial aid, but to no avail. North Korea makes Cuba look like a booming free-market economy. Just as China and Taiwan reflect their economic systems, the differences between North and South Korea are stunning economically."

"In a rally in San Francisco today, Senator Le said that in the interest of world peace, we need to endeavor to get along with the communist Chinese. His quote was that 'We should show favoritism to no nation and peace to all.' He also has indicated in past weeks that he believes the president needs to be more conciliatory and understanding toward Tehran."

Camelia had returned to Dr. Jellen's office and was standing in the doorway listening. "Has she said anything about how Senator Le is doing the polls?"

"President Kozdronski is still leading in the polls," Dr. Jellen said, "but Senator Le is gaining ground quickly. The trade issues with China are heating up, which might be a negative for Kozdronski. Le is very charismatic, and he might be able to trump his heritage in dealing with them. His parents were native Chinese who moved here before he was born. I like the guy. He's good."

"You like him because he's just like you," Camelia said knowingly. "Why anyone trusts him is beyond me."

"Because he's so good at selling himself," Dr. Jellen answered. "People believe every word he says. . .like he's a god or something."

Camelia nodded. "He is a fantastic liar, I'll give you that. Did you and he go to the same school?"

Dr. Jellen chuckled, appreciating the compliment, then turned back to the television interview.

5

*It's no wonder that truth
is stranger than fiction.
Fiction has to make sense.*

Mark Twain

★ ★ ★ ★ ★

CHAPTER 5

WHEN DR. JELLEN'S FOCUS returned to his big screen TV, Camelia went back to the reception area. Ambassador Richards was talking again. "We have always endeavored to get along with every nation. But like a successful marriage, the other party has to have a similar desire or it doesn't work."

Signe Larson glanced up from her papers and said, "The Chinese are angry that U.S. companies continue to increase the outsourcing of manufacturing to other countries, especially Africa. You have said they blame *that* on former President Jenkins. Is that true?"

"Yes, it's true," Richards said. "What President Jenkins did was great for America, tapping into the cheaper labor in Africa as labor costs in China were rising. It is all about money to the Chinese. When I served in China under President Jenkins years ago, one of the Chinese embassy staff, after one too many drinks, told me, 'That *black* president has cost us a lot of money. We do not favor anyone like him ever again.' He was dead serious."

"Mr. Ambassador, that lends itself to the ongoing conspiracy theory regarding the would-be assassination attempt upon President Jenkins when he was in office. The official story was that the white supremacist who shot and wounded the president was working alone, and that the assassin was killed almost instantly by a bullet fired by the Secret Service. You were the chairman of the special committee to investigate the assassination plot. Given your experience as a CIA operative, what can you say about that?"

"As you know," the former ambassador responded, "we interviewed thousands of people and spent a good deal of resources on independent research. Initially, it seemed as simple as a deranged racist who managed to get past security, shot the president, and then was shot dead. As with the assassination of John Kennedy, though, there were inconsistencies the committee could not resolve. For example, was the fatal bullet from a Secret Service .357-chambered SIG Sauer P229 pistol, or was it a 7.65 millimeter caliber bullet often used by Chinese secret agents? The problem is that the bullets are very similar, and the recovered bullet that passed through the supremacist was damaged from ricocheting on the pavement, which made a positive identification impossible."

The reporter continued, "What about the assassin himself? The unsuccessful shooting seemed to be meticulously planned, but the supremacist was described by his own mother as not 'the sharpest knife in the drawer.' No one believes he just decided that morning to load his gun, go to town, and shoot the president."

"Yes, that is another point of contention. The would-be assassin knew exactly where the president would be, who would be around him, and when. That depth of knowledge was far more than was generally known by the public. Also, the media surrounding the president that day provided a wealth of high-quality still photographs and video recordings. Most of the people around the president at the time of the shooting were later identified. Clearly, no other white supremacists were anywhere in the crowd that day. There were, however, two people of Chinese heritage standing next to the shooter. Neither was ever identified, but both had heavy overcoats with long sleeves that could easily have concealed a weapon."

"What about the analysis of the direction of the shot that killed the would-be assassin."

"In a normal situation, that would be of value. But the instantaneous chaos after he shot President Jenkins made an analysis impossible. So many Secret Service agents and bystanders tackled the shooter to the ground, and one agent discharged his sidearm while wrestling with the perpetrator. A lot different than when Jack Ruby shot Lee Harvey Oswald."

"Mr. Ambassador, the Chinese immediately spun this as a white-black racial issue. Does that imply their involvement?"

"Well, only in that their propaganda came out so quickly. But there was at least one Iranian nearby the president as well. We identified him as a member of the Iranian embassy staff to Canada. Unfortunately, he flew back to Tehran before we could question him, and Iran has never allowed us to interview him."

"But the Chinese were thoroughly embarrassed by what followed. Do you really think that when their propaganda machine planted stories about worsening American race relations and fabricated hate stories in both the U.S. and international media, the Chinese actually thought it would start race riots and weaken President Jenkins' administration?"

"There's no question that was their intent, though they badly miscalculated race sentiments here at the time. Their attempt to make old race riot footage appear current was beyond ridiculous. Besides, President Jenkins was the antithesis of a racist, and his administration was so clean that race relations were at an all-time best here. There was no real racial fuse to light by a single white supremacist."

The reporter said, "I once had a Chinese diplomat ask me, off the record, 'What were you Americans thinking when you went outside your *dominant race* for a president?' To him, the American Dream of equal opportunity for all was simply some opium for the masses. Do the communists still hold to that?"

"They haven't tossed Karl Marx off the bus yet. They don't understand the vast freedoms we take for granted or the racial equality we enjoy compared to other countries. Our children are able to pursue their dreams, which isn't possible in China. . .or to listen to a news program like yours. Even our poorest people live better than the vast majority of the rest of the world."

The reporter asked, "Would you remind our viewers of what happened between the NRA and ACLU after the assassination attempt?"

"It was unprecedented and symbolic of what was happening across America. As you recall, Signe, the NRA, wanting America to know that the shooter was *not* an NRA member and that President Jenkins was a hunter and a *devoted* NRA member, kept a 24/7 prayer vigil outside the White House during the president's recuperation. The NRA put up a million dollar reward for any coconspirators who were apprehended and convicted.

"The president, who was a bit unconventional, was also an *active* ACLU member. The ACLU decided that if the NRA could keep a vigil, they could as well. Suddenly. we had the NRA and ACLU side by side around the clock in front of the White House. At first there were concerns that the groups might clash, but just the opposite happened. With so much time to kill, members from both groups began talking for the first time in decades and found they agreed on a number of issues—most issues, actually. But each had a different way of getting to their goal.

"The NRA members actually strongly believed in free speech as long as it was applied to all media venues, not just the print media. Meanwhile, the ACLU vigorously agreed that the Second Amendment to the Constitution, the right to bear arms, was precisely that; they just didn't want anyone indiscriminately shooting anyone else. The NRA members didn't want their guns confiscated any more than the ACLU members wanted their free speech confiscated. The NRA people defended their right to own firearms as well as protect themselves and their families with force as a last resort. And the ACLU conceded that the criminals seemed to be able to get guns even in states where it was illegal for people to have guns. Being in the District of Columbia, where gun ownership for the average citizen is suppressed and yet its murder rate was sky high seemed to make the definitive case for the average citizen being accorded their right to own, conceal, and carry."

The reporter added, "And once the president was clearly on the way to recovery, this unlikely alliance was the fodder for unending jokes and satire by comedians and TV late shows."

"But the Chinese didn't get it and still don't quite comprehend what happened. They can't understand the value of diverse groups dialoguing and solving problems."

"Senator Le stated that since his family was more recently American citizens than other candidates, he is more sensitive to global needs and attitudes. What do you think of that?"

"I agree that immigrant families have a different perspective, but President Kozdronski has shown great empathy for all types of ethnic groups. And his parents were born in Poland, so Senator Le has no advantage over him in that regard."

"Do you think there's anything to the rumors that the Chinese and Iranians are secretly providing financial aid to Le's campaign, thinking he will have an easier foreign policy toward them?"

"I can't comment on the campaign finance rumors. But clearly the Chinese would like Le to win, since they view him as more pro-Chinese. However, given the stated reason that his parents left China, they should be careful what they wish for. While he may be more sympathetic to *Chinese people*, Le may not be as sympathetic to *communist Chinese government officials*.

"When President Kozdronski was first elected, a Chinese official said to me, 'Thank Mao, Kozdronski is a white Catholic.' The Chinese view Catholics as more naïve than others, assuming the basic good in everyone, and therefore easier to manipulate. However, they don't like his Polish heritage, since the Poles are much less tolerant of communism following the Russian occupation, economic decimation, and murder of millions of Poles until the late 1980s. And Kozdronski has continued Jenkins' policy of encouraging the outsourcing of manufacturing to Africa. In terms of Iran's preference in a president, they would embrace *anyone* who is more conciliatory toward them. Kozdronski has frustrated their state-sponsored terrorism, whereas Le wants to extend them an olive branch, so clearly Iran wants a Le election."

Signe Larson glanced down at her papers and asked, "What about the occasional Chinese threat to unload their trillions of dollars of U.S. Treasury notes—the so-called 'economic nuclear threat'?"

"Certainly a concern, but this might backfire and hurt the Chinese more than the Americans. There is symbiosis here, too. Who will buy their goods if there is no America? China now is an oligarchy—basically a dictatorship run by a small group who have become extremely wealthy thanks largely to the United States. They are CINOs—Communists in Name Only. Why would they kill the golden goose? And worst-case scenario, America could simply not honor the bonds held by the Chinese or print so much money that inflation would kill their value."

"One last question, Mr. Ambassador. What do you think about the possibility that Iran was involved in this morning's explosion at the University of Minnesota?"

"My sources indicate the sponsor of the research group, a man named Adel Jalili, is of Iranian descent. I'm told he has abruptly disappeared, and that the FBI is searching for him. We don't know if he is a private citizen, government official, or even if Jalili is his real name. We have no photographs of him. Unofficial reports are that the funding for the project that he sponsored flowed directly from an Iranian bank. This is quite concerning. If indeed Tehran is involved, they can expect a decisive retaliatory strike from our military. This type of terrorism works against Iran and would strengthen the public behind Mr. Kozdronski; so if it is of their doing, it may really be their *undoing*."

At the mention of the name *Jalili*, all the blood had drained out of Dr. Jellen's face. "Oh my God. I can't believe it's him," he whispered, closing his eyes and recalling his brief encounter with a man named Jalili. Then he heard Camelia's footsteps.

Camelia stepped quickly into his office, looking concerned and a bit frightened. "*He's* back again. And I don't like the look in his eyes. What did you do?"

6

*A good plan, violently executed now,
is better than a perfect plan next week.*

General George S. Patton

CHAPTER 6

I N A PLUSH GOVERNMENT office beyond the borders of the United States, others were watching the satellite feed of the American election news with great interest.

"How do you think it is going?" the first official asked.

"Better than anticipated so far, but still early," the second official replied. "Overall, the *New America* project has gone well. It was a magnificent stroke of luck that the Finance Minister's son was doing research and stumbled across the work that had already been done. And then for him to realize the potential value of how it could fit into our comprehensive plan was brilliant."

"It is humorous that the Finance Minister himself is concerned about how much this is costing after his son was the one who came up with the crucial piece."

"It is," the second official agreed. "But we have worked for over a generation to make this happen, and although these operations are expensive, the returns will be unimaginable, if we succeed. Meanwhile, the Americans have trained our assets in their finest universities, often through American scholarship money in engineering, finance, political science, computer science, and information technology, including the Finance Minister's son. And the research information he found was done by the Americans themselves. The Finance Minister must get some amusement from all that."

"I know it does amuse him. *Only America* trains its enemy's freedom fighters at its own expense," the first said and chuckled. "But we need the plan to succeed for our future."

"Are the assets in readiness?"

"We are in the process of activating them. We must be careful so as not to raise suspicion. We have dedicated too many years and too much money to become impatient now and miss our opportunity."

"Can we recall our assets if it fails?"

"Yes. Although activated, they will remain hidden until success is certain," answered the first, "so their risk is small. In fact, with few exceptions we could leave them in place even in the face of failure. If we lose a few, the Americans are far too squeamish to use effective interrogation techniques, so they won't find any others. And their courts and newspapers have eliminated any threat of profiling. If Pearl Harbor happened today, their media would make them interview as many Eskimos as Japanese. So if the plan fails to achieve our primary goal, it will not appear as anything out of the norm. But the time is now. We must get rid of Kozdronski. We can't wait any longer."

"We all agree on that," answered the second official.

"After the explosion, do you think Kozdronski will go through with the presidential debate?"

"We believe he has no choice. To not participate will make him appear weak. But security will be tight."

"Do you think going ahead with the explosion was wise this close to the upcoming debate?"

"The debate location was just announced, whereas the explosion had been planned for a long time and could not be put off. Nothing ever goes exactly according to plan," the second observed. "It won't affect the next phase of the project. It does present some immediate opportunities, but we must be patient and execute the plan."

"What is the latest information on Mr. Jalili?"

"I have heard nothing new. The Americans are saying he has vanished, so it appears we are successful there."

7

Caution is a most valuable asset in fishing,
especially if you are the fish.

Author Unknown

CHAPTER 7

*H*E DID NOT have an appointment with Dr. Jellen, but *He* had not only insisted on being seen but that the remaining scheduled patient for the day would be canceled. *He* occasionally dropped in unannounced, but as the most important patient Dr. Jellen had ever had, *He* was always seen and given VIP treatment. *He* was the one patient who had turned Dr. Jellen's narcotics business into a cash cow.

"Bring him back," Dr. Jellen spoke in a thin, rasping voice after Camelia had stepped into his office and announced that *He* was waiting.

"You look as if you just saw a ghost," Camelia said quietly, glancing back down the hallway. "What's going on? What have you hidden from me now? You're not trying to shut this guy's pipeline down, are you?"

"No, no," Dr. Jellen sputtered; his face was flushed and his broad forehead was furrowed with anxiety. She had no idea of just how much he hadn't told her. "Shut up and let me think."

Dr. Jellen could hear his heart pounding in his head as a knot swelled in his throat. In that moment, his mind flashed back to an earlier conversation they had in this very office.

He had started out as a regular pain patient a few years before and was one of the first to participate in Dr. Jellens' narcotics-for-resale business, although *He* never used them himself. Although *He* didn't seem all that excited about the drugs and money, Dr. Jellen was certain from their first meeting that this guy was an astute businessman, a big fish he could use to reel in even bigger fish or at least large schools of smaller fish; the cash flow was the same either way. If he played the guy right, and was slow, steady, and patient, and used the right lures, mostly money, at the right moment he would set the hook and make a killing.

It didn't matter to Dr. Jellen that he didn't actually know where *He* was from. *He* said *He* was from St. Paul, a community that had welcomed more Somalians and Hmongs into Minnesota than any other city in the United States. What difference did it make if *He* was Hmong or Korean or whatever Asian descent? All that had mattered was that *He* quickly helped Dr. Jellen build his business through referrals and shrewd advice. *He* rapidly built his own list of clients and faithfully paid Dr. Jellen a percentage of the transactions. After a while, *He* knew almost everything about Dr. Jellen's business.

Then one day, after *He* delivered a huge wad of cash to Camelia, *He* had sat down in Dr. Jellen's office and said, "I hope you are pleased with my performance, Dr. Jellen. I have learned much from you, and now I come asking for a favor. I want to do some research on the effects of magnetic fields on the brain."

"What?" Dr. Jellen asked with a hint of the laughter he was trying to restrain. "The effects of magnetic fields on the brain. Why would that interest you?"

"It is of no interest to me," *He* spoke flatly as his dark eyes narrowed slightly. "I have a party that is interested, and they have more money than you've ever dreamed about."

"You're kidding, right?" Dr. Jellen rushed his words, realizing that *He* never kidded. "Look, I'd like to help, but I don't do research."

"I know," *He* had said. "But I also know that you are a friend of Dr. Gene Yone at Minntronic, who is a Senior Vice President as well as an M.D. and Ph.D."

"That's true," Jellen said, wondering how *He* knew that. "We went to medical school together, and you might call him my friend. We're not exactly buddies, though."

"I would like to pay Minntronic to do the study for me."

Dr. Jellen ran his fingers through his dark hair, then rubbed his cheek in thought and said, "From what I know about them, there's no way they'll do that type of research. You'd be better off going to the University of Minnesota Neurology Department and working through them. You might even get a National Institute of Health grant if your research fits their criteria."

He shifted his position in his chair and replied, "I see it as a joint venture between Minntronic and the Departments of Neurology and Electrical and Computer Engineering at the University of Minnesota. And I have enough money lined up to pay for it without all the time and aggravation of going to NIH or some other outside agency. The cash is available immediately. So that should appeal to the researchers."

"How long have you been thinking about this?"

"Longer than you can imagine. You and I can walk away from the pharmacy if we make this happen."

"Have you spoken with Gene?"

"I sent over my associate, Mr. Jalili, but Dr. Yone won't see either me or Jalili. We have called and written, but your friend says he is not interested. Mr. Jalili even stopped by in person without an appointment and waited all day without success. Dr. Yone said they are quite busy with their own product development, and this is outside the parameters of electrical stimulation they have done of neural tissue."

"You didn't go yourself? Gene won't deal with anyone but the top dog."

"No," *He* answered, never changing his expression, "for now I prefer to work through Mr. Jalili. Until we have a deal in place, I do not wish to sign my name on Minntronic's computer, which also takes a digital photograph while the guard is watching at the entrance door."

"What's the big deal?"

"Just being careful. You insist that I be careful in all my work for you. And the financiers demand the same of me for this."

"So what does this have to do with me?"

"You will do it for me."

"What can I do about it?"

"Ask Dr. Yone to have lunch with you, me, and Mr. Jalili. And if you can persuade him, which you are a master at doing, I will reward you handsomely."

"I can do that, most certainly," Dr. Jellen said almost brashly, "but I'm not sure it will change his mind. Do I still get paid if he finally says no?"

"Set it up, please, Dr. Jellen, and I assure that you will be paid. Then let me handle the rest. When Dr. Yone hears what I have to offer, he will say yes."

If only it had all ended there, Dr. Jellen thought as his thoughts returned to the situation at hand and what he should do. He looked around his ornate office, suddenly realizing that he had reached a turning point, and *He* held all the cards. Then he turned back to Camelia, who looked as though her composure was slipping away fast.

Dr. Jellen summoned what little strength he had left, fixed his eyes on Camelia, and said, "Send him in. It'll be okay. I'll explain tonight."

Camelia looked as though she was going to challenge him for a moment, but then turned slowly and walked stiffly back down to the waiting room where *He* was waiting.

8

Tell me what you eat,
and I will tell you what you are.

Anthelme Brillat-Savarin, *The Physiology of Taste, 1825*

★ ★ ★ ★ ★

CHAPTER 8

C AMELIA SEEMED TO BRACE HERSELF as she made her approach. *He* stared at her the entire way to the reception's desk. "Please come back," she said, then turned and walked him to Dr. Jellen's office as she had dozens of times before.

He sat in one of Dr. Jellen's overstuffed red leather chairs before she could offer it to him. "I think Dr. Jellen has gone to the bathroom," she said with a tremor in her tone. "He'll be with you in a few minutes. Would you like some water, coffee, or soda?"

"No, thank you, Camelia," *He* answered and smiled. "Please close the door, though. And don't let anyone disturb our meeting. We'll let you know when we are through. Has the last appointment been canceled?"

"Yes. She'll come tomorrow morning."

"Good. You may go."

Camelia breathed a sigh of relief, turned, and made her exit, closing the heavy mahogany door behind her.

He stood up, stretched his legs, and walked to the office window as he waited for Dr. Jellen to come in. Staring blankly out at the quiet street, *He* thought back again to the lunch meeting that Dr. Jellen had arranged some years ago. *He*, Mr. Jalili, Dr. Jellen, and Dr. Yone had sat down to lunch in a private dining room at the Minneapolis Club where *He* was a member. They made some small talk, mostly about when Jellen and Yone were in school together, ate some appetizers, and sipped their drinks.

Once the wait staff was out of earshot, *He* said, "Dr. Yone, thank you for coming today. I wanted you to personally meet Mr. Jalili and me. Unfortunately, Mr. Jalili has another commitment, so he is going to leave now, and we can talk in detail about the proposal."

With that Mr. Jalili left, after saying his good-byes.

He wasted no time, getting right back to business. "I know, Dr. Yone, that you have not been interested in my project, but I had hoped a private, face-to-face meeting might convince you otherwise."

Dr. Yone pursed his lips and responded, "It isn't that the project might not be worthwhile, but it is well outside Minntronic's normal comfort zone of new product development."

Undeterred, *He* went through the project in detail with Yone and Jellen, stressing the basic research advances it would bring as well as the ultimate help it might bring to humanity with various brain disorders.

"Dr. Yone, not only could this research help humanity, but Minntronic will be compensated at the highest level of research dollars. Minntronic is a public company, and not only did *you* not make a profit last year but *you* may not this year. I will pay Minntronic 80 percent of the money upfront to undertake the project. I can't believe that an infusion of cash wouldn't be welcomed with respect to your bottom line or that it would help to more fully employ some underutilized engineers. If you are not the decision maker for this project, who should I call?"

"I have the authority to do it," Yone said, quickly defending his stature, "and it sounds like a fascinating project. But I ultimately have to defend it to the Board of Directors, and I don't know that I can. Minneapolis is called 'Medical Alley.' There are a number of med-tech firms here run by brilliant physicians and engineers. In fact, at least two of our top engineers who left us are working for CNS, a company here locally that develops and manufactures computer-based equipment for brain monitoring as well as for diagnoses of brain diseases. I could arrange an introduction for you."

"Thank you for the offer, but I have talked with CNS already. They have morphed into Breathe Rights® and are in the process of divesting themselves of the brain monitoring division. I have researched every firm, and Minntronic is the best by far. You have the depth and breadth of engineering and manufacturing that makes you perfect for the task, along with your substantial size."

Dr. Yone held out his hand in resignation and replied, "I'm sorry, but I'm afraid I can't do it. It's just not a fit with us."

He sat forward in his chair and leaned in tighter against Yone. "Dr. Yone, I know about the cover-up for your wife's felonious drug issues."

His words struck the two other men like the sharp blow of a hammer on an anvil. Both Yone and Jellen were stunned by the revelation. Little did Dr. Jellen know that *He* had brought his "son" into the office once, and while *He* distracted both Jellens, the computer whiz copied Jellen's books from QuickBooks. All of the Yone cover-up was in Word files that he thought he'd copy for good measure; they were rich with exacting details.

"This meeting is over!" Yone shouted and started to get out of his chair.

"Sit down!" *He* commanded, flashing his black eyes. "I have enough evidence to put away your wife in federal prison for a very long time. Not only was she using, she was also selling, and some of it was to minors. The federal prosecutor will not cut a deal when it comes to minors."

"You know nothing!" Yone shot back, though his tone had changed.

He then calmly pulled out of his briefcase a packet of documents and plopped them down in front of Yone.

Dr. Yone looked at them as one dazed by a horrible dream. "Where did you get these?" he demanded as he slumped back in his chair.

"It doesn't matter. The charges against her were for using and transporting illicit drugs when she was tried and acquitted. These documents have to do with drug dealing and distribution to minors, so there is no escape through double jeopardy. I have a list of the minors; having talked to their parents, they will all be made available to testify."

"My wife was in a bad place at the time. She has been totally clean now for a long time. This would ruin her and the children!"

"Precisely. And it wouldn't be the best for your aspirations to be CEO of Minntronic, either," He ventured. "I have no desire to hurt you, your wife, or those two beautiful teenage girls of yours. I only want you to do the project." As He leaned back in his chair, He made certain Dr. Yone saw the concealed pistol when his suit coat opened slightly.

Dr. Yone sat like a man who had been stricken dumb, furious but crestfallen. "I'll go to the police and have you arrested for blackmail," Yone warned, forcing out the words. "Besides, Dr. Jellen's testimony will clear her again!"

Jellen had perjured himself and received a lot of cash from Yone for the testimony.

"The police won't prevent what I have on her from coming out, even if I am arrested. And they will never be able to arrest me," He said, then turned his gaze on Jellen. "I'm sure Dr. Jellen will corroborate whatever I say."

From the first revelation, Jellen had felt almost dizzy and disorientated. His face was blotched and glistening with perspiration. "Why would I do that?" he asked lamely.

"Please, Dr. Jellen, no more games. First, I have evidence that you committed perjury in Dr. Yone's wife's case. Second, I have copies of all your accounting records, including the hidden set on narcotics sales. There's enough there to make the *StarTribune* headlines and to put you and the whoring Camelia behind bars for life. No more piña coladas on the beach in Grand Cayman for the two of you! Oh, and your accounting shows sales that involve distribution to minors as well. Prosecuting you and all the rich folks in your system could be the conviction of a lifetime for some politically ambitious young prosecutor in the Hennepin County Attorney's Office."

Dr. Jellen sat very still, stunned, as though he was watching the castle he had worked so hard to build come tumbling down and wash away.

"Gentlemen," *He* went on calmly after having paused to let his documents and words have their maximal effect, "there is no need to despair. I have a project that I must have done. If you cooperate, these records will never be released. It can be an enjoyable experience, if you do.

"As far as what you tell the Minntronic board, Dr. Yone, I will give you a pro-forma financial projection that will impress them, and you will bring in so much money with this project that it will boost your standing at Minntronic. I do insist that you personally run it, and I will put in a generous bonus for you personally if you finish on time. I will also make it financially rewarding for the University of Minnesota neurologists and engineers.

"However, Mr. Jalili will be your liaison with me. Neither of you will tell anyone about my involvement. Mr. Jalili knows nothing of what I know about you, and it will stay that way if you keep your part of the bargain. In addition to absolute confidentiality, at the end of the project all the files will be electronically shredded from your computers and those of your colleagues. All materials will be given to Mr. Jalili.

"Dr. Yone, I saw you staring at my handgun. Yes, it has been used many times on those who were uncooperative over the last twenty-five years. But I don't think we need to go there, do we?

"Should we have lunch?" *He* asked rhetorically as he picked up the menu. "The 'Walleye Milanese with Tomato Basil Sauce' is excellent here."

*Estimated amount of glucose
used by an adult human brain each day,
expressed in M&Ms: 250.*

Harper's Index, October 1989

★ ★ ★ ★ ★

CHAPTER 9

*H*E WAS STILL STANDING at the window in Dr. Jellen's office when a group of kids walking through the parking lot distracted his thoughts momentarily. *Dr. Jellen must have an enlarged prostate, He* thought and laughed. *He* walked slowly back to the leather chair and sat back down, and his mind wandered back to Dr. Yone and the project.

Yone had quickly assembled his team of two other Minntronic engineers, then he called the Professor and Head of the Department of Electrical and Computer Engineering at the University of Minnesota. Three engineering professors jumped at the chance to tackle this new research. Likewise, a private grant of this sort excited three neurology professors as well. As *He* had predicted, the engineers and medical doctors were interested, once Dr. Yone presented the details and got the project rolling. They were intrigued enough to do the research and cooperate without knowing the desired end result. And *He* kept his promise to provide more than enough funding and incentive for the project.

Mr. Jalili had video recorded the sessions for *Him*, and *He* recalled the very first session where one of the university neurologists was instructing the three engineers from the university and the three from Minntronic.

"The nervous system is a biologic computer," the neurologist said, "that adapts to experience with learning and memory storage as well as making new connections called *synapses*. It has a hundred billion nerve cells called *neurons*, each receiving inputs from a thousand synapses coming in from other neurons. Every neuron could output via synapse to multiple neurons. Functionally, the brain is in essence a binary-based computer system, not purely, but quasi-digital, at least in terms of the output of the neuron which either *fires*—a binary "one"—or *doesn't fire*—a binary "zero"—depending on the integration of the inputs from the thousand synapses connecting to that particular neuron.

"In simple terms, the nervous system has a central computer, the brain, with a direct extension of the brain that inputs huge amounts of visual data from the eyes. Optic nerves and pathways project connections to ninety percent of the brain. In the central nervous system, there are the neurons themselves, essentially the computer chips; there are wiring trunks, the white matter tracks, and there is cabling, the spinal cord. The peripheral nervous system begins as the wires leave the cable and become the peripheral nerves leading to various parts of the body. There are peripheral inputs; for example, the sensory nerves from the ears, muscles, joints, skin, and internal organs; and wiring to peripheral outputs, the motor nerves to muscles. The inner ears provide, in addition to hearing, valuable balance information. Various feedback loops work together as automatic control systems. The autonomic nervous system is what works primarily behind the scenes, controlling essentials such as temperature regulation, perspiration, vasoconstriction and vasodilatation, balance, cardiovascular pulse, blood pressure, cardiac output, and automatic breathing."

A second neurologist broke in and said, "It has been said that we only use ten percent of our brain capacity, which is a naïve, older view. Up to that point, researchers may have only fully understood and measured what ten percent does, but one hundred percent was there with a purpose, not simply to take up space. The human brain is not as fast in tasks such as number crunching as a traditional digital computer with a CPU. But the digital computer can't adapt its hardware by creating new circuitry, that is, synapses. Nor does it make new software on its own. Much of the brain's strength comes from its *adaptive* ability to make new hardware connections automatically and generate new software not just from experience but internally from thinking. Much behavior, perhaps eighty percent, is hardware-driven and preprogrammed or with software genetically burned-in. But perhaps twenty percent of behavior can be altered."

The other neurologist nodded and continued, "The brain can also reprogram certain neurons to act as other neurons whose normal function is different, particularly in young individuals—this is called 'plasticity.' You can't do that with computer hardware. The brain does a great deal of automatic parallel processing, a technique used by the British intelligence at Bletchley Park for their parallel processors to great advantage during and after World War II; for the code-breaking tasks for which these processors were designed, they still beat modern general purpose laptops with a half-century newer technology."

Dr. Yone had then stepped forward and addressed the neurologists. "Electromagnetic waves consist of an electrical wave in synchrony with a perpendicularly oriented magnetic wave. Theoretically, both would carry the same information from the sources that created them, but would have different transmission characteristics; that is, they would be affected differently by the substances through which they pass. Researchers learned about some of the electrical properties a century ago. As you know, this resulted in electroencephalography, or EEG, the analysis of brain electrical activity that is widely used today, and magnetoencephalography, or MEG, the analysis of brain magnetic activity, which has never found widespread use.

"Other than electroshock therapy, electrical stimulation of the brain has had limited use; recently, however, studies on lower strength electrical currents through deeply implanted electrodes help certain patients with Parkinson's disease and other movement disorders. Epilepsy patients have been helped by electrical stimulation of a number of parts of the brain. For example, magnetic stimulation has been used to measure the speed of a signal through the brain itself, which is called central conduction time. Magnetic resonance imaging, or MRI, has been used to give a much greater understanding of brain structure and abnormality by using a pulsed magnetic signal and observing the reactions of normal and diseased tissue with sensors and computer analysis.

"So in our project, we will need to decide how to apply the magnetic field. I am assuming it will be pulsed. We will need to decide the location of application, strength of the pulses, and duration of the pulses. Or do we use a continually present field that is modulated?"

In watching Jalili's videos, *He* had noted that as long as Dr. Yone stayed in charge of the project and reined in the engineers, it went smoothly. Jalili was primarily there to record and make certain the process did not bog down. At one point, though, Jalili said to the research group that he thought a digitally pulsed signal would be a better design; he was, in fact, correct, and that is what was done, although the pulsed-digital request really came from *Him,* not Jalili.

The neurologist and engineers were deeply interested in research, and it wasn't long before the research consumed their days. Dr. Yone was relentless to make the project successful in the shortest time frame and drove the project passionately toward its goal. Despite the precarious situation he was in, which he desperately wanted to rid himself of forever, Yone was as fascinated with the project as any of the researchers.

He seemed to have limitless deep pockets that made the chronically financially strapped university researchers ecstatic, and the considerable advance money helped turn Minntronic's R&D department from being a longtime cost center to a profit center that immediately changed the company's bottom line. Granted, *He* and his entities would retain all patent rights, but that wasn't unusual.

The project went well, and *He* was very pleased. Although what *He* wanted to do with the results was never clear to researchers, it was a highly intellectually stimulating project for the entire team, which showed in the results. They were way ahead of schedule, which made Dr. Yone even happier than *He*. Although the researchers could not use any of the results, they knew that what they learned would help them someday with another project. That part they didn't have to give back to *Him*. That had actually been part of the allure of Yone's sales pitch to the other eight.

With the click of Dr. Jellen's office door handle, *He* was instantly snapped back into the present moment.

Dr. Jellen stepped back into his office and immediately said, "I apologize for making you wait so long. I'm afraid I wasn't feeling so good. Did the wild rice soup from Byerly's ever give you diarrhea?"

"Dr. Jellen," *He* said, disregarding the apology, "we had an understanding that you were never to disclose anything about my research to anyone. In return, I agreed to tell no one about your narcotics business or your perjury. On top of that, I turned over all my drug clients to you, allowing you to take all the profits. Am I right about that?" *He* knew from their many discussions that Dr. Jellen considered himself above agreements, having never followed them, and despite the much more serious sub rosa agreement, Jellen liked to impress various people about what he knew. It was partly ego and partly business.

"I didn't tell anyone, including Camelia. I didn't dare."

"Dr. Jellen," *He* said, leaning forward in his deep leather chair, "do you think I'm really as stupid as you are? Do you believe I haven't been listening and watching? I have eyes and ears in your office and home and even your phone, and the two of you have more than loose lips. You are loose cannons rolling around on my deck, and it's time you stopped."

"You heard wrong," Dr. Jellen continued to lie, but his face was white and his lips trembled. "Besides, I really didn't know much about it, other than setting you up to meet Gene."

"Actually," *He* countered, "you took your friend Gene, who is no longer worrying about his wife's drug problems, out several times to see if there was anything you could exploit for your personal gain. Both you and Camelia shared and embellished stories about everything you knew about the project. Fortunately for me, nobody who knows you believes a word you say, so most of the stories were lost in the retelling; unfortunately for the two of you, I was listening."

Dr. Jellen's whole body seemed to shrink and sag with every word *He* said. His chest rose and fell heavily with labored breathing. "Look, okay, so we made a mistake. You and I have been partners for a long time. I'll do anything you ask. What can I do to make it right?"

"Please have Camelia come back and let's settle this."

Dr. Jellen picked up the phone on his desk and called for her to come.

Camelia came quickly, opened the door, and peered in.

"Please come in and close the door, Camelia," *He* said as she stepped inside, then slowly shut the door. "Did you ever tell the good doctor about all the times we met when you told him you were going out with your girlfriends? In your house, and your bed."

Seeing the light literally go out of her face, *He* broke into a shrill, mirthless laugh that betrayed his spirit for the very first time. Ten minutes later, with the issue put to rest, *He* walked out of Dr. Jellen's office and glanced back and forth around the parking lot. The final solution hadn't been in his original plan; however, the grin on his face said it was a fitting ending, after all.

10

*Don't live in a town
where there are no doctors.*

Jewish Proverb

★ ★ ★ ★ ★

CHAPTER 10

I T WAS LATE IN the afternoon, and Jack Stevens, M.D., was sitting in his office in Wayzata, due west of the Twin Cities of Minneapolis and St. Paul, trying to finish his notes from a busy day of seeing patients. But for the moment, his attention was focused on his flat-screened LCD television and an update regarding the explosion at the University of Minnesota Neurology Department that happened the day before. Names had been released to the public in the morning hours, and he knew all the neurologists and two of the engineers who had been killed, as well as some of the support staff in the areas immediately adjacent to the blast. It had been nearly impossible to keep his train of thought on patient care throughout the day. It wasn't until the last patient was gone that he dared to turn the television on, as he found himself deeply disturbed and agitated by the news.

At forty-two years old, Stevens had traveled extensively around the world, both when he was training as a neurologist and recently to attend medical seminars as well as teach them. He could have moved his practice to almost anywhere he wanted, but had spent most of his life in the Twin Cities area because he loved it, and he and his wife felt it was a great place to raise their children. Although it was seldom acknowledged, he had found Minneapolis and St. Paul to be thoroughly sophisticated and cosmopolitan cities yet wonderfully pleasant as well. His wife had often reminded him that they had more Broadway theaters per capita than New York City.

While he acknowledged to colleagues in warmer climes that Minnesota winters included a lot of snow that often blew *sideways* in storms and a lot of cold that could freeze your hair almost instantly at thirty degrees *below zero* and even cause it to *break off* if it was long and wet when you ran out, he loved engaging in the recreational activities during all four seasons. Minnesotans were hardworking and well-educated, and it wasn't a surprise to him that the headquarters of Pillsbury, Target, Northwest Airlines, General Mills, Cargill, Honeywell, Medtronic, Minntronic, 3M, and other Fortune 500 companies had been based here.

Jack also had fallen in love with the suburb of Wayzata since the day his parents had moved there when he was in high school. Located on the north side of Lake Minnetonka and only fourteen miles straight west of downtown Minneapolis, it offered a more relaxed living style from the fast pace of the big city. One of the wealthier cities in the United States, Wayzata was quiet and beautiful and had a low crime rate. In just a matter of minutes, he could be on one of the more than ten thousand Minnesota lakes or out of the city in the rich prairie farmland to the west. Jack's flight instructor once told him that *in winter,* there were ten thousand runways in Minnesota.

Always the amateur historian, Jack enjoyed describing Wayzata's past as the site of the summer White House in the late nineteenth century and a destination vacation as well for the United States. The railroad tracks built by J. J. Hill in 1857 began bringing large groups of people on special boat/cars from Minneapolis that were then disconnected from the train and, via a side track, launched directly into Lake Minnetonka. The group would cruise around the one hundred ten miles of shoreline and learn about the fabulous houses on the lake and the people who built them, then the boat would get hooked back up to another train to be brought back to Minneapolis. Some of those large cruise boats with their heavy steam engines had ended up on the bottom of the lake from various accidents. One boat, the *Minnehaha*, was sunk in 1926, raised in 1980, totally refurbished, and carries riders around the lake once again as it did a century before.

Jack had often taken friends in his own boat from the Wayzata docks, gone a few minutes west to the beautiful lakeshore of the Lafayette Country Club, golfed its nine holes, almost all of which are on or have views of the lake, then enjoyed the superb cuisine at the Lafayette Club. If a friend was a diehard golfer, he would take him to enjoy eighteen holes of championship golf at the Wayzata Country Club, followed by a casual lunch from the Grille while sitting on a dining deck with a spectacular view of the club's famous eighteenth green and sipping a mojito under umbrellas.

Over the years, Jack had built a steady practice. Unlike some of the other doctors he knew who considered patients who brought in printouts from websites about their problems to be nuisances, he found it helpful that his patients were well-informed and cared so much about their medical care. His most common problem was when patients obsessed about medication side effects. An inexperienced reader of package inserts would be scared off even by aspirin, which, if invented today, Dr. Stevens reminded his patients, would be a prescription drug. He found people's fears interesting, since almost all his patients drove cars that brought a national death rate of over forty thousand per year; yet no drug was allowed to be on the market that had one ten thousandth of that rate, and those drugs that do have a certain fatality rate are usually for life-threatening diseases with no alternative therapies. His patients found this analogy comforting, none of whom ever considered giving up their cars, not even the ones who drove small two-seaters that performed so poorly in crash tests.

Detective John Spencer, a short and broad-backed officer from the Edina Police Department, had just stepped into Dr. Steven's second-floor office on Lake Street. He presented his card and badge to Karen Sjogren, Dr. Stevens' long-time secretary. "Nice location," he said, gazing through the large floor-to-ceiling glass windows in the waiting room that provided a panoramic view of Lake Minnetonka across the street. Too cold to be butt glazed, the windows had only minimal dividers. "Nice office," he added, glancing around at the office décor.

"Thank you," Karen said, handing him back his card and badge. "Do you have an appointment, Detective Spencer? Dr. Stevens has already seen his last patient for the day, and I'm sure he's getting ready to leave. I didn't notice you in the computer."

"Well, I can't be in the computer, because I'm standing here," Spencer teased.

Karen responded with a courtesy smile, but it was a joke she'd heard too many times before.

"No, I'm here on police business."

"Is it about a patient? Do I need to pull a chart for Dr. Stevens? If so, I'll need a signed release or warrant."

"I don't think the person was a patient, just someone Dr. Stevens knew."

Karen reached for the phone and pushed the speed dial for Dr. Stevens' extension.

Stevens was seated at his desk, looking at electronic charts on his computer, but also listening to the latest news about the explosion. He picked up the telephone. "Yes, Karen?"

"Dr. Stevens, there is a detective here from the Edina Police Department who would like to talk with you."

"Did he say what it is about?"

"No."

"Okay, bring him back, Karen."

Karen led Detective Spencer down the hallway to Dr. Stevens' office, then knocked on the door. Although she knew Stevens was alone, it was always a courtesy, just in case he was in consultation with a patient or on his cell phone.

"Come in," Stevens said.

Karen opened the door and said, "Dr. Stevens, this is Detective

Spencer. If you need me for anything, please let me know." Then she turned and walked back to her desk.

"Dr. Stevens, I apologize for stopping in so late in the day," Spencer spoke flatly, his wide cheeks showing a light shade of red. "May I have a few minutes of your time?"

"Certainly, Detective. Have a seat." Dr. Stevens minimized the electronic patient charts he was reviewing so they would be secure from view. "Would you like something to drink?"

"If it's after hours, rum and coke will do," Spencer spoke a little too brightly, then laughed and added, "No, thanks, I'm fine. You have a nice office, Doc! What are the fish in the waiting room aquarium?"

"Those are Butterfly Koi, or Dragon Carp, an ornamental breed of the common carp, noted for their elongated finnage. I suppose I should have some walleyes, too, in order to be more Minnesotan."

"Walleyes would be illegal, so I don't recommend them," Spencer replied with a bit of a smirk, stepping toward the west wall of the office that displayed many plaques. "What are all these?"

"Some are awards, some diplomas."

"Where is the Institute of Neurology, Queen Square?"

"It is in London," Dr. Stevens said.

"Why would you go there when there is a great neurology program here at the University of Minnesota as well as the Mayo Clinic in Rochester? I did a little research, Doc," he added, "and Minnesota has always had one of the highest numbers of the best-trained clinical neurologists in the country. Did you know that the original Chief of Neurology at the University of Minnesota, A. B. Baker, was also a founder and the first president of the American Academy of Neurology, in 1948? The AAN is still based here and is the dominant neurological professional organization in the world with over ten thousand members."

"You've been doing your research, Detective," Dr. Stevens observed, "but not enough. As you'll see from the diplomas, I also studied at the Mayo Clinic after being at the University of Minnesota. I went to Queen Square for the same reason I went to the excellent neurology program at Mayo Clinic, for a Fellowship. There is still some art in medicine and neurology. Styles are a little different in each place. Queen Square had a long and prestigious past history with some of the world's legendary neurologists. Patients who have been everywhere else in the United Kingdom without results go to Queen Square as their last hope.

"Actually, while I was there, I saw my only case of leprosy, which involves the nervous system. That patient was from a former British colony in Africa. His case reminded me about just how little we understand about the workings of the brain. I tell patients that God gave us the human body, but not the operating manual. It's as though we've been given a computer that works on its own, but no instruction or repair manual came with it. Queen Square also had some interest in the effects of magnetic fields on the brain, which is a personal interest of mine. Besides, the Brits have a neat accent! Their version of English always sounds more erudite than ours, doesn't it?"

"I'll have to look that one up, but I'm guessing that yes it does, especially as compared to my English." Detective Spencer was still smiling and looking over Stevens' various diplomas and awards.

Dr. Stevens had done a year's internship at Hennepin County Medical Center, a Level I Trauma Center in downtown Minneapolis. The teaching and learning opportunities there were outstanding. He had more direct life-and-death responsibility in his first year than programs at other well-known institutions have in their last year of residency. HCMC is integrated into the University of Minnesota, such that the staff physicians are also professors at the university. Many of the residents at the U in various programs, including neurology, rotated through HCMC. When Jack was there as an intern, or PGY 1, rotating through Internal Medicine, he might be on thirty-six hours straight, then off twelve hours. He figured up his hours once and discovered that for this brutal schedule he was paid about ninety-two cents an hour!

Abe Baker, whom Detective Spencer referenced, had actually been Stevens' Chief. Dr. Baker always felt that in order to be a great neurologist, you had to be a great general doctor first. So at that time, internships were still somewhat separate from the rest of the training program. He wanted interns to learn some internal medicine, radiology, psychiatry, and other non-neurological fields. The trauma aside, the county patients at HCMC were generally the sickest around. Many used a lot of alcohol, drugs, and cigarettes and often had a general disregard for their own health.

After his internship at HCMC, Stevens' next three years of neurology residency were through the University of Minnesota. Although most of his time was spent at the U, he spent three months back at HCMC as a Junior Resident, or a PGY-2, three months at the U, three months at St. Paul Ramsey Hospital (now known as Regions), and three at the Veterans Administration ("the V.A."). This was a huge strength of the program for learning how to take care of patients and becoming a "clinical neurologist." HCMC and Ramsey had generally the sickest, most acute-care, and most trauma patients; the V.A. had primarily chronic-care patients; and the U had the most academically interesting neurology patients, the "fascinomas," and the most severe conversion hysterics, who were totally psychiatric in the basis of their complaints.

Stevens' PGY-3 year was spent mostly learning subspecialty fields and doing academic work at the U—neurochemistry, neuropathology, and so on, although he had classes all along, especially on Saturdays. He spent some of that year at Queen Square, focusing on Electromyography (EMG) testing, which assesses the workings of the peripheral nervous system—the nerves in the arms, legs, and chest. EMG also evaluates the integrity of muscle function. The nerves and muscles are electrically charged, so to see how they are working, a small electrical or sometimes magnetic pulse is applied and measured for the response.

In his PGY-4 year, Dr. Stevens was the Chief Resident at HCMC and then Chief Resident at the U. When at HCMC, he wrote the protocol for the safe handling of the fluid from spinal taps of patients with Creutzfeldt-Jakob disease or its variant, "Mad Cow." The Chief Resident generally runs all of the neurology at a training hospital and oversees not only all the patient care, but also the education of the junior residents, interns, medical students, and doctors from other specialties rotating through neurology. Part of that year he also spent in academics. After he completed his residency, he was accepted for a Fellowship at the Mayo Clinic, then entered private practice in Minneapolis.

Detective Spencer finally turned toward Jack and said, "Doc, this is a lot of education! How old were you when you got out?"

"That's exactly what my mother asked about a hundred times. She thought I should stop with college! I was thirty when I entered private practice," Stevens replied. He then paused and looked Spencer directly in the eyes. "So, Detective, I'm sure you didn't come to talk about my education. What can I do for you?"

11

Bulls make money;
Bears make money;
Pigs get eaten.

Author Unknown

★ ★ ★ ★ ★

CHAPTER 11

ETECTIVE SPENCER REMAINED STANDING in Dr. Stevens' office, then crossed his arms and fixed his gaze on Jack's face. "Doc, did you know that Dr. Geoffrey Jellen died yesterday between four and five p.m.? I am here because I am investigating his death."

"Wow!" Stevens gasped, shaking his head, which was already reeling for the loss of life at the university. "No, I didn't. I'm sorry to hear that. What happened to him?"

Spencer continued his long, searching look of Jack's expression. "We aren't certain yet. To be complete, *both* Dr. Jellen and his wife were found dead in his clinic last night by the cleaning crew. They were lying on the floor in his private office, side by side."

"Oh my God!" Jack blurted out, his eyes registering complete bewilderment. "How did they die?"

"The scene gave the appearance of a murder-suicide."

"*The appearance?*" Stevens questioned. "Doesn't sound like you thought it was conclusive?"

"The case is still very fresh, Dr. Stevens. Have to get the autopsy and toxicology results. The CSIs are still doing their thing as well. I find it best to interview people as soon as possible, which is why I'm here. I don't like to mentally box myself in. You M.D.s call it a 'differential diagnosis,' I believe. I understand you knew Dr. Jellen and his wife."

Jack looked at him as though he'd been dazed by an unexpected punch. "Detective, I knew them. . .slightly. . .and that was many years ago. Why do you ask?"

"Just doing my job," Spencer replied. "I talked with some of the directors of the past clinics where Jellen worked, and when I talked to the clinic manager of the Twin Cities Clinic of Neurology, your name sort of came to the top of the list. I—"

"What list?" Stevens broke in, shaking his head. "Am I suspect? Do I need a lawyer?"

"You can call a lawyer if you want, but like I said, all we know is the two of them are dead by gunshot wounds. I'm just gathering information at this point. What I was told, though, was you more than knew Jellen slightly. . .that you and he had an altercation that got ugly, and that it continued long afterward."

Jack sighed deeply, then said, "Look, I hardly knew Dr. Jellen or his wife. . .Camelia. There were rumors among the staff at TCCN, followed by complaints about Jellen's freewheeling narcotics prescriptions. I was a board member at TCCN, and, unfortunately, I was assigned by the board to confront Jellen and to terminate him if I thought it was necessary. Jellen reacted in a completely unprofessional manner, refused to discuss the specific prescriptions that the staff questioned, and so I did what I had to do and fired him on the spot."

"It got ugly?"

"He was very angry and verbally abusive, but he left voluntarily, and his office possessions were boxed up and delivered to his house."

"Our records show that you filed a formal complaint against Jellen three days later. What happened at your house?"

Dr. Stevens leaned back in his chair, crossed his arms, and closed his large blue eyes as he recalled the scene. "My wife and daughters were out shopping when Jellen showed up at the back door of my house. I never figured out where he parked his car. He was desperate to get his job back, said he'd lose his house if I didn't figure out a way to get his position back. He threatened to kill me as well as torture my wife and girls. When I refused, he pulled a pistol out of his jacket and pointed it at my chest. When I again refused, he started yelling at me and waving the gun around, threatened my family again, but seemed to get nervous. Then he just took off running out the back."

"And the police didn't believe you?"

"No, it wasn't that. They investigated, but could find no evidence that he'd been at my house, so it was his word against mine. I was, however, able to get a restraining order against him."

"And since then? The director at TCCN tells me that you received anonymous phone threats over the years."

"Not in a few years. But, yes, I suspect it was Jellen who made several calls after the restraining order."

"Dr. Stevens, you are registered, I saw, to conceal and carry a weapon."

"Correct. I believed Dr. Jellen posed a real danger to me and my family. I also have to work late at times. When working late at a hospital in Minneapolis, I had a couple of incidents with muggers in the parking lot. And two of my past patients brought guns into my office in order to try to intimidate me to sign off on disability claims. I don't believe in being a victim, unlike a lot of people I hear about on the news."

"Doc, you know that as policemen, we officially don't like a lot of extra guns on the street. However, I remind my colleagues that the states that legalize 'conceal and carry' for the average citizen experience significantly lower rates of murder and all violent crimes, and it's bull when somebody says the rate of accidental shootings goes up. The average citizen does not shoot people because he has a gun, but if armed he provides a definite deterrent to criminals. So what type of a gun do you own?"

"I own several, actually. I am not a hunter, because I don't personally believe in killing animals for sport. But I do skeet shoot, so I own a Browning Gold "Golden Clays" Sporting Clays 12-gauge shotgun. I also shoot pistol at a range. I usually carry a Glock 27, .40 caliber."

"Nice gun, Doc. Accurate and dependable. Ever shoot anyone?"

"No, never. In the twenty years I've had a pistol, the most I've killed was a rabid raccoon that was threatening one of my daughters in my backyard. I hope to never need it. I only carry it for insurance. I don't like having to carry a handgun to ensure my safety, but I'll use it if I must."

"Do you own a small caliber gun, like a .22?"

"I do own a Kimber 1911 A-22 Rimfire target pistol, which I keep at home, but I've never used it much. It was the first pistol I ever owned. .22s are not very good for self-defense, but good at close-up executions. They do a lot of brain damage, if used right."

"Now how do you know *that*, Doc?"

"I saw several victims at HCMC," Dr. Stevens said, "and as a boy I grew up in Chicago, where it seemed to be the preferred close-up and personal execution choice of gangsters who were good at it."

Spencer looked again at Stevens' wall. "Board Certification in Neurology. Looks like the one I saw on Dr. Jellen's wall. . .except for the blood. Why does it come from the American Board of *Psychiatry and Neurology*?"

"To be nationally board certified in neurology, you must pass both neurology and psychiatry testing."

"Why psychiatry?"

"Because they both deal with the brain but in different ways. I tell the medical students I teach that in a way neurology deals with the *hardware* and psychiatry deals with the *software*. And many patient complaints of neurologic symptoms in reality have a psychiatric basis. So to be good at neurology, you must be able to recognize psychiatric issues that mimic neurologic complaints and disease. The two fields grew out of the same origin. In years past, specialists did both neurology and psychiatry."

"Pretty complicated stuff. I'm thinking Dr. Jellen should have used some of that psychiatric stuff on himself. As it turns out, Dr. Stevens, the Jellens were the subjects of a secret ongoing investigation for selling narcotics. In looking through their office records, there are high numbers of prescriptions for narcotics as well as discrepancies in their records. And it appears they kept two charts on everyone, and two sets of accounting records. Is that one of the reasons you fired him from TCCN?"

"No, we couldn't prove it, but that was a long time ago," Stevens responded. "There were rumors back then that he was selling prescription narcotics, and I've heard more rumors through the years. As a chronic pain specialist, he presumably saw a number of patients with intractable pain, such as terminal cancer patients who are just being kept comfortable in their last days, so he would have written more prescriptions than most doctors."

"How can we tell what's legitimate?" Spencer said.

"Get a chronic pain specialist to be a consultant and check through that avenue," Stevens answered. "That doctor could look through the patient charts and quickly tell you what Jellen was doing."

"Good idea. Thanks. Do you prescribe many narcotics in your practice?"

"No," Jack stated. "I occasionally get drug-seeking patients, which is never fun, but they stop seeing me when I won't feed their habit. In my type of practice, we use a wide variety of non-narcotic medications that usually do the trick. You should also be going through Jellen's patient list for ones who might have had a reason to be mad at him. Then there's the possibility that he was a problem for the local drug dealers. It's a slippery slope, that kind of business."

"No question about it. Doc, I must ask you a few more questions. Where were you yesterday between four and five p.m.?"

"Here, doing charts." Jack picked up the landline and speed dialed Karen's extension. "Karen, can you come back, please?"

Karen's footsteps could be heard immediately coming down the hall. When she stepped into the office, she said, "Dr. Stevens, what can I do?"

"Karen," Detective Spencer responded, "where was Dr. Stevens yesterday between four and five in the afternoon?"

"He was here, until at least six p.m. when I left."

"Could he have left the office without you knowing?"

"No, not possible. We had patients straight through until five p.m. I check everyone in, instruct them to fill out a medical questionnaire at the computer, alert Dr. Stevens of their arrival, weigh and measure them. Then I call Dr. Stevens again to tell him when they are ready to see him. And I usually sit in to assist during the physical exam. There may have been five to ten minutes when I was not talking with Dr. Stevens or physically in his presence, maybe less, all afternoon."

"Thanks, Karen," the detective concluded. "Dr. Jellen's office is twenty minutes away, one way. Sounds like you are accounted for, Doc."

Dr. Stevens said, "Detective, any more questions for Karen?"

"Karen," the detective asked, "did you know Dr. Jellen and his wife, Camelia?"

"Not personally," Karen said. "I was working for Dr. Stevens, though, when he fired Dr. Jellen at the Twin Cities Clinic of Neurology. And I took the subsequent threats seriously."

"Can you think of any reason someone would want to kill them?"

"Kill them? Heavens, no. You can't be serious."

"Oh, I'm all too serious, and I'll call if I have more questions. Here is my card," Spencer said. "If you think of anything else that might be relevant, please call me."

"I certainly will," Karen said as she slowly turned to leave, obviously shaken by the news. She closed Jack's door and walked back to her desk.

"Dr. Stevens, I checked you out a little as you know, and you live well, even for a neurologist. You have beautiful homes in Way-zata and Scottsdale. Is the money that good?"

"You missed the condo in Puerto Vallarta, Mexico," Jack added. "If you're asking me if I've ever been involved in the alleged drug business, the answer is no. I do live somewhat better than the aver-age neurologist. If you checked me out, then you probably know that I have several medical device patents, and the payments from them have been a good source of income, much better than medi-cine. I had also founded a public company to market some of my inventions."

"Actually, I do know all that. So why do you work at medicine if you have the income from the patents?"

"Because I enjoy taking care of my patients. Reimbursement for physicians gets worse every year, especially considering all the non-income-producing years of education and the cost of the edu-cation itself. But I am fortunate to have found this other source of income, so I can practice medicine without worrying about income and still live comfortably. I would not consider myself wealthy, but I am comfortable. Nothing makes me happier than helping a Par-kinson's patient who can't walk to walk again through treatment."

Spencer looked at the photographs on Stevens' desk and wall. "Nice photographs, Doc. She is a beautiful woman. Your wife?"

"Yes, she was. But she died of a kidney cancer a few years ago."

"Oh, I'm so sorry," Spencer quickly added. "Remarried?"

"No, Anne was wonderful; the best thing that ever happened to me. My friends want me to date because it's been a few years since Anne's death, but I just have no interest in anyone else. I can't think of anyone and have never met anyone who could hold a candle to her. If I get introduced to a woman, I find myself mentally compar-ing her to Anne. As long as I'm doing that, it wouldn't be fair to any other woman, either."

"You're probably right. Are these three your daughters?"

"Two daughters; the third was Anne again. We were born the same year, but she always looked young enough to be one of my daughters, and people often asked that question." Jack broke into laugher. "They never ask in that picture of me over there with my daughters if I am the brother! Anyway, the daughter on the left lives out East. The other is in San Francisco."

"So, Doc, I also found that you had been a Director of the Twin Cities Clinic of Neurology for many years and then quit. Was that your idea or were you asked to leave?"

"Before Anne died, she made me promise that I would enjoy life more and work less. Anne was more worried about how I would do after she died than her own health. The only way to fulfill that promise was to break away and start my own practice at a slower pace. It was hard, because I had, and still have, many friends there. But she was right, and I am definitely happier having more time for myself and my children."

"Sounds like a fabulous lady," Detective Spencer added. "But I should be going, Doc. I've kept you super late. Your secretary has my card. If anything else comes to mind, please call me."

"I will, Detective. And if you think of any other questions, don't hesitate to call me," Stevens said. "But I do have one question. How exactly did Dr. Jellen and Camelia die?"

"Handgun. Given the specifics of the wounds, it appears that he killed her, then shot himself, since the gun ended up nearest to him. But it could be the other way around. At this point, we'll have to wait for some of the test results. But why would a pain doctor sell drugs when he's already making good money?"

"Greed. Habits to support. Status. Camelia wanted everything fast, and Jellen told me he had prior wives and children to support. He believed he deserved to live better than his colleagues and that he was grossly underpaid."

"Well, maybe we'll never know," Spencer stated. "So, okay, Doc, I'm going to take off now. Thank you for your cooperation."

"No problem, Detective," Stevens replied, standing up to shake the detective's hand.

With that, Detective Spencer left.

Stevens sat down at his desk. He picked up one of Anne's pictures and studied it for a while, then said, "I have slowed down, Honey. I know you wanted me to remarry because you thought I'd be happier not being alone. Don't be mad that I've never found anyone even close to you. It's all your fault, you know."

12

*Choose the environment
that will best develop you
toward your objective.*

Clement Stone

CHAPTER 12

D ANA LAFONTAINE turned her salsa red Lexus GX 470 SUV into the Minneapolis Club ramp, took a ticket, then drove up to the third level and pulled into a empty space that another car had just vacated. The Club was a premier gathering place for business, civic, and community leaders in the downtown area, but she used it primarily as a convenient parking place. Gathering her leather portfolio, she stepped out of the car, locked it, and turned to walk the several blocks to the IDS Building, the tallest building in Minnesota at nearly eight hundred feet, where she was having her third meeting with a new client.

As an award-winning and highly regarded commercial interior designer, Dana looked ten years younger than her thirty-eight years. No one who met her for the first time ever even came close to guessing her age, and she would never tell. She credited it to good French genetics, a hair stylist who gave her thick, dense, shoulder-length brunette hair just the right highlights, and her unwrinkled skin and face that she had never allowed to be damaged by the sun or by doing drugs or smoking.

Dana had trained at the University of Minnesota, one of the few schools in past years that offered a university-level degree in interior design. She had been offered academic jobs by her professors, and one of her retiring professors had even set her up to take over his job at a leading private Minneapolis design firm. But Dana had preferred to start her own business, despite the risks. She came from a poor rural family, had borrowed money and worked to finance her way through college, and was used to making her own way.

Having tried both residential and commercial design, Dana preferred commercial and seldom did any residential work anymore. She found that most of her commercial clients were businessmen who rarely fought among themselves about the color of drapes and carpeting or if they were spending too much on furniture and not enough on big screen plasma TVs. Some of her clients took her kindness for weakness, but she was tough as nails if someone tried to take advantage of her.

After she had been written up in local and national publications and won a number of awards, Dana never had to advertise. She worked on referral, usually from prior clients, architects, and builders, and was busier than ever, which suited her just fine. She was so busy, in fact, that she could even choose the clients with whom she wanted to work. Had she wanted to expand her business, she could have done so exponentially, but she preferred keeping it small—just herself, a few assistants, and an occasional intern. Dana was asked frequently to be a guest lecturer at the U and to take interns.

Ever since her husband, John, had died three years ago in a car accident, she devoted herself to her business more than ever. While she never said it, she realized the busy schedule was her way of keeping John off her mind. They had both been twenty-two when they got married, fresh out of college. He went into business, as did she, and she had gotten her ASID while he got his MBA at night school. They had paid off their student loans, and with their two incomes had been modern-day DINKs (dual incomes, no kids). They built a fantastic house on Lake Minnetonka, which Dana designed and received a number of awards on its interior design, and the house was featured in the prestigious *Architectural Digest*.

After thirteen years of marriage, they finally felt their finances were secure, and they decided it was time to get serious about having children. But on a routine business trip to Atlanta, John was struck on the door side of his small rental car by a truck that ran a red light and was killed instantly. Dana's strong, but passionate heart had nearly been shattered by the sorrow. With time the weight of suffering had rolled back, and she moved ahead with courage and hope.

Athletic and trim, Dana quickly arrived at the IDS Center, caught the next elevator for the tower, and began the ride up to the fiftieth floor where ChiFone occupied most of the space. *Definitely the high rent district,* she thought. The office space was already tastefully decorated by the prior tenant, but ChiFone wanted a completely different look, and she had been called through a referral from another client whose offices she had redesigned on the thirty-ninth floor. A mix of Asian and Western, something showing the harmony of both, she had been told.

Dana was surprised that a Chinese firm would settle in Minneapolis. Although Minneapolis was home to a number of Fortune 500 companies, they were homegrown firms. Most companies would have picked New York City, and Asian companies nearly always went to San Francisco. With private jets, the Internet, PDAs, video conferencing, and fax machines, it really didn't make that much difference; but there was still a perception in the business world that a major player had to have an office on the coast. The CEO of ChiFone, Mr. Chan, had told her that they liked the Midwest work ethic and values, and it helped project the image they wanted.

ChiFone Electronics was the U.S. operation of a Chinese manufacturing and distributing firm that had a booming business in cell phones. They were relatively new in the U.S. market, reliable but cheap, and apparently very well financed. In doing her homework on them, Dana had tried to find out who had the deep pockets, but Chinese firms always kept that close to the vest. For a new player in the cell phone market, they had done amazingly well, even for one well capitalized. In a little over a year they had achieved a significant market share.

Dana looked down at the ChiFone that Mr. Chan had given her personally—a gold-plated one with her name engraved on it. It represented one aspect of their market strategy that was already regarded as a classic move: free units to celebrities, newspaper editors, television news editors and anchors, and other thought leaders to get them to be early adopters. A major advertising campaign featured glowing endorsements by paid celebrities and deep discounts to first-time users. The phone had the usual games, calendar, e-mails, texting, plus free GPS and automatic updates at no charge. And it came with a hands-free ear bud at no extra cost. Customers had to use the Chi-Fone network if they wanted some of the free extras, but that was a bargain as well. If a person lost his phone or it was damaged, they would give him a new one if he renewed his contract for two years.

There were, of course, different levels of phones given to different people. Congressmen, for instance, got free ChiFones with a Congressional emblem, while a military officer recipient's phone was emblazoned with his or her service symbol and rank. There were no strings attached—no one called on the people to pester them to buy more service. ChiFone called occasionally to check on how the phone was working but did not try to sell more features unless asked. They did send out a 1099 for the gift, but the tax amount was nominal. Politicians often "bought" theirs for a minimal price with a concomitant large contribution to their reelection campaign that seemed to show up subsequent to purchase.

Dana got out of the elevator when it opened on the fiftieth floor and walked through the etched-glass doors into the large reception room. "I'm Dana LaFontaine, and I have an appointment with Mr. Chan," she told the receptionist.

"Thank you, Ms. LaFontaine," said the receptionist, an American of Chinese heritage. "Please sit down. May I get you something to drink—coffee or bottled water?"

"Water, please," Dana said.

"Certainly," the receptionist said as she entered into her computer that Dana had arrived, which immediately showed up in Chan's computer.

"Mr. Chan will be right out," she said, reading the return message on her screen. She turned to the credenza behind her and pulled a bottle of water out of a small refrigerator and gave it to Dana, then handed her an ice-filled glass etched with "ChiFone."

In her second meeting with Mr. Chan, they had met in his office. His large desk was made of exotic African lacewood with inlaid leather, and his file cabinets, small refrigerator, and walls were matched in lacewood as well. He had laughed when he told her that he didn't care what it cost. The first thing to go was to be the African lacewood, and he wanted nothing in the entire offices that came from Africa. On his desk he had photographs of his wife and one grown daughter. On his walls he had signed photographs from the Chinese premier, a host of European political leaders, several American senators, and other notables. Dana had gotten the clear message that Mr. Chan was a significant player.

The heavy lacewood door to Mr. Chan's office opened, and he stepped into the hallway and walked down the hallway to the receptionist desk.

"Ms. LaFontaine," Chan greeted her with a warm smile, "nice to see you again."

"Mr. Chan, nice to see you, too." Dana extended her hand and shook his firmly. "I brought the new proposals."

"Ah, good. Let's go to the conference room, Ms. LaFontaine," Chan said. "It will be more comfortable there to spread everything out." He led the way into the all glass room with a stunning panoramic view of the city's western suburbs. The large conference table, chairs, and the walls were also of lacewood. "As you can see," he said, "this wood has to go."

"Right," Dana said, finding a coaster for the table and setting down the cool glass of water. A smile crept across her face. "No African connections, as I recall."

"Exactly," Mr. Chan added.

Dana began to spread out the proposals on the table in the conference room. In their first meeting, Mr. Chan had called and made an appointment on the hurry up to meet with Dana in her office. While she had almost no time to get some background on ChiFones, it was clear that Mr. Chan had gone beyond her referrals, had researched several of the offices she had designed, and wanted to see Dana in her own setting. Despite feeling somewhat intimidated by the intense businessman, she was pleased to have won Mr. Chan's confidence and the opportunity to meet the challenges of the project.

In Dana's first visit to the ChiFone offices, she had toured the affected office areas, interviewed Chan to learn his goals for the project, and gotten some ideas about the budget and timelines. He left no doubt that he was the decision maker, and that she would be accountable to no one other than him, which is exactly the way she wanted it to be. And she was very pleased with his sizeable budget, which meant she could add some design touches that she almost never had the chance to even consider.

Since that meeting, Dana had spent several weeks in putting together the design. As she systematically laid out her color samples on the table, she said, "Just give me a minute to get everything spread out before you try to evaluate it. It all has to work together, and if you look at only one aspect of it, it probably won't make sense."

One by one, the samples of the carpet, drapes, wall coverings, and furniture came together, and even the untrained eye could see how each color complemented the others. Taken separately, the colors didn't look like they would complement each other. Together, they were magnificent.

At first Mr. Chan's expression was that of a stoic questioning gaze, but then a little smile deepened the crow's-feet at the corners of his eyes. When she pulled out her last sample of carpet with "ChiFone" woven in for the lobby and the conference room, he smiled and whispered, "Spectacular. . .spectacular work."

Dana's own expression lightened, as her trump card had obviously won the job. She showed him a complete rendering of the office as designed, but he was already sold on it.

"I love the design, Ms. LaFontaine!" he said after studying it for a while. "I can't believe you could accomplish so much in just so few weeks. The textures are soft, soothing, high-touch, and rich, and the colors are brilliant, bold, and creative—they have a high-tech appearance. I think it reflects well the image we want to project. Reliable, but creative. Forward thinking, but trustworthy. People have to like our product, but also trust it."

"I wanted the company to project ingenuity and cutting edge tempered by a Midwestern appearance of 'old-shoe' trust," Dana said, surveying her work. "Cell phones are about as necessary now as shoes, right?"

"That fits perfectly," Chan said.

"Thank you."

"Let's go to the next step. Get me pricing, more samples, and a projection of timing. When can we meet next? "

"I can have more information in another week. You tell me the time, Mr. Chan, and I'll adjust my schedule accordingly."

"Very good," Mr. Chan responded. "Let's meet one week from today at the same time. The sooner we get this moving, the sooner ChiFones will reflect all that I want it to become. By the way, how do you like your cell phone?"

"Very much," Dana answered honestly. "So well, in fact, it may not be good for me. I've been using it so much that I'm wondering if it might be giving me a headache. Maybe too much of a good thing! Thank you again. And also for the free minutes."

"My pleasure. You have an impressive client list, credentials, and honors. *You* are the type of person we want to have showing off our phone. I am sure your clients will be soon getting phones from us because of you."

"No doubt," Dana continued. "I've been telling everyone about this phone. It's an easy sell with all you offer. No wonder I see them everywhere now."

"Thank you," Mr. Chan acknowledged. "Tell me. May I keep these samples here to show my staff?"

"Certainly, I've got a second set in my office."

Chan walked her back to the reception area, but she needed to freshen up for her next appointment and decided to stop in the ladies room. "I can show myself out, Mr. Chan. Have a super day!"

"You, too, Ms. LaFontaine. See you next week." Chan turned and walked back to his office.

Dana was always impeccably dressed and was as careful with her appearance as she was with her work. It wasn't an ego thing; it all reflected on her professionalism. After a few minutes of touch-up in the bathroom, she stepped back out into the hallway and headed toward the elevator. Passing by a large wall mirror, she noticed that the back of her hair wasn't falling right, so she stopped to fix it.

Once her hair was fixed, she blinked her long-lashed brown eyes and gazed momentarily into her heart-shaped face, wanting to congratulate herself for having won this large project. Then out of the corner of the mirror she noticed a door opened to a back room she had not seen during her previous tour of the offices, and she wondered why the room had been left out. Curious, she stepped toward the backroom, caught a glimpse inside of a wall full of television monitors of dozens of news programs and several rows of desks with people staring at computer screens that looked as though they were monitoring data, then heard someone say something about the presidential elections. Something about it didn't make sense, but she couldn't place it. Then a tall Chinese man stepped suddenly into the doorway, stared at her briefly through suspicious eyes, and quickly closed the open door.

13

Every head has its own headache.

An Arab Proverb

CHAPTER 13

T HE NEXT MORNING after her meeting with Mr. Chan, Dana drove her Lexus north up County Road 101 over the Gray's Bay Bridge toward Wayzata. She loved the SUV's salsa red color and the design lines, but she liked it even more because it was always reliable, even on the winter's coldest and snowiest days. It always started, cruised through deep snow with its automatic all-wheel drive, and more than one client had been impressed by its stylish interior.

It was a gorgeous August day, with a blue, blue sky and a few sailboats already out slicing their way across the lake. *At least the neurologist's office is close to home,* Dana thought. She lived in the tiny city of Woodland on the south side of Wayzata Bay on Lake Minnetonka. Situated on only approximately .8 square miles with around eight hundred people, Woodland is the wealthiest city in Minnesota, but not nearly as well known as Wayzata, except to some of the immediately adjacent communities. Wayzata, being the home of the Daytons, Pillsburys, and other local celebrities, always got the attention which suited the Woodland residents just fine.

Woodland is a bedroom community; there is no downtown, no commercial property. The police are contracted from Deephaven and the fire department from Wayzata. One nice thing living right on a big lake is that the fire department could take water right out of the lake and not have to locate a fire hydrant, if there even was one around. "The Lake," as Lake Minnetonka is generally called by locals, has over 14,500 acres of surface area and 130 billion gallons of water, which could put out a lot of house fires. On a hot summer day it can evaporate over 50 million gallons per day and drain another 26 million gallons into Minnehaha Creek, which flows east to Minnehaha Falls, one of the sites referred to by Longfellow in 1855 in his poem *Song of Hiawatha* and specifically viewed by President Kennedy at his request during his presidency.

Minnesotans are proudly spoiled with all their water; unlike some states, you own the water under your land. In drilling for water in Minnesota, it is never a question of "if," only "how deep?" Most of the residents in Woodland have their own wells and septic tanks. Ironically, the only sanitary spills into the lake in recent years had been from the city of Minnetonka, which prided itself on its city sewer and water and forced its residents to give up their safe septic systems. Raw sewage from a broken city sewer pipe by the Gray's Bay Bridge had spilled into the lake. Some residents suspected that the mayor wanted to degrade the property of some immediately adjacent property that the city wanted as a boat launch and ultimately bought, presumably at a reduced price. Woodland residents kept their private systems whenever possible, knowing that medically it had been proven that in the United States, citizens who own their own private wells have fewer heart attacks.

Dana could care less about Woodland's notoriety or politics. She and John had built a house there because it was quiet and beautiful. They lived in the Maplewoods' section on three acres. Heavily forested as Woodland's name suggests, it has great fall leaf colors, is safe and serenely located on a not-well-known peninsula. She could have moved to a smaller house, but theirs was special; it had been a labor of love with John and reminded her of those happy days. He had been well insured, which had paid off the mortgage and millions more, so Dana was now independently wealthy, of which no one knew but her and her lawyer. John had insisted that if, God forbid, he died young, she would never lack for the rest of her life. *Hell of a way to make money,* she thought, thankful for his love and care and yet ever regretful the life insurance had ever come into play. *I'd give it all back and much more to have him alive.*

Dana had been getting migraine headaches for a number of months. At first she thought it must be stress-related, but she couldn't actually put her finger on any new stressors in her life over the past six months. After John had died, she experienced severe headaches for a few months, but those had ceased as her grief diminished. She had had migraines as a teen, mostly pre-menstrually, but seemed to outgrow them and rarely experienced any during her twenties and thirties.

She did wonder at times about the cell phone from Mr. Chan as the cause, since the onset of her headaches came about the same time she started using it. She loved the phone, used it a great deal more than her last cell phone, and her assistant had helped set it up to make her more efficient. She knew she should use a headset, but it never seemed to work right, and she had never been enough of a techie to solve the problems, whether it was Bluetooth stuff or computer software issues. So she would scrunch the phone between her left ear and shoulder, which clearly didn't help her neck. She always kept it on the left side, which is where the migraines seemed to start. She hoped it would be that simple—just a cell phone issue. But even when she tried to not scrunch it between her ear and shoulder, that didn't seem to lessen the headaches.

Getting close to the neurologist's office, she checked her makeup in the mirror, then wondered what the neurologist was like. She had heard great things about him from her girlfriends—that he was like a detective in the way he went about diagnosing medical problems. They thought he was good looking as well, and *single.* If he could help get rid of her headaches, Dana didn't care if Stevens looked like a frog; she would even kiss a frog for *that.* Her girlfriends said he had suffered from migraines, which she thought was good if he was treating her. *He better be good,* she thought, *because it took weeks to get in to see him.* And that was with her girlfriends, who were established patients, calling on her behalf. He didn't take many new patients, they said.

She turned left at the stoplight at Eastman and McGinty, went over the railroad tracks, then headed west on Lake Street in Wayzata, on the north side of Lake Minnetonka. She loved the shops and restaurants there, one more reason to live in Woodland. It was only four minutes straight across "The Lake" by boat, about twice that around Wayzata Bay by car. Seeing Dr. Stevens' office, which is where the old Wayzata movie theater had been, reminded her of John. When first married, she and John lived on Peavey Lane in Wayzata, on the west side of the downtown. They would often eat at Hart's Café, then walk to the theater. One snowy winter night when there was a foot of new snow in a warm March, they walked to the theater. The owner was there and put on the show for them and one other couple, with free popcorn. Hart's was now Sunsets, and the theater was now shops and offices.

Daydreaming about the old movie days, she parked her car on the side of the building, made her way inside, and walked up the stairs to Dr. Stevens' office on the second floor and a solid glass door that was etched with the words:

Wayzata Neurology
Jack Stevens, M.D.
by appointment only

She opened the door and walked slowly toward the reception desk, taking her time to first observe the office itself. Glancing at the lake through the floor-to-ceiling windows, she noticed that Dr. Stevens had a private balcony that was the length of the office even closer to the lake. *Nice touch,* she thought. *No more beautiful place during nice weather than that!* She liked the décor in the waiting room; *someone did a nice job, although a little updating would help.*

"Good morning, I'm Dana LaFontaine," she said as she stopped at the desk. "I have an appointment with Dr. Stevens."

"Welcome, Ms. LaFontaine," Karen said, whose bright smile always accompanied her greeting. "Would you please sit down at the computer and fill out the questionnaire? And we have a couple other forms on the computer as well. If you're not a computer person, I'll be glad to assist you."

"I should be okay," Dana responded.

"Good. Once you've done that, we'll put an electronic copy of your questionnaire and forms on a password protected USB memory stick that will be yours to keep. As times goes on, we'll download all your data and tests each time you come back. Then you'll have your medical records for any other M.D.s whom you might see or if you travel and became ill. If you forget your memory stick, we can e-mail a secured copy to your doctor if you are at another office. Your other option is that at anytime you can log onto our secure website, and with the unique password I will give you, you can always download any of your information. But if you keep this particular USB memory stick, it has a program on it that will self-load whenever you plug it into any computer that is connected to the Internet. It will automatically go to our website, seek your record, ask you to put in the password, and update itself with your latest dictations and laboratory information."

"Thank you," Dana said, not expressing how impressed she was with Karen's professionalism and the customer service. She sat at the keyboard and quickly worked her way through the forms, but needed to clarify one statement before printing it out and signing.

"Karen," she said, "the acknowledgment form says that Dr. Stevens is serving as a consultant only and does not take emergencies, weekend, or night calls. He is in the office only, not in the hospital. Isn't that unusual for a doctor?"

"That's true, and Dr. Stevens worked long hours for many years, especially when he was a Director of the Twin Cities Clinic of Neurology. But after his wife passed away from cancer a few years ago, he slowed down his life a lot. I have been his assistant for fifteen years, and it's a good change for him. Also, as medicine has changed, he felt emergencies should be covered by emergency doctors and inpatients by internists or neurologists who are intensivists. He believes they should focus on inpatient care, and he should concentrate on outpatient care. Overall, he has concluded it's best for his patients."

Dana nodded and turned back to the computer. She was sorry to hear about his wife and could immediately empathize with his loss. She finished up her inputting, which sent a message to both Karen's and Dr. Stevens' computers. Then she printed out a copy of the acknowledgment page, signed it, and brought it over to Karen.

Going back and sitting down again at the computer, Dana clicked on the Backgrounder on Dr. Stevens that she had noticed on the clinic's website. She read about his training and experience and his years at the Twin Cities Clinic, which had been founded in 1955 and grown to become the largest private clinical neurology practice in the United States and probably the world. *No wonder the guy worked long hours if he was—*

"Ms. LaFontaine," Karen interrupted Dana's reading, "I'll take you back to Dr. Stevens' office now, if you would kindly come with me. I scanned in your signed forms, and they will be on your memory stick."

As Karen walked Dana back to Dr. Stevens' office, she admired the light, airy, professional layout, especially the energy-efficient solatubes in the hall. Minnesotans love bright, natural light, especially in the winter. At Dr. Stevens' door, they stopped, and Karen knocked.

"Come in," Dr. Stevens said.

Karen opened the door and motioned for Dana to go in.

"Hi, I'm Dr. Stevens, Ms. LaFontaine," he said as he rose from his chair, came around his desk, and shook her hand. "Nice to meet you. Please sit down."

"Thank you," Dana responded as Karen closed Dr. Stevens'

door and returned to her desk, and Dr. Stevens returned to his desk. She quickly glanced around the office and noticed that all the diplomas had been etched in bronze. She saw a number of pictures of his daughters, one son-in-law, and his late wife. *My goodness, she was beautiful, and her smile was gorgeous*, she thought. He had photographs of his wife everywhere, including his desktop for his computer; family photos adorned the screensaver. *I don't think he's over losing Mrs. Stevens yet.*

Dana smiled at the picture of the gray and white Havanese male on the wall. She owned a white Havanese female, as luck would have it, and she loved the dog. It usually slept on the bed, didn't shed, barked as necessary, and every morning went through and around the house, still looking for John, probably thinking he was on a very long business trip this time. There were also pictures of Dr. Stevens and his wife with two U.S. presidents and a former British prime minister. *This guy got around some*, she thought. The pictures of him with his daughters in front of the pyramids of Giza in Cairo appeared to be more recent.

"So, Ms. LaFontaine," Dr. Stevens started, "I hear you have some migraines. You seem to have a lot of friends who wanted to get you in."

Dana laughed out loud and said, "That I do, and they gave you high marks. By the way, I like the diplomas etched in bronze, Dr. Stevens. I'm an interior designer, but I've never seen those before."

"Thank you. A birthday present from my wife. She had them custom made."

Poor guy, she thought, *memories of her everywhere. I bet she gave him that engraved sterling silver fountain pen, too. I won't ask him about that one.*

Dr. Stevens turned to his computer screen that was positioned on his desk so that he could look at it while still seeing his patients. He could also review their history, put in clarifications of their answers to the questionnaire, and later mark down physical exam findings. He thought it was rude whenever a doctor turned away from a patient to write into the computer. Stevens read out loud through her entire present and past history, medications, allergies, personal habits, review of systems, family and social/occupational histories, making a few additions as Dana made comments.

Once he finished the preliminary information, he said, "Ms. LaFontaine, let's get back to your description of the headaches themselves. How often do these headaches occur?"

"Pretty much daily," Dana responded.

"Any particular time of day?"

"I'm usually fine in the early morning, but worse when I start driving to work or get to work. They worsen as the day goes on, until I am at home, then they seem to lessen."

"Where are they located?"

"Pretty much right there," Dana said and pointed to the posterior temporal area, just above the left ear.

"Always on the left?"

"Yes. Does that matter?"

"It may," Stevens answered. "Do they throb? That is, do they feel pulsatile like your heart?"

"Yes, generally."

"Any associated visual changes?"

"Sometimes when I'm looking at something, high up in my right field of vision, I think I see flickering lights," Dana said. "And also my talking may be affected or my understanding of something or someone I am listening to."

"Are you right-handed?"

"Yes, why?"

Dr. Stevens clicked his mouse on an icon that opened a side view of the left half of the brain, then turned the screen so Dana could see it, and said, "The left side of the brain generally controls the right side of the body. Here, look at this. In a right-handed person, the part of the brain near where you pointed controls speech—both actual speaking and the interpretation of spoken language. And part of the visual pathways, the connections from the eye to the brain, go by there. Specifically, it is what we call the upper, outer quadrant of the visual field, the part of the world you see high up and to the right. Some neurologists call it 'the pie in the sky.' The temporal lobes are intimately involved with memory and emotion in conjunction with the limbic system. So I'm trying to do what we call 'localization'; that is, I am trying to put your symptoms together so that they correlate with a certain part of the brain. Yours seem to involve the back of the left temporal lobe, which is also approximately where your headaches are, just above the left ear. Are you experiencing any emotional or memory changes or difficulties?"

"Not really," Dana replied. "Is this left temporal localization a good thing or bad thing, Dr. Stevens?"

"Neither, in and of itself. Just a piece of the puzzle. Sometimes, knowing the part of the brain that seems most or initially involved can help identify what is causing the problem. At least we can try to correlate the symptoms and possible localization with the objective data from the results of testing we may decide to do. Does anything make the headaches better?"

"Ibuprofen helps sometimes."

"You said you had migraines in the past, right?"

"Yes, but they stopped long ago and returned only for short time after my husband, John, died in a car accident a few years ago."

"I'm sorry to hear that. The pattern you describe is common in migraines. Anything that makes the current headaches worse?"

"In the past, drinking alcohol at times might bring them on, especially red wine. Cheese or processed meat sometimes. Chocolate might bring them out. These days, none of them seem to matter. However, I got a new cell phone that I'm using a lot more than my old one. I almost always hold the phone on the left side, and I tend to scrunch my shoulder up and my neck sideways to hold it against my ear. I tried an experiment where I didn't scrunch it that way, but that didn't help. When I went on vacation and didn't use the phone, the headaches seemed to go away. Do you think that could be it?"

Dr. Stevens raised his eyebrows, which produced several lines on his forehead. "Strain on the muscles on the side of the neck can cause headaches, but normally that causes what we term *muscle contraction headaches*. Unlike your symptoms, those headaches are usually constant, not throbbing, dull, and not associated with visual or language disturbance. If anything, your current headaches sound *migranous*. Migraines are a type of vascular headache that can come and go during your lifetime. They can act just like this, but there are many other considerations. Does the cell phone figure in? It might be coincidental. Perhaps you're just busier and using the phone more, and it is the stress related to how busy you are that is the real cause of the headaches. The cell phone may be a red herring."

"What's that?"

Dr. Stevens smiled and sat back in his chair, relaxing a bit for the first time. "Oh, just something I picked up when I was training in England years ago. When the British would chase after a fox with dogs and horses, a 'red herring' was a fish that someone would drag across the path to try to throw the dogs off the scent and add to the difficulty. It would help the fox to confuse the pursuers. So in medicine, a red herring is something that is true, but unrelated, and throws you off your path to the correct diagnosis."

"Medicine isn't exactly straightforward, is it?"

"No, not hardly. God invented the body but didn't give us the operation or repair manual. Imagine trying to operate or fix your computer without instructions."

"I have enough trouble running my computer *with the manual!*" Dana laughed.

Stevens gave a little gust of laughter as well, then stood up and said, "Time to do a closer exam." Then he walked Dana across the hall into the exam room.

"Please put this on," he told Dana as he handed her a long exam gown. "There is a hanger and hooks there for your clothes. Karen and I will be back in five minutes. There are magazines in the rack to the left, if you are interested. The thermostat by the wall switch is for you to reset if you're not comfortable. The TV is tuned to cable news, but the remote is attached, so feel free to change stations." He walked out and closed the door upon exiting.

I'm impressed, she thought. *Really impressed!*

14

*If you believe the doctors,
nothing is wholesome.*

Lord Salisbury

CHAPTER 14

D ANA TOOK OFF HER CLOTHES, hung them up, and put on the dreaded gown. Rather than sit down and watch the television, she surveyed the windowless examination room and meandered around the room. She first noted four large framed paintings that looked as though they were done by a ten-year-old were hung around the room—two each were done and signed by each daughter. There were also etchings of French castles in the Loire Valley and the medical school at the Sorbonne. One wall had a large photo of the National Hospital for Nervous Disease, Institute of Neurology, Queen Square, London, apparently in recognition of a monetary donation to the institute. Another wall had a lovely watercolor painting of the old Wayzata train station that had been built by the railroad mogul J. J. Hill, which was now the location of the local historical society.

There was a knock on the door, followed by Karen's voice. "Ms. LaFontaine, may we come in?"

Dana opened the door, and Karen entered with a PDA-looking device in her hand, followed by Dr. Stevens.

Hearing the television news, Dr. Stevens asked, "Who is winning in the presidential polls?"

"Oh, I wasn't listening closely," Dana answered, "but Senator Le seems to be coming from behind in the polls. It's sort of weird.

I didn't think he had a chance, and I didn't care much for him. But my thoughts have changed, and I don't know why. I get these images in my mind of him and feel good about him. I almost feel as though I know him."

"Perhaps that's the power of the media, Ms. LaFontaine," Dr. Stevens continued. "They're certainly giving the senator enormous amounts of airtime. Would you please sit up on the exam table?"

Stevens already had done some of the physical exam, unbeknownst to Dana. Neurologists observe patients the minute they walk into the office. The symmetry of their movement, the way someone sits, and how they get up and down from a chair are all carefully noted. The cadence and character of their speech is examined. Facial symmetry is viewed during speaking as well as the coordination of their eye movements. A good deal can be noted about intellectual ability by talking to them. These are valuable evaluations, because the patient is more relaxed, not knowing they are being visually examined.

Over the years, Dr. Stevens had constantly worked to sharpen his observational skills. A patient's *intellectual* or *higher cortical function* can be assessed for forgetfulness or dementia at the bedside in various ways. Generally, he would ask his patients for the date, place, and their name. Assuming they were wide awake, they would be described in his notes as "Alert and oriented times three." He often did a whole variety of other tests, such as asking serial seven subtractions from 100, current events in the news, names of the president and other well-known figures, or seeing if a patient could remember three unrelated words. If warranted, a more in-depth testing involves a Mini Mental Status test. But the crown jewel is the neuropsychological testing done by a board-certified Ph.D. neuropsychologist.

Language function is often observed during the history. If someone has experienced *aphasia*, or the loss or impairment of the power to use or comprehend words, usually resulting from brain damage, more specific testing might consist of following verbal commands, testing for *receptive aphasia*. Hearing is one thing; processing the sounds into understandable language is another. The command "Touch your right ear with your left hand" is tough for some receptive aphasics.

Expressive aphasia means to have difficulty speaking in a specific way. The patient knows *what* to say, but can't say it. This is different from *dysarthria*, or slurred speech, and the difference is important because true aphasia generally comes from a very specific part of the temporal lobe. Once again, the neurologist is attempting to localize an abnormality. Aphasics have trouble with certain simple, but intrinsically complicated, expressions, such as repeating "No ifs, ands, or buts." Equally hard is "If they come, we will go."

Dr. Stevens checked Dana's blood pressure with an electronic device, which automatically synched wi-fi with Karen's PDA, which in turn she would sync with her computer record on Dana when she was done. During the exam, Karen could input any pertinent findings manually on the PDA to upload later.

"One hundred over sixty. Nice blood pressure. You'll live a long time with that one!" Dr. Stevens always chatted to keep his patients at ease. The physical exam was more reliable in a relaxed patient.

Dr. Stevens palpated her head through her thick and dense brunette hair, then worked down to her neck. "No unusual lumps or bumps in your skull."

Boy, that's a relief, she thought.

"Good range of motion," he said after he had checked her neck. "Neck problems can cause secondary headaches, but none are obvious."

Dr. Stevens then carefully checked her *cranial nerves*, the twelve nerves about the face that exit the brain directly, technically from various parts of the *brainstem* except for the first two. The first one, Cranial Nerve I, does the sense of smell. Cranial Nerve II, the optic nerves, are technically not nerves, but actually are a direct extension of the brain. That allows vast amounts of visual information to be gathered at fast speed. Comparatively, it is the difference between a high-speed broadband Internet connection and dial-up. The visual input is delivered to the thalamus and onward to the primary visual area. All in all, visual information is delivered to about 90 percent of the brain. The neurologist can see the end of the optic nerves as they come into the retina with the ophthalmoscope. This is the only part of the brain he can see normally at the bedside. This tells him about pressure in the brain. The retina gives information on hypertension, diabetes, and other diseases. It also is the first level of visual filtering. Perhaps only 15 percent of visual information gets through the retina to the inner workings of the brain. The retina is preprogrammed for danger, often associated with movement as well as certain shapes; but it "learns" what is important and can adapt throughout life to change its filtering.

Cranial Nerves III, IV, and VI do pupillary functions and control the six tiny *extraocular* muscles that make each eye move. Cranial Nerve V, the Trigeminal, gives facial sensation, while VII, the Facial Nerve, gives facial strength and taste to much of the tongue. *Bell's palsy* is a generally temporary weakness or paralysis of Cranial Nerve VII. To test the facial nerves, Stevens asked Dana to smile; then he pulled out a funny photo of a cat whose head was covered with a tennis ball cut in the fashion of a football helmet, which made Dana laugh. When she laughed, he noted that the right side of her face was minimally weaker than the left, but only at that time. It was subtle and usually means nothing and was called *an emotional VIIth.*

VIII, the Acoustic, gives hearing and vestibular balance. IX, the Glossopharyngeal, and X, the Vagus, mostly work the soft palate and help with swallowing and also inputting taste from the back of the tongue. Actually, the Vagus has a great number of autonomic functions, including the heart and gastrointestinal tract. It also helps regulate blood pressure from impulses from the carotid bulb. XI, the Spinal Accessory, makes us shrug, and XII, the Hypoglossal, gives us tongue function. Our tongues are mostly muscle, about a pound or so. The tongue sometimes gives an early indication of Lou Gehrig's disease, amyotrophic lateral sclerosis, or ALS.

Dr. Stevens chuckled to himself as he recalled how hard it was for medical students, including himself at one time, to learn even basic neuroanatomy, a course well-feared by students. The brain is still one of the more mysterious organs, which makes neurology a tough specialty. In medicine, there are mnemonics, or mind memory and/or learning aids, for cranial nerves and many other systems. Cranial nerves have roman numerals, and each has a name; you are expected to learn both. There is the clean version mnemonic, starting "On Old Olympus' Towering Top As Fine A..." for *olfactory, optic, oculomotor, orochlear,* and so on. The dirty version, starting with "Oh, Oh, Oh to Touch and Feel a Girl's..." is much easier to remember. There are clean and dirty versions for other nerve groupings as well. The naughtier it is, usually the better remembered.

Then Stevens performed a *motor exam* on Dana. This looks at muscle strength and tone relative to size and age. Dana was strong relative to her size and obviously physically fit. If there was any sign of weakness, Stevens might do some other bedside tests. Patients with Parkinson's disease might have a rest tremor and also increased tone called "cog wheeling" in their muscles, which the experienced neurologist could feel while moving the arm at the elbow.

Then he checked her *deep reflexes*—three in each arm and three in each leg, and much more in-depth than just knee jerks. He used a Mayo Clinic hammer, which most non-neurologists never use. The hammers many doctors use are way too small to get reliable results. On really decreased ones, Stevens might use his long Queen Square hammer. After he checked Dana for minor reflexes, such as jaw-jerks, Hoffman's, and palmomentals, which aren't generally done in normal patients, he moved onto the Babinski reflex.

"Now," Dr. Stevens said, taking Dana's right foot in his hand, "I'm going to check your Babinski reflex, based upon what the big toe does when the sole of the foot is stimulated. It was named after the Polish neurologist a century ago. Even now, if the MRI scan is normal but the Babinski is abnormal, the Babinski carries precedence in considering normality and diagnosis."

"So what do I do?" Dana asked, looking down.

"Just relax and watch." Applying firm pressure with his right thumb, Dr. Stevens began the stimulation back at her heel and moved forward along the outside edge of the sole to the base of her toes. "See, that's how it's done."

"You're kidding, right? Nothing happened."

"Which is good," he responded with a gentle smile. "If your big toe had gone up, that might mean trouble. If you do the same things to most newborn babies, they show a Babinski response because they are not neurologically mature. Upon stimulation of the sole, they extend the great toe. Many young infants do this, too, and it is perfectly normal. However, in time during infancy the Babinski response vanishes and, under normal circumstances, should never return."

"If my big toe had gone up, what would that indicate?"

"The presence of a Babinskis reflex is a sign of damage to the nerve paths connecting the spinal cord and the brain. Not what you want. . .at any age."

Gait and station, or how someone walks and stands, requires the integration of brain, spinal cord, muscle, motor, and sensory nerves for starters. Neurologists can often be fairly certain of Parkinson's disease just by watching someone walk. People forget how long it takes children to learn to walk. Those who are *broad-based* often have peripheral neuropathy, meaning they can't get sensory information to their spinal cord or brain, so they widen their stance and walking to balance better. People with muscular dystrophy may have a distinct gait often described as *waddling*. When the neurologist has them do a deep knee bend, they have to bend over to straighten up, because of the usual pattern of weakness. Then they take their hands and push themselves up to a straight standing position. Named after another neurologist, it was called a Gowers' sign.

Coordination is tested in upper and lower extremities. Testing might consist of putting your finger to your nose with eyes closed or lying flat and rubbing your heel up and down your foreleg, always keeping it on the front of your shinbone or tibia. Or you might be asked to alternately slap your palm and back of hand on the front of your thigh, called *rapid alternating movements*. Walking a straight line and heel touching toe are hard even when you are sober.

The *sensory exam* looks at such things as light touch, pinprick, position/vibratory sense, and temperature. If abnormalities are found, they might be assigned to a *dermatome*, which is a part of the skin supplied by a very specific nerve or nerve root. For example, the little finger is from the C-8 root, the 8th nerve exiting the cervical spinal cord, coming through the bony spine between the C-7 and T-1 vertebral bodies.

Once Dr. Stevens had completed the exam, he said, "Okay, Ms. LaFontaine, Karen and I will step out so you can get dressed. Then I'll be back in five minutes, and we'll sit down and talk."

As the door clicked shut behind Dr. Stevens and Karen, Dana began to change, thinking about how good Stevens' bedside manner was. *But did he find anything serious?* she wondered. *He has such a good bedside manner, I can't tell.*

You must go to bed at 9 p.m.,
give up drinking and smoking. . .
You won't live longer,
but it will seem like it.

An Anonymous Doctor's Counsel

CHAPTER 15

D R. STEVENS SAT DOWN at his desk. In a couple minutes, Karen's information was there on his screen, which he reviewed and edited. Some of the exam was prompted as a macro, upon which Jack amplified. He then listed his initial *Impressions*—his best assessment at that point in time of what problems Dana had or might have.

Stevens then began to type his *Discussion*, his plan for what testing to do and what other action steps to take. He would add more after talking further with Dana.

When five-plus minutes had passed, he got up, walked across the hall, and knocked on the exam room door. Dana walked out and followed him into his office, sitting down again where she had sat during the initial interview.

"I suppose I'm terribly normal, Dr. Stevens?" Dana kidded nervously.

"Horribly normal, I'm afraid," he joked back.

"So it's all in my head?" Dana asked.

Jack laughed heartily, which seemed to put Dana a bit at ease. "Yes, actually it is. But you're not crazy. . .if that's what you're wondering. People who ask if they are crazy almost never are. It's the ones who say there *can't* be a psychological component that usually have psychological issues. But clearly, your problem *is* in your head, or perhaps more correctly, genetically written into your DNA."

"How so?"

"You told me during the review of your family history that both your mother and maternal grandmother had migraines, which statistically gives you a fifty percent chance of inheriting the gene. Migraines will come and go throughout your lifetime; you never outgrow them. They just vary as to how much you are affected at a given time. My mother had them until she died at age ninety-three—not as bad in later years, and so they obviously don't shorten your lifespan. And she is likely the reason I have them."

"So I'm one of the unlucky ones?"

"In one way, but in another you get a bonus. People with migraines tend to be more successful and harder working than average."

"Well, at least I got the hard-working part."

"Your girlfriends told me you are very successful, although stressed with a booming business and because of the loss of your husband. Those are significant factors as regards headaches."

Dana sighed deeply and sat motionless as she was suspended over the thought for a moment. "Well, I certainly miss John, but I'm so busy now. I have a huge office redesign going at the moment. . .for the company that makes my cell phone, but that is going far smoother than I anticipated. I honestly don't think those are the triggers. So what can I do about the headaches?"

"First, be aware that there is no direct way to diagnose migraines. That is, there is no test I can do that will determine with certainty if you do have migraines. It is based on history, physical, blood testing, and imaging of the brain to exclude other problems that may mimic migraines or cause other headaches. And even then we always have to be open-minded to other diagnoses. Second, realize that they come and go throughout your lifetime and are often influenced by age, season, hormones, and foods, among other things. I'll print you out a list, though I know you're aware of what has influenced them in the past. And the medications for prevention are pretty good, although they can take a month to work. We'll draw your blood and run tests, some of which get sent to Mayo Clinic or the University of Minnesota and can take a month to come back. And we'll set you up for an MRI scan of your brain and an EEG."

"I hate to ask, but do you think I have a brain tumor? I have a cousin who—"

"Don't jump to conclusions," Dr. Stevens broke in, holding up his hands. "Everyone knows someone who got a dreadful diagnosis when they weren't expecting it. All these tests are routine, and while a brain tumor is possible, with your family history and what I've observed so far, it's unlikely. Still, we can't evaluate all of the brain easily at the bedside. These tests will help us eliminate a number of potential causes." He already had ordered all these tests, and they had shown up on Karen's computer. He picked up the telephone and said, "Karen, will you please come back?"

Within thirty seconds, there was a knock at the door.

"Come in, Karen," Jack said.

Karen opened the down and stepped into the doorway and stopped.

Jack looked at Dana. "Ms. LaFontaine, Karen will coordinate your tests and give you a return appointment. Call if you have any problems in the meantime. Let Karen know how you want to receive your medical records. We log your testing on the website as it comes in, so you can check it and download it as often as you wish. If a test indicates something important, I'll call you personally. As far as the new cell phone, let's try an experiment, if you're willing."

"Sure, what do you need?"

"Rather than start you on medication, I want to get you away from the cell phone for a while."

"Why?"

"Well, we know two things: first, that when you forgot your phone when you were out of town, you felt better; second, when you just tried to not hold it between your shoulder and neck, you did not get better. So why don't you go without your cell phone for a few weeks?"

"Are you serious? I don't know how I'd function!"

"Back to the old days. Pre-Blu-ray is what I tell my daughters."

She laughed. "Okay, but how about a compromise? I used a cell phone for years without a hint of a problem. I still have my old cell phone. How about if I set the new aside and use the old one?"

"That's not as good," Dr. Stevens shook his head. "It could be—"

"Seriously," Dana interrupted, "if the headaches continue, I'll ditch the cell phone. But I really, really need it. You have no idea."

"It's your head. It could delay discovering the culprit for a couple of weeks."

"I'll take the risk."

"It was a pleasure meeting you, Ms. LaFontaine. I hope the experiment works for you. See you in a few weeks."

"Oh, just one more thing. I'll only come back if you agree to stop calling me Ms. LaFontaine. People whom I know and trust call me 'Dana.' Does that work?"

Dr. Stevens chuckled and looked over at Karen. "What do you think, Karen?"

Karen was clearly amused as well. "Well, it wouldn't be the first time you violated your own office policy over the years."

"Okay, then, but it has to cut both ways. You have to call me 'Jack,' or it's no deal."

Dana nodded, and her eyes sparkled with pleasure. "Good-bye, Jack."

"Good-bye. Have a nice weekend, Dana."

Dana walked out of the office with Karen, still chuckling to herself by his reaction. Karen gave her a special USB memory stick, which had *Wayzata Neurology* engraved on the outside. It already had her records on it. Karen gave her written instructions as well as the password both for it and her place on the website, in case she didn't want to wait to use the auto play and download features.

After they concluded Dana's future office and test scheduling, Dana put the information into her purse.

"Ms. LaFontaine, we—"

"Dana."

Now it was Karen's chance to laugh out loud. "Dana, on the day before your appointment, I will also send you an e-mail reminder."

"Thank you, Karen," Dana said. "Have a nice weekend."

"You, too."

Back in his office, Jack looked up from his computer screen and stared at the pictures of Anne and their daughters. Whenever he looked at his daughters, he could see Anne in them—in their appearances, mannerisms, and personalities. He glanced back at his favorite photo of Anne and said, as he often did, "Honey, I slowed down, and I'm seeing the girls more, just as I promised you. I know you wanted me and the girls to be happy after you were gone, and I'm trying."

Then he recalled his final promise to her that he hadn't fulfilled. Anne was in the final stage of cancer and at home in bed with hospice care. Jack was sitting on the bed, holding her hand and trying to hold back his tears.

"I know you, Jack Stevens," Anne said though a gentle whisper. "Promise me you'll move on when I'm gone. You're going to be lonely, and you'll need another loving woman to be with you. You won't do well alone. I want you to remarry."

Jack could only nod; his throat was choked with tears.

"I want you to remarry, Jack," Anne repeated, squeezing his hand with what little strength she had left. "But you have to let the girls meet her and approve. Understand. You have to."

Again, Jack could only nod and try to chase away the tears with his hands.

"Promise me. Say it out loud."

Looking into her beautiful hazel eyes, he did what he knew he must and let go. "I promise," he finally choked out.

After she died, he had put that promise on the farthest back burner at the lowest heat. What he hadn't figured was that Anne had also made *the girls* promise that they would make Jack get remarried. Anne knew that as lonely as he might be, he would not want to get remarried out of love for her.

Anne always did things like that, and Jack could never lie to her. He was bad at lying anyway, and when she did catch him, she'd say, "I see your nose wiggling!" Anne used that expression on the daughters, too, when they were growing up. When they were going to try to fib to their mother, they actually would cover their noses so that she couldn't see them wiggling!

God, I miss her! Jack thought.

16

*There are more horses' asses
than there are horses in the world.*

W. Albert Sullivan, M.D., Associate Dean,
University of Minnesota Medical School

CHAPTER 16

M R. HAN, as Mr. Chan was known in Beijing, walked quickly into the Ministry of State Security (MSS) after going through the security area and being hand checked by the guards, even though he was well known to them as the Head of the Second Bureau for the United States. He hurried to the Minister's office and was greeted by the secretary, who immediately escorted him to the Minister's private office. The Minister was there as well as the Director of the Second Bureau of the MSS, who oversees and directs Chinese spies in foreign countries, as well as numerous other agents and assassins.

"Director Han, welcome!" Minister Hu exclaimed as he and Director Chao rose out of their chairs.

"Thank you, Minister Hu. My privilege to see you and Director Chao again," Han said as he took turns shaking their hands robustly. Although all three men bowed as Han greeted them, Han's bow was deeper out of respect for their position and age.

"I understand our time is brief," said the Minister as he and the other two men sat down. "Your flight is in less than two hours?"

"Yes, Minister," Han replied. "Too many meetings in a single day, and keeping out of the eye of our enemies requires many extra hours of travel."

"So how is our American project going, Han?" Director Chao asked.

"Ahead of schedule, significantly, Director. Every aspect of the plan has escalated with flawless precision and great success. You would be proud."

"The write-ups in *Forbes* and *Fortune* were impressive about ChiFone."

"Thank you, Minister Hu. The sales growth is beyond any product the Americans have ever purchased, and it is no surprise the magazine editors became so favorable toward us after they had used the special ChiFones we sent them. The result was better than free advertising. Your courage to move forward and extraordinary financing will accomplish all that our fathers sacrificed their lives for."

"I didn't think we would get it done in time," the Minister reflected, "but it has been worth the time and money. I am aware, Han, of how hard you have worked on this. Are you confident that the testing was accurate?"

"As you know, we thought it would take many years of research to reach our purpose, and no one anticipated we could move ahead so quickly. There simply was not enough time to do the large-scale testing the engineers wanted. The acceleration of the research team and the need to utilize the results in March forced us to move ahead. However, the research on small groups has gone smoothly. We can magnetically induce some memories and emotional associations through the skull and into the brain. We are limited now in the type and complexity of the memory and emotion. Obviously, this worked with the nomination of Senator Le."

"The Party will remember your perseverance and success," Director Chao said. "Getting Senator Le nominated was amazing! He was clearly what the Americans would call 'a dark horse' who is suddenly seen as 'the white horse.'"

"Thank you, Director Chao. We did not have the time to get widespread usage, so we targeted the delegates to the party convention. Not only on this project, but in future days, we can control some thoughts or emotions of selected people throughout the world. We may be able to do larger groups and more complicated thought and emotions from there. No one knows how far we can take this."

Minister Hu's grave, steely eyes were set deep back under his brow. "Han, we must not fail. The economic crisis here in China has deepened, and the Americans have slowed their production significantly. We have millions of starving unemployed workers, and hundreds of thousands are rioting in the streets, despite the force of two hundred fifty thousand of the People's Armed Police and the most capable secret police and vast network of informers in the world. Our past tactics of 'political decapitation,' quickly arresting protest leaders and leaving their followers disorganized, demoralized, and impotent, are not as effective as they once were.

"Every year, our labor market grows by more than ten million workers, most of whom are leaving the countryside for urban areas in search of employment. Each percentage point of GDP growth translates into roughly one million new jobs a year, which means that we need the GDP to rise at least ten percent every year in order to absorb the influx of laborers, and we have currently dropped to four percent.

"The Premier has made it known that the Party's finances have suffered greatly, and we must engage every measure to stop the transferring of American manufacturing to Africa, Vietnam, and Cambodia. Some of the higher-level work that we should be getting is going to India or the Philippines! We are better than the Indians and Filipinos."

"Han, let me echo what the Minister has said on your successes," Director Chao said. "You were one of the thousands we placed in various positions in the United States over the years. Many of them we just ordered to get American citizenship for use at a later time when we would determine their assignment. We have now activated many of these sleepers for your use and instructed the moles to increase their rate of espionage collection. So we have put most of our long-term United States assets at your disposal, but also at a much higher risk. We believe we needed to do something now, before our economic situation deteriorates even further. Your successes allow us to fast track our long-range plans, years before we expected to be able to activate our plans."

"Director," Han responded, "if this continues to go well, you can tell the Premier that he will have the American economy, military, and workforce at his disposal within the next few years. We will enhance our technology for thought and action control as well as saturate it into the depths of the American society. The Americans have no inkling as to what we are doing. We are using them to do our agenda within their system of government, so they and their media actually believe it is simply 'democracy at work,' as Americans would term it. They will look at what we are doing and not know it is anything but an evolutionary change in their perspective toward us. At least they won't know until we have strong control of their military and economic systems."

"We are already making plans to apply this same research to other projects," the Director added. "We can change the thinking in every country in the world that has a major population group that uses cell phones. Third World countries have leapfrogged into cell phones to get around the immense infrastructure costs of landlines. All we have to do is to gather the frogs in our net."

Han couldn't smile any brighter at the Director's words. He added, "The Americans like to tell the story about a frog that is in a pot of water and doesn't know that the water is slowly being heated to a boil. The Americans won't know the water is boiling until it's too late. We might be able to spread the People's Revolution to the rest of the world without ever firing a shot, using their own infrastructure to make it happen! And even if our plans are disturbed, we will soon have the American military, medical, and scientific might at our disposal."

"No nation in the history of the world has ever had such power to rule the world," Minister Hu spoke slowly. "The fools who thought we had become an entirely free-market economy and that capitalism would one day erode our values will find out the truth. If this works well, Han, I will personally nominate you for the 'Hero of the Revolution' recognition."

"I would be honored, Minister Hu," Han said, bowing deeply in his chair.

Director Chao glanced at his watch and said, "Before you go, we need updates on some operational matters, Han. Tell us about the bomb at the University of Minnesota."

"It was an essential strike that could not be delayed," Han replied. "The entire research and development team was killed instantly. Americans like their little parties, so the end-of-project celebration was ideal. They had already shredded the data electronically and returned all information. The nine people who knew the scope and nature of the research all ended up in tiny pieces spread on the university lawn. None ever knew the end product they were helping us build. We told them it would be used to speed learning and help rehabilitate those with stroke and mental deficiencies. Unknown, except to the Minntronic group, we actually were able to convince Minntronic to manufacture the key component. We did that to speed up the process, but we will now make the circuit boards in our own facilities here. We have other options as well for backup plans."

"Can they trace the bombing back to us?" the Minister inquired.

"No, the FBI was asked to investigate it as a presumed terrorist attack, until proven otherwise. That is the American protocol. I hired an unsuspecting Iranian to take the fall. He had no clue, and with the amount of money I offered him, he asked no questions. He was convinced that I had personal reasons for remaining in the background. Our liaison with the researchers was entirely through the Iranian, except for our initial contact with the key Minntronic officer."

"Why the other contact?"

Han nodded and said, "Normally, I would have had the Iranian do that too, but with so little time and the delicacy of the project,

I was forced to use another doctor to establish the contact. I spent countless hours securing this relationship. The Minntronic man knew me, but was one of the nine in the explosion, and I can guarantee that he never spoke a word about me. The FBI has tracked the project to the Iranian who wasn't at the party and searched his house. The fact that he has disappeared inflamed their immediate suspicions. The Americans' paranoia over Iran played perfectly with the ruse. We had cleaned out his house, bank accounts, and everything else about him. The FBI will find bank accounts that had money transferred through Iranian banks, untraceable to our banks. We had money wired to known arms dealers for the explosives from his accounts, which were funded from Iranian banks."

"And what about the C-4?" the Director asked.

"The explosive detecting dogs have already smelled the plastic explosive residues we smeared around poor Mr. Jalili's apartment. However, the FBI investigators will not find a taggant either there or at the University of Minnesota, which is consistent with an Iranian source for the C-4. The bank accounts for the explosives all came to a post office box in his name, although I insisted he give me the only set of all the keys. Then from the master bank account, controlled only by me, but also in the Iranian's name, I electronically transferred funds to the only account over which he had control whenever he needed them. So the money for the Minntronic people and the University of Minnesota engineers and neurologists all came through that."

"Wise precautions, and your usual thorough job and analysis, Han!" Director Chao exclaimed. "And what of Mr. Jalili's body?"

"They won't find a trace of him, I guarantee. One of our fellow patriots in St. Paul has a tree removal service. His wood chipper reduced the Iranian to a red spot, and a large bonfire turned red to black. So after the Americans convince themselves that the explosion was orchestrated in Tehran, they will also tie up their best investigators, trying to figure out Iran's motive and whether they can expect future attacks in the near term. That alone could take a couple years to analyze."

Minister Hu added, "And they will also be forced to determine what their response will be to the Iranian attack. Moreover, the American media is thundering about another terrorist attack on American soil. Senator Le's accusations yesterday that the current administration is soft and ineffective on terrorism will further focus their government and the American people on that. That should keep them from ever checking out what you are really doing at ChiFone."

"Truly impressive, Han!" Director Chao said. "You are certainly doing better than your predecessor and that botched assassination of their African president."

"Thank you, Director," Han responded. "At this time, a word from the Premier regarding China's sorrow over the explosion would be good. Then, at some time before the election, a word from the Premier that China feels that terrorist nations need to be restrained internationally and that China will allow more free speech internally will further soften the Americans toward Senator Le. The only downside of the explosion is that we now have a lot of federal agents in Minneapolis. But I think that after they gather their information, they will return to D.C. It's sometimes better to do business right under their noses."

"What about the doctor who brought you Minntronic, Han?"

"The drug doctor and his wife complicated the project more than I anticipated. Unnecessary executions increase the risk of discovery, but they were loose-mouthed and forced my hand. Actually, I did the Americans a favor; they were significant drug dealers. He was what the Americans call 'a real loser,' so no one will miss him or her, for that matter. They were a low-life couple. She cheated on him, and so I made it look like he killed her out of jealousy and then killed himself."

"And you enjoyed her company, I'm told," the Director said through a smirk.

"I did. Many times."

"That's good. A fringe benefit for the long hours."

Han and the Minister both laughed out loud with the Director.

"One nice part of having a cell business," Han continued, "is that we were able to log numerous additional phone calls to the other man with whom the doctor's wife was having an affair. We actually made the calls from our office with her phone number as the ID. When the police checked phone records, and already have subpoenaed ours, I wanted them to find her frequent calls to him and to find her number matching up on his landline printout of incoming calls as well as his cell phone."

"Excellent. Anything else before we close," the Director asked.

After reflection, Han added, "There is a woman whom we are monitoring closely. She is an interior designer who came to our office and may have accidentally stumbled onto something. She may have overheard Hai talking to one of the other agent techs about the next thoughts we are going to implant in certain individuals as we move the project along or about the Senator Le campaign in general. She may not know anything and is harmless enough."

Director Chao ran his fingers through his short dark hair and said, "Better to be safe, Han. If she suspects anything, she is too high a risk to not be removed immediately."

"Understood. Just a risk-benefit ratio we have to consider. Minneapolis is a very safe city, and too many deaths under unusual circumstances to upright citizens without any known enemies will be suspect. The explosion at the university, the death of the doctor and his wife, and then the death of a highly respected interior designer who has been working in the ChiFone office would bring the police too close for my comfort. But we will do what is best, and if necessary, we will make it look accidental or perhaps tie her to Mr. Jalili. She has one of our phones, so we can spin it any way we want. But if she doesn't do anything in the next week or so, she obviously knows nothing."

"Carry on, Han," the Director said. "I trust your judgment. Do you need any more assets?"

"I don't think so. I moved several up from Chicago. We have more than enough there in reserve if we need more talent."

"Han, I promise that you will be decorated and return to a high position in the Party when this is over," the Minister concluded as Han stood up to leave.

"Minister Hu, I look forward to watching the takeover of the capitalists from a front row seat and having a continued hand in it. We have all worked very long and hard for this. Thank you again."

17

Politicians are the same all over.
They promise to build a bridge
even where there is no river.

Nikita Khrushchev, Russian Soviet politician (1894–1971)

CHAPTER 17

SENATOR JAMES LE WAS PREPARING for his next major speech in his San Francisco presidential campaign office headquarters. If elected, he would be the first American of pure Chinese descent to be president of the United States. In 1958, his parents had entered the U.S. through lenient refugee policies by way of Taiwan, having escaped from Beijing. In the previous year, Mao Zedong, the Communist Party leader, who had been unable to overcome the deep-seated mistrust and lack of communication between the urban/educated and rural/illiterate communists, had sounded out the opinions of the Chinese intellectuals about the party. When the criticism was much more extensive than he anticipated, he decided to stop the critics by labeling them *rightists*. Historically, *left* was associated with radicalism and *right* with conservatism, so the label *rightist* implied over-conservatism in a radical socialist society. Rather than be thrown into prison or sent to labor camps with their fellow rightists, Le's parents had escaped.

At least that was the fabricated story that had been repeated thousands of times over the past years as Senator Le's political career developed. What was certain was that the senator's public relations people told the media his parents hated the Chinese communists vehemently, had come to America seeking freedom, had worked hard to gain citizenship, and that their son was born several years after they were safely established in California. Most Americans were here because their parents happened to be Americans. James Le was American because his parents *chose* to be Americans, his campaign alleged—an old but always effective slogan.

Le was excited, and for good reason. Six months before he had not been penciled in on any political analyst's short list; now he was his party's endorsed candidate and riding a wave of popularity that hadn't been seen on a presidential level for many years. It really wasn't about his Chinese heritage, for very few Americans cared about racial backgrounds as much as the media constantly proposed. There had already been presidents of African descent and a female Jewish president in years past. Rather, the issues against him were his lack of foreign experience and time in government in general. He was only forty-five years old and had served in the House of Representatives and most recently in the Senate. He had never held an executive position, and none of his committee time was in foreign relations.

He was well-educated, did political science at Berkeley, but unlike most of his fellow graduates, Le entered the military for four years as an officer. This was at the instruction of his parents, who had groomed him for political office from his birth. Military service always got at least some rating points. He served in no war theaters, but was adequate in his job as an intelligence officer with a top secret security clearance. He was honorably discharged after four years. He was then twenty-six, tried his hand at business for a few years with no apparent success, then to everyone's surprise Le became a representative from California, appointed out of the blue by the governor of his party to fill a vacancy. Some newspaper articles stated that one of Le's college professors pulled some strings with the governor, but it was never clear what brought Le to the governor's attention. What was clear was that once Le was in the House of Representatives, he caught the public's attention with his speeches and style. He won reelection easily, which eventually led to his becoming one of California's two senators.

Le never wrote any bills of substance, but he managed to secure a large amount of pork for California, and was frequently absent so he could campaign. His voting record was left of center but unpredictable, and he often missed roll calls. The media loved him though, and he had something for both ends of the political spectrum, while declaring himself a moderate. He portrayed himself a fervid anti-communist, a retired military officer, and a small businessman, which endeared him to the right wing. The left wing savored his California and Berkeley roots, his diversity, and most of his voting record.

Part of Le's appeal was that he had been the underdog through every stage of his life, and there are few themes that appeal to Americans more than seeing the underdog win. Part of his appeal was his Chinese heritage. It was put out by Le's team that he *needed* to be elected to prove that there was no American bias against the Chinese. The media ran with the race card, and it immediately helped newspaper sales and television market shares. And as long as there were profits and ratings, they were more than willing to keep pushing the racial aspect. It didn't need to bleed to lead the news; media profits were good on this one. This, of course, was a good thing for Senator Le. His rise had been meteoric. No one knew exactly why, but whatever he had going for him was definitely working. Political analysts focused on his marketing group and advisors. Those stories all made great evening news as well.

Ray Collins, Le's vice presidential nominee, was a milque toast politician from the Old Guard, as well as from a strategically necessary New England state. He had been a lackluster but gregarious governor and had found a way to stay on the national political stage forever. Collins had also served as a congressman and an ambassador to France. He was the perfect picture of a party loyalist, and being picked as Le's running mate was partly payback for long service. His age, executive and foreign experience, as well as general demeanor complemented Le well. And he was a WASP, which helped counter some of the issues of ethnicity and religion; it also was an endorsement from a Mayflower descendant.

Le was tall, well groomed, handsome, confident, and extremely articulate in English as well as fluent in Mandarin Chinese. He had a broad smile and warm handshake when necessary. He looked presidential, was an impeccable dresser, and was the rage of Hollywood. He had intense, piercing dark eyes, but his emotions were entirely controlled, and he was an impossible read. He was an excellent poker player, although he preferred mahjong and chess. Le enjoyed the planning of multiple sequential moves and the permutations of those. Having been well groomed by his parents through many years of homeschooling for his role, he had the perfect skill set for what they needed. He was convinced that America was evil, but he would lead a vast network of other sleepers to liberate the workers. He just needed to be patient a little longer.

Le's wife was part German and part Mexican, looking mostly Latino and always looking slender and beautiful. She was a lifelong Californian and a devout Catholic. She added diversity, which was the key that most people loved about Le. They had a dog that was a lovable mutt and a son and a daughter who were well-mannered, respectful, and outstanding students. Children and dogs were also campaign assets. None of the family knew Le for who he really was; they only knew the pseudo-Le. He was a great natural actor, and he never stopped acting or being aware of his purpose. He was like a hologram—very few knew where the real, not the projected, image really was, and there was no real substance.

No American president had ever been an atheist, and there had been no reason to push the envelope just because of their personal convictions. Le claimed he was a Buddhist, the religion his parents had chosen after coming to America, but no one ever noticed that he practiced it. No president had been Buddhist either, which added to his appeal in academic circles and especially in Hollywood.

There was a knock at his open door, and Le's campaign manager, Joe Secef, stepped in his office. He was a short, skinny young political whiz who worked tirelessly and had the entire campaign pushing to the max. "Senator, the latest network polls continue to improve, and not slowly but surely anymore. If the trend line continues, you are unstoppable. We are building up a critical mass, and it appears that you will peak just before the elections. And you will likely bring with you the Senate and House on your coattails. You are going to be owed a ton of favors down the road."

Le would never show it, but he got a continual rush seeing the numbers change and the trend lines and hard data swinging his way. He had no time for small talk. Performance and bottom line were the only real measure of success. All his years of preparation and hard work and his parents leaving their families behind was paying off; the long plan was working.

His campaign was a bit lacking in flesh, but had a lot of bone, and the flesh he showed had a lot of sizzle. Somehow it not only had appeal, but he was gaining widespread grassroots acceptance. There was no reason to change what he was doing, but he wanted to ratchet up the intensity. Le had played his foreign-relations card, that Sino-American relations could and must be improved, and that he was the one to do it. Given the economic interdependence between the countries and the continuing effects of the recession, he had made his case powerfully.

Secef pushed up his reading glasses and said, "Senator, I want to go over your travel schedule. California is already in the bag, and Governor Collins has secured the Northeast. We need to concentrate on the South and Southwest. Our polls show that they are wary of your lack of experience and pro-Chinese policies."

"Joe," Le said, hardly taking his eyes off his computer screen, where he had been working on his speech, "just let me know where I need to be and when, what I need to say to win them, and I'll be there."

Secef had worked with Le long enough to expect this answer. He had found Le to be a hard-working, driven man, who expected him to set the agenda and make it operational.

"Senator, your next stop is going to be Phoenix and Tucson. The media there are offering to give you coverage like I've never seen before."

"And what about guaranteeing crowds?"

"You just wait and see," Secef answered with a nod. "You'll be speaking just before a free rock concert in both Phoenix and Tucson. And get this—the cities are paying for the entire event. We figure you're going to have 70,000 young people who are crazy about you. The media will skip over the associated concert and just make recordings that show you with huge crowds. And our follow-up ads will show you with all the concert crowds in front of you. That was my idea."

Le was delighted that his go-to-guy had no moral reservations. There would be a place for Secef in his administration, despite the fact that he was white. "Then what?"

"We will go through Santa Fe and down to Albuquerque. In Santa Fe, we'll focus on a local eco concern. We'll use the rock concert in Albuquerque."

"And then?"

"And then we bring the big show to Texas, which is going to take some doing to win over. We'll go to Austin, Dallas, and Houston, with similar marketing execution there; that is, concatenate with concerts, leading off, if possible. Louisiana is pretty much in our pocket, so maybe spend a little time there, but not much. Their voting habits are well known. The Deep South—Alabama, Georgia, Mississippi, the Carolinas—we have to discuss further, but we aren't done with our research there as to what our message should be."

"And plans for my wife and children?"

"They are an asset we need to keep using selectively, Senator. No questions that we'll need them onstage for every event in the Deep South. Maybe as a follow-up to your Southwest visit. Voters love your family."

"How are we doing on money?" Le asked, though he knew the answer. Secef would never know that he wasn't concerned about his finances in the least.

"That's never been a problem, sir. Whenever we need money, there is a flurry of contributions from various untraceable sources, and literally millions of dollars show up. I honestly don't know how you do it, but you've got your fingers around some mighty big purse strings!"

"I am glad it's working," Le responded. He loved that his parents had moved to America and would live to see the takeover of the biggest capitalist government in the world. This couldn't have happened if they had stayed in China. He chuckled to himself, thinking Secef would be less worried if he knew about the campaign behind the campaign. But Le needed the best campaign manager that money could buy. This would help explain the "miraculous" win in November. Secef was expensive and was, in fact, an extraordinary manager. And Le would, of course, let the manager take the credit. If he used an inexperienced manager, especially one of Chinese heritage, it would have raised too many questions.

Senator Le was constantly reminded of the bottomless source of money pouring into his campaign from the Chinese government. There was some work in making it untraceable, but others took care of that. *Funny,* he thought, *America spends its money on Chinese imports, and we use their money to do a legal, bloodless coup. And if we are really good, they'll never know what happened. Over eight years, who knows what can be done?*

Le reached into his front pocket and pulled out his gold-plated cell phone, a ChiFone, of course.

18

*Politics is supposed to be
the second oldest profession.
I have come to realize that it bears
a very close resemblance to the first.*

Ronald Reagan

CHAPTER 18

PRESIDENT FELIX KOZDRONSKI was sitting in the Oval Office, looking at their party's polling data with his campaign manager, Charles Barth. At sixty-three years old, the wear and tear of four years as the president had added a lot of gray to his once pitch black hair and several lines of wrinkles to his forehead.

"It's not good, I'm afraid, Mr. President."

"I don't understand how this could be possible," the president mused. "When Le was endorsed at the convention, I was ahead by fifteen points over him and by more than that over all the others."

"Agreed," Barth said, staring at the numbers that defied explanation. "Your approval rating had been quite high, especially for an incumbent president. And nothing should have changed that. Although the economy is in a mild recession, employment still remains high, we have no major troop engagements, and the stock market is good, particularly in light of the recession."

"So what could have happened?" asked the president. "What are you hearing? What is the team saying? We have to turn this thing around, and fast."

"I don't know what happened, exactly. Part of it is simply that now that the other party has an endorsed candidate, it is normal that his ratings would come up, but that is typically a marginal gain.

The team doesn't agree on this, but I think it's the media. You were as popular with the media as any president in recent years. But after Le's endorsement, I noticed a radical change. Actually, I thought I first saw the same shift by the media against the other party's candidates well before their convention. At the time, I thought it was a good thing, because I thought Le was a weak presidential choice."

"You know, I thought the same thing," Kozdronski said. "And before their convention, everything was fine for me with the media. Then suddenly I'm facing a string of invented charges from one unnamed source after another, and the reporters run with every one of them. Normally fair editors and newspapers are writing editorials that are vicious. Reporters, with whom I've had good relations for twenty years, including the ones I had given exclusives, won't even talk with me, except to ask hostile questions. And I thought we clearly won the debate at the University of Minnesota. What are we up against, Charles?"

"Our whole team thought you scored a knockout, but the media reported the opposite! I hate to say it, because it's going to sound like you need a new manager," Barth responded, "but if I didn't know better, I'd say the media is under a spell. Maybe a Buddhist thing. They believe in spells, don't they?"

"Which part of that are you serious about?"

"The spell part. Something changed, and the media is killing you. . .without a single legitimate issue. I was kidding about the Buddhist part. Le is about as much of a Buddhist as the man in the moon."

"And yet the media never mentions that, and we don't dare say it. They're pushing his ethnicity and the Buddhism to the max."

"It's a good tactic, although not quite as effective as in years past. Still, it makes great coverage. Le is a feel good, American Dream story about how anyone can become president, and he is super smooth. And Le is well financed, although from where we can't tell. The changes in the laws regarding campaign financing have left loopholes big enough to drive armed trucks through. If you ask me, I think the media is being paid off, big time! But there's no investigative reporters chasing down that story."

"Well, it is a little over two months until the election, we're still leading," said the president, "and we can't start making unsubstantiated accusations, or we'll drop off the planet. What is my travel schedule?"

"We need to concentrate on the states that are swinging to Le right now. We have enough electoral votes to win, assuming our projections are correct, *if* we can get a critical number of those states on Election Day."

"Charles," the president said, "I've been in politics for over forty years now, and I know how to play catch-up, and I know how to keep a lead. I still don't always understand the polls or the sentiment behind them, assuming they are valid data. But I have never lost an election, although some were real squeakers. *I have no intention of losing this one.* So what's the plan?"

"Mr. President, I have you going to Ohio with your family this upcoming week, then Michigan and New York. We'll never catch Le in California, although you have more support there than people thought. You're solid in your home state of Illinois, and Le's ethnicity doesn't play as well in the Midwest as it does on the West Coast. Your family, of course, is tremendously popular with the people of America."

"That's a bit encouraging."

"Indiana, I think is strongly in our column. The Deep South still has some traditional concerns with someone from a communist country; some of our polls indicate that they aren't buying the tale about his parents' immigration. Texas has been yours, but there's slippage there that we've got to repair. Same with Florida. We still have two more debates coming up which may help."

"How are the workers doing?" the president asked.

"Hanging in there. A bit confused with the polls, just as we are. We need to give them something to get excited about. Some good news."

A knock at the door interrupted their conversation. Glancing up, they saw the president's secretary at the door.

"Yes, Phyllis?" the president asked.

"Mr. President, I have the secretary of state on the phone. She says it is urgent."

"Thank you," the president said and picked up the phone.

Barth could see from the doubled lines on the president's forehead that he might as well leave, because the phone call would take a while. As he stepped away from the president's desk, he thought about how few Americans knew how many crises the president faced every month. Kozdronski was especially adept at knowing how to deal with the bad guys and wasn't afraid to use a big stick to deal with them. But this was a new day, and Barth had a feeling the bad guys were playing by a new set of rules that meant no rules.

19

*Medicine is the only profession
that works unceasingly to annihilate itself.*

Martin H. Fischer M.D.

CHAPTER 19

D ANA LOOKED AT HER ORGANIZER, thinking about all the tasks she needed to work on for the ChiFone project. It was going to be a long, long day. She was seated in Dr. Stevens' office, waiting for Jack to come in. Four weeks had passed since her first visit, and she was a bit apprehensive of what she might find out, even though nothing had been flagged as a problem to this point.

"Well, good news, Dana," Stevens said, walking into the office with papers in hand. Setting them down on his desk, he sat down in his chair and continued, "Your blood tests and the MRI of the brain were all normal. How are you feeling?"

"I'm clearly better, but I miss my ChiFone."

"Good to hear you feel better," Jack said. "Let's review a bit. After talking to you on the phone three weeks ago, you wanted to go further, so we did a positron emission tomography, or PET scan, which showed an area of increased glucose metabolism with the radioisotope we injected in you. The PET scan was originally useful for certain types of cancer, especially to look for metastases. It's not used as much in clinical neurology except for some dementias, which you don't have. You also had a slightly abnormal EEG. EEGs look at the electrical waves generated by the brain."

"What did you say my PET scan showed?"

"It showed a small abnormality in your left temporal lobe. Right about there," he said, pointing to a model of the brain on his desk. "This is an area of increased neuronal activity consistent with increased brain processing, although there are other differential considerations. But correlating with that is your EEG, which was mildly abnormal because of some definite asymmetry. In the left temporal lobe, you had significantly more beta; that is, more high frequency brain waves."

"So. . .what does that mean?"

"The EEG would confirm that there is increased processing in the left temporal lobe. Exactly what it means is a little unclear, especially in face of a normal MRI and a large battery of blood tests. Had we found the abnormality first, we still would have done all those blood tests to work it up, so we have already done that. There were reports of abnormalities in rats when exposed to higher strengths of electromagnetic waves in the frequency spectrum of cell phones. But this was never seen in humans during life or at autopsy, even among heavy cell users. On the other hand, we sent you for the latest generation PET scan, and maybe we are seeing the effects of that; that is, maybe it is there in all cell users, but we never had the technology to detect it. The scans get more sensitive all the time. It is on the side of your preferred cell phone use."

"Dr. Stevens, I have been doing some reading on the web. Could it be an artifact?" Dana wondered.

"Yes, we always have to consider that, especially in smaller abnormalities like yours. In MRI scanning, as it has progressed in sensitivity, we frequently find tiny abnormalities, particularly as we age. Technically, there are broad differential diagnostic possibilities, but usually they are age-related microvascular changes. We often call them *UBOs* for *unidentified bright objects*, since on T2 imaging they are brighter than the background."

"Sounds like I have aliens in my head. . .and I'm just getting old," Dana said, raising her eyebrows.

"No aliens were detected, and we're all aging, but I don't think this is related to aging. You only had one UBO in an unusual location, you had a normal MRI, and you are not diabetic or hypertensive. So it's isolated, and what we call a *focal abnormality*."

"Could it always have been there?"

"Yes, absolutely. But I don't like your history of this having started with the new cell phone, being on the same side and about where you are holding it by your head. Also the EEG correlates with it, so I think it is real, not artifactual. What is strange is that in *structural* lesions in the brain that are usually *destructive of neurons*, there is usually a shift toward slower frequencies, especially what we call *delta*. Your shift was toward faster waves, that is *beta*. To be honest with you, Dana, I have never seen anything like it, and my Medline search showed no articles in the medical literature regarding this."

"Great. I'm a freak. Why is it significant?" Dana asked.

"Because areas of increased beta are areas normally of increased brain processing are not consistent with a structural lesion. Here," he said and turned his computer screen toward her and began pointing. "This is your EEG. I am the one who interprets them. Here is your posterior left temporal lobe, and there is your right. Can you see the difference?"

Dana laughed and said, "Not really, Jack, but I'll take your word for it. Looks like what we called *chicken scratching* back on the farm."

Now it was Jack's turn to laugh. "I guess it does. Have you heard about alpha waves?"

Dana nodded. "Yeah, I have. Isn't that connected with gurus and meditation?"

"Alpha is what I call an *idling frequency*. So if you have your eyes closed, are relaxed and not thinking too hard about something, I will see alpha especially prominent in the back of the head. Then, when you open your eyes, your alpha goes away and your beta increases as your brain processes visual information. The primary visual processing areas are in the back of the head. Years ago, I did research when I was doing a patent that demonstrated this in other areas, such as the temporal lobes, that there was a shift toward beta, that is higher frequencies when using them."

"What do the temporal lobes do?"

"Both are intimately involved with memory creation and storage. In a right-handed person, the left temporal lobe also is crucial to speaking and understanding; that is, deciphering speech. It's normally reversed in lefties. The right temporal lobe is generally more involved in nonverbal information, for example, reading music. Interestingly, in highly trained musicians, the notes become 'language' and are more processed on the left. There is a certain amount of plasticity in the brain, especially in young individuals."

Dana sat back in her chair and was surprised by her thoughts. She liked Jack's manner and approach, his easy smile, his calm and confidence. She had never had a doctor who actually took the time to explain things, which she really wanted to understand. And it didn't hurt that he was tall, in good physical shape, handsome, although his dark blond hair was thinning. "You called, and we repeated the PET scan and EEG yesterday. How did they turn out?"

"Normal, now, both of them. So your first scan was done only a week after you stopped using the new phone, so presumably still showing the effects. But after you were off the cell phone almost four weeks, it was normal, as was your EEG."

"So it was something in the ChiFone, even though I used my old phone?"

"It would appear so."

"How can we know for sure?"

"You are doing well, Dana," Jack said. "But it could be coincidence. For example, you could have had a viral infection of the brain particularly affecting the left temporal lobe, but coincidentally clearing up at the same time as you stopped using the new cell phone. If you are still game, let's do one more thing. I want you to use your new cell phone again for two weeks, and we'll redo your PET scan and EEG. If your headaches get worse again, and the PET scan and EEG are abnormal, the cell phone goes way up on my short list as the culprit."

"I'm game. But I'll bet a hundred bucks it's the ChiFone. We'll run the tests to satisfy your curiosity. You are one of the most curious persons I've ever met."

"I'm a doctor. A doctor who isn't curious isn't going to be that helpful. Karen will set that up and then a follow-up appointment with me."

After Dana left, Dr. Stevens began to think of some of his other headache patients. He decided to change his standard question-naire to ask about cell phone type, usage, and which side of the head it was mostly used on. He also asked Karen to do some research on their patient database.

Jack had never seen or read anything like Dana's case. While it didn't appear serious, it made no sense. He was betting on the ChiFone as well, but he wasn't about to tell Dana that.

20

If you are too smart to pay the doctor,
you had better be too smart to get ill.

African Proverb

★ ★ ★ ★ ★

CHAPTER 20

D ANA RETURNED in three weeks.

"How do you feel, Dana?" Dr. Stevens inquired.

"You owe me a hundred bucks, Jack," she said with a smile. "The headaches are back. I think I know the answer, but how was my PET scan?"

"Abnormal, and so was your EEG."

"I'm pitching this darn phone," Dana said, pulling the ChiFone out of her purse and setting it on Jack's desk. "Do you want it?"

Jack shook his head. "Actually, I hate to ask you this, but I'd like to get to the bottom of this and eliminate any possibility that the phone use is coincidental. If you're willing, the definitive way would be to have you use the new cell on the *right* side, never the left. A month should be enough. Then we'll do your PET scan and EEG once more. If it appears again and is on the *right* this time, that will be highly suggestive, although still anecdotal. I suspect I won't be the favorite M.D. with your insurance company."

"Oh, I don't know, Jack. Sounds like you want me to be the guinea pig," Dana said, squinting her eyes at him. "I've got a lot of projects at the moment, and these headaches are taking their toll. How might it affect my diagnosis?"

"It will be one more piece in proving that there's nothing wrong with you other than your phone," Jack answered. "But it's possible that there's something bigger at play here. I did a literature search and can't find anything like this. The ChiFone wasn't ever tested when the last research was done on cell phones a few years ago, and there's been no new research since. If there is a problem with this phone, people should know about it."

"ChiFone is my client," Dana said before she'd really thought about it. "Are you serious?"

"Absolutely," Jack said, clearly determined. "If they are a credible company, it should not change the work you are doing for them. You'd be doing them a favor."

"Oh, man, you need to come out of the ivory tower once and see what happens in the trenches. Still, you're right. If the ChiFones are doing in other people's heads what it's doing in mine, it needs to stop."

Jack turned to the phone and speed dialed Karen's extension. "Karen, would you please set Dana up to get a PET scan and EEG in three weeks? Clinical information: 'prior left temporal abnormality on PET; please compare.' Then have her see me afterward."

Dr. Stevens walked Dana out to Karen's desk and said, "See you in a few weeks."

"I look forward to it, Jack. But this is it for me as far as the phone."

"Understood," Jack said. "See you then."

Jack walked back to his office and sat down, then immediately called his former colleague and friend, Andrew Don, M.D., who was still working at the Twin Cities Clinic of Neurology.

"Barbara?" Jack said to Andrew's secretary, "this is Dr. Stevens. How are you?"

"Dr. Stevens, so nice to hear your voice! I'm fine, how are you?"

"Doing okay, Barbara. Missing you, of course."

"Jack, we've really missed you around here. And no one teases Andrew the way you used to. How are the girls?"

"Annalisa still lives in D.C., and Whitney lives in San Francisco. How are those two wonderful golden retrievers?"

"The dogs are great, and, no, I've not taken their pictures from my desk or walls or screensaver, as you used to joke about. Did you need to talk with Dr. Don?"

"Is he available? It's not an emergency."

"I think he's between patients and a meeting. I'll check. Say hi to Karen."

Jack waited for Dr. Don to pick up, then heard the click.

"Jack, old buddy, can I call you back on my cell? I need to run to a meeting."

"Sure, dial my direct number."

"Will do."

Within fifteen seconds, Jack's phone rang again. He picked it up and said, "Andy, how are you?"

"I'm good, Jack. Are you calling because you want your old job back? We couldn't pay you much—you were always such a slacker!" Jack had been the highest producing neurologist there every year.

"You can't afford, me, Andy! Besides, I'd never work for such a group of second-rate neurologists!" The clinic's neurologists were among the highest respected in the U.S., but he needed to return the insult.

"What can I do for you, Jack?"

"Andy, I have a puzzler, can't find anything in the literature, and wondered if you had seen or heard of it." With forty neurologists with various interests and subspecialties, there was a huge data source of information by the clinicians doing the day-to-day work of taking care of patients. The clinic also had monthly meetings, and one or more members would present interesting cases such as Dana's.

"What's the history?"

"Thirty-eight-year-old right-handed white female with distant history of migraines, positive family history for migraines, now with recurrence of headaches, but with a few different twists. Lost her husband in a car accident a few years ago, but seems to have coped well with that. Husband left her in excellent financial shape. Busy interior designer, but doesn't appear stressed. Doing a big project for ChiFone's CEO, and he gave her a free cell phone. No other significant symptoms or past medical history. Physical exam is normal. MRI of brain is normal. Usual blood tests are normal."

"Okay, Jack, so likely going through peri-menopause with hormonal instability and resultant reactivation of her migraines. You see that all the time. So what's the twist?"

"I did an EEG, and she had some focal left posterior temporal *increased* beta compared to the right. Looked real, not artifactual. Otherwise nonfocal and normal. No epileptiform or structural abnormalities. No skull defects to explain increased beta on one side."

"Doesn't sound too concerning with everything else normal."

"I agree. Anyway, she had gotten a new cell phone, used it a great deal more than the prior one, and always on the left. Used to scrunch it on her shoulder, but that doesn't seem to be it. Not holding it like that didn't help. However, going on vacation without it for a week did."

"If you're thinking of the rats with exposure to cell phone transmission frequencies, we have never seen that in humans."

"I know. I just rechecked the literature. And, of course, we never knew if the rats suffered from headaches, since they never complained of it."

"Right, Jack, so doesn't sound too serious. How is she now?"

"Well, I had her not use the phone for a while, and she improved rapidly. The hooker is, and maybe a red herring, she had an abnormal PET scan with a focal area of hypermetabolism in the left posterior temporal lobe, exactly correlating with the EEG."

"Now, Jack, *that* is interesting. Why did you even do the PET?"

"Andy, she had the abnormal EEG, and wanted to investigate further, so I ordered the PET."

"Fascinating. I didn't think they did PETs on the rats. I'll have to check. We have a Section meeting tomorrow, Jack. Want to come present the case to the guys?" They always called the neurologists "the guys," male or female.

"I have a conflict tomorrow, Andy, would you mind presenting?"

"No, we need another good case anyway."

"Andy, there's more."

"What?"

"I had her stop using the ChiFone and wait a few weeks and repeated the PET and EEG. Actually, she used an older cell phone."

"And?"

"And the defect is gone both on PET and EEG. Then had her use the ChiFone cell once more on the left, and the PET and EEG again showed the same abnormality."

"What are you doing with her now?"

"Taking it one more step. We decided to have her use the phone only on the *right* side for three weeks, we repeat her PET and EEG, and she follows up with me."

"Great idea, Jack. Let me know how it turns out. If it's not a red herring, you realize that Chinese fox isn't going to be happy."

"Yeah, Dana said the same thing."

"Who's Dana?"

"The patient."

"You sound like you have a—"

"Simmer down, Andy. I said she's the patient."

"Ah, but I hear it in your voice. Are you—"

"No, for crying out loud. It's a long story. She is attractive, though."

"And twenty years younger than you."

"She looks twenty younger than me, but that's the story of my life."

"Well, come over to the clinic sometime. We'd all love to see you. Or let's go to dinner sometime."

"Love to do it," Jack said. He avoided the clinic because it reminded him of Anne. "Let me know what the guys say about the case."

"I will. I may have to ditch my ChiFone if this is related. Have a great one, Jack."

"You, too, Andy. Thanks for talking."

"Anytime."

Jack listened as Andy hung up the phone, then he hung up his phone.

Others listening in did not hang up as quickly.

21

No man is a good doctor
who has never been sick himself.

Chinese Proverb

CHAPTER 21

JACK HAD KAREN SEARCH the office computer database of those patients with new-onset or worsened headaches within the past two years. He then had her do secure e-mails to them, inquiring about whether they had obtained a new cell phone prior to the onset of the headaches. If they had, they were asked to list the manufacturer and model. For those who responded with new phones, he ordered PET scans and EEGs, which he knew would and did result in an immediate list of insurance company medical directors to call. They wanted to know why he was suddenly ordering all these expensive tests for no reason.

Just part of the deal, Jack thought as he sat as his desk reviewing their charts. *Semi-Socialized medicine, although Big Brother had other names for it.*

"Dr. Stevens?" Karen said through the telephone intercom.

"Yes, Karen," Jack said as he picked up the phone.

"Dr. Don's office had e-mailed that he was free this morning. I know you had wanted to talk with him, so I called his cell phone for you. I have him on the line for you."

"Put him through, Karen."

"Jack," Andy said, coming on the line, "sorry I didn't get back to you sooner. Been busy. I think you have the right idea trying to have a life outside neurology!"

"No problem, Andy. Thanks, for calling."

"Jack, I'm afraid I am not going to be of much help. I presented the case at the monthly group meeting. We had a good turnout. No one has seen or heard of anything like this. Neither the headache nor the multiple sclerosis subspecialists can tell me what it is. Thanks for sending the CD copy of the PET scans and the EEGs. What might be helpful to you is that the group pretty much thought the abnormality was real in both the PET and EEG, especially with the clinical history. They are intrigued by the case."

"Thanks, Andy. It's nice to get a number of second opinions from the guys, so that helps."

"They all say 'hi.'"

"Say 'hi' back, Andy. By the way, I'm just reviewing the charts of headache patients with a similar history to my first patient. I've sent them all for PETs and EEGs."

"Anything back?"

"Not yet, but I'll stay in touch." Jack looked at his calendar on the computer. "Should be back over the next few weeks."

"You're going to tick off the insurance companies again."

"Already accomplished that much. Same old story."

"Our headache guys are intrigued. They are looking at getting an NIH Grant to study it further, but you know that will take at least a year before we even get approved. But in the meantime, we'll keep an eye out. I did an e-mail to everyone, including the partners who weren't there, restating the case and asking them to let me know if they get anything. I think we'll be ordering more PETs in suspicious cases, even before we get a grant."

"Don't tell the insurance companies I told you," Jack kidded. "I have a long list of medical directors to call already! Although maybe if your clinic does more, they'll accept it more easily as clinically indicated. They are just doing their job, but sometimes it really slows you down."

"Tell me about that! With forty partners, we have one of the support staff whose entire job is to do pre-authorizations now!

You know that fifty percent of the nation's health cost is 'watchers and checkers' who work for the government or insurers. And they blame it on us."

"Andy, I added cell phone use to my intake questionnaire. Should speed up the process of identifying these patients."

"Good idea. I'll tell our registration staff to do that as well. Call or e-mail when you know something, Jack."

"I will. Keep your synapses firing in synchrony!"

* * * * *

Over the next few weeks, Jack had Karen set up follow-up appointments for those with abnormal PET scans so he could do a bedside neurologic exam in the office. He also had Karen set them up for EEGs.

Jack saw a lot of patients with headaches, mostly because he was a neurologist, but partly because everyone in his family had headaches, going back as many generations as he could determine. He could empathize with the patients, Anne used to tell him, since he had migraines too. He used to joke that if his dog, Machiavelli, could talk, he'd probably complain of headaches too. So he thought he wouldn't be surprised if he saw a lot with cell phone use, regardless of type. It was the twenty-first century, and he didn't know anyone above the age of twelve who didn't have a cell phone.

Headaches are a common problem. Most people have them, but generally they are tension or other headaches, can be handled at home, and rarely require seeing a neurologist. Recurrent migraines affect about four percent of the population in the United States, afflicting women more than twice as much as men. They are often found to be genetic, if one probes enough; although without a careful family history taken by the doctor, the family trend is often missed.

There are interesting influences. In women, they often start in the teenage years and are frequently seen monthly just before a woman's menstrual period. They tend to simmer down in a woman's twenties and thirties, although the birth control pill might bring them out again. Similarly, with hormonal instability around menopause, they worsen in the forties. They never go away entirely, but might be much better and mild enough that they aren't termed migraines.

There are seasonal differences, occurring more in fall and spring. Classic food influences are cheese, chocolate, processed meats, and alcohol, especially red wine, but there are numerous others. But in women, they are influenced also, again, by hormones. So for most women, chocolate is great during most of the month, except at the point often before the period, when the smell of chocolate alone may cause a migraine.

Men tend to get migraines more in their thirties; they are more seasonal and tend to be milder. One exception is a nasty subgroup called *cluster migraines*. Typically affecting males and occurring spring or fall, they are of short but intense duration, usually around one eye, and occur many times a day for six weeks, and then are gone for months or years.

Since men's generally are milder in terms of pain, they tend to be forgotten or dismissed as *tension headaches*, and many men with migraines deny that they have them. They tend to have more associated "auras," especially dizziness and visual symptoms without the headache pain, often incorrectly diagnosed as other things. Partly it is a testosterone thing.

Jack looked at the results of his patients with the new headaches and cell phone use. It was consistent. There were ten of them. *Everyone used the ChiFone.* Each had a temporal abnormality. And each was on the side of the brain where they used the phone.

Jack picked up the phone and speed-dialed Karen. "Karen, can you please get Dr. Don on the phone? Try his cell. He seems to like that better."

"Right away, Dr. Stevens."

A few minutes later, she rang back with Dr. Don on the line.

"Hi, Jack, what's up?"

"Andy, I just got the little retrospective study I did on my recent headache patients going back two years."

"And?"

"And the ten with new or recurrent headaches who used Chi-Fones were the only ones associated with cell phone use."

"Really!"

"It gets better, Andy! All had abnormal PETs and EEGs. Not only that, they were lateralized to the side of dominant phone use, mostly left temporal, of course."

"Wow, Jack, you have to publish this! It's a major deal. Maybe you could do a quick 'Letter to the Editor' of *Neurology*. I've got to think it would get published immediately. It's October now, so the January issue might already be finalized. So far your one case was reversible, but this new data is enough for a significant case study report. Did her retrial come back?"

"She is supposed to have that this morning along with her EEG. She's been a real trooper in trying to find the answer!"

"Let's see, the next American Academy of Neurology annual meeting is in April. You could certainly get a poster presentation, if not a platform talk. Actually looks like it is in Minneapolis this time. I wonder if we should tell the Minnesota Department of Health?"

"Not sure, Andy, that I have enough data yet. But will you pass it on to the clinic? I think you guys better start looking closer at PET scans and EEGs."

"Jack, I think I'll start with me. I have a ChiFone, although no headaches. Actually, I have a shirttail relative who works at the FDA. I'll call him unofficially and see what he says. We may need to get them involved."

"Andy, how are 'the guys' doing?"

"Usual stuff, Jack. Many are worried about the election. Le seems intent on cutting reimbursement even more than before. It'll be a challenge to keep trying to afford the best docs and support staff with less money than ever! Funny, though, I've come to like Senator Le. I have never voted for anyone in his party, but I might give him a shot. My father would roll over in his grave! Mimi can't believe it. I just have these positive images of him lately. Go figure!"

"Given the polls, I think you have some company in terms of people who are intending to vote for him. Bye, Andy."

"Bye, Jack. I'll be in touch."

"Let me know how your own PET and EEG turn out. You should get checked immediately. My patient said something similar about Senator Le when she was using that phone. Maybe the phone makes you think funny and like people like Le."

"That's funny, Jack, but a bit of a leap of logic. I will get tested out of curiosity, if nothing else."

22

Politics is war without bloodshed
while war is politics with bloodshed.

Mao Zedong

CHAPTER 22

A FEW MILES AWAY in a back office on the 50th floor of the IDS Building, Hai, the chief electronics intelligence officer for ChiFones, was on the phone. "Mr. Chan. We have a problem. Can you come to my office?"

"I'll be right there, Hai."

Hai had spent his entire life in pursuit of an assignment of this magnitude, even leaving his family behind in China for as long as it would take to fulfill their purpose. Before he came to Minneapolis, he disliked Americans. Having spent several years in a downtown apartment, he now hated Americans. He hated that they were so smug, so comfortable, so lucky. All that was about to change, he hoped. In Hai's book, the only thing worse than Americans were the Chinese who became Americans. No, actually, the worst were those who married Americans and had children—all of substandard intelligence, he was sure.

Chan walked into the room. "Hai, what concerns you?"

Hai said, "Mr. Chan, as you know, we record and computer scan all the calls made on our network for keywords, much like the American NSA, but on a much smaller scale, since we don't have to interpret as many. They have much bigger computers, but we have all we need. The last few weeks, the word ChiFone has been correlated with words mentioning some government agencies, which is one of the algorithms we use. There is one such series of conversations, right here in Minneapolis, that concerns me. We received several hits from one person."

"Have you listened to the raw conversations?"

"Yes. There is a Dr. Don with the Twin Cities Clinic of Neurology who is talking to a Dr. Stevens about reporting the phone to the Food and Drug Administration or taking other steps to stop its use. I have downloaded the conversations for you to listen to from our offline storage."

Hai played the recordings of Andy and Jack for Chan, whose face turned progressively grimmer the deeper he got into the conversations.

"This is a problem," Chan said to Hai, who was familiar with the entire operation. "We rushed the phone into production from research without all the testing we would have done had we had more time. The trials at the university gave us the results we needed. We did do MRI scans of the patients in our experiment, and they were all normal. But we skipped doing EEGs because of the time constraints. And no one even brought up the issue of PET scans."

"So there *was* a glitch, after all."

"Unfortunately, and worse than we anticipated as a possibility," Chan stated. "Well, the stakes are too high, and it is too late to alter the main plan. Who is Dr. Stevens?"

"He appears to be a former colleague of Dr. Don," said Lam. "Don has our phone, so we can track him as well as listen. Unfortunately, Stevens doesn't. And Stevens has always called Don. Stevens' own line is blocked, so I can't tell where it originates. Don is a Director of the clinic and is about to tell his group of forty neurologists that Stevens has found abnormalities in the brains of numerous patients who are using our phones. Don's is the largest neurological clinic in the United States, so they can quickly look at hundreds of patients, both past and present, as well as rapidly test and analyze them. I heard Don say they were just celebrating their millionth patient. And they have national credibility—one of their first presidents was a founder of the American Academy of Neurology, and their doctors are highly regarded. So Stevens wants Don to tell his partners to start looking for abnormalities. And Don wants Stevens to write an article for their national journal, *Neurology*, as well as do a presentation at the Academy's upcoming annual meeting. They don't know the underlying workings of our cell phone, but they could move quickly to have it taken off the market as a medical hazard."

"Good work, Hai. Don needs some immediate attention. This Stevens can wait. Two connected deaths will bring too much attention. Find out what you can about him in the meantime."

"Will do."

"Don said he was turning off his phone. It was wise of you to suggest that our engineers modify the GPS so that it is always on, even when the user thinks they have turned off the phone! He will be easy to locate."

"Who will you send?"

"Lam. He has performed the strike many times without detection."

Hai nodded. Lam was a rough looking man with a badly scarred hand who stayed in the background as much as possible, but was always ready to act.

"Give me Don's GPS setting."

"I thought you'd want it," Hai said, slipping Chan a small piece of paper with the coordinates written on it.

Chan pulled his cell phone out of his pocket and quickly sent a text message to Lam. Externally, his cell phone was identical to any other ChiFone, but it was a bit lighter because it wasn't built quite like the other ChiFones. Software-wise, it worked on a frequency close to the other ChiFones, but Chan's was encrypted.

Then Chan called Lam's phone and heard him answer. "Lam, I have a problem that needs your immediate attention."

"Mr. Chan, I saw the GPS coordinates, and I'm in the car now. What needs to be done?"

"There is a doctor in his car, who's just leaving his office in Golden Valley."

"I have him on my screen."

"Lam, this needs to be his last car trip."

"Mr. Chan, I'm actually quite close to there. I'll call you when it's done. What's his name?"

"His last name is Don. Why?"

"I enjoy it more, when I know their name. Dr. Don. I like that name."

* * * * *

It was still a warm fall day in Minneapolis, and Andy Don was driving his red Miata with the top down. His wife had bought it for him in the spring. She called it his "fun car," and it was relatively inexpensive. She complained that he drove it too fast, and his partners were worried it was so small. He occasionally wished that it had some real storage space in the trunk.

Oh, well, Don thought. *It's fall and will be snowing soon. I'll put it away for the winter and start driving the winter car.* Many Minnesotans have "winter cars," often "junkers" that they don't care if they get rusty or rustier from all of the salt used on the roads. Some Minnesotans, such as Don, called them "summer cars" because, like the Miata, they had no chance of getting through deep snow. Don had a white four-wheel drive Tahoe that his wife and partners liked better.

Andy was headed south on Theodore Wirth Parkway toward Highway 55, slowing for the stop sign by the golf course clubhouse. He never saw the large black Suburban waiting at the T-intersection at Plymouth Road just before the clubhouse until it was too late. Striking the Miata on the driver's side, the Suburban collapsed the whole driver's side, slammed it into the curb, where it flipped the Miata over onto its top, crushing and killing Andy instantly.

Lam jumped of the SUV and could immediately see from Don's smashed head that he was gone. *That was too easy,* he thought.

Running back to his Suburban, which had no real damage, he backed up and drove away. His SUV had steel bars in front of the bumper covered with chrome, a look popular with some, but this bumper was meant to look harmless. In Lam's case, it was heavy steel and functional; good for ramming without damage to the vehicle itself. The Chinese frequently hit cars driven by dissidents living in the United States to harass them; in their cases, it simply caused light damage to their vehicle. Sometimes, as with Don, more force was necessary. Although it was a pleasant day, there were no golfers out today. No witnesses. Lam's kind of deal.

He encrypted texted Chan: *Dr. Don done.*

23

Physicians and politicians resemble one another in this respect, that some defend the constitution and others destroy it.

Author Unknown

★ ★ ★ ★ ★

CHAPTER 23

STEVENS WAS AT HIS DESK, reviewing Dana's electronic chart before she came. He had come in earlier than usual, because his cable service had gone out at home and with it his TV, Internet, and phone. He felt a bit cut off. On his wall he could see the cable news on the flat screen that was hanging behind the computer. With only four days before the election, the talking heads were offering up the usual political stuff. Jack was tired of it all, and he hoped the election would hurry up and be over, so the ads and coverage would stop. He surfed to another channel with local news.

Jack put down the remote and stared at the flat screen. He couldn't believe that he was seeing a horribly crushed red Miata and hearing the reporter say, "Doctor Andrew Don, a prominent Twin Cities' neurologist, was killed in a hit-and-run accident. Minneapolis police are investigating this tragic death, but have no leads on the driver of the other vehicle. They are asking the public's help for any information regarding the accident that happened in the afternoon on Theodore Wirth Parkway. Please call the Minneapolis police with any information."

He just continued to stare as the scene of the accident faded away. Jack had just talked to Andy shortly before. "Oh, dear God," he whispered. "How can this be? Why, Andy? This isn't possible! Who would leave him for dead?"

His thoughts were interrupted by the phone. He turned and picked it up. "Yes, Karen?"

"Dr. Stevens, you came in bright and early! I thought you were busy, so I didn't want to interrupt. Dana is here and ready."

Jack took a deep breath and tried to regain his focus. "Okay, bring her back, Karen."

Shortly after, Jack heard footsteps, and then there was a knock on the door. "Come in, Karen."

Karen opened the door and let Dana come in, then she closed the door and walked back to her desk.

"Hi, Dana," Jack said as he picked up the remote and turned off the television. "Have a seat. How are you feeling?"

"I'm. . .aaah. . .Jack, are you all right?" Dana asked, studying his face. "You're as white as a ghost. Are you sick?"

"No, I'm. . .sort of in shock," Jack answered, lifting his hand to his face and rubbing his cheek and mouth. "I just saw on the news that a good friend of mine was killed in a car accident, a hit-and-run. I'd just talked with him. I. . .can't believe it."

"Oh, I'm sorry," Dana said. "I heard about it on the radio. A terrible scene. What kind of a human being would leave someone to die like that? Perhaps we should reschedule for another time? This isn't urgent."

"No, no, no," Jack replied, holding up his hands. "There's nothing I can do at the moment, and his partners will take care of matters. I'll be okay. Let's do this. What did you find out?"

"Well, I did as we planned and continued to use the ChiFone for the last month, but only on the right side. And the headaches are back. How were my PET scan and EEG?"

"Abnormal again, I'm afraid," Jack said. "But this time it involves the *right* temporal lobe. Those on the left have gone away. Let's go across the hall and have a look at you."

Karen joined them in the exam room to input any notes for the records.

"You don't need to get into a gown, Dana. Just kick off your shoes and socks," Jack said, then he repeated the physical exam in just the same manner as he had the last two times, working quickly without much explanation.

"So how do I look?" Dana inquired when he finished the last reflex test.

"You look great at the bedside, just as before," Jack said. "A small temporal lobe lesion might not show anything on a physical exam. I tried to talk myself into some minimal abnormalities, but there is nothing I would usually say was abnormal in looking at you. Let's walk across to my office."

Dana put her socks and shoes back on. Jack led Dana back to his office, and Karen went back out front to input the data into Dana's records.

"So what's next, Jack?" Dana asked. "I'm done with the ChiFone. I can't take these headaches."

"I understand, and there's no reason to continue. I feel bad about asking you to go this long with them. We know that whatever the abnormal PET scan and EEG means, it seems reversible once you stop using the ChiFone, so that's good news. Since I last saw you, I researched my records for patients with headaches like yours who also used cell phones. Among the group, I found ten other patients who, after bringing them back for PET scanning and EEG, had the same abnormalities as you, but only those using a ChiFone."

"So it *is the phone!*" Dana said.

"I would think so. Although it's a small number of incidents, really like a pilot study, it's pretty persuasive to at least do a large scale study. We're considering reporting it to the Center for Disease Control in Atlanta or the FDA. The CDC, as you may know, is a federal agency charged with overseeing particularly infectious diseases and preventing epidemics. This is different than their usual deal, but we may have a different type of epidemic—an electronic one, if you will. The FDA normally doesn't get involved with cell phones, but we think they would in a case like this."

"I'll just throw the darn thing away and go back to my old one.

I think I told you that it was a gift from the CEO of ChiFone. Maybe I should tell him we have a problem."

"Dana, you should go back to your old phone immediately. But don't get rid of the ChiFone. I was a computer engineer many years ago, and I still tinker. If you don't mind, I want to give it a look. And I might bring it over to an old friend who is a top design engineer. Your cell phone might be needed for testing purposes."

"Here," Dana said, handing him the phone. "I'm glad to see it go. What about talking to Mr. Chan about it?"

"Before we falsely accuse him or get him upset, let me check this out a little bit more. Bad news like this can destroy a company, so we have to be careful as to how we approach it. I was in the midst of that with my old colleague from the Twin Cities Clinic of Neurology, who was just killed in the car accident."

"He was the one helping you with my case?"

"Yes. I had a feeling that there might be many others out there like you who are flying under the radar, because it's so unusual. Andy was going to have all forty of his doctors in the clinic take the same steps with their patients that I took, and he is also well connected and could help in getting some national neurological societies and magazines involved. He was just going to call someone he knows at the FDA. . .on his ChiFone, of all things."

"Oh, my goodness. That's makes it even more bizarre."

"It is bizarre. I told him he had to be the first one to get tested. Then he told me something else that was strange. He said that although he'd never voted for a left-of-center politician in his life, he thought Senator Le was great and was going to vote for him. That's not like my friend Andy. Didn't you say something like that as well?"

"I did, and it's been the weirdest roller coaster ride. When I first got the ChiFone, I couldn't stand Senator Le, but then I started liking the guy, even though I didn't agree with him on most of his policies, though it's hard to figure out what he actually believes. When I stopped using the phone, I went right back to not liking the guy. And, now, after using it again, I think he's the best, and I can't give you a single reason why."

Jack shook his head and said, "I couldn't begin to guess. But it's strange."

"You don't ever guess, do you?"

"Not often. I hate when people jump to conclusions without getting the facts."

"I like that in a person, but I also like to guess and to make bets. So, now what?"

"Well, I was a partner of Andy's at TCCN for many years. I know most of the people there. In a few days, after things settle down from Andy's death, I'll propose we look at this with the entire group at the clinic. As I told you a few weeks ago, your case was presented to the group, and no one had ever seen anything like it. But I have much more conclusive evidence now."

"That sounds like the right thing to do. And am I done? Is this it?"

"No," Jack replied, "we need to run final tests in a month and make sure that everything moves back to normal. There's no reason to think it won't, but it's important to verify it."

"Sounds good. I wasn't looking forward to this ending. Having all the PET scans and EEGs has been so much fun."

Jack chuckled, but wasn't sure if she was completely joking, and he wasn't sure how to respond. "Nothing like a good PET scan to make your week, I'm sure. We'll see how you are doing then, I guess."

"Looking forward to it."

24

High-Tech Run Amok

Anonymous Comment about Frustration with High Tech

CHAPTER 24

DANA WAS AT HER OFFICE in Deephaven, looking over her notes regarding the ChiFone office and some additional carpet samples that she wanted to show Mr. Chan. Picking up her cell phone, she dialed his direct number to confirm their next appointment.

"Ms. LaFontaine, so good to hear from you," Chan said. "How are you?"

"I'm doing well, thanks. I'm looking over some new carpet samples that came in that I thought you might want to see before we commit to the original choice, and I wanted to confirm our appointment at your office at 9 a.m., November 9, the day after the election."

"Let's see," he responded, quickly checking his planner. "That's correct. I look forward to finalizing our decisions and getting the remodel started. By the way, how do you like the phone, Ms. LaFontaine?"

Dana had desperately hoped that the cell phone would not come up in their conversation, and she shifted nervously in her chair, searching to find the words that would help avoid the full truth. "Mr. Chan, I liked the phone a lot, but I ended going back to my old phone, I'm afraid. The old one had served me well for so long that I guess I just couldn't get away from it. I'm not very high tech."

"Yes, actually I saw a printout of your account and that your use of the phone has been off and on recently," Chan replied, his words cutting like a scythe into Dana. "I'm very disappointed, and there's no comparison on what the ChiFone gave you over your old phone. Surely you must have had a problem with it, and I have no doubt we can do better."

"Mr. Chan, I appreciate your concerns, but. . .really. . .I'm happy with the old phone."

"But if there is a problem, I need to know. Our company is only as good as the product we provide, and I take it as my first responsibility to make certain our phones are the best. . .no matter what the cost. So was there a problem?"

"Well," Dana said, grimacing, "I think the ChiFone gave me headaches, so I switched to my old phone, and the headaches stopped. I just didn't want to risk continuing to have headaches. Perhaps it was nothing."

"Did you see a doctor? How do you know it's the phone?"

Dana coughed slightly and tried to clear her throat. "Mr. Chan, I didn't want to bring this up at all at this point. I wish we could wait until later."

"Ms. LaFontaine," Chan said with a tone of severity, "your problem sounds serious, and I really must know the extent of it. My company's reputation would be damaged by even one credible medical complaint, and I will do whatever it takes to resolve yours. Have you seen a doctor? What are the facts?"

"Mr. Chan, please, I am trying to spare you any anxiety over what still is not a proven problem."

"I appreciate that, but now I am aware of your problem, and I know you are the type of person who would never make false accusations," Chan replied. "But there's no reason now to not tell me exactly what the situation is. What proof are you looking for?"

"Okay, you're right," Dana conceded, taking a deep, labored breath. "I have seen a neurologist, Dr. Stevens, and he has determined that the phone was a problem for me and at least ten other of his patients. He didn't want to bother you until he knew more. He was going to do a broader study with his friend, Dr. Don, the director at the Twin Cities Clinic of Neurology, who was killed in that terrible traffic accident."

Chan's hands knotted around his ChiFone, and his knuckles turned white. "Ms. LaFontaine, I'm so relieved that you sought medical attention and feel better. I truly wish to get to the bottom of this immediately as we have not received one such complaint. Please bring your ChiFone phone with you so that my engineers can find out if there is, in fact, a problem. And I will provide you with a new phone."

"I'm sorry, Mr. Chan, but I gave it to Dr. Stevens. He and an engineering friend wanted to take it apart and study it. Trust me, I only wanted to make certain there was credible evidence that was worthy of your attention. I can call him and ask to get the phone back."

The muscles in Chan's jaw were tense, and his eyes were clear and smoldering. He swallowed hard and said, "No, Ms. LaFontaine, that's okay. Let them study the phone. We can attend to that later. In the meantime, it is Monday, and I insist that we get you a new phone. Are you in your office tomorrow afternoon? I'll have one of my colleagues, Mr. Lam, run one over to you."

"Sounds fine, Mr. Chan," Dana replied, not telling him that she had no desire for a new ChiFone, but that she would keep it. "My assistant has the afternoon off, but I'll be there. Just tell him to knock on the door."

"Excellent," Chan said, relaxing his grip on his phone. "I guarantee that you will never experience another headache because of a ChiFone, Ms. LaFontaine. Look for Mr. Lam in the afternoon."

"I will, Mr. Chan. Thanks. Good-bye."

Chan walked to his window and looked across the expanse of suburbs in the direction of Deephaven, then he nodded to himself and called Lam.

"Lam, I have another project for you. A Ms. LaFontaine needs a visit from you tomorrow afternoon. She will be alone in her office, and I will get you the address. She will be expecting you and thinks you're bringing her a new phone, so this should be an easy mark. Just knock on her office door. Ms. LaFontaine has an appointment with me next week on Wednesday, Lam. It's imperative that she not meet with me or anyone else again."

"Can you also provide me with a floor plan, Mr. Chan?" Lam asked.

"I can. . .but she'll be alone."

"Mr. Chan, I never go in unprepared, and I never take anything for granted."

* * * * *

Dana wasn't pleased that Chan had put so much pressure on her to talk, but she was relieved that he had not been defensive and seemed earnest to deal with the problem. He had always been completely straightforward and honest in all of her dealings with him. She thought about calling Jack, but seeing as Chan didn't ask for the phone immediately, she decided to not bother him.

Later in the afternoon, she got a call from her previous client in the IDS Building who had referred her services to Mr. Chan. They were a wonderful client, a law firm, and always seemed to be adding a new partner who wanted his or her office updated, no matter how nice the existing office was.

"I know it's ridiculous, but could you come tomorrow morning?" was the request from the law firm head. "It's the old story, Dana, we have to get this partner in place as soon as possible so we can start bringing in some cash. He didn't come cheap."

Dana had laughed and said, "For you, Bill, I'll drop everything in my hands and come on a run. I'll be there."

The next day, as Dana drove down Interstate 394 and headed toward the IDS Tower, she called Chan's office. He was gone for the day and unavailable, but his secretary was in.

"Hi, it's Dana LaFontaine," she said. "Mr. Chan was going to have a Mr. Lam courier a phone to me this afternoon. I have an appointment in the IDS, this morning, and I can just stop by and pick it up. No sense in Mr. Lam wasting a trip."

"I'm sure that will be fine, Ms. LaFontaine. I will get a phone from Mr. Hai and have it at my desk. How soon will you be here?"

"Well, the freeway is clear as a bell, so I can be there in fifteen minutes. Is that too soon?"

"No, that should be fine. I'll have it ready."

Chan's secretary walked to Hai's office, knowing he wouldn't be there, because he was in a meeting with Chan. Stepping into his office, she saw that there were several phones on his desk that had been programmed. Knowing that Chan considered Dana a local VIP, she picked up one to give Dana and would tell Hai later. He could program Dana's number from his office. It was a routine that she had done dozens of times for Mr. Chan, and Hai was often gone from his office.

When Dana arrived and got off the elevator, she walked directly to the secretary's desk.

"Good to see you, Ms. LaFontaine," the secretary said. "I have the new phone for you right here." Then she handed the phone to Dana.

Dana held it in her hand momentarily and was struck immediately that it was lighter than her first ChiFone. "Thank you," she said. "I'll see you next week when I meet again with Mr. Chan."

"Good-bye, Ms. LaFontaine. I understand this phone has our latest technology. I hope it works better for you."

Dana walked out of the ChiFone offices, took the elevator down to the law firm offices, and met with the new partner who surprised her by actually wanting to retain much of the décor of the existing office. After she had taken notes and greeted several of the other law partners whose offices she had redone, she walked back to her car and drove toward her Deephaven office.

* * * * *

Just before noon, Lam walked into the ChiFone offices and

approached Chan's secretary. "Mei, Mr. Chan said he had left an envelope for me with you."

"It's right here," she said, handing him the envelope that contained Dana's office address and floor plan.

"Thanks, I have a delivery to make this afternoon."

"Mr. Lam, are you referring to Ms. LaFontaine?"

"Yes, how did you know?"

"She came in earlier this morning, and I gave her a new phone. Mr. Chan wanted her to have it. We thought it would save you a trip. Is there a problem?"

"I don't know. Is Mr. Hai in?"

"He's in a meeting?"

"Get him out—now!"

Lam marched down the hallway toward Hai's office, where he was soon joined by Hai.

"Are you missing a phone, Hai?" Lam asked, pointing to the desk.

Hai surveyed the phones on his desk, and his expression changed to that of a thundercloud. "Yes, I am. What did you do?"

"I did nothing. Mei gave it to the interior designer."

Hai shot a fearful sideways glance at Lam and caught the man by the forearm. "Lam, get it back at once! It's one of our secure, encrypted phones, only for those involved in the Project. If I lose that phone, I'm done."

"Don't concern yourself about it," Lam reassured him, prying Hai's fingers from his arm. "She is next on my list for a final visit."

Lam quickly exited the offices and drove toward Dana's office in Deephaven, where the GPS said she was. Although the new encrypted phones were secure, they, like the other phones, had the GPS on all the time. A quick study of the office layout should be all that he required to finish the task.

25

*It's funny how dogs and cats
know the inside of folks better
than other folks do, isn't it?*

Eleanor H. Porter

CHAPTER 25

D ANA HAD SET ASIDE the notes from her meeting with the law firm and was back at her desk, reviewing her designs and plans for the ChiFone offices. There was a knock on the outer door, which she always kept locked when she was alone, even during the day. Her husband, John, had always insisted that she do that, even though she protested that Deephaven, just south of her Woodland home, was a very safe community in the western suburbs.

Her Havanese, Remy, all fifteen pounds of her, sprang to the door and started barking.

"Remy, chair!" Dana commanded, and Remy jumped back onto her favorite chair. It wasn't unusual for Remy to be alarmed when someone knocked like that.

Dana walked to the door and opened it without looking in the peephole. John had also told her *never* to do *that*. Seeing the Chinese man, she immediately noticed the scar on his hand and said, "Yes, may I help you?"

"Ms. LaFontaine? I am Mr. Lam. I believe that Mr. Chan told you I would be stopping by. I have a new phone for you."

"Oh, goodness. I thought they would tell you. I picked up a new one this morning, when I was downtown."

"Yes, they told me, of course. But Mei, Mr. Chan's secretary, gave you the wrong one and apologizes for the inconvenience. I have brought a replacement."

"Come in, Mr. Lam," Dana said, moving aside as he came into her office, then she closed the door, which automatically clicked into the locked position.

As he followed Dana to her desk, Remy remained sitting on her chair but began to growl.

"Remy, quiet," Dana commanded, turning to the white Havenese and shaking her finger. Then out of the corner of her eye, she saw the reason why. Lam stood behind her, having pulled out the newest version of the Chinese 7.65mm pistol with a built-in silencer, which was quieter, smaller, and easier to hide than the old models.

"Do you like your dog?" Lam asked coldly. "If so, you better make sure she stays where she is."

Dana stood there, staring at Lam, dumbfounded, trying to process what was happening. For a moment she felt dizzy and disorientated, the same as she had felt when she got the call that John had been killed in the car accident. But the image of John was accompanied by a flash of anger and indignation. John would never surrender without a fight, and neither would she.

Her heart that had been throbbing so wildly slowed, and she took a deep breath. "Who are you, really? And what do you want?"

"I am who I said I am, and I want that cell phone."

"It's in my desk," she said as she willed herself to take another step toward her desk. "Mr. Lam, I would have given you the phone gladly. What else do you want?"

Remy growled again from her chair, but didn't move, since Dana had told her to stay.

"Get the phone now or the dog is dead." Lam's voice was tense with emotion, and he glanced menacingly at Remy, though he never took the gun sights off Dana.

"Okay, settle down, Mr. Lam. I think I have the phone right here," Dana said and pulled open her right upper desk drawer. She took out the new phone, looked at it, then tossed it to Lam, who caught it with his left hand. "Now, will you leave? You must really want that phone."

Lam stuffed the phone in the same coat pocket that he'd pulled the gun out of and said, "The fun is just starting, Ms. LaFontaine. This can't just look like a random murder, so let's start with you taking off your clothes." He motioned with his gun. "Now!" he yelled.

At that moment, Remy, sensing the danger and unable to hold back, jumped from her chair and dove straight into Lam's left ankle, biting down with the ferocity of a small tiger. Lam screamed and swiped down with his gun, striking Remy on the head, then kicked her across the room, where she lay there motionless.

"Now for you, bitch!" Lam spat the words in a fury as he turned back to Dana, who was still more than clothed.

The ChiFone wasn't the only thing that had been in the opened desk drawer. Years before, John had given her a Smith & Wesson aluminum-framed .38 five-shot revolver with a built-in laser and made her take shooting lessons with it. It was, as he said, the lightest, most compact gun he could find that still had stopping power. And despite her protests of hating guns and violence, she had promised she would always keep it in her desk drawer. She always feared the day might come when she had to use it, and wondered how straight her aim would be in an emergency.

Remy had distracted Lam long enough for Dana to grab the .38. The button for the laser sight was built into the grip. In one motion she aimed the laser sight, somewhat shakily, right under Lam's breastbone, precisely in the spot where John had taught her. She could hear his military instructions still ringing in her head, "If you're off by shooting high, you'll get him in the chest; low, and you'll get him in the abdomen. You won't miss, and worst case you'll slow him down enough for the next shot."

Lam saw her Smith & Wesson and began to pull up his 7.65mm as Dana fired. The sound was deafening compared to the sound when wearing ear protection on the shooting range with John. The .38 bullet, a hollow point, went a bit low and to the right of Lam's midline, piercing his abdominal wall then liver, cutting part of his portal vein, an ultimately fatal shot.

The liver has two "intakes" for blood. The first is the hepatic artery, which supplies oxygenated and nutrient-rich arterial blood from the heart via the aorta. The second intake is the portal vein, with lower pressure than an artery. The portal vein brings venous blood into the liver primarily from the large and small intestines so as to allow the liver to process and detoxify ingested materials, the main function of the liver. All ingested solids and liquids, after being broken down by the gastrointestinal system, first must pass through the liver before entering the bloodstream. Lam would die soon from this shot, but not soon enough.

Lam looked bewildered and dazed. He wasn't used to having his victims shoot *at him*. Momentarily stunned, he lowered his gun, and Dana hesitated, thinking he would drop, but with an adrenaline surge he stumbled forward, raised his gun, and fired. His aim just grazed Dana on the left chest, fracturing her left lateral 7th rib just to the outside of her breast, but not entering her lung. Dana stiffened from the acute pain but stayed on her feet, unsure of what exactly had happened.

Still staggering forward, Lam's movements slowed markedly as the portal vein emptied blood into his abdominal cavity and the blood loss caused significant less blood flow to the brain, making him instantly lightheaded. With Lam only four feet away and trying desperately to raise his hand to shoot Dana in the heart, Dana aimed the laser between Lam's eyes and pulled the trigger. John had taught her, "Avoid head shots unless absolutely sure," but as the scene passed before her as though in slow motion, she had had no doubt.

A little low, her second hollow point went through the lower part of his nose and ultimately went through his left cerebellum. Lam stiffened, but still stood like a statue, his dark eyes not blinking.

Dana never hesitated, but fired again, with the laser near the same place. This time her shot was more midline and forehead, and the bullet coursed through the frontal sinus, then between the hemispheres of Lam's brain, and exited through the back of his skull. Lam fell over with blood rapidly pooling on Dana's custom made wool carpet that she had designed.

"That's for killing Remy, you son of a bitch!" Dana cried as she dropped the gun on the desk and ran over to Remy, who had not moved. Remy had been knocked out by the blow to the head, but was still breathing. Dana scooped Remy into her arms, then heard a slight whimper as Remy started to come to consciousness. "You saved my life, Honey!" Dana cried out as she held Remy tight.

As the adrenaline and endorphin rush from the incident wore off, Dana slowly realized that it hurt to breathe, then she noticed that her white blouse had a large patch of crimson on the left side that was expanding. Remy licked her face, but was still unsteady. All things considered, Dana was a lot more worried about her dog. Remy was the only living thing that still linked her to John, whose prior actions had also saved her life.

She walked back to Lam, with the quickly growing pool of blood underneath him, and was surprised by the complete indifference she felt toward a human being she had killed, as though her brain refused to think about the horror of it. She kicked his leg, instantly realizing she should not have done that unarmed. No movement.

"That was lucky," she said to Remy, then set the dog down on the floor and was relieved to see that Remy could walk gingerly. She picked up her pistol again in her right hand. With her left, she felt Lam's carotid artery as she did to count her pulse when jogging. *Definitely dead. Good riddance.* Lam wasn't going anywhere but the morgue.

She picked the new ChiFone up off the floor and reached in Lam's pocket and took out his ChiFone, then stuck them both in her purse and took out her old cell phone. If they were so desperate to get it back, she knew there must be a reason. She'd keep them and figure that out later. She hit the call button on her phone, thinking she hit 911, then listened.

"Dr. Stevens' office," Karen said.

"Oh, I'm sorry, Karen. It's Dana LaFontaine," her voice wavering from the adrenaline.

"Are you all right, Dana?" Karen asked. "You sound upset."

"I meant to call 911. I should talk to Dr. Stevens, though. I have an emergency!"

"Actually, he is free," Karen said. "Please hold on." She put Dana on hold and told Jack immediately.

"Dana," Jack said, coming on the line, "Karen said you had an emergency. What's up?" Over his years of practice, "emergencies" ranged from a numb finger to life-threatening brain hemorrhages. The patients who were talking for themselves were usually in better shape.

"Jack, I just had a man try to kill me in my office!"

"Say, again? Dana, are you all right?"

"He shot me, but I don't think it's serious, but I'm bleeding, and my heart and mind are racing! It hurts to breathe. I shot and killed him."

"Dana, I'm on my way!" Jack said as he reached into his desk, grabbed his compact .40 caliber Glock 27, and put it in his sport coat pocket. "Are you able to call 911 right now?"

"Yes, sure."

"Then call immediately, and stay with the 911 operator, and they'll tell you when the police are at your door. Don't let anyone else in. I might beat them there. Keep the gun in hand—in case he's not alone. Sit down; don't stand. If you feel faint, lie down flat. Hang up, and call 911 now."

Jack then ran down the hallway to the reception desk, where Karen was already standing.

"Karen," Jack called out as he approached and kept right on racing toward the door. "Cancel my appointments, but first call 911, in case Dana isn't able to. Give them her office address, tell them the perpetrator has been shot and is believed to be dead, and the victim is wounded and needs an ambulance. She appears to be alone inside the locked office, but the first responders should not enter without the police."

Jack shoved the entrance door to the office open, raced down the stairway, and ran out of the building toward his parked older Mercedes SL 500, a two-seat convertible, that he drove for the fun of it, but this trip was anything but fun. Dana's office was only a few miles south on county road 101, which was sometimes slow, as was getting to it from his office, but Jack had driven it thousands of times and knew the route best suited for any time of day. Dana was in a small quaint refurbished office building just off 101 and Minnetonka Boulevard.

Two more minutes, Jack thought as he gunned the Mercedes over the Gray's Bay bridge. He was aware of where the police hid with the radar and had not gotten a ticket in twenty years, and not because he was a slow driver. He hoped to find a police escort to bring him to Dana's, but the police were nowhere in sight.

Jack's mind raced ahead of his car to what he would find at the office. He didn't like what Dana had told him of her own condition, but had said nothing to keep her from worrying.

26

*A doctor must work
eighteen hours a day
and seven days a week.
If you cannot console yourself to this,
get out of the profession.*

Martin H. Fischer, M.D.

CHAPTER 26

JACK SWUNG HIS CAR into Dana's parking lot, skidded the car to a stop by the front entrance, then grabbed his medical bag and a small first aid trauma bag that he always carried in the car. Running in through the entrance door and up the stairs, he pounded on Dana's door, then called out, "It's Jack Stevens."

Jack could see from the light change that someone was looking through the peephole. The door opened with Dana there, holding a cordless phone in her hand, and Remy standing guard, barking. "Oh God, Jack, thank you for coming!" she said as she reached out and then nearly collapsed in his arms.

Jack hugged her back, which caused her to grimace in pain. "Dana, you're bleeding! How bad is it?"

"I think I'm okay, but my ribs on the left hurt when I breathe!"

"Are you feeling like passing out?"

"Some. . .and just really hyper. My heart and brain are racing!"

"You need to sit down, Dana!"

Jack led her to a chair and carefully helped her sit down as the door shut and clicked locked behind them. He looked around and saw no one else there. Dana, despite the slowly enlarging blood spot on the left side of her blouse, looked stable. Jack watched her breathe, and both sides of her chest seemed to expand well. She was tachypneic, breathing fast, her pale "shocky" skin was a contrast to the bright red blood spot. Jack had seen a lot worse in his trauma hospital days.

Dana could hear the voice of the 911 operator on her cordless phone continuing to talk. "Ms. LaFontaine, are you all right?"

"Yes," she said, "Dr. Stevens just got here."

"The police are a few minutes away," the operator said. "We had another call requesting an ambulance, and they should be there within ten minutes."

"I. . .don't think I need one," Dana said.

"It's already on the way."

Jack knelt beside Dana and said, "Dana, can you lift up that side of your blouse?"

Dana set the phone down, then lifted the blood soaked corner of her blouse. Jack saw the wound, still bleeding, a bit ragged, just below the left part of her bra, with what appeared to be a glistening part of a rib visible. Reaching into his small first aid trauma bag, he pulled out a "four by four," a standard sterile gauze pad, which he opened carefully and folded, so that the part he put on the wound was untouched by his hands.

"Dana, hold that with your right hand and put some pressure on your chest to stop the bleeding. Are you in a lot of pain?"

"Not bad."

Then Jack got his stethoscope out of his medical bag and listened on both sides and front and back of her chest. "You have good breath sounds—no sign right now of a collapsed lung. You look much better sitting down; your color has come back."

He then pulled an aneroid blood pressure monitor from his bag and took her blood pressure, talking out loud as he worked. "158 over 96. Pulse. . .130. Respiration. . .24."

"Isn't that high?" Dana asked.

"Not considering what has happened here. I'd be more worried if it wasn't. Your body is responding appropriately to the stress. Blood pressures and pulses are higher than when you exercise. But you need to get a chest x-ray, have the wound treated, and probably be watched overnight."

"I really don't want to go to the hospital!"

"I'm afraid you have to go," Jack said in a strong voice. "You could still get a pneumothorax or what we call a hemopneumothorax, where you bleed internally between the chest wall and the lung, which collapses the lung."

Jack picked up the cordless phone and said to the 911 operator, "This is Dr. Jack Stevens. Please patch me through to the HCMC ambulance dispatcher."

When the dispatcher came on the line, Jack explained precisely what he needed, then the call was switched back to the 911 operator.

Remy, doing better, had jumped up onto Dana's lap. Jack bent down to pet the Havanese, who licked his hands and face.

"You can tell she knows you are one of the good guys," Dana said. "She bit that bastard on the ankle and saved my life," she continued and pointed to Lam's body. "We have to get her to the vet. He hit her on the head with his gun, knocked her unconscious, and kicked her across the room. I thought she was dead!"

"I'm not a doggy neurologist, but overall she looks good. I can take her to the vet after we get you to HCMC."

"I don't want to be alone, Jack!"

"I'll stay with you until we get you into the ambulance to HCMC."

"Oh, look, I got blood on your sport coat," Dana lamented, pointing to a red blotch on the right side of his jacket.

"Don't worry about it. I'll bill your health insurance company," Jack joked, then looked over at Lam. "Looks like you spilled a bit more on this beautiful carpet, though."

Jack pulled his gun from his pocket, walked over to Lam, and kicked him hard. Not what he was taught in medical school for checking a patient who was "down," but proper protocol for a killer, who might still be armed and dangerous. No movement. Jack had been watching him the whole time since he entered Dana's office, so this was no surprise, particularly with amount of blood on the floor. Jack crouched down to check his carotids, stepping into the pool of blood. *Just like my days moonlighting for the HCMC ambulance,* he thought. No pulse, pupils fixed and dilated, no spontaneous breathing.

"He's dead," Jack announced to Dana.

"No kidding, Sherlock," Dana responded, then winced as she laughed out loud.

Jack stood up and turned to Dana. "Who taught you to shoot?"

"My husband. He made me take the conceal-and-carry course given by a Hennepin County deputy sheriff. He wanted me to be comfortable with a handgun if I ever needed it. I passed the written and shooting accuracy courses and actually got my handgun permit. I hate guns, and I've never carried it, but if John hadn't insisted I learn to shoot and keep a gun here, I'd be the one on the floor."

"What's in back there, Dana?" Jack asked, looking down her hallway.

"Conference room, bathroom, and storage."

"I'll check it out," Jack said as he turned and walked cautiously back to the other rooms and searched them. "It's clear," he said later as he came back down the hallway. "Just thought I'd be sure we didn't have any other uninvited guests before we let our guard down."

"You're just as anal as John was," Dana said quietly, which Jack did not hear.

Suddenly there was a loud knock on the door, followed by a shout, "Police."

"The police are at your door, Ms. LaFontaine," the 911 operator said. "I'll hang up now."

"Thank you so much," Dana said.

Jack looked through the peephole. "Looks like the police," he said to Dana as he opened the door, but kept his right hand in his coat pocket holding the Glock 27.

"Who are you?" the policeman demanded, his 9mm Smith

& Wesson drawn, as he looked over the scene and immediately noted Jack's hand in his pocket.

"I'm Dr. Stevens, a friend and her physician," Jack said, not moving.

"Where is Ms. LaFontaine?" the policeman asked as he stepped into the office, then saw her. He kept his gun at the ready and kept Jack at a place where he could watch him easily until he was certain who all the players really were.

"I'm here," Dana said. "And I'm fine now. Yes, this is Dr. Stevens. The man who tried to kill me is dead on the floor. Dr. Stevens just checked him."

The policeman reholstered his 9 mm, walked to Lam's body and bent over to feel his carotid artery. "Whoa! Looks like you are a good shot, Ms. LaFontaine! I don't think he is going to be trying to kill anyone else." He called back to the dispatcher, "We won't need an ambulance for the perp, but we'll need to notify the coroner and pick up a body."

"I have had HCMC dispatch an ambulance for Dana," Jack said.

The policeman took brief statements from Dana and Jack until the ambulance arrived. The paramedics checked her vital signs again, started an IV line, put a pair of low flow oxygen prongs in her nose, and helped her up onto the gurney, while Jack talked to the ER Attending Physician.

"Here's what you're dealing with, Dr. Barnes," Jack said somewhat clinically. "Ms. LaFontaine was shot by an intruder. She is awake, oriented, and alert. Glasgow Coma Scale of 15. Vital signs are stable, color is good, breath sounds are normal. Breathing is slightly impaired because of pain from what may be a fractured rib on the left lateral chest, about T-7. She is otherwise in excellent health. I'm concerned about a possible hemopneumothorax developing, so you'll probably need to keep her in overnight. She's not going to want to stay."

"I understand, there's good reason to keep her," Dr. Barnes replied, quickly typing notes into the electronic medical record regarding what Jack had said and repeating back to Jack the blood pressure, pulse, and respiratory rate for confirmation.

As the paramedics began to push the gurney toward the office doorway and stairs, the policeman said, "Ms. LaFontaine, it looks like a simple case of self-defense. We are going to need more information, so we will contact you. You are a very brave and resourceful woman. From what you have said, your husband would have been very proud of how you defended yourself. I will check on you in the morning. I am assuming you will be admitted to HCMC."

"Thank you for coming so quickly!" Dana said.

"I'm going to have to keep your gun for evidence for now, and we'll process the crime scene. I hope you feel better soon!"

When the gurney was just outside of the ambulance and the paramedics were about to load Dana into the rig, she suddenly waved her right and said, "One second, please. Can I have a moment of privacy with Dr. Stevens?"

The paramedics and doctor nodded and walked around to the front of the ambulance.

"What's up?" Jack asked, coming alongside.

Dana turned to Jack. "I have only agreed to go to the hospital if you take Remy to the veterinary hospital."

"Dana, I promise that as soon as I settle things here with the policeman, I'll take Remy to get checked out, and then I'll drive down to HCMC to see how you are doing. You are in great hands, now."

"The other thing is that you have to bring me my purse from the desk," Dana said emphatically.

"I don't know," Jack said. "It's a crime scene. He isn't going to—"

"Jack," Dana whispered, looking to see where the paramedics had gone, "the killer came to get back a new ChiFone that I picked up this morning. We have to find out why that phone is so important. And I got his phone as well. You have to get my purse out of there."

"I'll do it. One way or another," Jack responded, not sure what to make of it all, but going with Dana's instincts.

Once the paramedics got Dana loaded, the ambulance took off, lights and siren going, Code 3.

Jack walked back upstairs and into the office and spotted Dana's purse opened on the desk. The officer was busy gathering evidence, but Jack was aware that he had seen the purse and would notice if he were to sneak it out. He picked up his medical bag and first aid trauma bag on the desk, then quickly grabbed one of the ChiFones out of Dana's purse, sliding it into his pocket, while the officer was turned around.

"Officer," Jack said, picking up Remy, who was completely comfortable with him, and his bags, "Ms. LaFontaine asked me to take Remy to the vet and bring her purse to HCMC. I was wondering if—"

"Just let me look through it quick," the officer said, stepping to the desk and opening the purse wide. Piece by piece he set everything in Dana's purse on the desk, including the new ChiFone. Satisfied, he started putting it all back and said, "Looks clean to me. I've been meaning to get me one of those new phones. I suppose you've got one already, Doc."

"Matter of fact, I don't," Jack said with a grin. "I'm holding off for now. I think this model may have more features on it than I want."

"Yeah, I know what you mean. My kids love 'em, though."

Jack added the purse to his bags and Remy, and walked out of the office quickly and went to his car. As Jack had just put Remy and Dana's purse in his Mercedes and his medical bag and first aid trauma bag in the trunk, both the coroner and CSI unit showed up. Jack had known the coroner for many years and stopped to talk with him. It turned out that the coroner had also gone to the accident scene of Dr. Don.

"You know, Jack," the balding coroner said when Jack was turning to leave, "you might want to think about a new profession, maybe become a fiction writer or something."

"Why's that?"

"Well, I've been around long enough to see patterns. Neurologists at the U, that drug dealer Jellen was one of yours, then Dr. Don, and now one of your patients. Seems like you're in the wrong business."

Jack nodded and said, "You know, you might just be right. It's all getting a little too weird these days."

Once he got back in his car, Jack opened Dana's purse and pulled out the new ChiFone. "Something's rotten here, Remy, and I don't like it," he whispered.

27

*If you pick up a starving dog
and make him prosperous,
he will not bite you.
This is the principal difference
between a dog and a man.*

Mark Twain

CHAPTER 27

JACK FIRST DROVE HOME to let his own Havanese, Machiavelli, out for Piddle Patrol and to get acquainted with Remy. The two dogs joined together for the "pee-pee and pooh-pooh" event, after a bit of getting-to-know-you sniffing and barking. Once that was done, they both hopped into the car, Mac on the passenger floor and Remy on the seat.

Driving east on Highway 12 to Interstate 494, Jack went north to Maple Grove and pulled into the Animal Wellness Center. He always took Mac there because one of the veterinarians personally bred Havanese, and Jack had gotten Mac from her.

Remy was pronounced in good health, but the vet wanted to observe her overnight. Jack also boarded Mac with them, since he knew HCMC wouldn't allow a pet dog in the hospital, and he wasn't sure when he would be going home, if complications arose with Dana.

He headed back south on 494 to Interstate 394 and proceeded east. Once in downtown Minneapolis on Hennepin Avenue, he turned right onto Eighth Street, parked the car at a meter near HCMC, and headed to the emergency room.

He walked through the automatic doors and straight to the tall dark-haired male receptionist. It was a secure area, much different from Jack's days at HCMC. "Hi, I'm Dr. Jack Stevens," he said, showing him his driver's license and medical license wallet card, "and my patient, Ms. LaFontaine, was brought in by ambulance a couple hours ago."

"Dr. Stevens, I was told you'd be coming," the receptionist responded. "Ms. LaFontaine is in the Medical Intensive Care Unit in satisfactory condition. Dr. Griffith is in the back. I'll buzz you in." With that, he pressed a button to electrically open one of the security doors. Jack didn't have to go through the metal detector, which was good, because he had forgotten the Glock was in his coat pocket.

"Dr. Griffith," the receptionist announced on the phone intercom, "Dr. Stevens is here, and I am sending him back." Turning to Jack, he pointed and said, "Dr. Griffith is down that hallway."

"Thank you," Jack said. He walked down the hall and was met by a 6' tall, extremely fit, middle-aged man in scrubs and a white coat. *Has to be an ER staff physician,* Jack thought.

"Hi, I'm Bill Griffith," he said, shaking Jack's hand firmly. "I'm the ER Director and worked up Ms. LaFontaine."

"Jack Stevens here. It's been a few years since I was here as an intern and resident. Still the best trauma hospital and ER in the city!"

"Thanks, Jack. Ms. LaFontaine is up in MICU, but let me give you an update. She was in basically the same shape as when you called: alert, oriented, with good vitals. Good breath sounds, a bit tachypneic but no real dyspnea. We put her in the Stabilization Room as a precaution, but she didn't turn a hair. On low flow O_2, her O_2 saturation was 97 percent. She was a little alkalotic with a pH of 7.49, so she probably is hypoventilating some from the pain and retaining a little CO_2. I did get her 5 mg IV of morphine sulfate times two, and she was much more comfortable. I also gave her 2 grams of Rocephin IV for infection prophylaxis, although, as you know, with the high muzzle velocity of pistols today, the bullet is so hot that it sterilizes whatever it goes through. EKG showed no abnormalities; no suggestion of cardiac contusion. CPK is up, but cardiac enzymes are fine. Chemistries, coags, CBC fine, except for a WBC of 14,000 with a shift to polys, probably a stress reaction. Chest x-ray with rib details showed a left lateral T7 fracture and a suggestion of a minimal pneumothorax. Chest CT confirmed the pneumo and showed a trace hemopneumothorax. We irrigated, removed some small bone splinters from the rib, and sewed up a 3 centimeter laceration from the gunshot."

"Any sign of bullet fragmentation?" Jack asked.

"No, not visually or on imaging studies. We saw no indication for a chest tube, but thought we would keep her comfortable, observe her overnight, repeat the bloods, chest x-ray, and CT in the morning. Probably discharge tomorrow with pain meds, if stable, but that will be up to the house staff to decide, of course. All things considered, she looks like a rose!"

Jack smiled that the ER was still using the same "looks like a rose" saying for someone in good shape, especially when some things can't be said better. He said, "Good work, Bill. Very good work. 'The County' has changed its physical plant, but not the quality of its care since I was here."

"Well, we try," Dr. Griffith replied. "We have more residents and medical students than you can count these days, and our motto remains that *nobody is going to die on us if we can prevent it.* We don't lose too many."

Jack looked around the hallways and thought back to his "County" days with warm sentiments. "We tried as well, and there were cases where it probably would have been more merciful to have let some of the terminally ill die. Back then no real advance directives on care existed, and 'brain death' was a new concept still, so we did full resuscitation on everyone."

"Better to save too many than not enough, I always say."

"I guess you're right," Jack said. "Thanks, Bill, for your help. Can I run up to MICU and see her?"

"Absolutely," Dr. Griffith responded and nodded to a teenage volunteer standing nearby. "Jenni, here, will take you up, just in case you have forgotten your way around."

"Glad to meet you, Jenni," Jack said, shaking her hand. "Everything looks different since the last time I was here. Are you thinking of a medical career?"

"Yes, sir," Jenni answered brightly, walking Jack to the elevators. "My counselor told me I needed to get in the 'trenches' and see if the blood and guts would scare me off. I like it, and I hope to be a doctor."

"It's a long road," Jack observed as they got on the elevator and went up, "but it's worth it. You'll do fine."

The elevators opened, and Jenni pointed down the hallway and said, "MICU is straight ahead, Dr. Stevens."

"Thanks, Jenni," Jack replied, then turned and walked to the nursing station and asked for the Charge Nurse. It was Cheri Rasmussen, who had been the youngest nurse on the neurology station when Jack trained there.

"Dr. Stevens, my goodness, coming back for a refresher in gunshot wounds?" Cheri teased him.

"Cheri, so good to see you! You look great, not a year older than when I first met you."

"You are still as good a liar as when you were here," Cheri fired back. "But flattery *will* get you *everything!* I read about Anne. I'm so sorry for your loss. I don't know what I'd do if my husband died. Are you doing okay?"

Jack and Anne had been married while Jack was in medical school. When Jack was at HCMC, they only had one car, so either Jack would take the bus home or Anne would come pick him up. He was always late, so Anne would park, walk up to the neurology station, and sit down and talk with the nurses.

"Thanks, Cheri. I'm doing all right. I have my own small private practice now, and before Anne died I promised her I'd lighten my schedule and see my daughters more. I'm trying to do that, but today and tonight do not appear to be a lightening of the load. Where is Ms. LaFontaine?"

"She's is in 6, resting quietly, except when she asks what time you are coming and about her dog. Vitals are good, and she is afebrile. What happened?"

"Intruder came into her office and tried to kill her. Her fifteen-pound dog, a Havanese like mine, bit the intruder, giving her time to get a gun that her late husband made her keep in her desk. Looked like the *Gunfight at OK Corral* by the time I got there. They shot each other, but she won."

"Wow! Good for her," Cheri said. "Pretty bad when Deephaven isn't safe anymore!"

"Right," Jack said as he started walking over to Dana's cubicle. "Everyone is so concerned about gun licenses. I'll bet the intruder didn't have one, of course. Fortunately, Ms. LaFontaine did, so she could defend herself."

Jack stepped into the doorway marked 6, and Dana smiled warmly as she saw him.

"Jack, how is Remy?" Dana asked.

"Fine. Like her master, getting observed overnight, but probably in better shape than you!"

"Thanks for taking her! And thanks for coming to the office and now here," Dana said, sitting up a bit more and trying to push some of the loose tendrils of her thick brunette hair back into place. "I didn't know doctors did house calls anymore!"

"I have many talents," Jack replied, taking a seat in a reclinable chair next to the bed. "Humans and dogs, both. I clean up dog poop pretty well, too!"

"Well, Jack," Dana said, her words slightly slurred, "I'm fine now. So why don't you go home. You'll need some sleep for your patients in the morning."

She's definitely getting her money's worth from the morphine, Jack thought. *Great stuff, used properly. The patients who don't use it regularly don't need much to have an effect.*

"Dana, you are a bit high on the morphine and won't feel so great after you're weaned off. I promised you I wouldn't leave you alone tonight, and that's all there's to it."

"What about your patients tomorrow?"

"My schedule is light, so I've already had Karen reschedule. With everything that's gone on, and the hospital being less busy at night, I not sure what is safe anymore. I just think it's good that somebody's here tonight."

"Where will you sleep?"

"This easy chair reclines. I've slept in a lot less comfortable places in my residency."

Cheri knocked on the door and came in with some scrubs for Jack. "Thought you might be more comfortable sleeping in these, like the old days!"

"Brings back a lot of bad memories, Cheri. Thanks."

"Except we won't wake you up for emergencies or new admissions! Here is a white doctor coat for over it so you can look like a real doctor!"

"I won't know what to do with myself," Jack said.

"If you get totally bored," Cheri teased, "I'm sure the nursing aides wouldn't mind help cleaning out the bedpans."

"Sorry, I'm afraid I'm not qualified anymore," Jack shot back.

"I'm sure I can find something you can handle," Cheri said with a laugh. "So, Dana, how are you doing?"

"Never felt better," Dana replied. "Jack says it's the morphine. So you were saying before that you knew Dr. Stevens as a resident and had some good stories about him?"

"Lots. His wife, Anne, used to sit around and wait for him. . .like for hours some times. So we'd tell her all the good stuff. She said some days she'd come early just to hear them. Let's see, one of my favorites was when he was on Internal Medicine, and I was one of the nurses. A man came in with a Coke bottle—"

"Cheri!" Jack interrupted. "Dana needs to rest."

"No, I don't," Dana protested, clapping her hands. "I have nothing to read and that sounds interesting."

"Actually, Dana," Jack replied, "as you can see, Cheri is a *hottie*. Better stories might be all the dates she had with the hospital staff when she was single, some of which seemed to begin or carry on to certain closets and empty patient beds. She married a very handsome radiology technician, after a *very torrid—*"

"Dr. Stevens is correct, I think you need rest," Cheri cut in quickly, then she stuck her tongue out at Jack. "Dana, I'll give you my phone number, and we can talk after you've recovered."

"She has my phone number already, Cheri," Jack returned.

"Ah, you win, just like you always used to," Cheri conceded, then turned and walked out of the room.

Jack took the scrubs, went into the bathroom, and changed. When he came out, Dana was fast asleep. He took his pistol out of his coat pocket, put the white coat on a wall hook, clicked off the overhead light, laid back in the recliner with the Glock in his hand under a light blanket, and soon was sound asleep as well.

28

You look familiar. . . .
Have I threatened you before?

Captain Jack Sparrow, *Pirates of the Caribbean*

CHAPTER 28

JACK AWOKE AT 5 A.M. He couldn't help it; he'd been that way for years. He walked over to the nurses' station, and Cheri was gone, but Connie Lindgren was Charge now. She was new to him. New nurses, including newly appointed Charge nurses, generally got the graveyard shift, 2300 to 0700. Some weren't recent hires and actually had enough seniority to work whatever shift they wanted. Personality-wise, some just liked those hours. Generally slower paced than "days"—0700 to 1500—or "nights"—1500 to 2300—it also gave them the ability to spend a good part of their days pursuing activities while others were working.

"Dr. Stevens, good morning," Connie said. "I'm the Charge. How did you sleep?"

"Better than when I was last here during training," Jack noted. "Do you have any coffee?"

"Sure do. Cheri told me to take good care of you. Just made a fresh batch." Connie went into the nurses' break room and brought out a Styrofoam cup with coffee. "Black?"

"Black is great, thanks. How is our mutual patient?" Jack asked and sipped the hot brew carefully. Just as he recalled, it smelled much better than it tasted. Definitely *not* Caribou or Starbucks! But a great *vehicle* for the caffeine he needed.

"She's doing well," Connie reported. "Slept through the night.

Vitals are stable: BP is down to 110 over 70, pulse 64 and regular. Respiration 18. Afebrile. O_2 sat is 97% on room air."

"Great. Can't beat that."

"Lab will be up to draw routine bloods in an hour. She's a little nauseated with the morphine, although she has tolerated it well. So, we're keeping her on clear liquids until after her repeat chest x-ray and CT."

"Sounds good."

"Cheri asked the resident staff, and you can use their shower in the call room. There are extra razors, shaving cream, toothpaste, and towels in there."

"Now a hot shower sounds really good about now. I'm a bit stiff from the recliner."

Jack first got his street clothes from Dana's room, then walked over to the residents' call room, tried to slip in quietly so as not to awaken the two who were getting precious sleep, and headed for the bathroom and shower. He took off his scrubs and threw them in the laundry basket, then stepped into the shower. *Nothing better to wake you up,* Jack thought, *than coffee and a hot shower.* He let the warm stream pulsate on his neck and back, as he had so often told his patients to do when they had back strains. He took some brand of the community shampoo he'd never heard of and hoped it wouldn't make any of his hair fall out.

After he finished the shower and had dried off, he lathered up with shaving cream, selected one of the disposable razors, and enjoyed a close shave. Once he was dressed in his own clothes, he combed his hair and headed back for MICU by 0615. Seeing Connie, he asked, "Is Ms. LaFontaine up yet?"

"Not up, but she's awake. The lab tech is in there now drawing blood. Why don't you get some breakfast until she's up. I've arranged a VIP pass for you at the cafeteria. Just scan it with the cashier."

"Sounds like a plan. Thanks, Connie." Jack walked toward the cafeteria, which hadn't moved, but had been updated. One perk of working at HCMC was free food for the house staff, which really helped, considering what they were paid. However, the demands of a county trauma hospital did not allow for savoring any meal, because you never knew when the next cardiac arrest or gunshot might arrive. So residents tended not to "eat," but rather to "refuel." That is, you ate your bacon, eggs, and muffin, washing it down with orange juice and coffee in five minutes or less. Then, if there wasn't an emergency of some sort, you could sit back, have a second cup of coffee, and talk to your fellow residents. This extreme method of eating persisted in Jack and many of the residents, whose spouses would have to continually remind them when off call that they could and should eat slower. Jack had tried to eat as much as possible at the hospital to save food money for Anne, but he learned the hard way that at the age of twenty-nine as Chief Resident, his metabolism had indeed slowed down, and he could no longer eat all the free food he wanted.

So Jack got his bacon, eggs, English muffin, some more coffee and orange juice, which all tasted exactly as it had years before, and he tried to take his time, chew his food, as though Anne was watching. Sitting at a table watching the early morning news, he saw a report on the shooting at Dana's office, though no details were given.

Thinking he had some time to kill until 0800, when they were going to bring liquid breakfast to Dana, Jack walked around HCMC and the neurology station and reminisced over one wild episode after another that he'd experienced there. When he walked back into the MICU, Connie signaled to him that Dana already had a visitor in her room. Quickening his pace, he stepped into Dana's room and a husky, powerfully built Chinese man in a very expensive black Valentino suit turned around to greet him. There was a huge bouquet of flowers in a vase now on Dana's nightstand.

"Jack, this is Mr. Chan," Dana said, motioning with her hand. "I have been helping him decorate his office in the IDS. He is the CEO for ChiFone."

Chan extended his hand to Jack, who shook his hand. "Dr.

Stevens, as I told Ms. LaFontaine, I can't find the words to express how badly I feel about what has happened. I am so glad you were there to help."

"You're welcome, and I'm glad as well, but Dana more than held her own," Jack replied, studying Chan's face and body expression. "Was Lam actually one of your employees?"

"Regrettably, yes," Chan replied, shaking his head. "I knew his family and gave him a job to help him out several years ago. Lam had psychiatric issues as a young man, but was never violent. He received continuing medical care, and to my knowledge has not had a problem since his late teens. He performs simple tasks around the office, such as delivering the cell phone to Ms. LaFontaine, since the replacement one she was given was accidentally taken out of a group of defective phones that needed servicing. Because she had had the trouble with the first phone that brought her to your attention, I didn't want her to have another bad experience. I was horrified when I heard what happened."

"Where would he get that gun?" Jack asked, well aware that Chan's eyes had not once looked away from him since he arrived in the room.

"I have no idea," Chan answered, shrugging his shoulder. "Perhaps he bought it on the street or at a gun show. There are so many guns here. Such a pity."

"That was no street gun," Jack said. "I've read about it in some gun magazines. It looked like the newest version of the Chinese 7.65mm pistol with the built-in silencer. Whatever it was, that was a very serious gun normally issued only to government agents."

"Perhaps he has connections from home," Chan reflected. "I'm sure the police will trace the source. His parents are from an influential family. If I had ever suspected he owned a gun, I would have fired him immediately. I have told Ms. LaFontaine that I have arranged for ChiFone to pick up all the expenses for her at the hospital and all of her follow-up care. We will also pay for any damage to her office as well as any lost revenue from her business while she is recuperating. If she needs someone to drive her and help her until she is better, we will provide that service as well."

Finally turning his gaze from Jack to Dana, Chan added, "And Ms. LaFontaine, if there is *anything else* ChiFone or I can do, you know how to find me. And I have a limousine on call to take you home, when you are discharged."

"I'll be driving her home, but we appreciate the offer," Jack said.

Jack thought Chan seemed a little unhappy with that, although there was just a flicker of expression on his face.

"Dr. Stevens," Chan said as he stood a bit taller and crossed his arms, "I have engaged a medical consulting group that does a lot of work with the FDA for safety. We aren't normally regulated by the FDA, but since there has been the concern with Ms. LaFontaine and apparently some of your other patients, I want to be sure that the ChiFone is absolutely safe. This seems like the group that would do the most extensive testing. Our customers' safety is our first priority above everything else. I can let you know when they are coming to Minneapolis, if you wish, and you can attend the meetings with the consultants."

"How do you know about my patients?" Jack asked, feeling the hair on the back of his neck stand up. "No one—"

"I'm sorry, Jack. It came up in a phone conversation yesterday morning with Mr. Chan," Dana broke in, "and I didn't get a chance to tell you about it. I explained that you wanted to make certain you had the facts before bringing it to their attention. He understood."

"Oh. . ." Jack said, glancing at Dana to try to read her face and make sure she was telling the truth. "Mr. Chan, if that's the case, I am reassured to hear about the consulting group and your attitude toward this issue. Please let me know when the consulting group is coming to town."

"I will, and I must go now," Chan said, turning to leave. "Again, I am so sorry. Good-bye, Ms. LaFontaine. Dr. Stevens."

After he left and was out of earshot, Dana said, "That was nice of him to stop by. He didn't have to do that."

"Perhaps it was," Jack replied. "Perhaps he was just covering his behind early. . .really early. There may be more liabilities that Lam has with ChiFone that Mr. Chan didn't tell you."

Just then there was a knock at the door, and a radiology aide stepped into the doorway with a gurney and said, "Ms. LaFontaine?"

"Yes," Dana said.

"I'm here to bring you down for your chest x-ray and CT scan of your chest. Let me check your wristband," the tech said as she took Dana's left hand and read her wristband for name and information. "Please give me your date of birth." The tech compared Dana's answer to what was printed on her wristband.

"Can't I go in a wheelchair or walk?" Dana asked. "I don't need the gurney."

"Sorry," the aide replied, now satisfied he had the right person. "Hospital rules."

"Jack, tell him—"

"Hospital rules," Jack confirmed. "Besides, you've got a lot of baggage to take with you."

The aide pushed the gurney against Dana's bed, locked the wheels, and Dana slid easily onto it. They hung her IV from the IV pole on the gurney, loaded the oximeter on the bottom of the gurney and the EKG monitor on top, covered her with a blanket, and wheeled her out.

"I think I'll come along," Jack said.

The radiology aide and Dana's RN pushed her on the cart, and Jack followed. They entered the elevator, went down to the ground floor, and over to radiology. They wanted to do an upright chest x-ray, rather than a portable, for its better quality. Dana stood up for the x-ray, then she lay back down on the gurney and was wheeled to CT for a CAT scan. As the CT scanner worked, images of the "cuts" progressively showed up at the CT tech's monitors. Jack and the tech compared the new cuts with those done the day before. *Good news,* Jack thought, *it looks unchanged.*

They loaded Dana from the scanner back onto the gurney

and followed their path back to the MICU. Once there, Dana was transferred with her IV, oximeter, and EKG monitor back into the MICU bed. Then her wires for her monitoring were connected to the wall sockets to be monitored by the central MICU unit at the nurses' station as well as displayed in Dana's room.

Soon afterward the staff attending M.D. came by, followed by the "house staff," namely the Chief Resident (PGY-4), the Junior Resident (PGY-2), the First Year (PGY-1), and a couple of medical students. The Charge Nurse entered last.

Jack laughed at the expression on Dana's face as the small parade of medical personnel surrounded her. "This is a teaching hospital, Dana," he reassured. "You're today's lesson."

"How are you feeling, Ms. LaFontaine?" the staff M.D. asked. Jack knew he already knew the answer, since Dana had been checked over already that morning by one of the medical students, the PGY-1, and PGY-2, who in turn reported the findings to the PGY-4. They then reported her status to the attending M.D. just before entering Dana's room. Patients who were observed by so many people got tired of it, but little was ever missed in this teaching hospital.

"A lot better than yesterday," she replied.

Although the house staff had already checked, the attending M.D. listened to her heart and lungs and checked her labs and vital signs. "Your chest x-ray and chest CT are stable. Your blood work was also stable; no sign of any significant blood loss, and your chemistries were good. Oxygenation looks good, and vital signs are stable. Chest and heart sound good. Are you having much pain?"

"Not too bad."

"Your hemopneumothorax will gradually clear up on its own. I don't want you to be doing any straining or heavy lifting for the next six weeks. Your rib will gradually heal. You had one bone splinter, but otherwise it is well aligned. I see no sign of infection. You should come back or have your personal doctor remove your stitches in fourteen days, then have a follow-up chest x-ray and

CT in six weeks. You'll be tender there for a while beyond that and likely have some minor pain with breathing. Should you have any fever, sudden shortness of breath, or extreme chest pain, you should immediately come back in. I'll give you some pain pills. But otherwise, I'll let you go home. Do you have any questions?"

"May I drive?"

"I'd keep it to a minimum, especially if you are on the pain pills and feel drowsy. You can gradually increase it if it doesn't make you feel worse. But have someone else load and unload anything from the car."

"Thanks for your help. How soon can you get me unhooked and on my way?"

"The nurses will free you up and give you written discharge instructions."

With that, the attending M.D. turned as did the others, as if on cue, and left.

Dana's treating nurse, who had entered shortly before the attending left, disconnected her IV, oximeter, and EKG monitor and remained with her, giving her written discharge instructions and prescriptions.

"Dr. Stevens," the nurse said, "I'll help Dana get dressed and bring her downstairs with her personal effects if you want to bring your car around and meet me at the Seventh Street entrance."

"The sooner the better," Dana said as Jack stood up to go.

29

Home Sweet Home

CHAPTER 29

J ACK RODE THE ELEVATOR down to the ground floor and walked across to his car. When he was walking around the hospital earlier, he had gone out to the street to feed some quarters into the meter. As he looked at the meter, he laughed out loud when he recalled what an archaeologist friend once told him about parking meters. His friends said that in a thousand years, when someone digs up the remnants of civilization, they will think the quarters were tokens paid to one of the many "street gods." Jack always thought the city of Minneapolis would make more money each time you inserted coins if the meter issued a written fortune like you might get from a fortune cookie.

He got into his Mercedes and swung around the block to the Seventh Street HCMC exit. The nurse, according to protocol, made Dana ride in a wheelchair, which she pushed over to Jack's car. She and Jack helped Dana into the car and strapped her in. He then put Chan's flower bouquet and vase on the floor, between Dana's feet.

"Thanks, again," Dana and Jack said together.

"You're welcome," the nurse replied with a wave.

Jack put the car in gear and slowly drove off. Back down the street, a black Suburban pulled out and followed. Driving up Seventh Street past Hennepin Avenue to First Avenue, Jack turned left and after a few blocks pulled onto Interstate 394 west. The Suburban dropped back several car lengths and followed in the right lane.

"Dana, we never talked about where you want to go? Should I take you to your home?"

"No," Dana responded, a troubled look settling on her face, "I don't want to be alone. I'm scared, and I really don't know what's going on. That guy was a cold-blooded killer, but I have to tell you, he seemed to be completely rational. I'm not a psychologist, but he absolutely convinced me that he was acting on somebody's orders. How do we know he was working alone? Let's go to my office so I can pick up the Lexus."

"I would be afraid, too," Jack reassured her. "Maybe you should stay in a hotel for a while, or I can stay at your house, or you can come to mine."

"Let's go to yours, Jack. God knows what these guys, if there are others, know about me. I'm sure they know where I live. What will your neighbors think?"

"About a woman staying with me?" Jack asked, starting to laugh. "First, they'll never even notice. But if they do, they'll be thrilled. Anne told them I needed to find a good woman after she was gone."

Jack got off the freeway on the Wayzata exit, went south on 101 across Wayzata Boulevard over the Gray's Bay bridge to Minnetonka Boulevard, then to Dana's office, where her red SUV was still parked. Dana got out of Jack's car slowly, and he got out and walked her to the car.

"Unlock the car with the remote, Dana, but let me look inside before you get in."

She clicked the remote, and Jack checked the inside of the car with his right hand in his sport coat pocket on the Glock .40. Seeing it was clear, he held the Lexus door open and helped her in. "Still have to take it a little easy with the pneumo," Jack reminded her.

"Jack, could you follow me home? I want to change into some fresh clothes and pack a few things."

"Of course. I'll follow you, but pull over and wait if we get separated."

"The house is only a couple minutes away."

Dana started the Lexus and put it in gear, and Jack followed in the Mercedes. She drove north on Minnetonka Boulevard to Maplewoods Road, entered Woodland, and then the Maplewoods section to her house. She pulled into the garage, and Jack parked just behind her. When she had pressed the garage door remote, the lights had gone on inside and out from the lighting system macro. They walked into the house together, then Dana pushed the garage close button and disarmed the security system. She then looked quickly at the security log and said, "Well, no one has been here since I last left. The system keeps track by code number of everyone who arms or disarms the alarm. Why don't you help yourself to something from the fridge if you want, or just sit down somewhere?"

"Thanks," Jack said. He walked into the kitchen, opened the refrigerator, and grabbed a can of pop. "What a great house! Mind if I look around? I've always wanted to see the inside. Anne was here once when you opened the house up for a fundraiser for the Havanese Rescue League and talked and talked about your entire house."

"Make yourself at home."

Glancing around, he understood why everyone thought she was the best interior designer around. The place was awesome. As Dana went up the large free hanging circular steel and concrete stair to the top floor master bedroom, Jack noted the guardian angel to Dana's left and asked, "Who's that?"

"That's Alice," she answered. "She was busy yesterday."

Jack walked past the kitchen's 15' long granite center island. The entire west side of the house was floor-to-ceiling windows with a spectacular view of Lake Minnetonka and evening sunsets. He passed through the Great Room with a large custom rug that Dana had designed and Brazilian cherry flooring and a huge spanned ceiling that flowed from the kitchen all the way into the study.

The study was done in zebrawood with a custom made matching 10' by 5' desk, with wall-to-wall carpeting that was also designed by Dana. The deck faced a gas fireplace with two TVs on either side of it and a large plasma TV over it. On one of the study's walls hung a framed cover of *Architectural Digest* with a picture of the house and a feature article on the house. There were numerous interior design awards on the wall concerning this house and some of Dana's other projects that filled the rest of the wall. Even so, in the corner of the study was an entire stack of other design awards. Books and artwork filled the floor-to-ceiling bookshelves on the two other walls, with a gorgeous view of the lake through floor-to-ceiling triple-paned, argon-filled windows.

Jack kept going through the south double study doors past the powder room and tandem glass front doors, spotting a 10' high, multi-level water fountain that was in the front courtyard. Walking under the onyx hanging lights to the formal dining room, he recalled Anne's description of the circular ceiling hand-painted by a French artist and designed by Dana around a central medallion. Clerestory windows were spaced around the ceiling with hidden, indirect lighting. Dana had designed the circular rug to match the ceiling, and the perimeter of the room was guarded by century-old seraphim statues from Italy. Toward the east side of the dining room was a granite serving counter with glass cupboards above that held original china from J. J. Hill's private railroad car. Near the east door was a 300-pound statue of "Rebecca at the Well," and the entrance to the butler's pantry with its own kitchen setup and numerous cupboards. The mudroom and entrance to the upper garage was to the right, a small office straight ahead, and a circular screen porch.

Turning left, Jack walked through the kitchen again, past the elevator to the stairs, which he walked down to explore the pool room, rec room, exercise room, two more bedrooms, and an 18 reclining-seat theater with an 8' by 12' screen. The walls of the theater were designed to absorb or reflect sound through an acoustically invisible red wall covering and were custom tuned to the center of the theater as well as soundproofed from the rest of the house. The concrete floor was free-floating so as not to transmit bass sounds outside the room. He also came upon a locked security room, telephone room, video storage room, and whole house electronics room. There were two mechanical rooms with a total of eight air handlers, three steam humidifiers, buried and vertical conduit that went everywhere inside and out to a pool, a tennis court, three additional underground garages, and a boathouse.

Meanwhile, Dana had put her bloody blouse in some warm water in a sink to soak, then felt nauseous as the water began to turn to red. She quickly pushed the drain plug up, scooped the wet blouse up and tossed it into the garbage bin, then pulled up the plastic ties on the sack and tied it tight. "God, I never want see that again," she whispered to herself.

Washing her hands quickly and the sink, she took off the rest of her clothes, put them into the hamper, slipped into some fresh underwear, bra, jeans, and a light sweater. Then she gathered up some clothes, makeup, and toiletries. Seeing John's photo on the nightstand, she paused, and her already ragged emotions filled with another wave of painful memories. Then she thought of the other upper bedroom, which was to have been the nursery had John lived, and tears began to track her face. Sinking to the floor, she gave an inarticulate cry, began to sob, swayed back and forth as all the pent-up emotions of the past day overwhelmed her, and sobbed until she felt drained.

When she finally was able to compose herself, she washed her pale face, dried it with a thick white towel, and sat down at her makeup table and redid her makeup. Gazing into the mirror, she lifted her sweater and stared at the sterile gauze pad and suddenly felt overwhelmingly grateful to be alive. She got up and went over to John's photo, gave him a kiss on the lips, and said softly, "Thank you, Love." Then she gathered her items to take to Jack's house and slowly walked back down the circular stairs to the main floor.

Jack was in the Great Room, looking at the gas fireplace.

"Fantastic house, Dana! I've never seen or been in a more beautifully designed house. I've been in bigger houses, but never seen anything as spectacular as this."

"Thanks," Dana said, her voice subdued. "Sort of big for one person."

"And lonely, you mean, right?" Jack added, eyeing her closely. "I know a few things about an empty house. How many square feet?"

"Depends on how you count. Roughly 12,000, or so. It's got three acres with 310' of lake shoreline."

"Very pretty and quiet," Jack observed. "How are the neighbors?"

"Generally quite nice."

"When I was driving in, there was one guy who reminded me of Lurch from the Addams family—tall, gawky, staring effect with a shuffling gait and a bit of a tremor."

"You noticed all that when we went past him?" Dana laughed, then groaned in pain. "I have to be careful not to laugh too hard. He lives down the road and is a paranoid schizophrenic whom everyone actually does call 'Lurch.' The kids run away when they see him coming. One young child asked me why he kept his Halloween costume on all year round. He's somewhat better when he takes his medicine, although then he looks even more like Lurch, because he gets Parkinsonian side effects and shuffles as well as the occasional shakes. He can kind of creep you out. I hate to say it, but he's as dumb as wood and has a bimbo wife who showed up one night to seduce him in a long coat but naked otherwise."

"You're kidding, right?" Jack asked, but could see she wasn't. "Why would anyone seduce someone like him?"

Dana smiled and said, "Good old inherited money. Works like a charm. Actually, a lot of people around here inherited their money, but most are pretty nice."

"Anne used to call them members of 'The Lucky Sperm Club.'" Jack burst out laughing, then said, "Sorry," as he saw Dana hold her side as she tried to not laugh.

"Jack," Dana pleaded, "you have to lay off the jokes for a while. I tell you, though, I used to think they were lucky, but I've seen a lot of extraordinarily wealthy people who are very unhappy. Not just Lurch, but nice, normal people. Money eliminates one problem but brings others. I call it suffering from 'affluenza.' Are you familiar with it?"

"Oh yeah. It's crippling, and hard to cure, too. I try to avoid it whenever I can. So, do you want to get going?"

"Yes, let's go."

Dana left her Lexus in the garage, turned the alarm system back on, and went out the back door. Jack helped her into his car and put Dana's overnight bag and computer briefcase into the trunk. Jack drove out the driveway, left Maplewoods, and headed west out on Breezy Point Road as a black Suburban pulled out of a side road and followed them westward.

30

I have been very happy with my homes,
but homes really are no more
than the people who live in them.

Nancy Reagan

CHAPTER 30

"**M**Y HOUSE HASN'T EVER been featured in *Architectural Digest*, Dana," Jack warned, "but I agree it's safer than yours at the moment. I've got three extra bedrooms."

"Oh, don't worry about me critiquing your house," Dana said. "I critique every house, so why should yours be different?"

Jack laughed and said, "Yeah, I'm sure you do, and I can see why with your talents. By the way, the vet's office called me earlier and said the dogs seemed really lonely. One of the employees lives by me and offered to drive them here. Overall, I thought both humans and dogs would be happier. Just promise you won't lift them up."

"I promise. It's a relief, really, because I hate to keep Remy boarded if I can possibly avoid it."

They went north on 101 to the stoplight at Eastman Lane, where he turned left, went across the railroad tracks, and finally to Lake Street in Wayzata. They continued west, then south across the railroad tracks again and onto West Ferndale. He turned onto Harrington Road and then a quick left into his long driveway. Jack parked in the garage, took a good look around the yard and road, but through the heavy woods couldn't see the Suburban that had stopped before turning onto Harrington Road. He helped Dana out of the car and took out her luggage, then opened the house door, and the two of them walked into his house.

They stepped into the kitchen, which had a generous expanse of glass opening south across Wayzata Bay on Lake Minnetonka. Dana looked across the lake and said, "My goodness, there's my house!"

"Yes, Anne and I always admired it and watched it being built. Now I finally know the person who owns it. Let me show you your choice in rooms."

As they walked, Dana looked around the house, which was airy and open. "Nicely decorated. . .I'd say about six to eight years ago," she said. "More recently I see a distinct testosterone influence in some additions. Nice tries, Jack, but you might want to think about switching back to the feminine touch."

"I was hoping you wouldn't notice," Jack replied, leading her to the second bedroom and setting down her bags on the bed. "You can have your choice. This one has the queen bed and is probably the most comfortable and has no testosterone influences, but you can have one of the others if you want. Settle in, and I'll grill some burgers on the deck. I'm afraid I really never learned to cook."

"I'm starving for some real food after clear liquids at the hospital!" Dana exclaimed. "Burgers sound great!"

Jack headed to the kitchen, and Dana opened her overnight bag and began to hang up her clothes in the closet. She looked around the bedroom and thought, *A happy room and house. Nicely decorated as well. Probably one of the daughter's rooms and left the way it was when Anne was alive. Very feminine. Pictures of Anne, his girls, and the dog in the bedroom. All happy photos, nothing forced. I feel good here. . .safe. Anne wanted him to carry on, to not be lonely, and to be happy. What a nice woman. I wish I had known her.*

The doorbell rang, which Jack answered. A few minutes later, as Dana went out in the hallway to see what was happening, she heard a thunder of small feet and barking, followed by Mac and Remy running toward Dana. They jumped up on her legs, but she didn't pick them up.

"This is Machiavelli," Jack said as he formally introduced his male Havanese. "We call him 'Mac.'"

Dana had recognized Mac from Jack's picture on his desk at his clinic as well as the bedroom. Dana reached down to pet Mac, who licked her hand, then hugged and kissed Remy.

They all went outside onto the deck, where Jack had heated up the gas barbeque. He put the burgers on the grill, where Mac and Remy hovered hoping for burger droppings or treats. Once some of the edges of the burgers were cooked, Jack gave them small pieces if they sat nicely. Jack then put some cheddar cheese slices on the burgers.

"Do you have any salad, Jack?" Dana asked.

"Yes. I call it corn on the cob!" Jack teased.

"You're like my husband was. He never met a salad he would order on his own," Dana said. "I went to his apartment once and found his food supply was Coke, chocolate, ice cream, and Noodles Romanoff. John had at least ten boxes of it. Just add to boiling water. That could be for breakfast, lunch, and dinner. John actually used to rank his favorite restaurants as to the 'worst vegetarian.' The worst, being his favorite, of course!"

When the burgers were cooked, Dana resigned herself to the burgers without buns, English muffins, and canned corn. *Men definitely are different,* she thought. *Must be genetic, or else they all take secret classes together.*

"Looks good, Jack!" Dana said. "I'm thirsty."

"What would you like?"

"I saw you had some Macallan 18."

"Okay, but no pain pills for two hours. As your doctor, I would formally advise against it."

"I know. So do you have any of the 25?"

"Yes, not a lot, but enough for two people for one night. Taken only medicinally and administered by a physician, I can give you a dose or two," Jack kidded and smiled. "If you can believe this, a few years ago I was inside a hospital pharmacy where some of the older generation doctors still ordered one and a half ounces of whisky at bedtime for patients who always had some. There were bottles of single malt whisky next to the Ambien and Seconal on the shelf."

"I think I'd prefer that to the drugs, actually."

Jack laughed and added. "When I was an intern at HCMC, I helped with a study while I was working in obstetrics. It involved giving IV pure alcohol to women in premature labor. When Anne went into labor at twenty weeks while we were vacationing on Easter Island, I gave her Macallan orally, and it saved my second daughter's life and Anne went to full term. I used to tease my daughter that she had lost ten IQ points. Not only did IV alcohol work at HCMC, but I never saw so many happy women. . .and no stomachaches!"

They sat down with their dinners sans salads. Actually, they were both very hungry. The Macallan 25 was smooth, and Jack gave Dana some 12 and 18 as well, for comparison. Like most observers, she noticed a distinct improvement going from the 12-year-old Macallan to the 25, and from the 12 to 18, but not from the 18 to 25.

Jack did have several cartons of chocolate chip/cookie dough and cherry chocolate chip ice cream in the freezer, and they shared one carton of the ice cream. Mac and Remy kept busy chasing each other around the house, with Remy being the first to run out of steam. As darkness settled in, the meat and alcohol and ice cream brought on a sudden tiredness. Dana and Jack walked outside and let Mac and Remy have Final Piddle Patrol for the evening, then they decided to call it a night.

"I have coffee that brews automatically at 5:30," Jack said, "but goes into an insulated carafe, so it doesn't matter when you get up. I'll have to go to the office tomorrow, but you can stay in bed as late as you want."

"Thanks so much, Jack," Dana said as she walked down the hallway to her bedroom. "This will be great. I feel safe here. It's going to be okay. Just give me a few days, and I'll be good to go."

"No hurry. Just get better," Jack replied, then walked to the master bedroom, closed the door, and used the remote to turn on the security system. Then he changed and went to bed. Mac hopped into the bed with him. "You like them, don't you, Mac?" Jack said, then looked at the picture of Anne on the nightstand. "Good night, Sweetheart. I love you," he said and turned out the light.

Dana changed into her nightclothes, took off her makeup, brushed her teeth, and got slowly into bed. Remy jumped up to the head of the bed on the right side, turned around three times, also moving the covers a bit with her snout into a more comfortable position, and, finally satisfied, curled up. This was the side John slept on. When he was out of town, Remy slept up by the pillow. Both Remy and Dana fell asleep quickly; they'd both had a tough couple of days.

* * * * *

Farther east in the downtown IDS ChiFone headquarters, a select company were not sleeping, particularly Mr. Chan. It was November 6, just two days before the election, and he couldn't have anything go wrong now, no matter what the cost. He could be Party Head if this campaign went right; if it didn't, the party might *have* his head!

On Chan's desk was the predrawn syringes of potassium and insulin, a very effective intravenous murder weapon, that he had had in his suit coat pocket when he went to see Dana. Between Stevens being there, which he didn't expect, and noticing the small camera in each cubicle that fed to monitors at the nursing station as well as concomitantly to digital video recorders, there had been no opportunity to use the syringes.

Chan turned to Wang and Xu, who had driven up from Chicago and had tailed Jack and Dana to Jack's house.

"Mr. Chan," Wang said, "Stevens and the woman are settled in for the night. We thought about running her over as she was wheeled to the passenger side of the Mercedes or to broadside the car, but in either case you told us to be discreet. There were too many people on the street for that, and there were cameras on the outside of HCMC, not just inside. With the GPS, we easily followed them to his house, via the locators in the phone and the bouquet of flowers. We decided to wait and review the situation with you."

"I'm glad you were discreet," Chan said. "How private is it around Stevens' house?"

"Extremely private," Xu reported. "We can get in and out quietly and quickly."

"You know what to do," Chan said as they stood to leave. "Stevens has to die, too. If you get the shot, take him out. Or wait for our man. He will take them into custody in the morning and turn them over to you. Then make them disappear. Also, I am sending out a Taurus to swap for the Suburban. Don't want the same car hanging around too long to get noticed; also, it's smaller and not so obvious."

Mr. Hai, his chief electronics intelligence officer, was still in the meeting. He said, "I have transmitted the thoughts you wanted to be implanted to the users in Wayzata. We also sent a fake written order to the one. If he is required to collect the marks, he will deliver them to Wang and Xu; then we will transmit a different memory in its place to him. We are fortunate that you gave him a special phone!"

"Hai, how certain are you that the transmissions will work?" Chan inquired.

"Mr. Chan," Hai answered, "we have to think of reasons to get him to use the cell a lot tonight. I will call him myself a few times under the guise that we have had problems with the local cell tower. Even so, to implant those thoughts in such a short time frame has an unknown probability. We are beyond cutting edge."

"Thank you, Hai. We have the backup plan, if it doesn't work."

31

How do you make God laugh?
Tell Him your plans.

Anonymous

CHAPTER 31

JACK WAS AN EARLY RISER, as are most M.D.s. While an intern on his internal medicine rotation at HCMC, he might be on 36 hours, off 12, and good luck getting any sleep during the 36. Anne said that if his family had had enough money to take him to a doctor as a boy, he would have been diagnosed Attention Deficit Disorder (ADD). One of his business CEO friends told Jack it was really ADA, Attention Deficit Advantage, since most entrepreneurs who were successful seemed to have at least some ADD, particularly the hyperactivity part.

He had already showered, shaved, and put in his contact lens. Jack was a monovision guy, meaning he only needed one contact for driving, leaving the nearsighted one for reading. Once he had put on a long, thick terry cloth robe, he walked quietly to the back door of the house with Mac trailing behind and let him out for a few minutes. It was a crisp, clear November morning and still very dark. The sun wouldn't rise until nearly 7:30.

After Mac had come back into the house, Jack went to the kitchen, poured himself a cup of French roast coffee that had automatically brewed earlier, started to cook bacon and eggs, some of which he would save for whenever Dana got up, and popped an English muffin in the toaster. Both the smells of the coffee and food always helped his mood in the morning, and he recalled that one of his psychiatry professors had said that studies showed that the smell of coffee, much more than the actual taste of the ingredients, was a mood elevator. Jack ranked the smell of bacon right up with that of coffee. He thought of it as sort of Pavlovian, but without the drool.

Just as Jack was turning off the stove burners, Remy came charging into the kitchen, followed by Dana in her robe.

"Good morning," Jack said. "How did you sleep?"

"Actually, great," Dana said with a restrained stretch. "Thanks again for letting Remy and me stay with you."

"I thought you might sleep in a bit more, after the past couple of days. Did I make too much noise?"

"Not at all. But Remy often gets up at the crack of dawn, especially if someone is *cooking bacon!* She has a great appetite."

"Oh, I should have thought of that. Well, too late. How many eggs and how many strips of bacon?"

"One and two."

"There is orange juice in the fridge, if you want some. Coffee?"

"Black is great," Dana said. She reached into the fridge for the juice. "Want one for you?"

"Yes, please. The glasses are in the cupboard to the right of the sink. Oh, and use the unopened one. I think I was short of glasses one morning with the open bottle of OJ."

Dana filled both glasses and put them down on the counter. *Just like John; drinks right out of the bottle. Well, he is the only one in the house.* "I completely forgot to bring food for Remy," she recalled.

Jack pointed to a door. "Mac's food is in the pantry. Hopefully, it will be good for Remy."

"Remy eats *everything*," Dana said. "Actually, I'll put Remy in the laundry room to eat, if you don't mind. Otherwise, she'll eat Mac's before he gets to it."

Jack handed her two ceramic dog bowls that said "MAC" on them, and she filled them, gave one to Jack, and put the other in the laundry room, with Remy in close attendance, turned on the overhead light, and put it on the floor. Then she closed the door behind her.

"Nice touch on the personalized dog bowl," Dana noted.

"Anne made those in a ceramics class," Jack replied.

"I'm sorry."

"Don't be. I like the memory of it. Hope Remy doesn't mind."

"Not a chance. She'd eat his name *and* the bowl if they were edible!"

Jack put down Mac's food on the floor. Then he pulled out two plates, put the bacon and eggs on them, carried them to the counter, followed by Dana with the carafe of coffee.

They were both hungry and ate their breakfasts quickly. As they were finishing, Dana said, "Where does your neighbor work? He gets going early."

Jack gave her a quizzical look. "What neighbor?

"The one who parks out on the street. I woke up a couple hours ago, and looked out the window and thought I saw him getting in his car. It was hard to tell in the dark."

"Is the car still there?"

"I don't know. I guess I didn't look."

Jack immediately stood up and walked quickly out of the kitchen, down the hallway, and into Dana's bedroom that had the lights all off.

He looked north out the window, which had a clear view of the top of his driveway, and the car was still there. Jack thought he could make out two people in the front seat.

Dana stepped into the dark room and said, "What's wrong, Jack?"

"The car is still there, with two men sitting it," Jack said with some hesitation. "No one ever parks on West Ferndale or Harrington. Never. This is not good, unless their car broke down and they're waiting for a tow. But it doesn't look that way."

Dana stood speechless and shook her head. "This can't be happening."

Jack drew back from the window and took Dana by the arm. "Keep the lights off and get dressed. They don't know that we've seen them, and we'll call the police. But let's get ready, just in case. Get dressed, pack your bag again, and meet me in the kitchen."

Jack went to his bedroom, got into a pair of jeans and a sweatshirt. He shoved his wallet and the keys to what had once been Anne's Suburban, put on a light jacket, and slipped the Glock .40 into one pocket. He took out some extra clips of ammunition from the closet safe and put them along with a box of hollow points into another pocket. He also took out Anne's Smith & Wesson .38, the same model as Dana's, and put it in a third pocket with an extra box of +Ps. *I always liked jackets with a lot of pockets,* he thought.

Next Jack went to a large safe in the walk-in closet and took out a 12-gauge pump shotgun and an Israeli semi-automatic Uzi pistol that he never dreamed he'd ever actually need. Carrying the guns to the garage, he put them in the back of the Suburban, then went to a storage closet in the garage and pulled out two boxes of buckshot shotgun shells and three 25-round box magazines of .45 bullets and put them in the back of the Suburban as well. No one would have ever guessed that Jack was something of a gun expert. There was a time not many years ago when the United States was on the verge of economic collapse from Congressional overspending and a president who was essentially espousing class warfare to get votes. Many normally peaceful Americans, fearful for their families' safety from mob violence, stocked up on various arms. Things were much better under President Kozdronski, but Jack and others still had the weapons.

Going back into the kitchen, he found Dana waiting with one of her bags on the granite counters. She had changed into her jogging outfit and tennis shoes, with a windbreaker, and a baseball hat.

"Okay," Jack said, "here we go." He picked up the portable phone and pressed a speed dial number.

"Emergency 911," said the voice on the other end.

"This is Dr. Jack Stevens, did my address show up?"

"Yes, Dr. Stevens. What is the nature of your emergency?"

"It may be nothing, but there are two men in a car on Harrington Road near the top of my driveway. I don't recognize them, nor am I expecting anyone. I have reason to believe we are in grave danger and request police assistance."

"We will dispatch Wayzata police right away. I'll be off the line for a moment. Do not hang up."

Jack looked at Dana and said, "I'm on hold. We need to figure this out. If those guys are connected to Lam, how did they find us? I have unlisted phones, my name is not on my mailbox, and all my mail goes to either the office or a personal post office box in Wayzata, so someone couldn't open the box on the street to look at names on mail."

"Maybe they followed us."

"No, I was watching. Nobody was that close," Jack replied, shaking his head. "All we have is the three ChiFones, but I turned them off."

"Chan told me they have GPS built in as a free feature for everyone."

"They could certainly track us with that, but only if the phone is on."

"What if they do it with the phone off?"

"No. . .but maybe. Sounds a bit paranoid, but what if when you turn the cell off, the GPS stays on?"

"What can we do? We can't give up those phones."

"Well, we can take out the batteries, but they may have hidden internal batteries, too. Or they may be able to monitor when that happens. But I have an idea. Here, listen for the operator. If she comes back on, call for me to come."

Jack ran out of the kitchen and down a hallway to his den, where he opened some cupboard doors and pulled his father's old metal film storage case that kept large 8mm reels of family movie film. He had had the films converted to DVDs, but still kept them in the metal case. Taking out the reels, he put them back in the cupboard, took the metal case to the kitchen and put the Chi-Fones in the case.

"How will that help?" Dana asked, still holding the phone.

"The solid conductive metal will prevent any cellular or GPS signal from getting out to the tracking equipment," Jack said. "If the phones are the source, they're now untraceable."

"Dr. Stevens?" the 911 voice inquired.

"One second," Dana responded, handing the phone to Jack.

"Dr. Stevens, are you still okay?"

"Yes. Nothing has happened."

"The police are two minutes away. They will come silently so as not to alert the prowlers."

"They'll be here in two minutes," Jack repeated for Dana, then noticed that both Mac and Remy needed to go out after their breakfast. "Here, take the phone," he said, handing it to Dana and grabbing the dog leashes. "I'm going to take the dogs out."

"You can't go out there!" Dana exclaimed as Jack hooked the leashes to dogs' collars. "You don't know what those men are going to do."

"It'll look normal, taking the dogs out," Jack replied, "and it will distract them from seeing the police car coming. But just in case, here's a gun exactly like yours. It was Anne's. Your husband and I must think alike."

"No kidding," Dana said, taking the gun and extra bullets and putting them in her windbreaker's pockets.

Jack opened the front door and walked the dogs out onto the front lawn right in front of the house, glancing down the long driveway. The police still were not there. The dogs did their business on the lawn, then Mac suddenly scared up a rabbit from under a bush and both dogs jerked their leashes, catching Jack off guard and jerking him forward. At that moment Jack thought he felt something brush his face then heard it strike the brick exterior and ricochet off. Pulling the dogs, he ran low to the ground and in through the front door.

"What was that?" Dana cried, slamming the door behind him.

"That was a bullet that missed me by a whisker or two," Jack responded, wiping his chin and cheeks to make sure there was no blood. "And that was a stupid move on my part."

"What's that?" Dana asked, hearing sounds coming down the driveway.

Jack glanced out the window and was relieved when he saw the Wayzata police car pull up to the garage.

"The policeman should be there, now, Dr. Stevens," the 911 voice said to Dana. "I will hang up now."

As Dana put down the phone on the granite countertop, Jack looked at her and said, "I'll put the dogs in the laundry room, just in case something happens and we can't take them with us. And I want you to hide in the den until I'm sure it's okay."

"Why, it's the—"

"Just trust me," Jack ordered, leading the dogs into the laundry room and closing the door. Dana hurried out of the kitchen and went into the darkness of the den.

When the policeman got out of his car. Jack saw that it was Wayzata's chief of police, Mark Weber, with whom Jack had graduated from Wayzata High School many years previous. Jack opened the door and said, "Pretty impressive that the Chief comes."

"Jack, I was actually on my way here anyway when I heard the call. What's going on?"

"Get inside, Mark! Those men at the end of the driveway just took a shot at me!"

"Hold on, now, Jack. I just talked to them—two Chinese men. Their car broke down, and they're just waiting for a tow truck. I didn't see a gun, for crying out loud. Are you sure?"

"I'm sure, but I don't think we should go outside for a second opinion," Jack answered. "I don't want to tell you how to do your job, Mark, but I think you need some backup. I would say they have a high-powered rifle, probably with a scope and a titanium silencer."

"Jack, I hate to say I don't believe you, but I have some bad news. I have a warrant for your arrest for harboring a fugitive, a Ms. Dana LaFontaine."

"A what?" Jack was incredulous. "Mark, someone tried to kill her two days ago! She was in HCMC until midday yesterday. The Deephaven police have our cell phone numbers, and she talked with the policeman from the crime scene yesterday morning at the hospital. Since then, no one has called."

"I have to bring her in, too, Jack," Mark said. "So you better tell her to come along, wherever she is here."

Jack looked at the Chief and noticed there was something odd about his old classmate's demeanor, and things weren't adding up. "Mark, how did you know Dana was here? We didn't tell anyone where she was or that she was even with me. In fact, the Deephaven police don't even know she had been discharged from HCMC."

"Sorry, Jack, but I have my job to do, whether I like it or not. We can keep this low profile if everybody cooperates."

Then Jack noticed the phone on Mark's belt and asked, "So how do you like your ChiFone? I've got one just like it."

"I liked it until last night! It was one phone call after another. Sales people, crank calls, then someone from ChiFone wanting to test their circuitry or something. I couldn't get off the phone."

Jack's gut told him something was very wrong, and the Chi-Fone had something to do with it, when Dana stepped through the doorway behind Mark and broke a large vase over his head, knocking him to the kitchen floor as well as unconscious.

"I thought you were overanalyzing the situation," Dana suggested. "Sometimes you just have to act first and figure it out later. I tried to choose a vase that was inexpensive. I can get you a good price on a new one."

Jack grabbed Mark's ChiFone, car keys, and police wireless. He cuffed his hands behind his back and opened one of Mark's eyelids. Pupils looked good, pulse was strong, breathing was good.

He'd have a bad headache, but he would be fine in a few hours. He threw his handcuff keys on a counter and kept the car keys.

"Nice job, Dana," Jack commented. "Good low-tech solution. He'll wake up after a while, but be confused and then find the handcuff keys. We, however, need to get out of here, now! Get the dogs, your bag, and bring them into the garage."

They loaded the dogs into Sherpa bags and put each of them on the floor of Jack's Suburban, securely in between the back and front seats, then he put Mark's ChiFone in his father's metal movie film case along with the others and set it in the midline between the bags. Then he and Dana jumped into the front seats, and he started the engine, which he knew the men in the car were too far away to hear. Back when the Suburban was Anne's vehicle, Jack had a switch put on to manually disable both front airbags, because if petite drivers like her are too close to the steering wheel, the airbags can seriously injure them. He punched the disable button, making certain he wouldn't have to contend with the airbags.

"Put your seat belt on and keep your head down where they can't see you," Jack commanded. "This is going to be rough. I'm going to disable their car. I'm glad I backed the Suburban in so I don't have to turn around."

With that Jack opened the garage door, hit the gas pedal, and roared out the garage and down the driveway. He caught the two men completely off guard outside their car stretching their legs, obviously expecting to have Jack and Dana turned over to them in an orderly fashion by the Chief. When they saw what was coming, they jumped into the car and could only try to block the end of the drive.

Jack saw the Ford Taurus stop in front of the driveway entrance, and he punched in the fulltime 4-wheel drive rather than stay on the continuous computer controlled automatic. *Never bring a Taurus to a Suburban fight,* Jack thought as he gunned it. When he reached the end of the driveway he was doing over 50 miles per hour and headed for the driver's front wheel.

"Brace yourself," Jack yelled.

The Suburban hit as planned, crushing the Taurus's left front end and wheel, spun the car completely around, and kept right on rolling, hardly slowed down by the impact. Jack had all he could do to hold the turn onto the street, then he gunned it again and disappeared down the road as the sun began to peek over the horizon.

* * * * *

The Chinese men were not seriously injured, but their airbags blew, and both men had sustained minor burns on their face. They were, along with their bruises, mentally stunned and in a crippled car. It took them a few minutes to get their wits about them.

Meanwhile, Chan and Hai had been monitoring the situation from Hai's office downtown. Xu had called just as the Suburban came toward them, and Chan and Hai heard Xu scream and a tremendous crash, then Xu's phone went dead.

"What happened? Where are Stevens and LaFontaine?" Chan shouted.

"I don't know," Hai replied. "They went off the grid a few minutes ago. Sometimes if there is a lot of steel in the house, we can't track them until they come out."

"They are out, and we need to find them. Our plan and backup failed," Chan said.

"They must have left the phones in the house. They are not in the vehicle."

Chan kept hitting the redial on his phone, and after several tries Xu finally picked up.

"What happened?" Chan shouted even louder this time.

"The Suburban came out of nowhere and disabled our car!" Xu cried. "They're long gone. You said the cop would—"

"We don't know what happened to him," Chan called out, "but the phones are in the house. Find them and bring them back!"

"What about the cop?"

"Shoot him with his own gun and make it look like Stevens did it," Chan ordered. "But get the phones out of there at any cost. If you fail, I'll kill you with my own hands."

Xu and Wang raced down the driveway, knowing the crash would soon draw the attention of the neighbors. Finding the house unlocked, they went straight in, not realizing that Jack had turned the alarm on so that if Mark left, help would come soon, but if the intruders entered with the Chief still unconscious, a different kind of "help" would come.

Jack deliberately didn't pick up the ADT call to his cell, so ADT called the Wayzata police, who had had a 911 call with no recent response from the Chief and now a second alarm call. This immediately got the attention of a several squads, one of which was cruising down Lake Street, just a minute away. When Lieutenant Kristine Smith arrived, she saw the busted up Taurus steaming in the street and then the Chief's car parked in the driveway.

As she pulled to a stop alongside the Chief's car and stepped out of her car, gun drawn and ready, she could see the two armed men going through the drawers and the cupboards in the kitchen, and the Chief lying in the foyer. She moved quickly in through the still opened front door, but Xu caught her reflection in a window and pulled his gun.

"Drop your weapon!" the officer yelled, watching Wang as well, who had turned around.

Xu spun around and lifted his gun but took three 9mm bullets to the chest before he could pull the trigger. His gun flew across the floor, and he crumpled onto Jack's kitchen floor and never so much as wiggled, with a pool of blood swelling out around from underneath his chest.

Wang might have pulled his gun as she was firing, but surrendered instead, obviously realizing the female policeman was an expert shot. She had him facedown on the floor and was cuffing him when the other police squads arrived.

"You okay, Smitty?" one of the other officers asked as he ran into the kitchen, gun drawn.

"Yep, but go check on the perp that's down over there. And somebody check the Chief and get an ambulance."

One of the other officers had already done that and was radioing in that an officer was down and an ambulance was needed.

"Haven't lost your aim, Smitty. He's dead."

After clearing the house, the small army of policemen helped get their chief into the ambulance, then continued to gather evidence from the house and the smashed car. They reported that Dr. Stevens, a longtime resident, was missing, as was one of his vehicles, and they also notified the FBI that Dr. Stevens may have been kidnapped by Chinese perpetrators whose connection and motivation were unknown. They did not know that Dana had been there or that she was "missing" too, so the Deephaven police were not notified.

32

*Courage is being scared to death,
but saddling up anyway.*

John Wayne

CHAPTER 32

JACK PULLED UP to an ATM on Wayzata Boulevard and said, "We have to get some cash before they start to trace our credit cards. It's only a matter of time before Mark will recall that he was there to arrest us, and they'll start hunting for us."

"How much are you taking out?" Dana asked.

"My daily limit—two thousand," Jack answered, entering his information. "I almost never use the card, unless it saves me a lot of money paying cash for something. Glad I have it today. This should keep us for a while."

Jack got back on Wayzata Boulevard and then headed east on Interstate 394 and then north on Interstate 494. "If we're going to be on the run, we have to put Mac and Remy in a safe place. Let's drop off the dogs at my regular vet again in Maple Grove," he said. "She specializes in Havanese and breeds them. They have a nice facility for boarding, and I totally trust them. I'll just tell her we have an emergency."

"Sounds like a plan," Dana said. "How long will you tell them it'll be?"

"I'll say three weeks," Jack replied, "but I know they'll take good care of them if it's six months."

"Good grief, you can't be serious."

"At this point, who can guess? We have to find out what's going on and blow their cover, or we're dead. How's your chest?"

"A little worse with your ramming through the Chinese Taurus roadblock," Dana noted. "I have some Vicodin in my purse from HCMC."

"I didn't unload the 12-pack of Coke I bought. It's in the back seat—warm, but good enough for your pill." Jack reached back, tore open the cardboard, and handed one to Dana.

"Thanks, Doc," Dana said.

"You're welcome. I run a full-service neurology clinic and a cozy bed and breakfast, plus Coke and guns."

As Jack drove to the vets, he made a call to his friend Bob Dolan, a genius design electrical engineer whom he had talked with a few days before regarding the ChiFones. Jack explained to him what had happened, and Bob had agreed that they should come to his house and stay with him.

As quickly as possible, they dropped the dogs off with the veterinary clinic. Dana met the vet and liked her instantly, so she knew Remy was in a good place. Then they got back in the Suburban, and Jack drove east on Interstate 694 across the Mississippi River then south on Interstate 94 to Minneapolis and finally east toward downtown St. Paul, the capital of Minnesota. While St. Paul is somewhat slower paced than Minneapolis and arguably more "family" as well as less "commuter" in recent years, there has always been a rivalry between the two "Twin Cities." St. Paul has the state politicians, governor, and Supreme Court. Minneapolis has the Minnesota Twins baseball and Vikings football and Timberwolves basketball teams; St. Paul has the Minnesota Wild hockey team. Minneapolis has the Guthrie Theater; St. Paul has the Ordway Theater.

"So tell me more about Bob," Dana said as Jack turned off the interstate onto Lexington Avenue and went south. "You're sure he's safe?"

"No question about it," Jack replied. "When I started my own company, I convinced Bob to leave Minntronic to come with me and rewarded him with stock options. Eventually, when I took the business public, it was acquired by a large pharmaceutical company, at which point Bob was financially independent because of the stock, so he retired, though they retained him as a consultant. Then he got a great deal on one of the grand old but somewhat rundown mansions on Summit Avenue and fixed it up. He set up an electrical and computer engineering consulting office there as well as an incredible lab, and he uses it as his residence as well."

"Why'd you call him 'Kluge'?"

Jack laughed as he turned east on Summit Avenue and replied, "Bob was affectionately known around the office as 'Kluge,' which is a noun that means a system made up of poorly matched components, only we turned it into a verb. So, for example, in the process of developing a new computer circuit board, Bob would 'kluge' together parts in an ungodly looking way, which performed in a godly manner. I've never seen so many computers with holes in the covers or without covers that were wired to extra circuit boards Kluge put in to speed up the computer or make it do something new. Once Kluge called IBM because he had sped up a PC so fast its CPU was unable to handle it. They told him they had no idea why it worked so strangely because no one, including any of the IBM engineers, had ever done that. I used to ask Bob if the electromagnetic field was strong enough around his customized computers that he should wear aluminum foil in his shorts to protect future children."

Both Dana and Jack burst into laughter as Jack slowed the Suburban and pulled into a driveway leading up to a stately stone mansion built in the Richardson Romanesque style in 1855 surrounded by large maple trees. He followed the driveway around to the back of the house and pulled to a stop.

"Wow!" Dana said, glancing around the property. "Looks like those stock options paid off handsomely."

"Wait till you see the sweeping twenty-six-foot high staircase and the dining room's white marble mantel inlayed with a geometric serpentine," Jack replied, stepping out of the SUV and pulling out their bags. "It's gorgeous inside. You're going to love it. Grand hallways, twelve-foot ceilings on the first floor, majestic fireplaces."

The back door of the house opened, and Bob Dolan stepped out. He was in his mid fifties with nearly a bald head and wire-rimmed glasses that sat low on his nose. "Jack, let's get your car into the garage and swap license plates."

"Nice to see you, too!" Jack said. "Bob, this is Dana LaFontaine."

"Forgive my manners," Bob replied, shaking Dana's hand. "Glad to meet you, Dana. I just thought we better get your vehicle hidden, or somebody might take a shot at my front door."

"Nice to meet you, Bob. Jack's been telling me all about you," Dana said.

"All lies, I'm sure. But it sounds as though we may have to get good at lying for a while. I've never had fugitives from the law or bad guys in my house! When I bought this house, I was told that in the 1920s and 1930s there were occasional gangsters who came up from Chicago and stayed here while they sold their illegal alcohol during the Prohibition."

Jack jumped back in the Suburban and pulled it into the garage, then he and Bob quickly changed plates.

"Not much bumper damage. That should slow them down some if they're running plates on Suburbans," Bob said as he put away his screwdriver. "If the police stop by, I'll just tell them I shouldn't have left you alone in my garage because you stole my license plates."

"Depends on which police department you talk to," Jack said. "I don't know what got into Mark Weber. He claimed he had a warrant for our arrest, although he didn't show it. When he woke up, I don't know how much he has remembered. But we've got problems with the good guys. They're acting like bad guys, and we're not sure why."

"I hear you're a pretty dangerous character, Dana," Bob teased her, leading them toward the house. "I hid all the vases. Can I get you guys some coffee?"

"Sounds good," Dana said, and Jack nodded the same. *Jack was right,* she thought. *Bob is like an old shoe, comfortable from the first.* "By the way, Bob, Jack loaned me Anne's .38, so I am beyond vases now."

"I hope you don't need to use it," Bob replied. "I heard on the news about the Chinese guy in your office. Horrible."

"So how are you, Bob?" Jack asked as they walked up a short stairway and entered a spacious kitchen.

"A little older and balder, but I'm okay," Bob said and invited them to sit down as he poured some coffee. "Dana, let me know if you like the coffee. I'll gladly make a fresh pot for a woman packing a .38!" Bob said with a big smile, pushing his glasses back up his nose and turning back to Jack. "What have you got for me, Jack? I'm ready to rock and roll."

"Something worthy of The Kluge, believe me," Jack said. "I told you about Dana's headaches as well as the other patients. I have no doubt that there is something in the ChiFones that is causing it. I started to research it in the typical way we would medically if we suspect our patients are getting sick from something they are exposed to, gathering data and then contacting the proper people. But now my old colleague from the Twin Cities Clinic who was going to help is dead, and I believe ChiFone is willing to kill anyone who threatens to expose whatever is going on. ChiFone probably has billions of dollars invested in this, and a recall of their product would be disastrous to them, not only in the cost, but the negative publicity would kill their entire product line."

Jack handed Bob the metal case that he had brought in from the Suburban.

"Run out of tin foil, Jack?" Bob asked and laughed. "Remember the patient you told me about who used to line his hat with tin foil so the radio waves couldn't control his thoughts?"

"Boy, do I," Jack replied. "I've been thinking about him the last few days, and I think the guy was just ahead of his time."

"Well, let's see what you got," Bob said as he got up and led them down a long hallway and into what had once been a huge bedroom, which was now one of his labs. Bob's entire basement, garage, and office were all covered with wires and high-tech gear.

"How is Fran?" Jack asked as he and Dana sat down and Bob closed the door. "I didn't see her. Did she finally have enough of all your mess and take off?"

"I wouldn't blame her if she did, but she's gone for a couple weeks visiting our kids in Chicago," Bob said, setting down the case and taking the phones out. "We had our first grandchild, and they asked Fran to stay awhile. I was there last week, and they kicked me out."

"Bob, it doesn't look like you're any less *klugey* than when I first met you," Jack said.

"It works for me," Bob replied. "Dana, when I bought this house years ago, the state of electronics was such that nearby radio stations would interfere with sensitive test equipment. So what was done commercially, and what I did here, was to tear out the sheetrock and carpet, then put a thin mesh of copper screen, all connected together, totally enclosing the room, and grounded. The door is also screened under the veneer. We did the same thing at Jack's business, because there was a radio station that interfered with their electroencephalograms that measure in millionths of a volt. Jack was still a *real engineer* then, but now he's relegated to changing light bulbs, and only incandescent at that."

"Be nice, Bob. I do recall that your test gear doesn't work as well with coffee poured into it. I think it confuses the electrons!" Jack said, holding his cup over a $50,000 piece of equipment. "Dana, if you look at your cell phone, you're getting no signal in this room. Nothing electronically gets out of the room. It's a giant version of my dad's metal box."

By this time, Bob already had the casing off of Dana's first Chi-Fone and started to take readings with his equipment. "This puppy is definitely putting out a signal, even though you had it turned off. Low level, so eats up very little battery. The user wouldn't even notice it as long as they were actively using and charging the phone. Very clever, but why would they do that, Jack?"

"Not a clue, but now I think that Dana's hunch was correct; probably the GPS. The bad guys seemed to be tracking her everywhere she went. I bet the FCC doesn't know about that!"

"There's a lot more, Jack. Take a look at Dana's original phone, the one you said caused the brain abnormalities." Bob stood up away from the lighted magnifying glass and pointed for Jack and Dana to have a look, then he started taking off the casings on the other phones.

Jack bent over and studied the phone's parts. "Looks like a tiny electromagnet. What is that for?"

"I don't know, Jack. But what is weird is the circuit board connected to it. The rest of the guts have all Chinese characters on them, but that board is in English. I've never seen a design layout like it. Look at the lettering on the edge of the board. Remember how we couldn't patent the unique connections on the electronic boards, but we could copyright the layout of the boards?"

"Yeah," Jack said as he moved the magnifying glass slightly, and he and Dana both read "MINNTRONIC" out loud.

"I didn't know Minntronic made components for cell phones," Jack said.

"They don't," Bob replied, checking the components of the other phones. "I still have close friends who work at Minntronic, and they've said all along that they didn't want to try to compete in the cell phone market. They're strictly medical. Now, look at this. Chief Weber's phone is identical to Dana's first phone. But the Chinese assassin's phone is the same as Dana's replacement phone that he was going to kill her to get back." Bob put Lam's exposed phone under the magnifier.

"There is no Minntronic board or electromagnet in Lam's phone or the second phone!" Dana exclaimed. "But there is another board with Chinese lettering in its place."

"Correct," Bob said, looking up over his glasses at Dana. "You had noted to Jack that the original phone was heavier that the replacement. It's the magnet. I looked at the earbud you had. It has an electromagnet as well."

"Why the magnet in some but not others?" Jack asked.

"Don't know," Kluge said. "But it gets even more mysterious. Lam's phone has a GPS, like yours. But on the side of the casing is a tiny toggle button. This phone can transmit on two different frequencies." He put the case back on Lam's phone. "Since we can't get a signal in this room, nor do we want to, I ran a wire from Lam's phone to your original. Pick up your phone and listen."

Dana lifted her phone and heard Bob's voice perfectly.

"Okay," Bob continued, "now I'm going to toggle this switch. Please listen again."

"It's all garbled," Dana responded.

"Now, I'm going to connect it to the second phone you were given, Dana." He made the adjustment and then handed her the phone. "Can you hear me now, Dana?"

"I hear you perfectly, again, Bob," Dana said.

"See, it's encrypted," Bob said. "That's why they didn't want you to have it. Someone gave it to you by mistake. The texting is the same: regular or encrypted. Very sophisticated in such a small case. Have to admire that technology!"

"Can you get into the stored text messages?" Jack asked.

"That will take a bit longer. . .maybe a lot longer. I'll work on it. I'll also print out a list of the stored phone numbers. Might be interesting," Bob said. "We still have a couple of empty bedrooms for when the kids visit that you can use. Why don't you get your stuff and make yourself to home."

Jack and Dana went back to the kitchen and picked up their bags, then each headed for an empty bedroom and unpacked their things.

A few minutes later, Bob walked by the two tandem rooms and knocked on the frame of Jack's open door. "Need anything, Jack?"

"Have any sterile 4 by 4s and some paper adhesive tape? And some triple antibiotic? I need to change Dana's dressing."

"What kind of doctor are you, asking the engineer for medical supplies?" Bob teased.

"One who ran out of his house in one hell of a hurry."

"Yeah, yeah. Okay, doc! The *engineer* will get you some."

Jack walked to Dana's room and knocked on the door. "House call," he said, smiling. "How are you?"

"Oozing some, but the Vicodin took care of the pain. Great stuff!"

"Yes, but a tad addicting."

"The way my life is lately, a little addiction is not a bad thing."

"No, probably not."

Bob reappeared with his first aid kit. "How's the wound, Dana?"

"Not bad."

"Better keep track of Jack's hours. He's very expensive, especially with house calls."

"I have good insurance, Bob," Dana shot back.

"Give it up, Kluge," Stevens said. "Come over here and be useful."

"Dana, can you lift your shirt up?" Jack said.

Jack took off the gauze pad. "Wound looks good," he pronounced. He carefully applied the topical antibiotic with part of the new, sterile 4 by 4, then covered the wound and taped it up. "Did you also bring the oral antibiotics from HCMC, Dana?" he asked.

"Yes, and taking them on schedule."

He felt her forehead. *Afebrile. No makeup, but she still looks great,* Jack thought.

The doorbell rang, and Jack automatically reached in his pocket for his gun.

"Whoa, there, Lone Ranger. I ordered a pizza," Bob said. "Hope that's okay with both of you." He knew it was fine with Jack.

"Fine with me," Dana said.

Bob went to the front door, paid the pizza delivery guy, and set it down on the coffee table in the living room.

"Fran's gone, so I think we can eat informally," Bob kidded as they sat down on a large couch and he turned on his 80" flatscreen.

"I see Fran still lets you have some toys outside your lab," Jack observed.

"She watches it more than me," Bob noted as he turned on the news.

After a report about Minneapolis homes sales, the newscaster said, "In local news, the Wayzata police have asked the public's help in locating Dr. Jack Stevens, a well-known neurologist and entrepreneur. Stevens is missing and police fear he was abducted. Early this morning, a 911 call from Dr. Stevens resulted in the shooting death by Wayzata police of an armed Chinese national and arrest of a second Chinese national at Stevens' residence in Wayzata. The chief of police of Wayzata is suffering from a concussion in the incident, but expected to fully recover. From his concussion he has retrograde amnesia that may last a few days. Stevens and his late model Suburban were found to be missing. You can see his license plate on the bottom of the screen. Anyone with any information regarding Dr. Stevens or his SUV is asked to notify Wayzata police. We will report further as more information comes in on this breaking story."

"I hope I didn't hurt the Chief too much," Dana said.

"He should be fine. But concussions can prevent recent memory formation, so the Chief may never remember the incident. This may slow them down in tracking us."

"So much for going home again," Bob said.

"No kidding," Jack replied. "But we've got a lot of work yet to do this afternoon. Can you use a hand on analyzing the phones and seeing if we can break into the encrypted texts?"

"Sure, and I can see Dana might enjoy checking out the house and offering some design ideas. Fran says it's getting outdated here."

"Gladly," Dana said.

"Jack, I kept my taste for the Macallan 18 you introduced me to," Bob said. "Could you use some later?"

"Purely medicinally, yes," Steven replied.

"Don't forget the patient," Dana complained. "My Vicodin will be wearing off by then."

"Still drink it neat?"

"It's a mortal sin if you don't," Jack said.

"Single or double?"

"Double for me, single for the patient," Jack said and winked at Dana.

As it turned out the encryption was far more complex than Bob had ever seen, and despite hours of trying, they couldn't break it. Frustrated in the later evening, they gave up and settled for the Macallan. With that and the day's activities, they were soon off to bed and sleep.

33

It's supposed to be hard.
If it wasn't hard, everyone would do it.
The "hard" is what makes it great.

Tom Hanks, *A League of Their Own*

★ ★ ★ ★ ★

CHAPTER 33

LATE IN THE PREVIOUS AFTERNOON as he and Jack worked on the phones, Bob had called his friend Leroy Walker, the Chief Operating Officer at Minntronic, and set up a 9:30 a.m. meeting at Walker's office in Fridley. Bob went alone, while Jack and Dana went to a meeting of their own.

Walker's assistant led Bob into his office, and he stood and shook Bob's hand. Walker stood 6'6" and was skinny as a rail, dressed in black suit, and had a long narrow face and bushy eyebrows.

"How are you, Roy?" Bob said. "Thanks for meeting on such short notice. You're looking more and more like an undertaker every day."

Walker laughed and said, "Nice to see you, Bob. I'm fine. Glad to see you haven't lost your sense of humor. Have a seat. What's up? You sounded a little upset yesterday."

Bob and Walker sat down on chairs at a corner table that already had carafes of water and coffee waiting for them.

"Just a question before we start, Roy. What kind of cell phone are you using now?"

"AT&T, like always. Why?"

"Not using the ChiFone?"

"Nope. I'm happy with my own, though I hear it's a good phone and a phenomenal price. Why, you selling ChiFones or something?"

"No," Bob said and chuckled. "I just wondered. You guys doing any work for ChiFone?"

Walker shifted in his chair and took a sip of coffee from his cup. "Bob, you know we don't do anything other than medical. What's with the evasiveness? It's not your style."

"Roy, we've known each other a long time. This has to be absolutely confidential."

"No problem, Bob."

Bob pulled out Dana's original ChiFone from Jack's metal case. "I found a board marked 'MINNTRONIC' inside this phone."

Roy studied the phone, then his pupils dilated and his face flushed. "Bob, where did you get this?"

"From a consumer," Bob said, pulling out a magnifying glass. "But I went into the ChiFone store and bought one myself. Same board. Check it out for yourself, Roy."

Roy took the magnifying glass from Bob and studied the board. "My God," he said, "how did that ever end up in there?" Roy handed the phone back to Bob, who immediately put it back into the metal case and closed it.

"You know the board, Roy?"

"I do," Roy said, shaking his head. "One of our Senior VPs got involved in a research project outside of our normal business, although centered around potential medical usages. The appeal was that at some time in the future we hoped we might integrate into our business what we learned through the research. Our SVP was initially reluctant to do it, but somehow got talked into it by an old friend, a Dr. Jellen."

"The dead drug dealer?"

"Yeah, that was him," Walker replied. "They went to medical school together, I guess, but I don't know exactly what transpired to get him more interested in the project. We helped in the R&D and sort of got roped into manufacturing a million boards, although we made a nice profit on the deal. The project director was an Iranian who arranged it with us and a team of electrical engineers and neurologists from the U of M. There was a team of nine."

"Not the guys in the explosion?"

"Exactly. Our SVP was one of them. The whole team died."

"Oh, my God. This is worse than I thought," Bob said. "What did it do, Roy?"

"Well, we had a confidentiality agreement," Roy replied, wrinkling his brow, "but I suppose I can talk with you. The Iranian disappeared, so I'm not sure where the confidentiality lies now. I had to approve the project at certain points. It appeared the Iranian wanted the research for something, was given all the data, we made boards for him, and the FBI believes he then killed the team and fled the country, presumably back to Iran. They found traces of plastic explosives in his apartment and bank records of transfers to arms dealers. The FBI has everything we know about it. The research team was using the technology to induce or create memories in the brain with a pulsed magnetic field, and apparently it worked to a certain level. The potential seemed unlimited. We never could convince the Iranian to let us get involved in further R&D. Once the research got to the point of achieving some success, he paid us in advance to make a million boards, and that was the end of it."

"What did he intend to do with it, Roy?"

"I don't know. Big on confidentiality, but he never patented it. Told the team he intended to finish the larger scale research trials elsewhere. I don't have much on the trials because we agreed to destroy all our files. But I can show you the layout of the board and the component parts, but how the prototype for the board was connected to whatever other devices they used, I never knew."

"Great. Looking at the components you included in the boards you made along with what I know about cell phone circuitry should help. I'll look for what's different from other standard cells. Actually, ChiFones makes at least two kinds of phone. One has your circuit board in it, and the other one is encrypted or at least can switch from the regular carrier frequency to another."

"Encrypted? How did that get through the FCC?"

"Good question. One of many. For now I'm going to see what differences there are between the two ChiFones. That should give me somewhat of a control case, allowing for the encryption circuitry. Can you burn me a CD of it?"

"Bob, I'm already over the line here. I can deny showing you the parts, but a CD puts me on the line. Why do you need it?"

"I'm not sure the explosion at the U was the last killing regarding your circuitry, Roy. Someone, we think people from ChiFone, just tried to kill two more people. One is a friend I've known for fifteen years. And the hit-and-run fatal car accident of the neurologist by Theodore Wirth Golf Course—I'm thinking it might not have been an accident. He had a ChiFone and had just finished talking to my friend about the ChiFone problems and was going to collaborate on a study. He was going to report it to the FDA, at least unofficially to a relative there, and was killed a few minutes after they stopped talking."

"My God!" Roy exclaimed. "What do the police say?"

"It's pretty complex, Roy. My friend is a neurologist and was the one who first noticed the abnormalities in his testing. The ChiFone apparently causes brain abnormalities and headaches. His primary patient was given a new phone by the CEO of ChiFone, but someone apparently gave her the encrypted model by mistake. Next thing she knows, a Chinese guy shows up, demands the phone back, and shoots her!"

"The lady in Deephaven who shot that guy?" Roy inquired.

"That's her. So the Deephaven police determine it's self-defense and clear her. She is afraid there might be more bad guys who know where she lives, so she asks my neurologist friend if she can stay in one of his spare bedrooms where he lives in Wayzata. He brings all her ChiFones with him, and early yesterday morning two Chinese guys show up at the end of his driveway. He calls 911, but takes the dogs out for a bathroom stop, and one the Chinese guys shoots at him."

"That was on the news last night."

"Right. Meanwhile, the Wayzata police show up, actually an old high school classmate of my friend's, who then starts acting strangely and tells him he is under arrest. The woman knocks the chief out with a vase, and they came to me with the phones to research."

"Remind me not to piss her off!" Roy said. "Where are they now?"

"I better not tell you. I've put you at enough risk. The problem is the Deephaven police cleared her, but the Wayzata police want to arrest them both. The Wayzata police chief had a ChiFone they brought to me, which has your circuitry in it just like the woman's first phone. So who do you call? Who do you trust?"

"I heard on the news that the Wayzata police killed one of the Chinese gunmen and took another into custody. They are listing your friend as a missing person, possibly kidnapped."

"That's what they're saying," Bob replied, "but can you believe them?"

"Gosh, I don't know," Roy said. "So why do you carry the phone in a metal case?"

"Well, there's also one more nasty thing. The phones all have a GPS, and it transmits even when you turn the phone off. So you need to have it in a transmission-proof, grounded room or a metal case like this if you don't want to be tracked. It's how the Chinese tracked my friends. Also," Bob added, "if any of your employees have ChiFones, I'd get rid of the phones, but very discreetly. I don't want you in the crosshairs next!"

"Bob, I know some people in Washington. Maybe I can help?"

"Roy, I might take you up on that later. For now, we're not quite sure who to trust. When an old high school classmate with a ChiFone comes to arrest my friend on an obviously false charge, we have to know for certain our next step is safe."

"I understand," Roy said. "Be careful. I've already lost three of my best employees at the University of Minnesota explosion. I will discreetly check with some other people who were peripherally involved in the project and see if they have ChiFones first. Why don't you just disable the GPS?"

"I don't want to tinker too much. This phone may have some valuable stored text messages. I haven't been able to get the encrypted ones out yet. If you find out anything from your other employees, let me know."

"I will, Kluge! If anyone can get into the text, short of the NSA, it would be you."

"Thanks, Roy, hope you're right. Now, let's get that CD burned of the circuit board design."

"No problem!"

34

*The difference between genius
and stupidity is that genius has its limits.
When you want to test the depths
of a stream, don't use both feet.*

Chinese Proverb

CHAPTER 34

WHILE BOB WAS MEETING with Leroy Walker at Biotrionics, Jack and Dana borrowed Bob's wife's car and arrived at Dr. Dwight Crandal's office at the University of Minnesota. Crandal was the university's Chief of Neurology and had been one of Jack's first attending staff physicians and somewhat of a mentor. Crandal was ten years older than Jack and looked it. He had a full head of white hair, deep, sparkling eyes, and reading glasses that hung on a string over his coat and tie.

"Dwight, so nice to see you!" Jack said after they'd shaken hands. "Thank you for seeing me right away. I'd like to introduce Dana LaFontaine."

Dana extended her hand. "Nice to meet you, Dr. Crandal."

"Dana, a pleasure," Dwight replied as he shook her hand. "I saw your photo on the news and heard about the terrible shooting. And, Jack, the news said you may have been kidnapped. You don't look kidnapped to me."

Jack shook his head and said, "Dwight, I'm not sure where to even begin. Like I said on the phone, what I am going to tell you cannot leave this room, or it may put you, your department, and others at grave risk. I'm asking for your complete trust in this."

"Jack, I'd trust you with my life. There's no problem with the confidentiality, of course. What is going on?"

"Dwight, I need to know everything you can tell me about the research project with Minntronic."

Crandal leaned back in his black chair and crossed his arms. "That's painful, as you can imagine, Jack. We lost a lot of good people here. We were contracted to do neurologic and neuropsychologic research for an outside party, an Iranian, Mr. Adel Jalili. All the original documentation was given back to Mr. Jalili, whom the FBI believe was responsible for the explosion. But I can tell you what I know from conversations with my team."

"Please do."

"The research that was being done involved magnetic information transfer to the brain," said Crandal. "It was intriguing, but primitive. The study group found you could transfer certain thoughts and feelings as well as associate them with certain people or events. For example, we discovered that we could create a positive or negative mood in a test subject in association with a magnetically encoded photograph, and then when re-presenting the actual photograph, which they had *visually* never seen before, have the person correctly identify the positive or negative emotion associated with it. The test subjects believed they had seen the picture or person before or met them in person, although they didn't know when or where. The test subjects didn't know why they had the positive or negative emotion, just that they did, and it was a fairly strong emotion. We had progressed beyond the study goals to seeing if we could cause the subject to perform a more complex response, that is, to spontaneously carry out a task or activity. It seemed to be working. However, the study had achieved its goal and was not continued further. It's too bad, as there was great potential."

"What parts of the brain did they stimulate, Dwight?"

"They guessed the temporal lobes would be a good place to start and got lucky. They could create memories in both the right and left side. As you might suspect, the left temporal lobe favored memories that required more verbal processing, and the right temporal lobe favored memories requiring more complex analytical, mathematical, or spatial-orientation skills."

"How did they test for adverse effects?"

"They did EEGs, physical exams, CTs, and MRIs. Also neuropsychiatric testing. We found no abnormalities. However, we did not do PET scans. Since you brought it up on the phone, we found some increase in headaches, but we did not, in our small group and limited study, find a statistically significant increase. And, now that I think about it, there was a suggestion of some faster processing in the posterior temporal lobes on the EEGs corresponding to the side stimulated magnetically."

"Dwight, as I mentioned, Dana came in to see me for headaches associated with ChiFone use, which went away with abstinence. Similarly, although the MRI testing was negative, the EEG had a suggestion of increased beta over the left posterior temporal lobe. The PET scan showed an abnormality in the same place. When Dana switched sides of cell use, the PET abnormality appeared only on that side. I went back over my other patient files and found ten others with the same findings. What do you think of my data?"

"Concerning, certainly. We don't, of course, know if they were exposed to stronger fields or for a longer period of time. Your first case with Dana is especially disturbing, since you used her as her own control subject from left to right as well as with and without the phone exposure. It is highly suggestive. The other ten make it very worrisome."

"What were the clinical applications for the research?"

"Theoretically, quite broad for applications. Faster learning, perhaps faster rehabilitation of stroke or multiple sclerosis patients. Possibly quicker treatments for psychiatric patients by implanting positive thoughts and associations. But potentially negatives as well."

"Such as?"

"It might cause depression if one implanted negative associations. No definite violence, but I think that is a potential. The implanted ideas were limited, but there certainly was the anticipation of much more to come. More complex thoughts and associations. Possibly induction of an action plan for the patient to carry out."

"Dwight, what do you think of the explosion?"

"Oh man, I lost two of my dearest friends in it. The motivation is unclear. The contact was Iranian, not Chinese, and he disappeared, apparently to Iran, a terrorist state. There was no known cell phone use or testing."

"Do you have the test protocols and raw data results?" Jack asked.

"We had to turn everything over to the sponsor. In fact, part of the contract was that we had to electronically shred that part of the disk where it was stored. So other than what I might recall from staff meetings, there is no chance of recovering anything off hard drives. Have you reported what you found to the FDA, FCC, CDC, or Minnesota Department of Health?"

"No," Jack said. "Your friend and mine, Andy Don, was about to call a relative at the FDA when he was killed. I'm trying to decide if we have enough evidence to go to one of the agencies. But this thing is so perverse, it is easy to get paranoid about telling anyone."

"Doesn't sound too paranoid given the fact that you and Dana were almost murdered."

"The problem is that if they have progressed to the point where they can cause a complex action, for example, to get the Wayzata police chief to try to arrest me without a warrant, I'm concerned about who else they might have provided ChiFones to, and what they have been programming through them. For instance, what if they used ChiFones to program a special SWAT team or FBI antiterrorist group to shoot Dana and me as terrorists on sight. How would one of those individuals not know we weren't dangerous terrorists?"

"Any ideas of what their specific goals are?"

Jack shook his head. "I can link ChiFone to the Minntronic circuit board, but Minntronic signed away patent rights to the Iranian.

He can do whatever he wants with the boards, including making more. And there is nothing illegal about him selling a circuit board to ChiFone, as long as it is deemed safe. However, that circuit board was probably not disclosed to the FCC, which would be a violation. ChiFone denied any knowledge of Lam's intent, who tried to kill Dana. From what I'm reading in the media, the Wayzata police have not associated the two Chinese operatives at my house with ChiFone, although the police chief may have some influence there. Dana and I are just being reported as missing."

35

Never give in. Never give in. Never yield to force. Never yield to the apparently overwhelming might of the enemy.

Sir Winston Churchill

CHAPTER 35

B Y THE TIME JACK AND DANA got back to Bob's house, Bob was already in his lab analyzing the data from the CD that Walker had given him.

"So what did you learn from Walker?" Jack asked as he and Dana joined Bob in his lab.

"Well, it is a Minntronic circuit board," Bob replied, "but they had no knowledge that it would be used in a cell phone. It was one of those hush-hush research projects, with a lot of money greasing the skids. This *was* the project that involved those who died during the explosion at the University of Minnesota, and the lead person was the Iranian the FBI is trying to track down. They never knew exactly what he intended to do with the board, and it was never patented in the United States. The Iranian insisted on retaining all rights and paid the researchers handsomely to do the research and make the circuit boards. Funds for the project seemed to come through Iranian sources, and the C-4 appears to have been made in Iran or some other country that didn't want it traced. Roy gave me a copy of the circuit board layout on this CD, which may indicate something more."

"I have a question, Bob," Jack said. "I thought Minntronic didn't do projects like this. How did they get involved?"

"They don't normally," Bob replied. "It surprised Walker, but he gave his SVP some latitude because the SVP argued strongly that it had broad medical applications, and it appeared to be justified. Apparently the SVP turned the idea down initially, but a friend, perhaps you know the guy. That drug dealing pain doctor named Jellen, who shot his wife and then himself, somehow talked him into it and introduced him to Mr. Jalili, the Iranian scumbag."

"Unbelievable!" Jack said with a gasp.

"What?" Bob asked.

"I was questioned by the Edina police the day after the explosion at the U," Jack noted. "The Jellens were found dead a few hours after the explosion, and I knew Dr. Jellen."

"Jack, you never mentioned that," Dana said.

"There didn't seem to be a correlation with you or the ChiFones, Dana," Jack said. "In fact, the investigator never connected them. Rather, they suspected more a murder-suicide or double murder. I had fired Jellen from our clinic many years ago, and it had gotten ugly, so the police wondered what I knew about the Jellens."

"This is too weird," Dana said.

"Jack, what did you and Dana learn at the U?" Bob asked. "Did Dr. Crandal give you any information you didn't already know?"

Jack sat down on a chair and said, "He knew more than Walker, that's for sure. Get this. What they made with Minntronic was an electromagnetic device that could induce memories and associated emotions by magnetic stimulation in the brains of the test subjects of their study group. According to Dwight, they were able to produce limited, primitive, but effective *thought control*."

"My gosh, what's next?" Bob asked. "Walking robots?"

"So what is this technology doing in a cell phone?" Dana asked.

"Nothing good, you can bet the farm on that," Jack replied. "It was promoted by the Iranian as a humanitarian device for rehabilitation of brain-challenged individuals as well as speeding learning in normals."

"*Uff da!*" Bob exclaimed. "So that might explain the Wayzata police chief who thought he was supposed to arrest you two. This is really scary!"

"I guess!" Jack replied. "Although Dwight indicated that the research was just scratching the surface, think about the possibilities it presents for thought programming, that is, twenty-first century brain-washing on an unsuspecting individual! What do you suppose their motives are?"

"I don't know, but let's put together what we know at this point," Dana interjected. "Bob, you have the whiteboard on that wall to help you visualize new projects. Why don't we start a list?"

Bob went over to the board with a marker pen. Together, they worked on the list throughout the afternoon and came up with the following points.

WE KNOW

✓ Mr. Jalili, Iranian organizer, source of funds for Minntronic circuit board development, suspected bomb maker, now missing, presumably fled to Iran.

✓ Entire research team killed by a plastic bomb, possibly of Iranian origin.

✓ All research data was given to Jalili and hard drives shredded.

✓ Dr. Jellen is dead, who introduced Iranian to Minntronic team leader.

✓ ChiFones cause side effects in Dana and other patients.

✓ Dr. Don, who had a ChiFone and was about to report the abnormalities to a government agency, is killed mysteriously in a traffic accident.

✓ A Chinese employee of ChiFone tries to kill Dana and retrieve her encrypted phone.

✓ Two other Chinese find Jack's house and try to kill them.

✓ Police chief believes he needs to arrest Jack and Dana without a warrant.

✓ Device shows up in ChiFones and all have 24/7 GPS.

✓ Two models of ChiFones—one with Minntronic circuit board, the other encrypted.

✓ The Minntronic circuit board in the ChiFone appears to be able to plant thoughts in the brain.

QUESTIONS

✓ Why would the Chinese use a circuit board designed and paid for by Iran?

✓ Was the ChiFone just a front for Iran, since Americans would never buy an Iranian cell phone?

✓ Were the Iranians just a front for the Chinese, who were secretly behind this?

✓ Who is Chan?

✓ Regardless, what is the phone for?

The three of them stared at the board and rehashed their ideas for hours and hours, but came up with nothing that any of them felt was even remotely close to an explanation. Nevertheless, all the data pointed to some kind of mind control for no good. Dana went into the kitchen and made them a late dinner, and Bob turned on the television as they sat down to eat.

"Gosh!" Bob exclaimed, seeing the host of news analysts gathered and voter numbers running across the bottom of the widescreen and "Election Day—November 8" across the top of the screen. "I never even thought about voting. Looks like Senator Le is winning handily. Not a great shock at this point, eh?"

"No, his numbers just kept rising every week," Jack replied, taking a sip of red wine and leaning back in his chair as the analysts chattered on and on about the senator's rise from obscurity to become the president-elect. "He caught a wave of popularity and seemed to peak at the perfect time."

"I'm so tired I can hardly stand to listen to another word," Dana added, looking away from the television. "I'm going to bed as soon as I'm done eating."

36

*Whether you deserve it or not,
there are times when you will get screwed.*

W. Albert Sullivan, M.D.

CHAPTER 36

J ACK AWOKE to the smell of fresh brewed coffee. By the time
he got to the kitchen, Bob and Dana were already eating and
watching the television.

"Welcome to the living, Sleepy Head," Dana said to Jack. "I
thought the HCMC nurses said you always got up early?"

"One of the best night's sleep I've had for a bit," Jack replied. "I
guess I'm slipping in my old age."

"Want some bacon and eggs?" Dana asked.

"Yes, please," Jack answered as Bob poured him a cup of
coffee.

They all sat at the kitchen table and silently listened as the cable
news reporters compared the huge upset and percentages from this
and past elections. They ran clips of the election parties from the
night before, including President Kozdronski's concession speech.
Kozdronski looked stunned, but pledged his complete assistance
during the transition. Then they ran Senator Le's victory speech.
Le had won the popular vote, although not by as much as had been
predicted the night before. The ballots from rural communities
and absentee ballots from people overseas as well as those in the
military voted so overwhelmingly for President Kozdronski that
no one could explain the disparity. Nevertheless, Senator Le had
won by 20 electoral votes—not a lot, but enough.

Then one of the network's political "experts" was interviewed who raised another statistic that had emerged from the exit polls and had most of the analysts shaking their heads. Over the three months preceding the election, record numbers of citizens who had traditionally voted for Kozdronski's party and intended to vote for President Kozdronski had changed their minds and voted for Senator Le. Most, the "expert" said, could not explain why they changed their vote.

"Wow!" Bob exclaimed. "That is a surprise. Who. . ." his voice trailed off as the screen switched to a commercial.

It was an ad for ChiFones, showing a clip from earlier television coverage of Senator Le with what was obviously a ChiFone, followed by the voice-over, "The cell phone that is good enough to be used by the president-elect!"

Jack, Bob, and Dana looked at one another with stunned disbelief. They all knew instantly the key purpose of the ChiFone.

"My God!" Dana shouted. "They stole the election!"

"A million circuit boards," Jack said, "and a significant number of which were provided to key people selected by ChiFone. A million phones able to individually plant thoughts in people's minds. And ChiFone targeted strategic people to get the phones. A president-elect who comes out of nowhere and runs the table."

"And Chan would have concentrated logically on the cities, not rural areas and not military, because it would be much easier. So that's why the huge disparity!" Dana observed.

"Who else had them?" Bob wondered, and the rest of the ad answered that question, too, at least to some extent. It showed a flurry of celebrities and well-known media figures endorsing the phone. "That's who. No wonder they sang its praises."

"We have to try to do something," Jack said.

"What can we do?" Dana asked. "The election is over."

"Maybe if we call some reporters or news anchors," Bob responded. "Jack, you have some local contacts from your company days. Plus, they always seem to call you when they need a television expert for neurologic problems. Or I could call a buddy I went to high school who's a political reporter for the *StarTribune*."

Jack took his last bite of bacon and chewed it down, then said, "Let's start with your friend. If ChiFone can scan calls and is listening for my name on their network, they'll track it to your house. But they have no reason to be listening for you. Give him a call and find out if he has a ChiFone."

Bob pulled out his cell phone and clicked open his list of contacts and scrolled down. When he found the name he wanted, he punched the Send button and waited. Then he nodded to them that there was an answer.

"Hey, Roger. This your old buddy Bob Dolan. How you doing?"

Bob listened for a short while, then said, "That's great. Glad to hear your family is well. Fran and I are doing well here, too. Say, you know I'm something of a gadget guy, and I'm looking for the best phone I can get. I know the newspaper always makes sure that you have the latest phone. What are you using, and why?"

Bob's eyes lit up by the response and nodded to Jack and Dana. "How about the rest of the reporters?"

Once again Bob listened, just shaking his head the whole time. Then he said, "Roger, I can't tell you how much I appreciate the advice. I'm sorry to be so short, but I'll call you in a couple days and we can talk about our kids. I'm on the run. Good-bye."

"What did he say?" Dana asked as Bob clicked his phone shut.

"Well, it's worse than we thought. Not only does he have a ChiFone, but several months ago they were handed out to every reporter at the newspaper, and they had to turn in their old phones. Roger said he thought all the media outlets for news had received ChiFones, and he couldn't say enough good things about his phone."

"That takes care of trying to get a newspaper on our side," Dana said. "We'd be crazy to call any reporter and try to explain the details."

"You know, we'd be crazy to call them even if they didn't have ChiFones," Jack added. "Let's face it, if we told them our story, they would tell us we're crazy, because the story is so farfetched. Who's going to risk their career for some wild-eyed conspiracy story? I have done work on *magnetoencephalography*, the study of the magnetic information in brain waves as opposed to EEG, *electroencephalography*, which looks at the *electrical* signals. When I was at the Institute of Neurology at Queen Square in London, we had done magnetic rather than electrical stimulation of the brain to measure the speed of a signal through it, but there's no way I would have believed it could advance so quickly."

Jack, Bob, and Dana sat dumbfounded, staring blankly at the big television screen. What Jack said was true. A president had been elected, defeating the outstanding current president by thought manipulation. This was outrageous, but no one would believe them. Or at least they wouldn't believe them until it was too late, and Le was in firm control of the country.

"Did you catch that part about Le?" Jack asked, after several minutes of silence. "It all makes sense. What if his parents, who allegedly fled from the communists in China years ago, were in fact sent here to raise their son to infiltrate politics for the communists? And let's presume there are many others who also came here from China with the same agenda. Some of the U.S. intelligence agencies in the past have said that there might be thousands living in America. Then someone stumbles on a scientific idea of speeding up the whole process of getting hidden Chinese elected."

"The Chinese I've worked with are very intelligent and very patient," Bob said. "They think over a much longer time span than most cultures. I've heard about Chinese sleepers for decades."

Jack nodded and said, "So have I, and I believe it. Let's say that suddenly one of their researchers comes up with an idea of implanting thoughts. People have tried various methods in the past, subliminals and brainwashing, but nothing of this scope. They had the idea, but neither the ability to test the theory nor to make the product. So they search for and finance an American med-tech company located close to a major university and medical center.

Minneapolis fits the bill well, and it's not a place known for sub-versives, so it's easier to hide out. It all fits."

"But we still don't know the Iranian-Chinese connection," Bob said.

Dana suddenly stood up and said, "I think the Iranian was a front for what the Chinese were doing at ChiFone. When I was talk-ing with Mr. Chan, he told me that part of their 'marketing strat-egy' was to target all the key media outlets. It's no wonder, if they implanted positive thoughts about Le, that every news story and article was favorable for Le and so rabidly negative for President Kozdronski. To the media, they actually believed they were doing their jobs correctly. And there was a room in the ChiFone office I noticed that Mr. Chan had not included in the office renovation, which I got curious about and peeked in to see why. A Chinese man saw me approaching and shut the door, but not before I noticed a wall full of television monitors of dozens of news programs and several rows of desks with people staring at computer screens that looked as though they were monitoring reams of data. I didn't know what it was at the time, but I'll bet they were analyzing the impact of the phones in the media and possibly scanning phone calls."

"Damn Commies, anyway," Bob whispered, pushing his glasses back up his nose. "Now we know who was funding Le's campaign. And, I think your observation, Dana, is correct. As an engineer, I have to tell you a cell company might have a lot of computer mon-itors for their network, but they wouldn't be monitoring multiple television shows!"

37

Heroism consists in hanging on
one minute longer.

Norwegian proverb

CHAPTER 37

THEY DECIDED THE BEST thing to do was to safeguard Jack's data until they figured out what to do with it. There was no reason to think that key members of the FDA and CDC were not using ChiFones. They needed to find someone who was in a position of power that one of them knew and would trust them implicitly but did not have a ChiFone. Jack and Dana would drive to Jack's Wayzata office, and Bob would stay at his house and try to unlock the access to the ChiFones' stored text messages that he hadn't figured out yet.

It was a little after noon when Jack drove his Suburban with Bob's plates down Lake Street, which had the most unique boutique and coffee shops in Wayzata. Despite it being early November, it was busy. Jack hoped they would blend in with the shoppers. He suspected that his house and Dana's house were under surveillance, but he thought the office would be safe. The day before he had emailed Karen from an internet café to cancel his patients indefinitely and close the office until he returned. When they got to Ferndale, the traditional "end" of Lake Street, he turned around to head east once more.

"I don't see anyone," Dana said, peering ahead. It was their third transit past or around Jack's office.

Over Jack's protests, Dana had insisted on coming along. *Something Anne would have done*, Jack thought.

Jack preferred the direct, natural approach. He parked the Suburban in the lead spot of four on Lake Street, right in front of another Suburban. *Easier to pull out quickly,* he thought. He and Dana got out of the car. Both wore dark sunglasses and light winter coats, and Jack wore a baseball cap as well, which also helped the disguise. It was cool and windy, and their outfits were appropriate "Wayzata-wear" for that time of year.

Looking just like any other couple there, they walked quickly from the south side of Lake Street to the north and entered Jack's building, while scanning the area intently from behind their sunglasses. They took the stairs, which they deemed safer than the elevator.

As they went up one flight to the second floor, they peered either way. "Coast is clear," Dana said.

Jack opened the door with his Medeco key. He still preferred low tech on some things, such as great locks. He turned to the alarm, keyed in his code, and continued in, closing and locking the tempered glass door behind them.

"I've always loved your waiting room, Jack," Dana said, glancing around the room. "With all the windows it has such great lighting even on cloudy days. Look, Lake Minnetonka has some thin ice on it already. I think your plants may need some water, though. Do you have a watering can?"

"Funny, here we are sneaking into my office at personal risk, and we're worried about the plants," Jack said and chuckled. "Let's see. Look in the closet behind Karen's desk. Might be some plant food, too. I'll be back in minute. I need to get the patient data from the affected cases, including the PET images, so we have some objective, undeniable evidence to prove our case."

Jack walked down the hall to his office. When he and Dana had run from his house, he took his PC, but for confidentiality reasons he kept all the patient data at the office. He had tried to get it downloaded from his website, but couldn't. He wasn't sure if that was just the electronic gods doing their usual thing about mucking up high tech or if someone might have disabled his system.

Jack could download their data from his office computer, but not knowing if it was corrupted, he went for the wall safe that was hidden behind a large picture of his extended family on the bookshelf. The cabinetmaker had done a great job of concealing the safe behind a bookshelf door that was a perfect match for any of the many other seams on the back of the bookshelf, so no one would ever suspect it was a door.

Everything on the bookshelf was exactly where he had left it, so if someone had been here, they were very careful replacing things. His safe was surrounded by concrete, quite fireproof. He kept sensitive data there, including information on patients of interest. He also kept Anne's engagement and wedding rings there. She had wanted the rings to eventually go to their girls, but they wanted Jack to keep them for now. Jack liked to look at the wedding ring. It had two large diamonds and a heavier ruby in the middle. They had started with one diamond, added a second with the birth of their first daughter, and the ruby, for color, with the birth of their second.

He opened the concealed door, then the safe, and found the Dell external hard drive cartridge, took it out, closed the safe, then shut the door. He put the cartridge in his briefcase, took the Dell external hard drive, USB, and power supply from his desk computer, and put those in his briefcase as well. Jack closed and locked his private office door and headed down the hall for the waiting room.

"Okay, I've got it," Jack called out to Dana as he entered the waiting room. Then he noticed she was sitting in one of the chairs with duct tape over her mouth and plastic cable ties that held her hands to the arms of the chair.

Before Jack could reach in his coat pocket for his pistol, Chan hit Jack with a tremendous blow to the back of his neck, and he collapsed to the floor and couldn't move. Chan knew the finer points of the killing trade. Hit the victim hard in the back of the neck, but don't break it unless you want to make fast work of it. A blow like this depolarizes or de-energizes the neural circuitry in the spinal cord temporarily, essentially producing a spinal cord concussion. The net result is temporary quadriplegia, which may last seconds to hours or longer.

Chan was a very large man and, although in his fifties, very trim and muscular, despite weighing two hundred fifty pounds. He stood over Jack and said, "You and your bitch thought you could disrupt the work of thousands of loyal Chinese who have worked for over two generations to take over this country. You came so close to exposing our plan and bringing shame upon me. Now it's time to clean up the mess you've made before the Inauguration. You've forced me to take matters into my own hands, and I can't tell you how much pleasure I will take in killing you both slowly with my bare hands. The stupid Iranian was enjoyable, but he died far too quickly. I'll be more careful with both of you."

Jack found Chan rolling him over onto his back, but he couldn't move his legs at all. His arms were barely moveable but weak. His hands tingled, burned, and were numb, feeling like they had heavy gloves on them—just as some of his patients with neuropathies described it. Jack knew he couldn't push Chan off him, as Chan straddled Jack's torso on his knees.

"Being a doctor," Chan said, "you realize there are a number of ways to strangle someone. My favorite is the direct compression and obstruction of the windpipe, the trachea. Ms. LaFontaine, I positioned your chair so you could watch the flawless execution. Note the length of time it takes to cut off the doctor's air, as I will use the same technique on you. He will have a brief jerking epileptic seizure toward the end; then we will know his brain is feeling the effects of lack of blood flow. Such a delightful way to kill a neurologist! No need to fear a sexual assault, Ms. LaFontaine, in case that worries you. The killing is a sufficient aphrodisiac. I don't like white women anyway."

That said, Chan slid his massive hands around Jack's throat and slowly compressed his trachea. Jack's breathing became stridorous immediately. Some of it may have been that his diaphragm, the main breathing muscle, got its nerve supply from the C-4 or fourth nerve out of the cervical spinal cord and likely had some concussion in the cord tracks going to it.

"Now, Good Doctor," Chan instructed, "I want you to slowly feel the cartilages that are imbedded in the trachea and hold it open, fracture one by one as I gradually increase pressure. I prefer this sensation in my fingertips to the 'shoot-them-and-leave-them' method used by our younger Party agents today. Much more fun in disabling a target than leaving them conscious while they die, especially if they have an audience such as Ms. LaFontaine?"

Think! Jack said to himself. He knew he didn't have long to live. He reached up for Chan, but he was too disabled to push the assassin away or gouge at his eyes or choke him back or do much of anything else. His one hope was to distract Chan as best he could with his left arm, and at least get that hand in Chan's eyes, while his right hand weakly reached up for Chan's carotid arteries in the neck. Neurologists always feel carotids; it's second nature. Each one provides 40 percent of the blood flow to the brain for a total of 80 percent. He could compress them, but Chan could overpower him before it would have an effect. What Jack could do, though, was better and didn't take much strength. Each artery had a *carotid sinus*, or *baroreceptor*. Basically, it measures the blood pressure coming into the brain. If it is too low, it accelerates the heart rate; if too high, it decelerates. In years past, doctors would use *carotid sinus massage* if they were in the field and someone had a dangerously fast heart rate, or *tachycardia*. Gentle massage of both could be lifesaving. On the other hand, too much pressure would slow the heart too much, a *bradycardia*. So medical students were taught not to press too hard on both sides simultaneously when examining patients lest they cause a cardiac arrest, which is precisely what Jack hoped to do—to induce at least a severe bradycardia, enough to make Chan pass out.

Chan laughed out loud as Jack was reaching out with his left hand. He felt Jack's right hand on his neck, but it was obvious Jack's hand was too weak to compress his trachea. The carotid sinus massage was so esoteric and irrelevant to Chinese agents that it was never taught. "Your nerves are still screaming, Doctor. You don't actually think you can choke me back, do you?"

As Jack's left hand brushed against Chan's face and then tried to get in the man's eye, his right thumb was on Chan's right carotid and his right index finger was on Chan's left carotid. He pressed mildly and moved his thumb and finger rhythmically up toward Chan's head and down toward his chest, but actually kept the same spot on Chan's carotid sinuses the whole time. Knowing where to press was critical, and it was obvious that Chan thought nothing of the mild pressure on his neck. With the stress and exercise, Chan's pulse rate had increased to 120, and as Jack felt the rate gradually fall, he had all he could do to keep from passing out himself. Chan was allowing only enough oxygen to keep him from blacking out. Slowly Chan's heart rate fell to 80, then 60, then 40, at which level Jack felt Chan's grip slowly weaken on his trachea, and the assassin quietly passed out and collapsed on top of him. Finally able to get a full breath of air, Jack kept up the pressure, not knowing exactly how long or hard to press, but knowing he couldn't risk Chan reviving. Usually he had feedback from the patient's pulse rate, but it was all he could do to focus on Chan's carotids. Finally, Chan's pulse rate decreased to 0, essentially cardiac arrest.

With every breath, Jack felt his strength returning throughout his body. He had all he could handle just in getting out from underneath Chan's large frame. He could only crawl to Dana, then he pulled himself up on her chair. With what little might he could muster, he caught a corner of the duct tape on her mouth with his trembling fingers and pulled hard.

Dana screamed and shook her head back and forth, as the tears started to roll down her cheeks. "Oh, man, that hurt," she cried, still wincing her face. "Jack, are you all right?"

"I've been better," Jack whispered, still leaning hard against her and the chair. His chest rose and fell heavily with labored breathing. "And so has Mr. Chan."

"I thought you were dead."

"Reports of my death were premature," Jack mumbled with a bit of a smile.

"Is he dead?"

"Very," Jack said as reached in his pocket and pulled out a jack-knife and began to cut through the cable ties on her hands.

"What did you do to him?"

"Something I wasn't taught in med school. I've never tried to slow down anyone's heart enough to make them pass out, and I may have pressed too hard. He has no pulse."

"Thank God!" Dana gasped as her last hand was freed from the cables. Then she reached out and hugged Jack tightly to herself. "Oh God, I thought we were dead."

"Close, but no cigar." Jack's voice was hoarse, and his body was still shaking. He returned the hug, buried his face in her hair, and closed his eyes. In that moment, for the first time in years, perhaps since Anne's death, he felt fully alive inside, the sheer joy of being alive. Some gladness had risen in his soul that had lain dormant for years, though he wasn't sure what to make of it. It just felt good.

Finally, he took a deep breath and pulled away.

"How did that bastard find us?" Dana asked as she stood up and rubbed her wrists. "Where did he come from?"

"I don't know. He must have electronically tagged us somehow," Jack replied. He finally had enough strength to get up and walk slowly back to Chan. He knelt down and felt Chan's carotids one more time. "Call the coroner. . .in a couple days."

"How can we find the electronic bug?"

"Bug or bugs," Jack said. "They are so small these days that they're tough to find. Someone who bumps you on the street can attach one to your clothing. Might be in a purse or briefcase or a pocket. Let's check what we have."

Dana and Jack emptied the contents of the briefcase, purse, and pockets, but found nothing.

"Okay," Jack said, "I have another idea. Come back to my office."

They walked back to his office. Jack went to a cabinet and rummaged around for a while. Finally, he pulled out a rectangular object with a handle that looked like a clothing iron, but about half the size.

"What is that?" Dana inquired.

"A bulk eraser for videotapes. Before DVDs, I had a large collection of VHS tapes. Although you can always record over a tape, this is more thorough and also allows you to erase a whole tape without recording over it. You plug the eraser into the wall, and it is a strong electromagnet. Then you move it for a few seconds over the tape slowly, and gradually withdraw it perpendicular to the tape."

Dana nodded. "And what does that have to do with electronic bugs?"

"I thought we could each move it over our clothes and hair, then the nonelectronic things in our bags as well as the bags themselves. It's not very kind to most electronic bugs, or credit cards, or watches. Electromagnetic fields *can* be your friend, as long as they're not coming out of ChiFones."

"How will we know if it works?"

"Hopefully no one follows us and tries to kill us anymore!"

"What if they bugged your Suburban even before the two Chinese thugs showed up at your house?" Dana asked.

"Good thought," Jack replied. "We'll stop at a carwash and try to eliminate that as a possibility."

"What should we do with Chan?"

Jack stared down at the large man whose body lay in a crumpled heap on the floor. "Check his pockets and take everything you find. We know we can't trust the police here in Wayzata. Chan is dead, so there's nothing we can do for him. I have the data we need, so we won't be coming back here. Let's let him rot here."

"You're kidding, right?" Dana asked.

"Yeah, of course," Jack said with a grin. "I don't want him messing up my carpet with a body stain. I'll turn on the alarm, then open the door and leave it open. The alarm company will not be able to locate me and will dispatch police, who will find Chan's body. Without his ID, it will slow them down some."

Jack took out his cell phone and took a picture of Chan and then a closeup of his face. "Someone might be able to identify who this guy really is," Jack said.

Gathering their things, Dana and Jack went out the front door and left it open, then walked to Jack's Suburban and got in.

"Let's drive to the carwash that's up the street. I'll be sure to get the underbody wash. If there's a bug attached, I'm hoping the pressure spray will either dislodge it or short it out. Then we are going to do a manual wash, including the engine compartment."

"Well, at least we'll have a nice clean car if we get arrested," Dana kidded.

38

If you have to swallow a frog,
don't stare at it too long.

Mark Twain, attributed

CHAPTER 38

D ANA ENDED UP DRIVING back to Bob's house, as the effects of the fight with Chan had taken their toll on Jack. He had reclined his seat back and fallen asleep on the long drive back to St. Paul. When she pulled into the garage and turned off the Suburban's engine, he never wiggled or blinked. Finally, Dana reached out and touched his shoulder, and his eyes popped open.

"Oooh," he said, sitting up slowly and holding his head. "Did I see a bottle of Ibuprofen in your purse? My head is ringing like a bell inside."

Dana lifted her purse off the floor of the Suburban and pulled out a bottle of Advil. Popping the top, she pulled out three tablets. "Here. Can you swallow these without water?"

"I think I could swallow nails if they'd get rid of this headache." He slipped them into his mouth and gulped them down. "No problem."

"You want some help getting into the house?" Dana asked.

"Ummm. . .can I stay right here?" Jack replied and opened his door. "I think I'll make it as far as the house at least."

Bob opened the back door to the house as Jack and Dana approached and said, "Jack, what the heck happened to you? You look like death warmed over!"

"I'm sure," Jack replied as he stepped slowly into the house. "Well, add another attempted murder by choking to Dana's list on your board. Chan was waiting for us inside my office, and he just tried to kill Dana and me."

"Thought you have a gun," Bob noted.

"I do," Jack said, stretching his neck and arms. "But it doesn't help when you get hit from behind in your own clinic. I never heard the guy coming, and he blasted the back of my neck. He could have killed us easily if he hadn't wanted to torture us."

"Where is he now?"

"He was on the floor in my waiting room, but the cops are probably there by now, collecting his remains."

"How'd you kill him?"

"These bare hands, buddy," Jack said, holding them out toward Bob. "Don't mess with me. I've got a sleeper hold that I took a little too far."

"He's telling the truth for a change, Bob," Dana added. "I saw him do it. He's guilty."

"Bob, I think we all have to get out of your house, and you better tell Fran to stay away until you call again," Jack said. "Chan somehow tracked us, and we don't know how. We checked our stuff and washed the car, but I can't guarantee this place is safe."

Bob's face began to flush, and he said, "We can go to—"

"Just hang on for a second," Jack interjected. "I think the knock on the head may have been a good thing. I can't believe I didn't think of this sooner, but when I was in my office I noticed an old photo of several of my high school friends that Anne had framed for me. One of the guys that I had lost touch with for years, Mike Lawrence, came to our last class reunion, and we had a great time together. Get this. He's a three-star army general from Wayzata."

"Good night, I should have hit you myself," Bob joked. "But then again, I get nervous about those hands of yours."

"Why should we trust him?" Dana asked.

"Good question," Jack said. "Mike's story is sort of ironic. His mother would never allow him to play football in high school because of a bad knee, but he joined the army and eventually was put in charge of the Jump School at Fort Benning, where he told me he did 6,000 jumps on that bum knee. Later, he did time in Vietnam and took shrapnel in the same knee and got himself a free knee replacement. He went on to become a general in the Pentagon and was in the western side of the building near where the 9/11 hijacked American Airlines Flight 77 crashed, killing 64 people aboard the plane and 125 Pentagon personnel. In fact, many of Mike's subordinates were killed. He was in the conference room with his men and had walked down the hall to get some papers when the plane hit. Mike is a diehard patriot who epitomizes why our military has provided the protection to allow this democracy to survive."

"Sounds like our guy," Bob surmised. "I say you should give him a call, and let's get out of here. I got a creepy feeling somebody's closing in on us."

"Me, too," Dana concurred. "Call him."

"I think he gave me his direct number," Jack said, pulling out his cell phone and scrolling down his list of contacts. "I had a couple drinks too many that night, so it's a little fuzzy. Oops, there he is." Jack pressed the Send button and waited, then whispered, "I got General Lawrence's aide."

"Hello, this is Dr. Jack Stevens, an old friend of General Lawrence. Is he able to talk? It is an urgent matter of life and death."

"Dr. Stevens," the aide said, "hold on, and I'll see if the general can talk with you, sir." A minute later, Mike came on the phone.

"Jack, how the hell are you?" Mike asked. "What's it been now, three or four years since I last saw you?"

"Mike, you wimpy, weak-kneed momma's boy. I'm fine, just a little hoarse. How are you and Gretchen? Does she let you go out alone?"

"We're just fine, you pussy. I can whip your butt anytime, pencil head. Why are you bothering me, anyway? What's this life-or-death crap? Is the foam on your cappuccino not stiff enough?"

"Mike," Jack said, taking a deep breath, "all joking aside, this is not a social call. First, I must ask, do you use a ChiFone?"

"What the hell is this, Jack? Why would you call to ask me that?"

"I know it sounds stupid. But I'm asking you to trust me for a second, and just answer that."

"You think I'd buy a damn Chinese phone, Jack? C'mon. I buy American."

"Good, good. That's a relief. Now we can talk," Jack said through a smile. "Mike, on my word of deepest honor, I'm asking you to trust me again. I have conclusive evidence of a serious national security threat that is already unfolding, and assassins are trying to kill me and two of my friends."

"Jack, don't say another word," Mike commanded. "These lines are not secure. Go to the 88th Army Reserve campus at Fort Snelling immediately. Bring your friends, and call me from there. They have a secure line, and I'll have them ready for you."

Without a moment's hesitation, Jack and Dana and Bob loaded up all the evidence into bags as well as their personal bags, locked the house, ran to the garage, and jumped into Jack's Suburban.

"Let's get out of here!" Bob said as he clicked his seat belt into position and scanned the driveway around the corner of his mansion.

There was a collective sigh of relief as they made it out the driveway without any shots fired or confrontations, and Jack drove south and west across the Mississippi River and past historic Fort Snelling, which was the first permanent fort in Minnesota, located at the confluence of the Minnesota River and the Mississippi River, and continued to the Army Reserve base. Major Sjogren was expecting them, and they were led to a private room with a secure line in it.

"General Lawrence," Major Sjogren said as he got Mike on the speakerphone, "I have Dr. Stevens here." He nodded to Jack and left the room, closing the door behind him.

"Mike," Jack said, "I'm back. Can you hear me?"

"Just fine," Mike said. "So you stepped into some shit, huh?"

"I did, Mike," Jack said. "Both feet and up to my ears. I wasn't trying. We just sort of stumbled into it, I'm afraid."

"Jack, you aren't shitting me, are you?" Mike shot back.

"No shit, Mike," Jack replied. "My life and the lives of my friends here are in the crosshairs, and our national security has been severely jeopardized. I have evidence the presidential election may have been rigged by the Chinese government, starting with the explosion at the University of Minnesota before the presidential debate—"

"Jack, everything we have ties the explosion to the Iranians."

"All a smokescreen, Mike," Jack retorted. "I can tie the Chinese to the bombing, to the killing of everyone who knew about the technology the research team had developed, to the production of at least a million circuit boards put into ChiFones that have the scientific capacity to effect people's feelings and thinking, and to the use of that technology to change the outcome of the election for Senator Le."

"Jack, if you're blowing smoke up my ass," Mike warned, "I will make your miserable life into a torture pit. I am the number two man in many of the army Pentagon ops, and while I take your statement seriously, we hear crazy shit all the time from seemingly credible people."

"Yeah, I understand. Like telling people at the gas station that their car was misfiring because it needed 'summer air' in its tires when you worked your summer job?"

Mike started to laugh out loud. "Touché, old friend. But. . .I'm not in the mood for your twisted sense of humor at the moment. You realize this sounds like one of the old *Twilight Zone* episodes you obsessed over. You're asking me to put my ass on the line here."

"Listen, I know who you are, Mike, and you know who I am," Jack answered. "My life and my friends' lives are in your hands. My friend Dana was shot and injured, I was shot at and then nearly killed by a Chinese assassin this morning, and one of my friends who was going to help me research what I'd found was killed a few days ago. What I said may sound a bit crazy, but do you think Senator Le won the election fair and square? How do you explain what you watched unfold? You don't believe it, do you, Mike?"

"No. Nobody here does. But it's a done deal."

"No, it's not. Not by a long shot," Jack countered. "But we don't have time to chit chat about it. We can absolutely prove the election was stolen. I'll hand over all my evidence and let the NSA confirm it."

"Okay, Jack, tell me one more time what you've got."

"Mike, I have evidence of a long-term, deeply imbedded and deeply moled Chinese conspiracy to take over the United States by pseudo-legal means, starting with the presidency. I can show that the lone Iranian in the university bombing was a paid front man by the Chinese, that the research developed was primitive but far more effective than even the researchers knew, and that the technology was secretly imbedded in at least a million cell phones and used to change the election. If the NSA opens up one of the ChiFones I have and looks at my findings regarding them, they will be instantly convinced."

"Oh, boy. This stinks to high heaven," Mike drawled. "Okay, here's what we'll do. You bring all your evidence and sorry asses to D.C. I'll send a jet for you and your two friends. Stay right where you are, don't even think about leaving the office, and keep your mouths shut. You'll be safer there. The chief of staff will tell you when the plane arrives. I'll take care of everything here. But if you—"

"I promise not to tell anyone that your mother wouldn't let you go out for football," Jack said and laughed. "I get it, Mike. I won't let you down. See you tonight."

"And I won't tell your friends about—"

"See you tonight, Mike. Good-bye." And with that, Jack punched the Off button.

39

It's not how often you fall down;
it's how often you get up.

An Author's Advice to His Children

★ ★ ★ ★ ★

CHAPTER 39

IN A LITTLE OVER AN HOUR, Major Sjogren drove Jack, Bob, and Dana to the airstrip, where they were cleared by the guards at the gate. Then they drove out to where an Army Cessna Citation Encore Jet (UC-35B) was waiting, with the pilot flanked by his copilot and two armed MPs in civilian clothes. The major pulled to a stop and popped the trunk as they opened their doors and stepped out onto the tarmac.

"Dr. Stevens?" the pilot asked.

"Yes?" Jack said.

"General Lawrence has asked me to fly you as fast as possible to Washington, D.C. He ordered two MPs to safeguard you. Is there anything I can help you with, sir?"

"No, thanks. I think we are fine," Jack said. "We'll just grab our gear quick. Maybe one of you could help Ms. LaFontaine with her bags. She was shot in the line of duty and hasn't healed yet."

"Ma'am, let me help," one of the MPs said as he stepped forward.

"Call me Dana, please, unless you want to call him Dr. Jekyll," Dana joked. "I can't tell if he's Jekyll or Hyde. One minute he's a neurologist, and the next minute he pretends he's James Bond."

One MP got on the plane first, checked around, then motioned them on. Jack and Dana got onboard the plane. Jack put his briefcase behind his seat, and they put on their seatbelts. The MP sat in the seat in front of them. Bob came onboard a few minutes later, carrying Jack's metal case with the cell phones inside. He sat in the seat across from them.

The copilot had just finished her preflighting as the refueling truck pulled away. She climbed back onboard and put her head into the cockpit. "Good to go," she said to the pilot. She stepped back out, motioned for the second MP to come onboard. He made his entrance and sat down across from to the first MP. The copilot then closed the hatch and sat down in the second seat in the cockpit.

The eight-seat Cessna, clearly underloaded, shot down the runway and lifted off quickly. In less than 2 hours, they landed at Joint Base Andrews Naval Air Facility Washington, formerly Andrews Air Force Base, just eight miles east of Washington, D.C. The MPs got off first and motioned Jack and Dana and Bob to follow. As Jack and Dana deplaned, an aide was waiting for them at the airplane with a car.

"Dr. Stevens?" the aide asked. Jack nodded. "General Lawrence asked me to take you, Ms. LaFontaine, and Mr. Dolan to his office."

The aide led them to the car, the MPs were met by a Suburban, and the two vehicles sped toward the Pentagon. When they pulled into view of the Pentagon, the headquarters of the Department of Defense, they came to a stop at a traffic light.

"Wow!" Dana exclaimed. "How big is this building?"

"Really big," Bob answered, staring out his window.

The aide laughed and said, "That's right. It's the world's largest office building by floor area. Obviously, it has five sides, with five floors above ground plus two basement levels, and five ring corridors per floor with a total of 17.5 miles of corridors. Just to give you an idea of how big it is, there's a five-acre central plaza."

"Ground Zero, as I recall from the Cold War days," Bob added. "We always thought the Soviets would drop a nuke or two right in the center of the plaza."

"So did we," the aide replied. "There is a coffee stand in the middle. The Soviet spy satellites saw large lines emanating out of people waiting to get served. So they thought it was an elevator down to the 'super secret' part of the Pentagon, which would be far underground. So when we debriefed some defectors, we learned that they had targeted that very spot for a missile. Good for a laugh, anyway."

"Tough on the cappuccino machine!" Dana laughed.

"How many people work here?" Jack asked.

"They tell me about 23,000 military and civilian employees and another 3,000 non-defense support personnel," the aide replied. "That's about twenty times the size of my hometown."

They went through heavy security and were given an escort through numerous corridors straight into General Lawrence's office.

"Mike, I can't believe I caught you working!" Jack greeted his old friend, who was 6'2" and broad shouldered with a definitively athletic countenance and a short blond hair crewcut.

"Jack," the general said as he stood up from his desk and greeted Jack, Bob, and Dana, "how the hell are you? You look a bit like something the cat dragged in!"

"Considering everything that happened this morning, I'm just glad to be even dragged in alive. This is Dana LaFontaine, of whom I spoke to you, and computer and electrical engineer extraordinaire and longtime friend Bob Dolan."

Mike shook hands and greeted them all. After greeting Dana last, he smiled and said to Jack, "Well, at least she was worthwhile sending a jet and a couple MPs for. I wouldn't have done it for you."

"Mike, I wouldn't have come, but Dana insisted, you prick," Jack fired back. He knew of no finer person than Mike Lawrence. He was the kind of officer a man would fight alongside and for whom he would risk his life.

"Sit down, Ms. LaFontaine," Mike said, pointing to a padded leather chair. "That's the most comfortable chair. Jack, you can have the one with the broken leg. Bob, have a seat there."

The general sat back down at his desk, and his expression changed from a smile to very grave. "Jack," he started, "they identified the dead body of a Mr. Chan in your office this morning. That was one little detail you didn't mention on the phone earlier. I assume that's the Chinese assassin you referred to. He was the CEO of ChiFones, and the company has already come out with a statement that you and Ms. LaFontaine were trying to blackmail the company and Chan went to your office this morning to discuss the medical findings with the two of you."

"Oh, before I forget, I have two pictures of Chan, in case you want to try to identify who he really is," Jack said and showed them to Mike on his cell phone.

"Don't you love cell phones," Mike said. "Or not, after what you told me." He downloaded the pictures into two USB memory sticks and gave the phone back to Jack, then called back an aide on the intercom.

"Yes, sir?" the aide said as he entered the office.

"Transmit this, highest priority, secure to CIA and FBI. Ask to try to identify this man," Mike said and handed one stick to the aide. "This one, run through our Army intelligence," giving him the second.

"Right away, General!" the aide said and hurried out of the room.

"He was at the center of it, Mike," Jack answered. "Either I killed him or the two of us would be dead."

"He's an American citizen, Jack. Born here. He's grown to be one of the most highly sought after executives in the world, and he's been written up in every major magazine in the country. Or at least he is supposed to be."

"Being a citizen doesn't mean he's one of us. You know that all too well," Jack replied. "The same is true of Senator Le, and a whole lot more of supposed citizens."

"Why did you leave your door open for the security system to trigger?"

"He didn't want his rug to get damaged, in case Chan started to rot," Dana replied, trying not to snicker.

"You meathead!" the general snapped. "You could have bought us some time. I can't hide you very long now. It's all over the news in Minneapolis. If we can't prove your claims quickly, I'll be peeling potatoes with Beetle Bailey and you'll be sitting with me. Show me your evidence. I need the entire story."

It was dark by the time Jack and Dana and Bob had finished methodically relating the story and showing the general all the data they had assembled. The general spent most of the time pacing around his office as they talked, sometimes staring out his window into the dark night and sometimes looking at the data. When they wrapped it up, Mike had sat back down at his desk.

Mike leaned back in his chair and rubbed his chin, then he exhaled heavily. "This is serious shit, Jack! We've feared and prepared for technological attacks for years, but our pants are down on this one. I don't think anyone was looking at cell phones."

"So you'll help us?" Jack asked.

"You're damned right I will," the general blurted out. He pressed the intercom and said, "Get me the Director of the NSA."

"Sir," a male voice responded, "I'm sure he's gone—"

"Track him down and tell him I've got an elephant in my office that we have to deal with immediately. Not tomorrow. Tonight."

"Yes, sir." Then he clicked off.

"Gosh, I didn't even offer you something to drink," Mike said. "Can I get you some water or coffee or something?"

"Water's good," Jack replied, and Dana and Bob nodded in agreement.

The general spun his chair around and reached down and opened the small refrigerator door that was beneath his credenza. He had pulled out four plastic bottles of water and set them on the desk when the intercom came on.

"Sir, the Director of the National Security Agency is on line two. He was still in his office."

"Thanks," the general replied. He put his phone on speaker and punched in line two. "Good evening, Director Handley. This is Mike Lawrence. I have an emergency security situation here I need to get in front of you and your best engineers immediately. I don't have time to explain, because I have an urgent call to make to Director Reson. I have some cell phones that have encrypted text of potentially serious nature and an electrical engineer from Minneapolis named Bob Dolan whom I'd like to send over to speed up the process. He knows the entire story as well as all the data, which is going to scare the hell out of you. Can you stay and fast track it?"

"If you say it's serious, Mike," the director answered, "I'll be here and have a team of our best engineers waiting in the lab."

"The package is on the way," Mike said. "Tell the gang it's going to be a late night."

"Will do. This better be worth it. We'll talk later."

"Yes, sir."

That said, the general punched the intercom again and barked, "Get a driver and car ready and two MPs for escorts. Tell them I have a delivery to Fort Meade, and the director of NSA will be waiting for them."

"Yes, sir."

"And get my assistant in here. I need him to escort Mr. Dolan to the car bay."

"Right away, sir."

"Okay," Mike said, looking at Bob, "you're taking all the evidence with you to the NSA. Jack and Dana are staying with me. Don't let the NSA boys take it over. You're in control, you know what you've got, and I need you to make sure they've fully seen it all before they jump in and confirm it. Do you understand?"

"Yes, sir!" Bob said, jumping up and all but saluting the general. "I've always dreamed of getting in the NSA labs and—"

"Spare us the chatter and get going," the general interrupted. "You can play over there later. Right now your only purpose is to save the NSA time. Every second counts."

"Make backup copies of everything. . .before they start," Jack said as Bob picked up the bags and headed for the door where the assistant to the general was already waiting.

"Go!" the general barked.

Timid men prefer the calm of despotism to the tempestuous sea of liberty.

Thomas Jefferson

CHAPTER 40

AFTER BOB AND THE GENERAL'S ASSISTANT exited the room, General Lawrence punched the intercom again and said, "Get me the Director of the FBI on the phone now. Tell him what you told the Director of the NSA. Don't take no for an answer."

"Yes, sir. Right away."

General Lawrence rubbed his forehead with his fingertips, then pressed his fingers against his eyes as though he was massaging a sinus headache. "What I won't do to keep you from telling the boys about my mother keeping me out of football," he said, shaking his head and casting a sour look at Jack. "I'm hoping when this is over that I can take you—"

"Director Reson is on line one, General," the male voice suddenly said over the squawk box. "He doesn't sound all that happy."

"That makes two of us," the general mumbled and picked up the phone. "Milt, it's Mike Lawrence. How are you tonight?"

"I was good, and I was just about to go home," the director shot back. "What's up with the elephant? You never call this time of night unless things are nasty somewhere."

"Milt, I'm going to put you on speakerphone." After pressing the speakerphone button, he said, "Can you hear me okay?"

"Loud and clear, Mike."

"Milt," Mike continued, "I have a lifelong friend, Dr. Jack Stevens, here from my old stomping grounds in the Twin Cities, and a patient of his, Ms. Dana LaFontaine."

"Hi, folks," Milt said, "welcome to D.C."

"Thank you," Dana and Jack responded.

"I hope you're sitting down, Milt," Mike said.

"I always sit down when you call at night. Let's hear what you got."

"Well, I wouldn't believe what I'm going to tell you except that it is coming from a source I would trust with my life. The short version is that Dana and Jack have provided evidence that the NSA will be examining within the next few hours that shows that the suspected Iranian bombing at the University of Minnesota was all a smokescreen, and that the presidential election was rigged in the most elaborate technological scheme I have ever heard, so that Senator Le would win, orchestrated in part or whole by the Communist Chinese in Beijing."

For what seemed like an eternity in the room, there was complete silence on the other end of the phone. Finally, the FBI Director spoke out in a low rasping voice, "My God, Mike, are you sure?"

"I've looked at the evidence. It's credible and with the NSA now. My people are credible. It's a nightmare, but I believe it's real."

Once again there was a long pause, then the director said, "Mike, I'm going to try to conference in the attorney general. Let's not waste time explaining this twice. From what you know, should the CIA be involved, too?"

"Right now," the general replied, "I think we'd have to classify this as domestic and probably keep them out. But you and the attorney general can advise on this after we talk. I did send over to CIA and your guys two photos of the main perpetrator for further identification."

"I'll put you on hold and see if I can get him on. I'll also have an aide see if we are making progress on the ID."

"We'll be here," Mike replied as the line went silent.

"If you need to go to the bathroom, now would be the time," Mike said to Jack and Dana. "Once we're on, it's going to be a long talk. The bathrooms are right outside my office."

Dana and Jack both got up and headed for the bathroom while the general stayed in his office to listen for the phone. Jack came back first, then Dana walked back in just as the phone came back on.

"Mike, are you and your associates there?" the FBI Director asked. "I've got Attorney General Tom Wright on the line."

"We're here, Milt," the general responded. "Tom, I have with me a highly trusted lifelong friend, Dr. Jack Stevens, from Wayzata, Minnesota, and a patient of his, Ms. Dana LaFontaine. Did Milt apprise you as to the situation?"

"He did, Mike," Wright responded, "but I gotta tell you that there are only about three people who could convince me to listen to this—you and Milt being two of them. The president's the third, so this story better be rock solid."

"Tom, let me first introduce Dr. Jack Stevens, a neurologist and computer engineer I've known since high school. He is of the highest integrity, even though he moved from Chicago to Wayzata. I've forgiven him for being from Chicago."

"Okay, Mike," Wright said, "just because I'm from Chicago, you've already raised his credibility. At least until he moved to that Wayzata place. You have to get over the fact that you were raised in a state with more fish and mosquitoes than people!"

"Tom and Milt, I'm going to turn this over to Dana and Jack. I've told them to be ready to be grilled and to give you only the facts."

Dana spoke first. "Gentleman, I am an interior designer who was employed by a Mr. Chan, the CEO of ChiFone, many months ago to redesign their corporate offices in downtown Minneapolis. He—"

"He is now dead," Wright broke in. "And Dr. Stevens is accused of murder. And you shot a Chinese man in your office. What—"

"Hang on there, Tom," Mike said. "That's later in the story. Keep going, Dana."

"The first day I went to their office, Mr. Chan gave me a ChiFone to use, and over the next weeks I developed severe headaches, so I went to see Dr. Stevens."

"Dana came to see me for migraine headaches," Jack interrupted, "and we found out that the ChiFone she was using consistently on the left side caused PET scan abnormalities in her left temporal lobe, which is important in memory function. I had her stop using the phone, and the PET abnormality disappeared. I had her start again, using the cell only on the right side. The abnormality reappeared on the PET scan, but this time on the *right*. This ties into the explosion at the University of Minnesota, Director Reson."

"How so?" the FBI director asked. "We could never track the source of the C-4, because it had no taggant, but the Iranian funded the study. We followed the money trail back to Iranian banks, but the trail went cold, as you might expect. The Iranian fled, and we have not located him. We still have a task force working on it. Iran is a manufacturer of untagged C-4, so the Iranian government is clearly on the short list of perpetrators."

"What's the connection to your migraines?" Wright asked.

"Mr. Wright," Jack responded, "I'm sure Mr. Reson knows in the course of his investigation what we discovered, that the nine researchers who died in the bombing were working on a confidential project to develop a product to induce memories in the brain. It was primitive but successful."

"That's correct," Reson said. "You talked with Dr. Crandal, I suspect."

"Yes, he was a mentor of mine at the university," Jack continued. "Minntronic, the biotech company whose engineers were among those who died in the blast, also made a million circuit boards of the electromagnetic product for the Iranian, Mr. Jalili, which are unaccounted for."

"Also, correct," Reson said. "But what is the connection to ChiFone?"

"What you don't know," Jack went on, "is that Bob Dolan, a computer and electronic engineer and friend who worked for me at one time and who is now at the NSA getting our evidence confirmed, took apart Dana's ChiFone at my request and discovered that the Minntronic circuit board that was made from this project was in the cell phone."

"*That* I didn't know," Reson replied.

"Neither did Minntronic," Jack added, "until Dolan showed it to their COO. They had no idea."

"How could they get away with that?" the attorney general wondered out loud.

"If the phone meets FCC emission standards, it is passed," Jack said. "Also, we don't know if the one they submitted to the FCC for review even had a Minntronic board in it. And the FDA normally does not get involved with cell phones."

"So, Dr. Stevens, did you report this to the FDA?" Wright asked.

"Let me backtrack some, please, Mr. Wright," Jack said. "Although it caused a problem with Dana, I wanted to be sure it wasn't an idiosyncratic side effect—that is, that it was not unique to her. So I reviewed my recent patients and found ten more with exactly the same results. I did PET scans on them, which we normally don't do to evaluate migraines. All ten were using ChiFones, none were using other cell phones, and all had results that were the same as Ms. LaFontaine's. So one hundred percent correlation with ChiFones in a small group of people."

"My God!" Reson exclaimed.

"You haven't heard most of it," General Lawrence added. "Go on, Jack."

"Since I am semi-retired and have a limited practice, I called a former colleague and president at the Twin Cities Clinic of Neurology, the largest private clinic in the United States, to see if they had any similar experience. The clinic president and I talked back and forth on a couple of occasions. His entire clinic was set to review their large group of migraine patients for cases of similar stories and do PET scans where indicated. He was about to call a relative of his at the FDA unofficially from his own ChiFone, when he was killed in a hit-and-run car accident."

"That could be coincidental," Attorney General Wright said.

"I thought so at first," Jack said. "But we discovered that all the ChiFones have a GPS in them, which operates continuously, even if the phone appears to be turned off. So if ChiFone was involved, they certainly knew where to find my colleague."

"Inconclusive," Wright maintained.

"True," Dana joined in. "But when Mr. Chan found out I had a medical problem with my phone and had given it to Jack to study, they mistakenly gave me a second different ChiFone that turned out *not* to have the Minntronic board. Rather, it was encrypted, both text and audio. It had a switch on the side that could toggle it to just a normal text and audio cell phone. And Mr. Chan sent out an employee who demanded I give back the ChiFone, then he shot me in the chest and almost killed me, but not before I killed him. Chan told the Deephaven police that this person had had past psychotic breaks. But later, two Chinese men somehow were able to know that I had been discharged from the hospital the day before when even the police didn't know it, and they determined we were at Dr. Stevens' private residence as well as located his house, which has no identification on it. Then one tried to shoot Dr. Stevens in front of his house, before we were able to escape."

"Didn't you report this to the police?" Reson demanded. "It should have concerned them greatly."

"We did," Dana responded, "both when the man tried to kill me and when the two men came to Jack's house. But the police department for the latter incident was in Wayzata, and the policeman who came to Jack's house was acting strangely and tried to arrest Jack and me without a warrant. And he told us that he was extensively using his ChiFone just before he came to us."

"Mike," Jack said, looking over at the general, "the policeman was Mark Weber, from our high school class. He thought he was supposed to arrest Dana and me, but he wasn't even rational. I believe he was reacting to thoughts implanted in his mind. Then Chan, the CEO of ChiFone, tracked us to my clinic in Wayzata this morning, when Dana and I went there to pick up the data we have turned over the NSA. After tying up Dana, he personally tried to kill me. As he was choking me, he stated unequivocally that he was involved in a plan that involves thousands of second generational Chinese who are set to overthrow our government. In killing Dana and me, he said he was mopping up on problems before the Inauguration of Senator Le."

"General Lawrence," Dana said, reaching in her purse and pulling out a pistol, "I neglected to send this along with Bob to the NSA. It's a 7.65 millimeter pistol with built-in silencer and Chinese characters engraved on it. I think that is what Chan hit Jack in the back of the neck with and caused him to be temporarily quadriplegic." She handed the gun to him. "I think it is the same kind of gun that Lam, the man who tried to kill me, shot me with. The Deephaven Police have it, so you can confirm with them."

Mike held it up to his desk light and said, "Tom and Milt, this is definitely a Chinese-made assassin weapon. It looks like the latest model. They have had them for years. These are closely controlled within their government. It likely puts Chan as a member of government, a secret agent with clearance to kill."

"Oops," Dana added, pulling something else from her purse, "I also have this."

Mike took it from her and studied it for a moment. "It's a Chinese diplomatic passport, fellas. It's a real one."

"That's Chan's photo," Dana said. "But the name is 'Han' on the passport. And here is a non-diplomatic passport with the name 'Chan.' And Bob Dolan has the ChiFone we took off of Chan this morning. We thought it might have the most interesting text messages of all, but Bob hadn't been able to crack into the messages."

"Mike," Reson said, "get the passports over to the State, right away! We need to know who this guy was."

"Sure thing," Mike said and summoned his assistant.

"You two are really scaring me," Reson said. "So you killed Chan or Han this morning and let your office alarm attract the police. Why not go to the police?"

Jack shook his head and said, "Mr. Reson, from what we can tell, ChiFones were distributed freely to all the media people, and the Wayzata police chief was given a ChiFone. We have good reason to believe there are a million ChiFones with Minntronic boards out there, and I assume the Chinese have flooded the market with their own knockoffs, so there may be millions more. When we were trying to figure out who we could trust, I decided to call Mike and hope he didn't have a ChiFone. So here we are."

"You two are a dangerous couple," Reson kidded. "Give me warning if I ever really make you angry."

"But how can you jump from your evidence to fixing the presidential election?" Wright asked. "What if Chan was just trying to protect his company from your allegations? He would lose his company if that news had gone to the FDA."

"I agree that is more circumstantial right now," Jack said. "But look at the evidence. Where did all of Le's secret campaign money come from? Why all the murders with clear implications of the Chinese government being involved? How does an irrelevant politician of Chinese descent come from nowhere and get elected president instead of an extremely popular incumbent? Might a million-plus cells make a difference in strategic swing states? Why did the media that widely used ChiFones turn rabid against the president and have nothing but praise for Le? Can anyone verify that Le's parents were truly Chinese Communist dissidents who 'saw the light' and immigrated here? And did you notice that Senator Le just happens to use a ChiFone? And we didn't mention that Dana observed a room in the ChiFone offices that had a wall full of television monitors of dozens of news programs and several rows of desks with people staring at computer screens that looked as though they were monitoring reams of data."

"Highly suggestive," Wright said, "but inconclusive. We are dealing with a situation that has never happened before, at least successfully, where a foreign government deliberately and maliciously tampered with a presidential election on such a scale. We have a potential constitutional crisis that we must resolve before the Inauguration, which is only two months away. This type of investigation normally takes years."

"Tom," Reson asked the attorney general, "do we have enough to get a search warrant for ChiFone's headquarters in Minneapolis? I'm concerned that we're already losing crucial evidence."

"I think so, Milt. We certainly have tied them to attempted murder times two at least. I'll put an aide on it now."

"Gentlemen," General Lawrence said, "I think, unless you feel differently, that we've done everything we can on the phone for now. What happens with the NSA will likely either leave us where we are or give us what we need to prove the conspiracy. Mr. Dolan did not get all of the information from those phones that the NSA engineers will surely crack. The army has trained in case there is ever a massive disaster and declaration of martial law. I am going to order some exercises to be done that I'll call a drill. Should we tell President Kozdronski?"

"Too early," Wright said, "and too risky. We need to have a stack of definitive answers and irrefutable evidence. The low level staff in the White House leak like a sieve, and we can't risk that. Politically, if it comes from us, doing our jobs, discovering a coup, it will be much more believable by the American public than if the incumbent president who lost the election tries to have it nullified. We could end up with a civil war on our hands. And we've got constitutional laws to review."

"Mike and Tom," Milt said, "how about setting a meeting for 0900 tomorrow unless something boils over before?"

"Sounds like a plan," Wright said. "Milt, make sure the NSA stays in that lab until they've cracked every seam. We need a gusher."

An aide came into General Lawrence's office.

"Sir, I have an urgent message from CIA. They said interrupt you, if necessary."

"Thank you," Mike said and read the paper. "CIA had identified Chan as indeed being known as 'Han' in China. They believe him to be the head of Chinese Intelligence in the United States. So, even more is falling into place. They said they were never able to determine where he might be in the U.S. He came through San Francisco on his diplomatic passport and disappeared."

"If I might make a final comment," Dana interjected, "everyone might want to figure out how many ChiFones are in each of your agencies as well as other parts of government."

"Phew! That's a good idea, Ms. LaFontaine," Milt said. "I'll put a task force on it. Who knows what crap they might sending out right now?"

"We'll talk to you tomorrow," Mike said and hung up the phone, then he pushed his chair back and leaned way back and crossed his long arms. "Well, Dana and Jack, I got a real bad feeling about all this. I think the shit's going to hit the fan, and it's going to get ugly."

41

Democracy is a very bad form
of government; but for all the others.

Winston Churchill

CHAPTER 41

I T WAS EARLY MORNING on December 18, the first Monday after the second Wednesday in this calendar year—the day upon which in each state capital the electors of the Electoral College would meet to vote. A Department of Justice jet, accompanied by two Air Force fighter jets, was on its way to Sacramento, California, where the state's electors would meet. The Attorney General of the United States, Thomas Wright, was about to outline the agenda with those onboard the plane.

Wright looked at those seated on the jet. "Let me just go over what we are doing today. Election Day is the first Tuesday after the first Monday in November in even years, and in those years during which we elect a president, it serves to select the electors who will meet today in each state capital. Today is the day set by the United States Constitution on which the Electoral College meets every four years. Constitutionally, this is when the election of the president and vice president really takes place. The president then will be inaugurated on January 20."

"Tom, I know it's an old question, but do you think this is a fair system?" Dana asked. Over the past weeks, she had gotten on a first-name basis with the attorney general.

"Dana," Tom replied, "my role is to enforce the law, not to try to decide its fairness. What I can say is that it has worked well for over two hundred years. Article Two of the Constitution defines this. It was originally a compromise between large and small states, and one could make the same argument today. Each state gets the same number of electors as it has U.S. senators and representatives, and more recently D.C. gets electors as well. The Constitution *never* intended for a direct, popular election of the president."

"You could argue about fairness all day," Jack said. "I think that in order to cast a ballot, voters should have some minimal competency to read, write, and understand the issues. Immigrants who want to become citizens are required to know much more than the average voter. Is that fair?"

"The questions are legion," Tom agreed. "But the voting process is as intended. That is, as an indirect election, really just another form of representative democracy. We don't have a direct democracy. Rather, we elect representatives to pass laws. In any event, the largest, most powerful democracy in the history of the world changes or retains its leadership every four years without bloodshed or revolutions. On that basis, I'd say it works very well."

"Tom," Jack said, "I realize you want to avoid the constitutional crisis that could happen if Le is elected, but why did you choose California today?"

"Your old buddy Mike said I should so we could fly here in the wee hours from D.C.," Tom joked. "He wanted to see if a semi-retired doctor really gets up as early as he always claimed."

"Did I tell you that his mother—"

"Get on with the agenda, Tom," Mike broke in, "or I may give the brain doctor a migraine of his own. So why California?"

"How electors are chosen is decided by each state, not by the federal government," Tom explained. "Most states require their electors to vote as a block, a 'winner-gets-all' vote; other states' electors vote proportionately, depending on each candidate's popular vote. However, prosecution of electors who do not vote according to their selection process are in violation of state, not federal, law, and it is up to the *attorney general of a given state* to decide whether to prosecute. In this case, the California attorney general, Arnold Yu, is a law school classmate of mine, and he is as honest as they get. This will be key, because we don't want the California electors intimidated by the threat of prosecution for voting their consciences. Although it may be constitutionally legal by each state to prosecute those who vote different than the general election, I'm not sure that was ever intended by the Constitution. California also has a total of fifty-five electors, but we don't need all of them to decide the outcome of the election. Also, California has a high cell phone usage and was an area with a great deal of ChiFone penetration, so I suspect your stories will resonate with them. Arnold had his staff collect all the ChiFones a few weeks ago from the Electors, telling them they may be a health hazard. And he cleaned them out of the State of California offices. So, if Jack's conclusions are correct as well as Dana's experience, their thinking will be returning to normal."

"Also, we found six states with secretaries of state who were part of the conspiracy," FBI Director Reson added. "Their states all went for Le, but we don't want to arrest them before the electors vote. It could look really bad if we arrested one. We are a bit on the edge with what we are going to be doing here. In California, we looked closely at the secretary of state, and he does not appear to have any ties to the Chinese conspiracy. So we thought we'd let those other states go and concentrate here. There are twenty California electoral votes separating Le from Kozdronski. If we pick up ten here, it's a tie, since Le would have gotten all California's electoral votes—this is a "winner-take-all" state. So even if a candidate lost in all the congressional districts except one, but won the popular vote overall, none of those districts would count toward selecting electors. It is the state as a whole. The big district/small district debate is like the large state/small state debate two hundred years ago. So if we pick up only eleven electors here, assuming the voting of the other states as predicted, President Kozdronski will win by two electoral votes. And we have agents waiting to arrest the secretaries of state who are coconspirators after the vote today."

When the jet from the Department of Justice landed in Sacramento, the U.S. attorney general deplaned first, followed by Dana, Jack, and Bob, and got into an armored Suburban. They were accompanied by an FBI antiterrorist task force in two Suburbans, one ahead and one behind. When they reached the building where the electors would meet, they found that the street had been cordoned off by Sacramento police. FBI sharpshooters were on that building and the surrounding buildings. Two army helicopters flew overhead. The FBI agents in kevlar jackets, with M16s, accompanied the group. Some secured the building from outside and others from inside.

They entered the room where the California electors were meeting. None of the California electors or any of the electors elsewhere in the United States knew what had happened or what was about to happen. However, in every state capital and in D.C., the electoral meetings were heavily guarded by both the local police and FBI. U.S. Marshals would guard the votes until inauguration.

The California Secretary of State convened the meeting, greeting everyone, then he reviewed the procedure for the election. But before beginning the procedure, he announced that there would be an informational session first. He then introduced the Attorney General of the United States, Thomas Wright, which sent a sharp ripple through the fifty-five electors.

Wright stepped to the podium and said, "I realize our presence this morning is a bit disconcerting for you as electors. We are here to announce that over the past six weeks the FBI has conducted an intense emergency investigation of the election process and discovered hard evidence of extensive election fraud. While our investigation began with what we considered a terrorist explosion at the University of Minnesota thought to be sponsored by the Iranians, through the heroic efforts of two civilians with us today, Ms. Dana LaFontaine and Dr. Jack Stevens, we have uncovered a massive conspiracy by the Communist Chinese to overthrow the presidency of the United States. Before the Director of the FBI explains what his agents have uncovered, both Ms. LaFontaine and Dr. Stevens will explain their roles."

Dana came forward, shook the attorney general's hand, then took her place at the podium. "Electors, I have never been active in politics other than to cast my vote. Several months ago I was hired to do interior design work at the corporate office for Chi-Fone in downtown Minneapolis. The company CEO, a Mr. Chan, whom the FBI has now concluded was really a man named 'Han,' the head of Chinese Intelligence for the United States, provided me with a ChiFone to use. Soon thereafter I developed migraine headaches, and after extensive consulting with Dr. Stevens, who is a neurologist, he found abnormalities in my brain directly caused by advanced technology in the ChiFone and consistent with false memories and emotions planted magnetically into my brain. When Mr. Chan found out that I was the source of the medical investigation and I was mistakenly given a second ChiFone with special encrypted capabilities, a Chinese operative was sent to my office to retrieve the phone and kill me. I was shot in the chest, but survived as you can see, and I was able to shoot and kill the assassin. Dr. Stevens will explain further."

Dana sat down, and Jack stepped up to the podium. "Good morning, I am Dr. Jack Stevens. Ms. LaFontaine was the first of eleven of my patients who used ChiFones that caused abnormalities in their brains shown on PET scanning and whose thoughts were manipulated by Chinese spies to vote for Senator Le. Researchers at the University of Minnesota participated in what they thought was a privately funded study by an Iranian man to help in improving brain function and learning. Mr. Jalili was the unwitting accomplice of the Chinese, who framed him for the explosion at the University of Minnesota, and then killed him. The primitive research was used in circuit boards implanted in ChiFones, which caused the abnormalities I discovered. The second ChiFone Ms. LaFontaine procured was a special type that had the ability to encrypt all of its telephone calls and text messaging and was designed only for those involved in the conspiracy. The NSA used that phone to reveal the scope and audacity of the conspiracy.

"Beginning in the 1950s, as a part of a long-range strategy, the Chinese government planted thousands of secret agents here in the United States as 'moles' to be activated at a future time. Senator Le's family never in reality renounced Communist China and was among those moles. Senator Le was groomed by his family to integrate into American society and enter government, as were others, such as Mr. Chan. Because of the booming African trade and resultant loss of manufacturing and recession in China, the Communist Chinese felt they must speed up the process. However, they needed American technology and medical researchers to develop their modern 'brainwashing'—something they had done in other, much less sophisticated manners for many years. Thus they equipped the ChiFone with the test circuitry developed for good, but now twisted to evil. They influenced voters, delegates to Senator Le's party convention, police, key media figures, and other officials, most of whom were strategically targeted in advance by the Chinese to receive free ChiFones. Right now, they have at least a million cell phones in use, all equipped to alter thoughts, many in the hands of average civilians, such as Ms. LaFontaine. So, in Ms. LaFontaine's case, she personally experienced a change in her thinking, such that she was going to vote for Senator Le instead of President Kozdronski. Once she stopped using the ChiFone, she shifted back to her normal thinking and would have voted for President Kozdronski."

Jack sat back down, and Thomas Wright took the podium again. "Thank you, Ms. LaFontaine and Dr. Stevens. Ladies and gentlemen, you are here at a historic moment in the history of the United States. What you elect to do here will change the future of the United States and the world. The FBI and Department of Justice have voluminous information indicating deliberate, widespread, illegal interference by the Chinese government to brainwash Americans to vote for Senator Le. We have investigated the voting for President Kozdronski and found no such illegal activities. We believe California was more influenced because of the high cell phone and ChiFone use. How many of you had ChiFones before Attorney General Yu collected them?"

A large number of electors raised their hands.

"Based on various data analysis," Wright continued, "we have concluded that but for the Chinese government's illegal interference, President Kozdronski would have won in a landslide. You have the power to correct a great wrong. Let me get Director Reson up here to outline some of the data that the FBI has collected."

Director Reson stepped to the podium and said, "We are still de-encrypting the data. But here is a summary of what we have so far." He then clicked on a Power Point page on a big screen behind him. "This shows the overall plan downloaded from the computer of Mr. Chan, the CEO of ChiFone. It shows the detailed plan for the election overthrow of the United States presidency by illegal means that dates back before the nominating conventions. This next document," he changed the Power Point page, "shows plans detailing the placement of 'deep cover' Chinese agents and families whose missions were to be 'sleepers' and act like normal American citizens over the past fifty years. They were strategically assigned to become positioned in government—executive, legislative, and judicial branches—as well as military, media, and industry, so together they would have broad potential power focused on a single goal. Many sleepers were activated in the nomination and election of Senator Le. Many more were to be activated when Le became president. One of them was the military officer whom Le selected to carry the 'nuclear football' at the president's side at all times. As you know, the 'football' is the transmission case to our nuclear missile locations that communicates the codes to enable launch."

There was a collective stir in the audience.

"It gets worse in terms of the breadth and depth of the conspiracy," the director continued. "The good news is that by the braveness and perseverance of Ms. LaFontaine and Dr. Stevens, we uncovered and destroyed this plot in time. What's more, the data shows the identity of every Chinese spy, and there are thousands, in the United States. We have arrested most of them and will arrest the remainder soon. When we are done, we will have cleansed the United States of virtually all Chinese spies by imprisonment, execution, or deportation. It will take the Chinese spy network decades to reassemble. One particularly nefarious twist is that there were also a number of Americans who were recruited by the Chinese and joined the conspiracy to be part of what the Chinese termed the New American Order. These unscrupulous men and women will be prosecuted as traitors, I promise you. They are perhaps the most disgusting of the lot. Let me turn the podium back to Attorney General Wright."

Wright stepped up again to the podium. "Electors," he said, "I can't make you do what I think is the correct action today. However, it is my strong belief that if the framers of the Constitution were here today, they would point out that this situation is one that supports an Electoral College. And my interpretation of the Constitution is that you are free to vote however you wish, and that that was the intent when it was written. Now, let me turn this meeting back to the Attorney General of California, Mr. Arnold Yu."

Yu stood up and came to the podium. "I am of Chinese descent and proud of my heritage. The Chinese are wonderful people, but the Communist Party is a ruthless dictatorship. Its puppet, Senator Le, is a disgrace to his heritage. I am here to tell you that the Attorney General's Office of California will not prosecute anyone here regardless of how you vote. So you are not bound by any state law governing electors as far as this office is concerned. The governor, who is ill and cannot attend, supports this. I will now pass out a letter from him as well as one from my office, detailing this, for each of you to keep."

Thomas Wright took over the podium once more. "Those of us who are not electors will leave you here. If there are any questions or clarifications, we will be in an adjoining room. I will turn the meeting over to the California Secretary of State."

Jack, Dana, Bob, Tom, Milt, Arnold, and Mike left the room.

"Tom and Arnold," Mike asked, "how long do you think they will take?"

"Hard to say, Mike," Tom replied, and Arnold nodded. "This is a first, for sure. Hopefully, a last! If we have made our case well, it should not take too long."

It didn't. About thirty minutes after, the California Secretary of State came out the door. "It's over, everyone! All the electors but one voted for President Kozdronski. I have talked to the secretaries of state throughout the country. Because of our vote, President Kozdronski has won the election. At least we will firmly believe he did anyway. Never in the history of America has the decision of the Electoral College been challenged."

"There is always one odd ball," said Mike. "No one tried to kill him for his dissention. Maybe that's why America is great!"

What no one knew was that that particular elector had a Chi-Fone, but also an assumed name. His ChiFone was encrypted, but it was such that it never showed up on the ChiFone network in a traceable manner. A Cal Tech Ph.D. in computer and electrical engineering who worked in Silicon Valley, he had been recruited by the Chinese to manufacture more boards if Minntronic fell through or they had trouble importing the boards from China and they needed a second source in America. He was never called on for that, but he had all the circuit diagrams and plans and knew well how to redesign it for other devices. He just needed more time, but he was a patient man and was not part of Chan's group. He was so deep-cover that he reported only to the Director of the Second Bureau of the Ministry of State Security in Beijing. The Director was a careful man who always had a backup plan. *And some backup plans you don't share with others.*

42

An honest politician is one who,
when he is bought, will stay bought.

Simon Cameron

CHAPTER 42

THE MASS ARREST of conspirators was elaborately choreographed. Although their messages were heavily encrypted, the Chinese never anticipated an intrusion into their offices without enough warning to destroy the data. It began with placing listening devices in and around ChiFone's IDS offices. ChiFone's landlines, including those used for fax and voice encryption, were wiretapped.

The evening cleaning crew at ChiFones was replaced by FBI and NSA agents, who also planted miniature cameras. Some areas were locked and secured by the Chinese. The federal agents made short work of that, but then left those areas with the appearance of being untouched.

One great bonus of Le's win on election day was that, believing they had achieved victory and that their communications were secure, the Chinese government literally flooded ChiFone with voice and data communication. At times there was so much, it had to be queued. And ChiFone reciprocated with vast communications back.

With all the listening and watching devices in place, it was better than could ever have been imagined. The NSA computers quietly processed all the data, and the FBI prepared their cases; the Attorney General's team prepared warrants. It would provide great training for years in the future for agents.

Not only did the FBI gather the names of all the coconspirators, some of whom were prominent politicians, military officers, State and Defense Department officials, and business executives woven throughout society, but also the names and locations of virtually all the thousands of Chinese intelligence agents in America. There were so many that it became a significant tactical problem as to how to arrest them all simultaneously, so as not to tip off the others before they were arrested.

Finally, after gathering so much data that further listening appeared unnecessary and redundant, the FBI obtained a search warrant and raided the ChiFone's IDS Headquarters. A few of the Chinese agents, including Mr. Hai, made the mistake of pulling their guns and attempting to escape. In Hai's case, he reached for his handgun, but never got it from his belt. A single spot-on shot meant he would fly back to Beijing in the cargo hold of an airplane. The FBI had all the data they needed from their surveillance and only needed to seize the physical evidence, particularly the computers, but also the mother-load communication voice and text encrypter. The conspirators would be blocked by diplomatic immunity from testifying, despite their heinous activities.

The receptionist was taken into custody for questioning and was one of the few workers who was not involved. In a funny footnote, she tried to call 911, thinking the FBI was a criminal gang. Agents had disabled all incoming and outgoing landlines to ChiFone's offices as well as jamming the cell frequencies in the local area.

Once the entire office was secure, the NSA agents entered. Unbeknownst to Hai, the NSA had disabled the electromagnetic feature in the phones by changing one line of software in ChiFone's computer. This was undetectable by the Chinese. They had observed how Hai and his ChiFone conspirators had texted encrypted messages and shut it down so it couldn't be used to tip-off the conspirators at the very end.

The FBI and NSA breathed a collective sigh of relief that there was no indication of their ranks being infiltrated by moles. It was true that their systems of screening had worked, but only partly true. The Chinese's primary method was to work from the top down. For instance, if they could get the "right" person to be the FBI Director, he or she could pull in cronies. However, neither the FBI nor NSA proved vulnerable at the top, so the Chinese focused on infiltrating other areas and getting Le elected.

When the NSA asked the FBI if they'd like the conspirators to come in voluntarily to be arrested, the FBI did not find it humorous until the NSA said they could actually pull it off *and all at once.* They discovered that the conspirators had a series of wheel-type configurations, basically a spoke and hub for each conspiratorial cell, with the hub being in a large central city. So utilizing the Chinese own system in Minneapolis through ChiFones, the NSA sent out a message for members of each cell to come to their central city for an urgent meeting. The cells had had meetings at specific locations at times before. Now that their main conspirator, Senator Le, had won, they knew it was time to activate the next stage of the plan. They would make decisions as to who each cell felt would be a candidate for various federal appointments or to be moved up the ladder in government departments.

So in each central city, the conspirators came into a designated location, voluntarily. Those whom the FBI knew were high up in the local cell and might have been too suspicious were rounded up ahead of time. The FBI thought a nice touch would be to celebrate with champagne. So as each spy or traitor came into locations used previously, they were give a flute of champagne and sat down in comfort, surrounded by familiar faces. It was hard for some of the FBI agents to resist laughing.

The FBI had a large number of patriotic Americans of Chinese descent in its ranks. They were assigned the rewarding task of impersonating some higher members, whose names were known to the rank and file conspirators, but whose faces had never been seen before. It was, it seemed, a celebration in part, so why shouldn't some of the higher-ups come to see them?

Each conspirator was asked upon arrival to turn in his or her ChiFone in trade for one the FBI named the "ChiFone II" that they were told was more secure. They were assured that any of their saved text messages would be downloaded into their new phones, but that the phone would not be activated until an hour after the meeting. This provided the NSA and FBI a great deal more of stored evidence to work on.

The loyal Chinese-American FBI agents were also given the honor of doing the actual arrestings. Each conspirator was brought into an adjoining room with the excuse that they were to be individually honored and interviewed as to their hopes for the New Order in America. In each case, they were charged, read their rights, and brought out another door to be put in a series of unmarked vans to local military bases for safekeeping.

Although the Chinese Communist spies would eventually be freed on diplomatic immunity, any who were American citizens had no such immunity and were, in fact, guilty of treason, punishable by death.

While the conspirators were out of their houses and being arrested, other FBI agents in harmony with local law enforcement officers simultaneously exercised search warrants of their houses and businesses. It was a sweep made in heaven and beyond any bust the FBI had ever made in its storied history.

The honor of the arrest of Senator Le was reserved for David Yang, the Special Agent in charge of the San Francisco office. Yang's parents had, in fact, fled China in the 1950s after the communist takeover, nearly being killed in the escape, and were fiercely loyal American citizens. Yang took particular delight in knocking on Le's door, surrounded by other agents who were spread out around Le's house. The Secret Service detail had stood down.

Le himself answered, somewhat surprised, actually expecting it to be someone from the Secret Service. "May I help you?"

"Senator Le, I am FBI Special Agent David Yang, and I have a warrant for your arrest."

"You can't arrest a U.S. senator!" Le answered tersely. "I have immunity under the arrest clause of the United States Constitution."

"We cannot for civil crimes, but we can for treason and being a conspirator to terrorist acts, including mass murder, Senator," Yang said without a hint of acquiescing. "Perhaps you're also familiar with Article One, Section six, Clause one of the Constitution? Please submit peacefully and put your hands out while I handcuff you." He then started to read the senator his rights.

"I am the President-elect of the United States!" Le threatened. "It is you who will be arrested for treason. I will personally punish you and your family for the rest of your lives."

"You won the election illegally," Yang countered. "You will never see the Oval Office from the inside. Presidents can't be traitors either."

"Protect me!" Le shouted to his Secret Service agents.

"Sir," the head Secret Service agent of the scene said, "we do not protect those who soil the office of the president; we help arrest them. We in the detail came to the conclusion some time ago that you were a fraud."

"One last chance to come peacefully, Senator," Yang said. He normally would have let his junior agent do that, but in this case, he reserved the cuffing for himself, as Le finally submitted, and Yang finished reading him his rights. Then Yang walked Le to the unmarked FBI car.

Le said, "Yang, you are a traitor to your race and ancestors. I was only here to spread to these ignorant capitalists the peace, harmony, and wisdom of our culture and political system! My colleagues will save me from your treachery."

Yang replied, "I am proud to be of Chinese ancestry. My parents made a decision before I was born to escape the tyranny of your communist dictatorship, which has set back the progress of China a hundred years. I am an American and proud to be so. I thank God for the day I was born in the United States rather than live under the rule of killer scum like you.

"In addition to the legal rights I read to you," Yang continued, "I should also inform you that as a traitor and terrorist who participated as a conspirator in mass murder, should you try to escape I have been empowered to shoot and kill you. And by the way, I wouldn't hold my breath waiting for your coconspirators to help you. They're already in custody."

"You are all making the biggest mistakes of your lives," Le screamed at all the agents.

"Sir," Yang replied, "I cannot tell you, since I am a professional, that I would wish they had public beheadings in the United States. I can tell you that I take pleasure as an American to be able to arrest you and bring you to justice. By the way, your parents have been arrested as well. But there won't be visiting privileges for a long time. Enjoy the ride. You also won't be seeing your capitalist private jet or limo ever again."

43

*We must learn to live together as brothers
or perish together as fools.*

Martin Luther King Jr.

CHAPTER 43

JACK AND DANA were relaxed on the government jet as it climbed to its cruising altitude. The plane was headed for D.C., but with a stop in Minneapolis.

Tom Wright and Milt Reson were on the secure phones on the jet. Wright motioned to Jack while Milt did the same to Dana for each to take a phone.

"It's the president," Tom said.

"Dr. Stevens and Ms. LaFontaine," President Kozdronski said, "I want to thank you on behalf of the United States of America. You both have done truly outstanding deeds in preventing a massive conspiracy in our history. It is difficult to think of two people who on their own have made such a difference in the history of this great Republic."

"Thank you, Mr. President," they both said together.

"I have been following your exploits," Kozdronski went on, "but I needed to keep my distance until the Electoral College had voted. I have conferred with the leaders of both houses of Congress. I would like you both to come to Washington in January, as my guests, to stay in the White House and then be awarded the Presidential Medal of Freedom, the highest honor I can bestow. Later that day Congress will award you with the Congressional Gold Medal, Congress's highest civilian award. There are very few individuals who have received both honors. I can think of no two people who deserve it more. Also, Mrs. Kozdronski and I would like to invite you to stay on and be our personal guests at the activities following the Inauguration of my second term. May we count on you both being there?"

After a bit of hesitation from the shock, Jack said as Dana nodded, "Ms. LaFontaine has indicated she would, and I think I can speak for both of us in saying we wouldn't miss it for the world!"

"Ms. LaFontaine, Mrs. Kozdronski and I have decided to redecorate the White House for our second term. We have seen some of your work, and we are wondering if you would consider being our interior designer?"

"It would be my privilege, Mr. President," Dana replied. "I won't be finishing my work at ChiFones, so I'm available."

President Kozdronski laughed and said, "Dr. Stevens, Director Reson will be talking to you about an idea I had regarding something else you might do to help us here in Washington."

"I look forward to talking to him about it," Jack said.

"Mrs. Kozdronski and I have a lot we'd like to hear more in depth about what happened to you the last several months. Is there anything I can do for either of you?"

"No, but thank you, Mr. President," Dana said. "I think we both just need a rest!"

"Well, get rested up the next few weeks. The story is starting to break, and I suspect you will both be very busy with the media for some time. I have asked the Secret Service to extend some coverage to you for privacy and protection. Oh, and I understand that you both have dogs," Kozdronski went on. "Bring them along. Mrs. Kozdronski and I love dogs!"

"Thank you, Mr. President," Dana and Jack said simultaneously.

"I'm looking forward to your visit when we can talk more. In the meantime, if you need anything, do call. As you might imagine, I have a few things that need my immediate attention both nationally and internationally. Good-bye for now." That said, the president hung up.

FBI Director Reson looked at Jack and Dana. "How are the two of you feeling?"

"Exhausted and beat up, but still upright and on the correct side of the ground," Jack said.

"Tired, hungry, and I miss my dog," Dana added.

Reson said, "After you rest up, Dr. Stevens, we could still use some more help from you consulting on the case. We took care of the crisis, but there will be years of digging through all the information we gathered. We would put you on a consultant basis consistent with what you are making in your practice. Also, I have some other cases where your input would be helpful. What do you think?"

"Wow! What do I think? I'm honored by the offer. I need a rest, some good comfort food, sun, and to get my dog and some normalcy back in my life. But I'm happy to help where I can. I'd like some time to think about it, though, and see how it would affect my daughters and my patients and so on."

"Jack," Reson went on, "here is my card with my direct telephone number and personal email address. I'd like to sit down with you when you come to Washington to see President Kozdronski. I think there are several invaluable ways you could continue to help the country. Given the power of this electromagnetic circuitry, we have to expand the power of the FDA. We will need someone new to run the FDA who has experience in this. You, of course, have the perfect training."

Reson turned to Dana and said, "Here is the same card I gave Jack. If you ever need anything at all, please call. Your country owes you and Jack a tremendous amount—more than any of us can fully imagine, I suspect." Then Reson went forward to talk to Wright.

Jack and Dana took the cards and flopped back into their seats.

"So, Jack," Dana said, "what are you planning to do in the next few weeks?"

"I'm still a bit hoarse and sore in the throat. Got a bit of a stiff neck. I'd like to start with a good night's sleep and some good food and nobody bugging me."

"Do you really think it's over? Are we going to be pursued still by the Chinese agents?"

"Can't rule it out," Jack said, talking like a neurologist. "But why would they bother us, other than simply for revenge. Our involvement is pretty much over. The FBI and NSA have all the data. I think this backfired so badly for the Chinese that they will be busy for years trying to reassemble their spy network here. And dealing with the worldwide political fallout of what they tried to do—that alone should keep them out of our hair. Director Reson said that this was the biggest spy roundup in America's history. And they have arrested some senators and representatives, judges, and others who are not of Chinese heritage, but rather opportunists who wanted to profit from the New Order. So, overall, a great day for America."

"It will be good to see Remy," Dana stated as she looked at her non-ChiFone cellular with Remy's digital photograph on the start-up screen. "Aren't you hungry, Jack. I'm starving. We haven't exactly had a lot of food the last few weeks."

"Yeah, I'm hungry all right," Jack said. "What do you like?"

"I feel like some Mexican. Do you know a good place?"

"I do. Best Mexican I've ever had!"

"Is it far?" Dana inquired.

"Depends on how you travel. Not far if you fly."

"I'm tired of flying and fleeing, Jack!"

"It's a four-hour flight to Puerto Vallarta. I have a condo on the beach with four bedrooms. I usually rent it out, but it's vacant now. The media and Chinese won't be able to find us. I think some heat might help my aches. It's warmer there than Minnesota in December!"

"That's what I hear," Dana continued.

"There are twenty great restaurants within walking distance of the condo. You'll get tired of eating before you run out of restaurants."

"I don't want to get fat before the Inauguration. I have nice clothes I need to fit into!" Dana exclaimed.

"As a medical doctor, let me assure you that Mexican food, if eaten in a Mexican restaurant in Mexico, has only one calorie per serving."

"I love guacamole, but it just beelines to my hips."

"If you wash it down with multiple margaritas, you won't notice it," Jack claimed.

"I'd miss my dog," Dana protested.

"I used to bring Mac, so bring Remy."

"You are making it hard to say no!"

"I'm trying."

"I don't have any clothes for Mexico."

"Like they don't have any stores there? If you'd rather, Dana, I could rent the condo below mine so you could have some extra space and privacy. My daughters have been quite worried and want to fly down too to be with me. They tend to dote on me a bit. What do you think?"

"If I go, will you finally tell me the story about the man with the Coke bottle?"

Afterword

★ ★ ★ ★ ★

AS A BOY, I was always "inventing" things. My boyhood dream was to take my preteen "inventions" and start an engineering company that designed and manufactured them. One of my fascinations was with the human brain, even though I made it clear during my career planning class at Wayzata High School that I *never* wanted to be a medical doctor.

In college, as an electrical engineering student, I looked at the brain as a biologic binary, i.e., pseudo-digital computer, and wrote a paper about the analogies for an engineering class. As a senior in engineering school, I decided to go to medical school so I could invent and manufacture biomedical devices. At the time, there was no school that I knew that offered biomedical engineering, and one of my engineering professors, Gerry Timm, Ph.D., himself a biomedical inventor and entrepreneur, gave me several reasons to apply.

This came as a surprise to my fiancée, who was helping me prepare for the Law School Admission Test (LSAT). She and I had been very active in local and national politics, and together we planned to save the world through politics (it was the 1960s). Law school seemed the proper road to politics. However, we found that saving the world was harder than we first thought and not all the world wanted to be saved, thank you anyway. So we thought we might save just a bit of the world by inventing biomedical devices to help people. We realized we could help more people inventing medical devices than we could in several lifetimes as a practicing M.D. Practicing medicine, as opposed to going to medical school, was another something I thought I would never do. Since then, I have now probably seen over 100,000 new and follow-up patients over the past thirty years. Things change.

When I applied for medical school, I had never taken a biology or quantitative analysis or organic chemistry course in my life. The Associate Dean of the Medical School at the University of Minnesota, Dr. Al Sullivan, thought that although few engineers attend medical school, they tended to do well with the coursework. However, they had never let anyone into it without those courses, so reluctantly I pithed frogs and did QA and O-Chem.

I found neurology to be every bit as fascinating as I had dreamed as a boy. The brain, as human organs go, is truly the last great unexplored territory. The brain circuitry emits electromagnetic waves. Electroencephalograms (EEGs) look at the data emitted electrically. Magnetoencephalograms (MEGs) look at the data emitted magnetically. Theoretically, EEG and MEG should carry the same information. However, there are different transmission characteristics from various brain structures through the skull, and MEG tends to be a weaker signal. This then may alter some of the information from deep brain nuclei versus neocortex. The EEG is also much easier to record. MEG requires more difficult recording tools but the signal may have different and potentially important information. There is a great deal of information—probably the majority—that has never been able to be used from either EEG or MEG.

For instance, what happens if you reverse the electromagnetic field? *Electrical stimulation* is used clinically for electroshock therapy (EST), also called electroconvulsive therapy (ECT). Although not used so much anymore, EST in the past was of great help for severe depression that was resistant to other forms of treatment. *Magnetic stimulation* of brain has been used to measure the speed of impulses inside the brain. Magnetic Resonance Imaging (MRI) actually involves low level magnetic stimulation to perform its testing. Magnetic stimulation may be safer fundamentally than electrical stimulation.

When I cofounded CNS, Inc. with another neurologist, before CNS developed the Breathe Right® Nasal Strips, our first patents were involved in brain monitoring during surgeries, analysis of brain processing as well as monitoring in ICUs and sleep labs. One night when we were working late and a bit tired, I suggested to our chief engineer that we could use *mu rhythms*, which had to do with a certain frequency spectrum in the motor strips of the brain, to control movements. We developed a program based on Pac-Man, popular in those days, which was moved left and right *by just thinking about squeezing* (but not actually squeezing) either the left or right hands. The change in brain frequencies would be sensed by the electrodes on my head, and I could move the Pac-Man left or right in response to brain frequency shifts. By combining sides or measuring certain other rhythms, I could stop the Pac-Man, move it forward or backward.

With this novel, I combine some fiction with fact and what I think could be some future brain devices and research. I hope you enjoyed reading it as much as I had writing it.

COMING IN LATE 2010

Book #2 in the Dr. Jack Stevens Novels.

Check it out at www.GreekFlu.com.

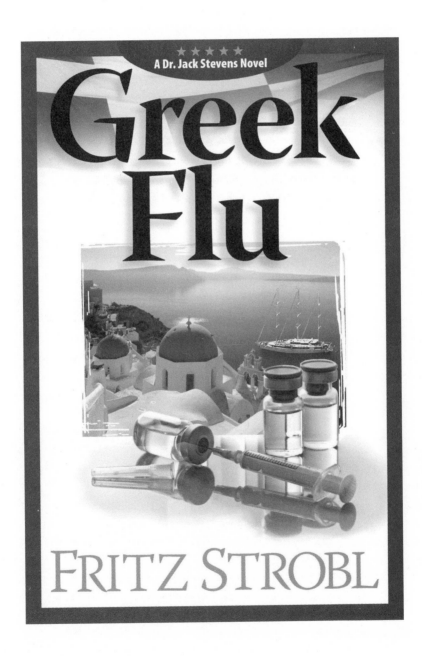

* * * * *

While Dr. Jack Stevens and Dana LaFontaine are in
Washington receiving the Presidential Medal of Freedom for
their past heroic actions for America, a deadly H1N1 virus that
causes a fatal brain infection is spreading through Greece at
an unusual time for influenza. Why are mysterious messages
coming out of the Cyclades Islands? And why are investigating
American agents in Greece being murdered?

When the president asks Jack and Dana to go to Greece to
help, can they find an answer in time and get home safely? And
can the U.S. get enough vaccine made to prevent a pandemic in
America despite the shutdown of its main vaccine producer?
In this thrilling second book in the Jack Stevens series,
Jack is asked to try to find answers before it's too late.

* * * * *

1

An association of men who will not quarrel with one another is a thing which has never yet existed, from the greatest confederacy of nations down to a town meeting or a vestry.

Thomas Jefferson

CHAPTER 1

JOHN DANIELS stood on the foredeck of the cruise ship, *The Kiklades*, looking across the shimmering blue water at the sacred Greek island of Delos, located in the center of the roughly circular ring of Mediterranean islands called the Cyclades, just west of Mykonos. An especially important archeological island, no one was allowed to stay there overnight except the guards and the current group of archaeologists who were working there. Inhabited since around 3000 B.C., it has priceless ruins and was the mythological birthplace to the ancient Greek god Apollo and his sister-goddess, Artemis.

The native Greek skipper, Yiannis Kostopoulos, stared at Daniels from the bridge and said to his first mate, "Who do you think he is? Some kind of VIP?"

"I have no idea," the first mate responded, barely looking up from his charts. "He's very quiet, that's for sure. He's either got a lot of money or he's a friend of the family who owns the Franklin Expeditions group. All I know is I took the call from the Expedition headquarters in Washington, D.C., stating to make room for Daniels and give him everything he wanted."

"He's one of the Lucky Sperm Club, no doubt," Yiannis replied with a smile. "Perhaps he needs a trip because he's stressed out trying to figure out if he should serve Tanqueray or Bombay Sapphire gin with the gin and tonics at his next cocktail party."

The first mate laughed and said, "Lucky Spermer or not, I don't really care, as long as the Expedition group keeps paying their bills. Eight ten-day sightseeing trips a year is a breeze, especially at the rates they pay."

"Sort of odd, though, that's he's alone. Most of these guys bring their trophy wives, sometimes the original issue, especially if she's the one with the money. Daniels brought no TWIT or TWIP."

"No what?"

"I just came up with it," Yiannis explained, noticing that Daniels had turned and was headed their way. "A TWIT is a Trophy Wife in Training who hasn't gotten her wedding ring but is working on it. A TWIP is a Trophy Wife in Practice who has the golden ring."

"I prefer the TWITS. They keep their men preoccupied in their cabins and off the decks. Cuts down on our work."

"*Kalimera*, Captain," Daniels said as he walked past the bridge and stopped. "Or is it *kalispera,* since it is toward evening?"

"*Kalispera,* Mr. Daniels," the captain answered with a nod. "You have been working on your Greek."

"Just a bit," Daniels replied. "Are there any messages? The email and cell and satellite phone don't seem to work in this bay."

"Mr. Daniels, I am afraid that the signals are too weak today. We are in between several islands, but the main problem is the remnants of the storm yesterday have done something with the satellite and cell communications. Your email goes through our satellite feed. I can offer you our radio, of course, but you are concerned with confidentiality, right?"

"That's right, I am, and I can wait, Captain. When do we weigh anchor and head for Mykonos?"

"Not until this evening. We have planned for a traditional Greek meal here for you while we are between these islands and safe from the winds."

"That sounds wonderful. Could someone let me know when you get a signal?"

"Of course, Mr. Daniels. I am sorry for the inconvenience."

"Certainly not your fault, Captain."

"Nonetheless, I am sorry."

"Your service has been sterling," Daniels added. "And the tour has been spectacular, despite the storm. I've never seen the Cyclades before, much less Greece."

"So glad to have you. The best is yet to come," Yiannis replied, smiling at his first mate.

Daniels had already been to Sifnos and then Milos, where the famous statue of Aphrodite, the "Venus de Milo," had been since 130 B.C., abandoned, then discovered by a peasant in 1820 and taken to the Louvre Museum in Paris. Widely renowned for the mystery of her missing arms, she is the epitome of graceful female beauty, made from marble from the nearby island of Paros.

Santorini, the island of Plato's Atlantis speculation, was Daniels' favorite, but he was interested in a different kind of scenery than the drop-dead beauty of these islands. He couldn't imagine that people still lived on the little island in the middle of its volcanic caldera. After all, an eruption there in about 1625 B.C., perhaps the largest in human history, wiped out not only the Minoans at the city of Akrotiri, but sent perhaps the largest known tsunami to obliterate the highly civilized Minoans at Crete. Four times more powerful than Krakatoa's eruption in 1883, its several tsunami, up to 500 feet high, made more modern tsunamis seem tame. The Minoans had the biggest fleet of ships in the world that protected them. When the tsunami wiped out the fleet, what was left of Crete was defenseless and became easy prey for waves of marauders.

On the previous day, they had seen the island of Naxos, but then ran into a storm with 50 mile per hour, Beaufort 9 gale winds and high seas, so they anchored in the safe harbor of Syros, the administrative center of the Cyclades, for the night. Fortunately, it cleared quickly, and they had headed for Delos where they spent the day.

Daniels had just gotten back onto the ship. He had planned to leave the cruise and fly out to Athens, as many of the islands have two flights a day, but he discovered that Delos didn't have an airstrip. It was critical that he get to Athens, but he'd just have to wait until they got to Mykonos.

The Kiklades was a sleek, modern cruise boat, only 185 feet long, and had room for 50 passengers and 16 crew members. It was easy to get in and out of port and could tie up directly to many docks, which made for easy access. This was not true at Delos, though, since it had about a 17-foot draft, so a tender had to bring them ashore. Although they usually cruised under power at 10 knots, the boat could make seven knots with its three masts, which it did intermittently. Radar, GPS, computer navigation, and radio all added to the safety, but Yiannis Kostopoulos could easily sail these islands on his own, day or night.

Daniels headed aft and down the stairs to the lower deck. One of the crew had given up a cabin for him. He could have had better accommodations, but he just wanted to fit in. His cabin was small with one window, unlike a large cruise ship cabin with a balcony. It had twin beds, a tiny shower, and vacuum toilet.

Daniels locked his door, went into the bathroom, which he also locked. He put his .357-chambered SIG Sauer P229 pistol on the sink. Next to it, he carefully placed his Nikon D-80 digital camera with the AF-S Nikkor 18-200 lens. He was dirty from the day's activities and needed a shower physically . . . and psychologically.

The bathroom had a musty boat smell to it, but Daniels thought he smelled worse. It had been a productive day, but he quietly cursed the time it took to get his digital photos and email where he wanted. He turned on the shower, used the supplied shampoo in the dispenser on the wall, and after washing his body, stood there for a while with the hot water running on his neck and back.

"A few hours won't matter," he quietly told himself. "I got in and out quickly and quietly. No reason to raise suspicion."

Feeling better, he turned off the shower and reached for the terry cloth towel. It was humid, but not bad. Once dried off, he slipped on the terry cloth robe provided with the room. He ran a brush through his short black hair to untangle it followed by his fingers to spread it out to the air to dry. His wife hated that part; she had thick hair that took an hour to dry. Daniels' hair would be dry by the time he had finished shaving. Putting on fresh clothes, he finished the therapy.

After a brief rest, he locked his doors and headed to the main deck for dinner, where he met the boat's restaurant manager.

"Mr. Daniels, how are you?"

"Better after a shower, Demetrius."

"Always better, isn't it? Are you joining us for dinner?"

"Yes, looking forward to it. I heard we're having traditional Greek food."

"Ah, the captain's giving away my secrets. Tonight, we start with a Greek salad with feta cheese and black olives and rolls or pita bread, freshly baked. We continue with marinated lamb chops, potatoes with lemon vinaigrette, and a Cretan variation of baklava that's to die for."

"I can't wait. I'm starving."

"Will you be dining alone?"

"Yes. May I eat on the upper aft deck? The evening looks beautiful." Daniels was more concerned with the possibility of getting a cell or satellite signal as the atmosphere cooled than he was about ambience.

"Of course, of course. Let's go out there now. I don't think anyone else will be nearby." Demetrius grabbed a placemat, utensils, and cloth napkin and led the way. "You have your pick, Mr. Daniels. Where would you like to sit?"

"This table with the aft-most cushions looks inviting."

"Excellent choice. A good place to unwind. Please sit down, and I will send Aggeliki to wait on you. She will take good care of you."

The manager left, and Daniels sat down. He put his cell and satellite phones down on the cushion and stared at them. "Damn. No signal!"

"Mr. Daniels, *kalispera*," Aggeliki said as she walked toward him with a carafe in each hand. "Red or white wine with your dinner?"

"Red, please."

Aggiliki was a young Greek woman, nearly six feet tall, slender and attractive. Tanned and muscular, she obviously helped with other chores on the boat. Although her hair was blond, her dark roots were showing that they needed a peroxide update. She had waited on Daniels on other evenings and was always attentive. After she poured his wine, she said, "I will bring back your salad."

"Thank you, Aggeliki."

Daniels enjoyed the quiet and solitude of being alone on the deck, slowly sipping his glass of wine and glancing at his phones. Aggeliki returned with his salad, then brought out one course after another until the fresh baklava was finally served. It was everything Demetrius had suggested and more.

★ ★ ★ ★ ★

The roar of the twin 650-horsepower diesel motors starting up caused Daniels to suddenly awaken. *Strange*, he thought as he willed his eyes to open. *I only had one glass of wine.* Daniels was always in control, but his head was spinning and his sight was dim. He tried to stand, pushing up against the table, but he was too weak.

"Mr. Daniels, may I help?" Aggeliki said as she approached, seeing his difficulty.

"I think I'm sick," Daniels said, trying to focus on her face but feeling as though he was going to pass out.

"Here, let me help you up," Aggeliki said, wrapping her long arms around him.

Daniels could barely hear her voice over the din of the engines and the anchor being lifted. "What's going on? Why are we . . ."

Daniels was the only one who heard the splash of his body into the clear blue water. Slowly he dropped motionless all the way to the bottom as though he was weighted down, a tiny stream of air bubbles the only indicator of life. He never saw the *Kiklades* pull away.